Tales of the Fays
Volume 1

Tales of the Fays
Volume 1

by
Marie-Catherine d'Aulnoy

Translated, annotated and introduced by
Brian Stableford

A Black Coat Press Book

ISBN 978-1-61227-836-0. First Printing. February 2019. Published by Black Coat Press, an imprint of Hollywood Comics.com, LLC, P.O. Box 17270, Encino, CA 91416. Printed in the United States of America.

TABLE OF CONTENTS

Introduction

This two-volume collection assembles all the published tales of the fays known to have been published by Marie-Catherine Le Jumel de Barneville, Baronne d'Aulnoy (1651-1705), presenting them as they appear to have been prepared by the author for publication. It is now impossible to determine with certainty the exact pattern of their actual publication; many modern reference books and critical studies assert that that originally occurred in 1697 and 1698, but none can name a publisher or give reliable details of the pattern of publication, because no copies of the supposed original volumes are accessible. The Bibliothèque Nationale does not have custody of any such editions, or any early reprints, and no copies can presently be located in any other library; all the bibliographical data in reference books appears to have been reconstructed by inference from the version of Madame d'Aulnoy's assembled works that was published in 1717, when Estienne Roger reproduced all the works included in the present collection in volumes 3-6 of his illicitly produced *Cabinet des Fées*. The same text was subsequently crammed into volumes 2-4 of Charles-Joseph Mayer's similarly illicit 1786 *Cabinet des Fées*.

Each of Roger's four volumes appears to have combined two volumes of the originally-planned editions, which were surely designed and perhaps issued as two pairs, a singleton and a three-volume work entitled *Le Nouveau bourgeois gentilhomme, ou fées à la mode* (tr. in Volume 2 as "The New Bourgeois Gentleman"; the subtitle translates as "Fashionable Fays"). In the *Cabinet* versions the second couplet is separately titled *Les Contes de fées*, but no individual titles are attached to the first couplet or the singleton. That title has therefore been speculatively attributed to the first part of the assembly, while the rest are sometimes listed as *Nouveaux contes de fées* or as *Fées à la mode*. That is a highly unusual and rather puzzling dearth of information, about the possible reasons for which we can only speculate.

The first bibliographer who attempted to compile a definitive list of *contes de fées* was Nicolas Lenglet Du Fresnoy, in the second volume of *De l'usage des romans, où l'on fait voir leur utilité et leurs differents caracteres, avec une bibliothèque des romans* [On the Usage of Romances, which shows their utility and their different characteristics, with a library of romances], illicitly published in 1734, allegedly in Amsterdam, with the by-line "M. le C. Gordon de Percel." In the section devoted to Madame d'Aulnoy's *contes*, the bibliography records eight volumes under the collective title of *Les Contes de fées*, allegedly published in Paris in 1698, but Lenglet Du Fresnoy might not actually have seen any such volumes, and probably had not seen a reported reprint of 1708, published in Amsterdam either; the latter edition certainly does exist, although other sources record that the two volumes published in that year by Pierre Mortier only feature the contents of the first five hypothetical 1698 volumes, the remainder following from the same publisher in 1711, in a two-volume version of *Le Nouveau bourgeois gentilhomme*.

Lenglet Du Fresnoy mistakenly attributes *Histoires sublime et allegoriques* (1699; actually by the Comtesse de Murat) and *Les Chevaliers errans* (1710; actual author unknown) to d'Aulnoy as well, illustrating the difficulties in determining authorship that existed at the time, which were to become even more complicated thereafter.

In view of the absence of reliable documentation, one of two things must be true: either the alleged 1697-98 editions of Madame d'Aulnoy's work do not exist, evidently having been refused a royal privilege for publication, or, having been printed illicitly at that time, the copies were all destroyed, immediately or over time. We cannot know for sure—and the fact that we cannot is a significant datum in itself—but the likelihood is that Lenglet Du Fresnoy's recording of an eight-volume 1698

Paris edition is fictitious, and that the first editions of Madame d'Aulnoy's work, perhaps consisting of a compaction of eight intended volumes, were printed illicitly in 1708 and 1711. What is certain, however, is that if it were not for editions belatedly published without the benefit of the royal privileges necessary for licit publication, Madame d'Aulnoy's contributions to the genre she helped to invent and form would have been obliterated from the historical record.

Very little is known, either, about much of Madame d'Aulnoy's life. Joseph de La Porte, the indefatigable historian of literary works by French women, devoted abundant space in his the third volume of his history, compiled in 1769, to Madame d'Aulnoy's travelogues and historical fiction, but only gave brief and rather dismissive mention of three of her *contes de fées*, evidently working from a contemporary compilation, and he claimed to have been unable to discover anything about her biography other than a (mistaken) birth date and the year of her death.

Subsequent researchers ascertained without much difficulty that Marie-Catherine Le Jumel de Barneville had been born into the minor nobility of Normandy, and married off by her family at the age of fifteen to the much older François de La Mothe (or La Motte), Baron d'Aunoi (or d'Aulnoy). She had four children in rapid succession, two of whom died in infancy, but her marriage effectively ended when the Baron was arrested on a charge of lèse-majesté and was sent to the Bastille on 30 September 1669, on the order of Jean-Baptiste Colbert, one of Louis XIV's principal ministers.

Baron d'Aulnoy eventually turned the tables on his denouncers and was released, after claiming vociferously that he had been stitched up by his mother-in-law, with the collaboration of a lover and another accomplice. His wife was arrested, and might have been briefly imprisoned, but was soon released if so. The truth of the matter is now impossible to ascertain, but the accusation routinely flung around in later commentaries that Marie-Catherine was one of the instigators of a plot to frame her husband is pure speculation; the probability is that if the baron really was framed, the reasons were political and undisclosed; Colbert is unlikely to have lent his hand to a petty family dispute. At any rate, the Baronne's mother, who became the Marquise de Gudanes following her remarriage, fled to Spain, and although there does not appear to be any reliable information as to where the Baronne was during the 1670s and the early 1680s, she was probably with her mother for at least some of that time. During that period she had two more children, but the identity of their father, or fathers, is unknown.

The widely-published speculation that Baronne d'Aulnoy spent time in Holland and England is devoid of solid evidence, and might be based purely on the fact that she published works of fiction that masqueraded as memoirs of those nations. The suggestion that while she was there she worked as a spy for the French government is pure supposition, although she does appear to have had considerable credit with some influential individuals when she resurfaced in Paris late in the 1680s.[1] At that time she began to write fairly prolifically, producing a fictitious *Relation du voyage d'Espagne* [An Account of a Journey in Spain] (1691), a series of equally fictitious "memoirs" of the Spanish, English and French courts, a couple of *nouvelles espagnoles* [Spanish novellas] and two historical melodramas set in Tudor England, *Histoire d'Hypolite, comte de Duglas* [Hippolyte, Earl of Douglas] (1690; the spelling of "Hypolite" varies in different editions) and *Le Comte de Warwick* [The Earl of Warwick] (1692). The last-named titles were apparently popular—La Porte describes the former as a "masterpiece of its genre"—and by 1695 the author had a solid literary reputation.

From the early 1690s onwards d'Aulnoy was an active member of a literary salon hosted by Anne-Thérèse de

---

[1] Jean-Baptiste Colbert died in 1683, but whether that had anything to do with d'Aulnoy's return to Paris, there is now no way to know. She was, however, definitely acquainted with Colbert's long-serving secretary, Charles Perrault.

Marguenat de Courcelles, Marquise de Lambert (1647-1733), along with the poet Antoinette Deshoulières, the poet and dramatist Catherine Bernard, and the tutor to the young Duc de Bourgogne, François Fénelon. The most prestigious member of the salon was Marie-Anne de Bourbon (1666-1739), a princess of the blood, then known as the dowager Princesse de Conti; she was accompanied there one of the ladies of her household, Mademoiselle de La Force, and the salon was subsequently joined by the latter's cousin, the Comtesse de Murat. Lambert's salon was also joined by Antoine Houdar de la Motte, a writer who became very successful after the turn of the century—when the salon reached the peak of its celebrity—but he was at the outset of his career in the early 1690s; he was presumably related to Baron d'Aulnoy, but perhaps only distantly. Madame d'Aulnoy also hosted her own salon in the 1690s, and attended the long-running salon of Mademoiselle de Scudéry, by then hosted by the latter's protégée, Mademoiselle de L'Héritier, which had a regular membership overlapping Madame de Lambert's.

In part two of *Hypolite, comte de Duglas* one of the characters relates an allegorical *conte* [tale], "L'Île de felicité" [The Isle of Felicity]; it is set against the background of Classical mythology, but the narrator says by way of introduction that it is a "*conte approchant ceux des fées*" [a tale similar to those of fays], implying that the notion of *contes de fées* had already been introduced to the Parisian salons as early as 1690, probably as a kind of calculated exercise or game, like the games described in Mademoiselle de La Force's *Les Jeux d'esprit, ou la Promenade de la Princesse de Conti à Eu* [Witty Games; or, The Princess de Conti's Excursion to Eu] (written before 1700, published 1865) and Catherine Bernard's historical novelette set in the mid-sixteenth century, *Inès de Cordoue, nouvelle espagnole* (1697; tr. as "Ines de Cordova"). The latter might well have owed some inspiration to d'Aulnoy's exercises in that vein, although it is very striking in its refusal of the happy ending characteristically attached to such stories.

A key passage from *Ines de Cordoue*, in which the young queen of Spain, Elisabeth de France, proposes a storytelling contest, is often cited as a representation of the way in which *contes de fées* must have been invented:

"She proposed, in order to create a new amusement for herself, making up gallant tales. The order was received with pleasure by all the ladies who composed the little court; rules were agreed for those sorts of stories, of which the two principal ones were that the adventures should always counter plausibility and the sentiments should always be natural. It was judged that the charm of the tales should only consist of making visible what was happening in the heart, and that there should also be a kind of merit in the marvelous imaginations, which would not be retained by the appearances of verity."

It seems highly probable that some such suggestion must have been made in one of the literary salons in Paris, most likely by Mademoiselle de L'Héritier, who became an ardent propagandist for the writing of *contes de fées*, and that it was imported at some stage to Versailles—almost certainly by the dowager Princesse de Conti, who was Louis XIV's eldest and favorite daughter, and who had a court of her own within the king's court—where it apparently became something of a fad.

The importance of the Bernard representation is not restricted to the suggested "rules" for the writing of such stories, although the assertion that "the charm of the tales should only consist of making visible what was happening in the heart" certainly needs to be borne in mind is examining Madame d'Aulnoy's work, as well as the specification that they must contain "marvelous imaginations." The implication that there was an element of competition in their composition is equally significant. Some of the writers who dabbled in the genre would surely have said, if asked, that they were not competing with anyone, but merely dabbling for the joy of taking part, but even if they meant it, the fact remains that they were operating within a competitive framework of sorts.

Given that implication of competition, it must have rapidly become obvious to everyone involved in the game, and everyone tempted to get involved, that there were only two serious contenders for the hypothetical prize: Baronne d'Aulnoy and the Comtesse de Murat. If that was not obvious from the very beginning, it certainly became manifest when those two writers became the most prolific contributors to the genre, effectively in control of its development. It became blatantly obvious toward the end of the competition, when both writers deliberately undertook to produce new versions of two stories borrowed from Gianfrancesco Straparola's *Piacevoli notti* [Facetious Nights] (1551-53), "Galeotto" and "Pietro." Straparola's tales are both short, but the new versions produced by d'Aulnoy and Murat are much longer and greatly elaborated; they were probably the last *contes de fées* produced by either author, and represent the ultimate stage of development achieved by the process of evolution they had directed and contrived. D'Aulnoy's "Le Prince marcassin" (tr. as "Prince Marcassin") and "Le Dauphin" (tr. as "The Dolphin"), and Murat's "Le Roi porc" (tr. as "The Swine King") and "Le Turbot" (tr. as "The Turbot"), were evidently produced in parallel, in the context of an overt or covert literary duel.

In retrospect, it seems probable that the frame story in which d'Aulnoy's two Straparola-derived tales were embedded, *Le Nouveau bourgeois gentilhomme*, was produced at the same time—in 1698—and in the same spirit as the frame story of Comtesse de Murat's *Les Lutins du château de Kernosy* (tr. as "The Goblins of Kernosy Castle"), although the publication of the latter was long delayed, until a version eventually appeared, fugitively, in 1710, without the benefit of a royal privilege. D'Aulnoy embedded some of her earlier tales in two *nouvelles espagnoles*, and the competitive stimulation of Catherine Bernard might well be visible in the fact that two of those tales—"Le Mouton" (tr. as "The Sheep") and "Le Nain jaune" (tr. as "The Yellow Dwarf)—refuse happy endings, as Bernard's do: a rare circumstance in d'Aulnoy's work, and even rarer in Murat's, although the latter probably produced the similarly-exceptional "Anguilette" at the same time.

If the salon writers really did start the game of composing *contes de fées* as early as 1690, the stock of such tales would have had seven years to accumulate before the floodgates of publication were suddenly opened by the immense success in 1697 of Charles Perrault's *Histoires et contes du temps passé*, better known as *Contes de ma mère l'oye* (tr. as *Tales of Mother Goose*). The latter was originally its subtitle, but became its title in the reprint editions that followed posthaste—to the authorship of which Perrault rapidly owned up, having initially tried to pass off the first edition, apologetically, as the work of his son. When the success of Perrault's collection became spectacular, the printers of Paris raced to obtain privileges to publish the similar works, of which a considerable treasure-trove was awaiting their attention.

That change of fortune was very dramatic; it seems probably that *contes de fées* had previously been produced with no real expectation of publication, although Mademoiselle de L'Héritier had included two paradigm examples in a 1696 collection of *Oeuvres meslées* [Miscellaneous Works], buried among poems, historical fiction, essays and letters, and Catherine Bernard had embedded two in her Spanish novella.[2] It seems likely that Madame d'Aulnoy intended to use the same tactic as Bernard when she embedded tales in two *nouvelles espagnoles* of her own, but the packaging must have come to seem irrelevant before she rewrapped the two novellas within a further frame, as they appear in the 1708 Mortier collection and the 1717 *Cabinet*. There seems to be little doubt that the six long *contes de fées* embedded in the three projected volumes of *Le Nouveau bourgeois gentilhomme* were intended to be the selling point for their envelope rather than *vice versa*. That particular enclosure, which includes more wry commentary on the writing of such tales than the earlier portmanteau,

---

[2] Mademoiselle de L'Héritier's two exemplary *contes de fées* are translated in the Black Coat Pres collection *The Robe of Sincerity*, and a translation of *Inès de Cordoue* can be found in the Black Coat Press anthology, *The Queen of the Fays*.

leaves no doubt as to the fact that it was difficult for *contes de fées* to be taken seriously even by their own writers, while they were regarded with sneering contempt by most "serious" people, as much because as in spite of the vogue that briefly boosted them to enormous popularity.

There is surely an element of disingenuousness in Madame d'Aulnoy's teasing protestations that her own works in that vein were mere play, essentially slapdash and rather silly, because she certainly poured a great deal of effort into them, and there is a naked determination in her later work not to be outshone by Murat, who was a more careful and more polished writer, and equally imaginative, although not as fluent or as rapid in production. Even if d'Aulnoy's earlier published stores are a trifle casual—but still brilliant in their fashion— her later work is certainly not lacking in application and intensity. If, as seems highly probable—although the order of composition of the works read in salons is impossible to determine—Charles Perrault stole freely from d'Aulnoy as well as L'Héritier and Bernard in shaping his much slighter and somewhat inept tales, it must surely have caused her immense chagrin to see him achieving astonishing popularity with material ineptly recycled from her superior endeavors, while she could not obtain a privilege from the royal censors to publish her own works.

In retrospect, d'Aulnoy and Murat can now be seen as the major contributors to the genre they helped to invent and largely took responsibility for shaping and developing, d'Aulnoy producing twenty-four *contes de fées* for intended, if not actual, publication in eight volumes, and the latter at least twelve, ten of which were published in three volumes in 1698-99, with two more added in 1710.[3] No one else managed to issue more than a single volume. Quantitatively, therefore, d'Aulnoy won the competition, and in terms of subsequent

---

[3] All of the *contes de fées* that Murat is known to have published during her lifetime are translated in the Black Coat Press collection *The Palace of Vengeance*.

popularity she held on to the laurels, although in terms of her influence on the writers of the second wave of production between 1735 and 1755, Murat was probably the more highly esteemed. That aspect of the competition is, however, of minor importance; the most interesting aspect by far is the effect that d'Aulnoy's endeavors had on Murat's, and vice versa. If they had not been consciously and manifestly in competition, listening attentively to one another reading their works and then trying to outshine them, *contes de fées* would not have undergone such a rapid and dramatic evolution, the nature and scope of which can very easily be seen by comparing the earlier stories in the present collection with the later ones, and comparing the six stories in Murat's first two published volumes with the four in the third. Although d'Aulnoy's stories were not necessarily written in the exact order that they appear herein, their sequence must be a close approximation of the order of their composition, and there can be no doubt at all that the stories in volume two of the present set were written later than those in volume one, in a markedly different frame of mind.

The extent of the fad for *contes de fées* and the rapidity of its spread is wryly indicated, albeit satirically exaggerated, in *Le Nouveau bourgeois gentilhomme*, set in d'Aulnoy's Norman homeland and featuring two deluded sisters addicted to the genre, one of whom calls herself Virginie, although her real name is Marie, and the other Marthonide rather than Marthe, in whom it is perhaps possible to find distant ironic echoes of d'Aulnoy and Murat as well as conspicuous echoes of Molière's scathing sexist satires of the salon culture promoted and shaped by Mademoiselle de Scudéry, *Les Précieuses ridicules* (1659) and *Les Femmes savantes* (1672). What the story could not contain, of course, is any comment on the fact that the production and publication of such stories in Paris soon came to a very abrupt end, and that from 1699 onwards, only a tiny handful of stories—five volumes in eighty years—received royal privileges, so that the entire genre was under effective proscription until the 1789 Revolution, and would have vanished entirely but for a trickle of illicit publications, at first unsteady but rebelliously robust for a while between 1735 and 1755.

Exactly why that sharp interruption happened, it is very difficult to determine, but it was certainly not spontaneous; the nascent genre was brutally crushed, and the complete absence of early editions of her works from the world's libraries leaves little doubt that d'Aulnoy was the principal victim, if not the primary target, of the suppression. As well as first editions of two of Murat's three volumes, the single volumes of *contes de fées* issued in 1698 by Mademoiselle de La Force, and two volumes nowadays attributed to Jean de Préchac and the Chevalier of Mailly are all in the Bibliothèque Nationale, but the absence of all eight of d'Aulnoy's alleged 1697-98 editions does occasion some pause to wonder whether other writers might have have been equally unfortunate. Lenglet Du Fresnoy's bibliography only lists one 1698 collection of *contes de fées* that seems to have vanished completely, by the historian Pierre de Lesconvel, which he dismisses as trivial (although he probably had not actually seen it and all other references seem to be copies of his allegation), but it is not impossible that other published volumes had left no detectable trace by 1734.

But what on earth happened to provoke that sudden suppression? What reason could Louis XIV's censors possibly have had for suddenly taking against *contes de fees* and maintaining that hostility for generations thereafter, leaving the genre to maintain a fugitive existence as literary contraband?

The first member of the coterie to suffer manifest persecution was Mademoiselle de La Force, who was banished from Paris even before her own collection appeared in December 1697, sent to a provincial nunnery from which she was not given permission to emerge for sixteen years. Some documentation survives of her protest against that imprisonment, including a letter addressed to the Prince de Conti, who had recently inherited that title from his brother, the late husband of her protectress—who was known as the "dowager" Princess de Conti because the new prince's wife was also a Princesse de Conti. Although La Force protests her innocence vigorously in the letter she does not actually specify what charges had been laid against her, nor does she name the individual responsible for her internment, although the suspicion is inevitably strong that it was probably either the dowager Princess or the Prince.[4]

Madame d'Aulnoy appears to have been the second of the three major writers of *contes de fées* to leave Paris for good, sometime in 1699, but no reliable information appears to be available as to why she left or where she went. Much was made by Charles-Joseph Mayer in the account of Madame d'Aulnoy that he included in volume 37 of the 1786 *Cabinet des fées* of the fact that an alleged friend of hers was executed for attempting to murder her abusive husband, and that the baronne might have feared implication as an accessory—and many subsequent commentaries copied that allegation—but it was mere gossip, and there does not appear to be any real evidence for the suspicion.

The Comtesse de Murat left the capital shortly after d'Aulnoy, having been under investigation for some while by the Lieutenant-General of Police, whose reports survive, and who continued to persecute her after she had left Paris, with the result that she was arrested in 1703 and committed to a state prison (without any formal charge or trial), where she spent the next seven years, only being released when her health had been comprehensively ruined. Why she was under investigation and who instigated the pursuit is unknown, but the Lieutenant-General's reports have survived; they consist

---

[4] The letter, along with the text of *Les Jeux d'esprit*, resurfaced in the mid-nineteenth century, when Louis-Philippe's personal library was sold at auction. It seems likely that both had been handed down from the possession of the Prince de Conti, although what that might imply about his relationship with Mademoiselle de La Force or his sister-in-law it is difficult to assess.

entirely of malevolent gossip, with not a shred of real evidence of any criminal conduct.

At the most, Murat seems to have been suspected of libertinism and lesbianism, but the former is an accusation to which few members of Louis XIV's court could have been immune, and the latter an inevitably vague suspicion. Some such suspicion might also have hung over Mademoiselle de La Force, Mademoiselle de L'Héritier and Catherine Bernard, none of whom ever married, but the "crime" was impossible to specify, let alone to prove, and it is not clear why, even if it were true, anyone should have cared very much. Mademoiselle de Scudéry had been calling herself "Sapho" for nearly fifty years, seemingly without attracting any particular hostility, or even comment. Baronne d'Aulnoy, who had borne six children, would seem to have had a ready-made defense against that particular charge, although the fact that two of her children had been born after her separation from her husband cannot have aided a reputation for virtue, and *Hypolite, comte de Duglas* includes a scene in which the heroine, who has attracted the passionate attentions of a marchionesss while disguised as a man, agrees to put on male attire again, briefly, purely for her benefit—a daring narrative move for the time. The frame story of *Le Nouveau bourgeois gentilhomme* includes some sly implications of lesbian lust on the part of Madame du Rouet and Madame de Lure, but they are not suggestive of anything except an awareness of its existence that must have been commonplace at the time.

It is not difficult to imagine a hypothetical scenario in which the relationships between the dowager Princess de Conti and her confidantes became suspect, and perhaps embarrassing, to the Prince—especially if the relationships in question became troubled—and that the suspicions then extended to the entire coterie, but it seems highly improbable that any such suggestion, no matter how well-founded, could have provoked such a blanket suppression. Mademoiselle de La Force, the Comtesse de Murat and Baronne d'Aulnoy must surely have been suspected of something worse than passionate amity with one another, or with a widowed princess of the blood, in order to provoke such sweeping reprisals. In any case, if their personal conduct was responsible for their exclusion from the court, that could hardly explain the extravagant subsequent persecution of the entire genre to which it belonged, which must have required a more general hostility.

One possibility is that it was not so much suspicions of lesbianism that attracted stern hostility to the salon coterie as suspicions of heresy, which had become subject to severe repression since the revocation of the Edict of Nantes in 1685. The ex-Huguenot Catherine Bernard had converted to Catholicism in order to avoid persecution, and Mademoiselle de La Force was also a convert, but such renegades were always open to the suspicion of merely putting on a show. A more relevant issue might be that the Château de Gudanes, to which d'Aulnoy's mother had fled, and where d'Aulnoy probably spent some time before her return to Paris, had long been the property of a powerful Huguenot family, and might well have served as a refuge for Huguenots fleeing France before and after 1685. It might also be significant, in this context, that one of the key features of the fictional world in which tales of fays are set is that it is utterly devoid of the Roman Church and its deity—with one significant exception.

The one prose tale that Charles Perrault published in advance of his 1697 collection was "La Belle au bois dormant" (tr. as "The Beauty in the Dormant Wood," but usually known in abridged English versions as "The Sleeping Beauty"), the opening sequence of which, when an evil fay gatecrashes an endowment party and sabotages the benevolence of a group of good fays, closely resembles scenes in d'Aulnoy's "Le Prince Lutin" (tr. as "The Sprite Prince") and "Serpentin vert" (tr. as "Green Worm"). Given Perrault's tendency to appropriate material, it seems highly likely that he stole that motif from d'Aulnoy rather than *vice versa*,[5] but either way, the signifi-

---

[5] D'Aulnoy was by no means above borrowing herself; "Finette Cendron" is a deliberate conflation of motifs bor-

cant difference is that in Perrault's version of the scene the interrupted ceremony is a baptism, and when the princess eventually recovers from suspended animation she is married to the prince by her almoner; in d'Aulnoy's versions, there is no baptism, and no priest. In spite of the presence of fays, therefore, Perrault's tale might well have seemed far less offensive to the bigoted Churchmen in Louis XIV's court than the works of Madame d'Aulnoy, the narrative background of which is blatantly pagan, and in which the most important deity by far is Amour, although the temples at which characters occasionally go to worship are sometimes dedicated to the goddess Diana.

Whether or not the "rules" drawn up for the production of *contes de fées* in the context of the salon game actually specified the rigorous elimination of Christianity from the conventionally-adopted background, it certainly became a significant paradigm feature of such tales. Although the principal motivation for the placing of a new and idiosyncratic version of *fées* at the heart of the genre was undoubtedly feminist, permitting the construction of a hypothetical world in which the most powerful agents of virtue and evil alike are women, the construction of the particular idea of fays employed by the salon writers also avoided, almost entirely, all the ideological baggage associated with the terminology of "witchcraft." D'Aulnoy's mention in a couple of her stories of "the apparatus of the Sabbat," is atypical, and perhaps undiplomatic, although the characterization of her evil fays is blatantly similar to popular conceptions of the typical appearance and conduct of witches.

---

rowed from Mademoiselle de L'Héritier's two paradigmatic tales, and "La Chatte blanche" (tr. as "The White Cat") deliberately recycles motifs from her own work as well as appropriating one from Mademoiselle de La Force, but d'Aulnoy never stooped to mere copying; she always wanted to extrapolate her recycled materials in order to draw more out of them. That cannot be said of Perrault.

The deliberate paganism of *contes de fées* might well have been instituted as a diplomatic move intended to deflect suspicions of Satanism, but if so, it might well have misfired badly, and made the tales seem more slyly suspect, and hence potentially more dangerous, in the eyes of devout readers. The royal censors were, of necessity "professionally devout," and perhaps the wonder is not that Madame d'Aulnoy was refused privileges for the publication of her work in the genre, but that other members of the coterie obtained a few in the wake of Perrault's breakthrough. Perhaps, had La Force and Murat not had the protection of a princess of the blood, at least temporarily, they would not have achieved that.

Given the forceful, if largely tacit, influence of the Church over the philosophy of censorship in the seventeenth and eighteenth centuries, and the inevitable wariness of the licensing bureaucracy in consequence, the taint of heresy is probably the likeliest hypothesis that could account for the almost complete removal of *contes de fées* from the protection of privileged publication. The overt feminism of *contes de fées*, although feeble by modern standards, might also have raised hackles on the part of Churchmen, who were notoriously misogynistic, and it is in that context that suspicions of lesbianism might have become a significant factor, infecting attitudes to the entire genre as well as occasioning particular reactions against its leading practitioners.

In terms of the feminist component of fay mythology, d'Aulnoy was not one of the more extravagant propagandists to begin with. In the early "Gracieuse et Percinet" (tr. as Gracieuse and Percinet") the agent of benevolent enchantment is male, and in "La Belle aux cheveux d'or" (tr. as "The Golden-Haired Beauty") the male hero is aided entirely by talking animals, without a fay in sight. Although the hero of "Le Prince lutin" makes abundant use of a fay gift, once he has received the gift in question, its benevolent donor disappears, and it is left almost entirely to his ingenuity to exploit it. In the fourth story in what was presumably her first collection, "L'Oiseau bleu" (tr. as "The Blue Bird"), which features the first of the grotesquely sadistic fays who were to become such a key feature of d'Aulnoy's work in the genre (Grognon, the archetypal harridan in "Gracieuse et Percinet," is not a fay), much of the magical opposition to the heroine's evil stepmother, repulsive stepsister and the latter's hagwife godmother, is provided by a frankly misogynistic male enchanter, which leaves the poor heroine a trifle short of female support by comparison with many of her peers, until the conclusion of her woes.

That attitude underwent a definitive shift, however, in her later work, and d'Aulnoy eventually provided some of the most extravagant models of female empowerment. In the spectacular "La Princesse Carpillon" (tr. as Princess Carpillon") the character identified as "la fée Amazone"—which can be construed either as "the amazon fay" or "the fay [named] Amazone"—functions in much the same fashion as a twentieth-century superhero, clad in a shiny costume and popping up when required to save the innocent from seemingly certain disaster, and to slay monsters and villains with her fiery lance. In "Belle-Belle, ou Le Chevalier Fortuné," (tr. as "Belle-Belle; or, The Cavalier Fortuné"), the heroine, clad in male attire, effortlessly outshines her rival knights in the arts of dragon-slaying and seduction, although she does have a harem of male sidekicks, each of them endowed with a particular superhuman talent, at her beck and call. Those examples, and the enterprise of several other heroines featured in volume two of the present set surely make up for the relative dearth of female heroism in volume one.

At no stage in d'Aulnoy's career as a writers of *contes de fées* did her absolute commitment to the ideals of virtue, fidelity and altruism waver, and she also offers conspicuous support to the policy of forgiving one's enemies. One might imagine that a reasonable Churchman would approve of that wholeheartedly, but in fact, it is entirely possible that a devout critic would think it pernicious, and dangerous, precisely because the tacit argument of the stories is that Christ and the Christian God are utterly irrelevant to virtuous sentiment and action; the world of the fays is not only a world replete with evil and with appalling actions committed simply for the love of evil, but it is also a world that has no need of assisted redemption, where the crucial opposition to evil is provided entirely by instinctive decency and the effects of a particular, and perhaps peculiar, notion of Amour. In a strict interpretation of Catholic dogma, that is definitely heresy, and no matter how corrupt and licentious Louis XIV's court might have been beneath its ostentatiously polite surface, it had no shortage of outspoken dogmatists and bigots.

Madame d'Aulnoy could easily be seen at the time, as she still can be, as the most extreme promoter of the moral ideology of *contes de fées*, as well as the most prolific. She probably did not set out to be, but she had little alternative to taking up the challenge, simply because she was consciously engaged in a constant competition in extremism. None of the leading writers of *contes de fées*, either during the 1698 boom of the mid-seventeenth century revival seemed to know the meaning of the word "excess" when it came to managing their imaginative extravagance, but no one else was as flamboyant in that excess as d'Aulnoy. Because her work lacked a little of the polish and narrative organization of Murat's, it also lacked Murat's delicacy and discretion, and that could well have been the reason why pious observers apparently drew the conclusion that d'Aulnoy was the most dangerous of an inherently dangerous bunch: the writer whose works ought to be first in the queue for banning or burning. At any rate, their early editions really do seem either to have been aborted before publication or burned afterwards, silently but thoroughly.

By 1734, as Lenglet Du Fresnoy notes, d'Aulnoy was being promoted defensively, in the shadow of Perrault, as a writer primarily fit for reading by children, and the entire genre was often regarded by subsequent commentators in the same light, but in fact, Perrault and Fénelon were the only writers involved in the initial boom who designed their work for the consumption of children, and it is by no means difficult to make out a case for d'Aulnoy's work, in spite of the routine attachment of specific (but highly unconvincing) morals, being blatantly unfit for children from any ideological or esthetic viewpoint. Like almost all of the other members of the coterie, she was a renegade female aristocrat writing tales for the select consumption of other renegade female aristocrats about a world the corrupt glamour of which female aristocrats understood only too well, with a depth of sarcasm that the innocent could not be expected to comprehend.

Madame d'Aulnoy was not the only writer in the genre to feature sadistic fays who take great delight in torturing their victims most extravagantly and most ingeniously, but she set the standard for such horrors with such characters as Carabosse in "La Princesse printanière" (tr. as "Princess Springtime"), Magotine in "Serpentin vert," Lionne in "La Grenouille bienfaisante" (tr. as "The Benevolent Frog") and Grognette in "Le Dauphin." Nor was she the only writer to deal extensively in unrelentingly vicious and murderous ordinary women—mothers and sisters as well as stepmothers and scorned lovers—but no one else matched the sheer nastiness of Duchesse Grognon in "Gracieuse et Percinet", the king's sister in "Belle-Belle, ou Le Chevalier Fortuné," and the queen mother in "La Princesse Belle-Etoile et Prince Chéri" (tr. as "Princess Belle-Etoile and Prince Cheri"). Nor did any other writer take generic work as far into the esoterically perverse realms of surrealism as d'Aulnoy did in the remarkable triptych of tales constituted by "Babiole" (tr. as "Babiole"), "Serpentin vert" and "La Grenouille bienfaisante." In all of that work, innocence, although completely admirable, is something that cannot endure without the aid of miracles: specifically, the miracles provided by fays, whose non-existence thus becomes a tragedy for any reader capable of seeing that tales of faerie—tales of enchantment—are, in their essence, tales of deep and chagrined disenchantment.

It makes far more sense, therefore, to regard d'Aulnoy and Murat as significant writers in the development of Decadent fantasy literature than as writers for children, and one is bound to wonder what they might have done had they been allowed to continue with the process of evolution that they had begun and taken forward with such rapidity. Having already moved from the production of novelettes to novellas, it seems highly likely that one or both of them might have progressed to the writing of full-length novels, or even works of more epic length, with plots of a complexity to match. Given that both writers had extraordinary imaginative range, it is hard to imagine that they would have run out of inspiration any time soon, had they not been violently stopped in their tracks, even without the spur of their ongoing rivalry. It was not to be, however, and we have to be content to be grateful that they contrived to publish as much as they did during their brief window of opportunity, leaving behind fugitive material that could be recovered once worst of the tempest of repression had blown over.

Considered separately Madame d'Aulnoy and the Comtesse de Murat were both great writers of imaginative fiction, but seen as a competitive collective they are surely unique in literary history, and it is as part of that collective endeavor that Madame d'Aulnoy became fully entitled to her classic status, even though her modern reputation is somewhat misrepresentative of her actual ability and achievement. One thing that ought to be borne very much in mind while reading the present collection as that its contents first reached print as literary contraband, which the censors of the day attempted with the legal might at their disposal to suppress and annihilate, as a dangerous encouragement to freethinking—but it survived, and thrived in spite of that, and to some extent because of it. It deserves to be considered in that light, and not as a set of "fairy stories" fit for children.

All the translations were made from the versions contained in of volumes 2-4 of the 1786 *Cabinet des fées* reproduced on the Bibliothèque Nationale's *gallica* website.

Brian Stableford

GRACIEUSE AND PERCINET

There was once a king and queen who had only one daughter. Her beauty, her mildness and her intelligence, which were incomparable, caused her to be named Gracieuse. She was her mother's entire joy. There was no morning when she was not brought a beautiful dress, sometimes gold brocade, velvet or satin. She was adorned marvelously without being proud or more vainglorious. She spent the morning with knowledgeable individuals, who taught her all sorts of sciences, and in the afternoon she worked in the company of the queen. When it was time for a snack she was served bowls full of sugared almonds and more than twenty pots of jam, so it was said everywhere that she was the most fortunate princess in the world.

In the same court there was a very rich old woman called Duchess Grognon, who was frightful in every way; her hair was flame-red; she had a terribly fat face covered in pimples; of the two eyes she had once had, only one remained, which was gummy; her mouth was so wide one might have thought that she wanted to eat the whole world, but as she had no teeth there was no fear of that; she had humps in front and behind and was lame on both sides. Monsters of that sort are envious of all beautiful persons; she hated Gracieuse mortally, and withdrew from the court in order not to hear her praised any longer. She had a castle of her own not far away. When anyone came to see her and recounted marvels about the princess she cried, angrily: "You're lying! You're lying! She isn't lovable. I have more charm in my little finger than she has in her entire body."

However, the queen fell ill and died. Princess Gracieuse nearly died too, of the grief of having lost such a good mother. The king regretted such a good wife greatly, and remained shut away in his palace for nearly a year. Finally, the physicians, fearing that he would fall ill, ordered him to go for walks and to divert himself. He went hunting, and as the weather was very hot, when he went past a large castle that he found on his route he went in.

As soon as she was informed of the king's arrival, Duchess Grognon—for it was her castle—came to greet him, and told him that the coolest place in the house was a large, well-vaulted cellar, very tidy, to which she invited him to descend. The king went there with her, and, seeing two hundred barrels lined up on top of one another he asked her whether it was for herself alone that she made such a large provision.

"Yes, Sire," she said, "It's just for me; I'd by very glad to let you sample some; there's Canary, Saint-Laurent, Champagne, Hermitage, Rivesalte, Rossolis, Persicot and Fenouillet; which would you like?"

"Frankly," said the king, "I hold that Champagne wine is better than all the others."

Immediately, Grognon took a little hammer and struck: *tap, tap*. A thousand pistoles emerged from the barrel.

"What does that signify?" she said, smiling. And she struck another barrel: *tap, tap*. A bushel of double louis d'or emerged.

"I don't understand this at all," she said, again, smiling more broadly. She went on to a third barrel and struck: *tap, tap*. So many pearls and diamonds came out that the floor was covered by them.

"Oh!" she cried. "I don't understand at all, Sire. Someone must have stolen my good wine and left these bagatelles in its place.

"Bagatelles!" said the king, who was quite astonished. "Damn it, Madame Grognon, do you call that bagatelles? There's enough there to buy ten kingdoms the size of Paris.

"Well," she said, "know that all these barrels are full of gold and precious stones; I'll make you the master of them on condition that you marry me."

"Ah!" replied the king, who loved money uniquely, "I'd like nothing better; tomorrow, if you wish."

"But there's one more condition," she said, "which is that I want to be mistress of your daughter, as her mother was, that she depends entirely on me and that you leave her at my disposal."

"You'll be her mistress," said the king. "Put it there."

Grognon shook his hand; they went out of the rich cellar together, of which she gave him the key.

He returned to his palace immediately. On hearing her father, Gracieuse ran to meet him; she kissed him and asked him if he had had a successful hunt.

"I caught a living dove," he said.

"Oh, Sire!" said the princess. "Give it to me, I'll nourish it."

"That can't be," he said, "for, to explain myself more intelligibly, it's necessary to tell you that I encountered Duchess Grognon and I've taken her for my wife."

"O Heaven!" cried Gracieuse, in her first impulse. "Can she be called a dove? She's more like a screech-owl."

"Shut up," said the king. "I intend that you love her and respect her as much as if she were your mother. Go and adorn yourself promptly, for I want to return to her today."

The princess was very obedient; she went to her room in order to get dressed. Her nurse read her sadness in her eyes. "What's the matter with you, my dear child?" she said to her. "You're weeping."

"Alas, my dear nurse," replied Gracieuse, "who wouldn't weep? The king is going to give me a stepmother, and to complete the disgrace, it's my cruelest enemy. In a word, it's the frightful Grognon. How can I see her in these beautiful beds that my good mother the queen embroidered so delicately with her own hands? How can I caress a she-ape who would like to have me killed?"

"My dear child," relied the nurse, "your intelligence ought to elevate you as much as your birth. Princesses like you ought to set fine examples for others. And what more beautiful example is there than to obey your father and do violence to yourself in order to please him? Promise me, then, that you won't give Grognon any evidence of the pain you feel."

The princess could not resolve to do that, but the sage nurse gave her so many reasons that she finally agreed to put on a good countenance and use it well with her stepmother.

She immediately put on a green and gold dress; she let her blonde hair fall over her shoulders, floating at the whim of the wind, as was the fashion in those days, and she put on her head a light crown of roses and jasmines, all the leaves of which were emeralds. In that state, Venus, the mother of the Amours, would have been less beautiful, but the sadness she could not overcome appeared in her face.

To get back to Grognon, that ugly creature was fully occupied in adorning herself. She had one shoe made half a cubit higher than the other, in order to appear a little less lame; she had a bodice stuffed over one shoulder in order to hide her hump; she put in the best enamel eye she could find; she put on make-up to whiten her face; she tinted her red hair black; then she put on an amaranth satin dress lined with blue, with a yellow skirt and violet ribbons. She wanted to make her entrance on horseback, because she had heard it said that the queens of Spain made theirs in that fashion.

While the king was giving his orders and Gracieuse was awaiting the moment to depart to go to met Grognon, she went down into the garden on her own, and went into a very dark little wood, where she sat down on the grass.

"Finally," she said, "I'm at liberty; I can weep as much as I want without anyone opposing it."

Immediately, she started sighing and weeping, so much that her eyes seemed to be two fresh-water springs. In that state, she was no longer thinking of returning to the palace when she saw a page coming, clad in green satin, with white feathers and the most beautiful head in the world. He put one knee on the ground and said to her: "Princess, the king is waiting for you."

She remained surprised by all the charms she remarked in the young page, and as she did not know him she thought that he must be in Grognon's retinue.

"Since when," she said to him, "has the king received you in the number of his pages?"

"I'm not the king's, Madame," he said, "I'm yours, and I only want to be yours."

"You're mine?" she replied, quite astonished. "But I don't know you!"

"Oh, Princess," he said, "I haven't yet dared to make myself known, but the misfortunes by which you are threatened by virtue of the king's marriage oblige me to speak to you sooner than I would have done. I had resolved to leave to time and my services the care of declaring my passion to you, but..."

"What!" cried the princess. "A page has the audacity to tell me that he loves me! That's the culmination of my disgrace."

"Don't be afraid, beautiful Gracieuse," he said to her, in a tender and respectful manner. "I am Percinet, a prince well enough known for my wealth and my knowledge for you not to find any inequality between us. It's only your merit and your beauty that can introduce any. I've loved you for a long time; I'm often in the places where you are without you seeing me. The gift of enchantment that I received at birth has been a great help to me in procuring me the pleasure of seeing you. I'll accompany you everywhere today in this costume, and I hope not to be entirely useless to you."

As he spoke the princess looked at him with an astonishment that she could not get over.

"It's you, handsome Percinet," she said to him, "that I've had so much desire to see, and about whom such surprising things are said. How glad I am that you want to be my friend! I no longer fear the malevolent Grognon, since you're entering into my interests."

They said a few more things to one another, and then Gracieuse returned to the palace, where she found a horse fully harnessed and caparisoned, which Percinet had brought into the stable, and which everyone believed to be for her. She mounted up. As it was a great jumper, the page took it by the bridle and led it, turning continually to the princess in order to have the pleasure of looking at her.

When the horse that was being led for Grognon appeared next to Gracieuse's, the latter looked like a mere nag, and the blanket of the handsome horse was so brilliant with gems that the other could not enter into comparison with it. The king, who was occupied by a thousand things, did not notice it, but all the noblemen only had eyes for the princess whose beauty they admired, and for her green-clad page, who was prettier than all those of the court.

They met Grognon on the road in an uncovered caleche, uglier and more ill-formed than a peasant woman. The king and the princess embraced her. Her horse was presented to her for her to mount, but seeing Gracieuse's, she said: "What! That creature will have a finer horse than me! I'd rather not be queen and return to my rich castle than be treated in such a manner."

The king immediately commanded the princess to dismount, and begged Grognon to do him the honor of mounting her horses. The princess obeyed without protest. Grognon did not look at her or thank her; she had herself hoisted up on to the beautiful horse; she resembled a bundle of dirty linen. There were eight gentlemen holding her, for fear that she might fall.

She was not yet content; she muttered threats between her teeth. She was asked what was wrong. "Being the mistress," she said, "I want the green page to hold the bridle of my horse, as he did when Gracieuse as mounted on it."

The king ordered the green-clad page to lead the queen's horse.

Percinet cast his eyes upon the princess, and she on him, without saying a single word. He obeyed, and the entire court set forth; drums and trumpets made a desperate sound.

Grognon was delighted; with her flat nose and her skewed mouth, she would not have changed places with Gracieuse.

At the time when it was least expected, however, the beautiful horse began to leap, to kick and to run so fast that no one could stop it. It carried Grognon away. She held on to the saddle and the mane; she screamed with all her might. Finally, she fell, her foot caught in the stirrup. It dragged her for a long way over stones, over thorns and through the mud, where she remained almost buried. Everyone followed, and had soon caught up with her. She was scratched all over, her head was fractured in three or four places, and one arm was broken. There had never been a bride in a worse condition.

The king appeared to be in despair. She was picked up like a shattered glass; her bonnet was on one side, her shoes on the other. She was carried into the city, she was laid down, and the surgeons were summoned. Ill as she was, she vituperated nevertheless.

"This is a trick on the part of Gracieuse," she said. "I'm certain that she only took that beautiful but malevolent horse in order to make me desire it, and so that it would kill me. If the king doesn't give me satisfaction, I'll return to my rich castle and never see him again as long as I live."

The king was informed about Grognon's anger. As his dominant passion was self-interest, the mere idea of losing the thousand barrels of gold and diamonds made him shiver, and would have brought him to any extremity. He ran to the bedside of the filthy patient; he put himself at her feet and swore to her that she only had to prescribe a punishment proportionate to Gracieuse's fault and he would abandon her to her resentment. She told him that that was sufficient, and that she would send for her.

In fact, someone came to tell the princess that Grognon was asking for her. She became pale and tremulous, suspecting that it was not to caress her. She looked in all directions to see of Percinet was apparent; she did not see him and walked very sadly to Grognon's apartment.

Scarcely had she gone in than the doors were closed. Then four women, who resembled four Furies, threw themselves upon her, on the order of their mistress, tore off her beautiful garments and ripped her chemise. When her shoulders were bare, the cruel Megaeras could not bear the gleam of their whiteness; they closed their eyes as if they had been looking for a long time at snow.

"Let's go, let's go, courage!" cried Grognon, from the depths of her bed. "Flay her for me, and don't let a little piece of that white skin remain that she thinks so beautiful."

In any other distress, Gracieuse would have wished for the handsome Percinet, but, seeing herself almost naked, she was too modest to want that prince to witness it, and she prepared to suffer everything like a poor sheep. The four Furies each had a fistful on frightful switches. They also had large brooms from which to take new ones, with the consequence that they thrashed her mercilessly, and at every blow, Grognon said: "Harder! Harder! You're sparing her!"

No one could believe, after that, that the princess was not flayed from head to toe, but they would be mistaken, for the gallant Percinet had fascinated the eyes of those women; they thought they had switches in their hands, but they were multicolored feathers; and as soon as they commenced, Gracieuse saw that, and ceased to be afraid, saying to herself: *Oh, Percinet, you've come to help me very generously. What would I have done without you?*

The flagellators became so tired that they could no longer move their arms. They stuffed her into her clothes and threw her out, with a thousand insults.

She returned to her room, pretending to be very ill. She went to bed and commanded that no one stay with her except her nurse, to whom she recounted the whole of her adventure. While telling the story she fell asleep; the nurse went away.

When she woke up she saw the green page in a corner, who dared not approach, out of respect. She told him that she would not forget the obligations she had to him as long as she lived; she implored him not to abandon her to the fury of her enemy but asked him to withdraw, because she had always been told that she ought not to be alone with boys.

He replied that she could remark the respect that he employed with her, but that it was only just, since she was his mistress, that he obey her in everything, even at the expense of his own satisfaction. With that, he quit her, after having advised her to pretend to be ill, as a result of the ill-treatment she had received.

Grognon was so glad to know that Gracieuse was in that state that she healed in half the time it should have taken, and the wedding celebrations were concluded with great magnificence. As the king knew that Grognon loved above all things being praised for being beautiful, he had her portrait painted and ordered a tourney in which six of the most adroit knights in the court would sustain, against anyone, that Queen Grognon was the most beautiful princess in the world

Many knights and foreigners arrived to sustain the contrary. The she-ape was present throughout, placed on a large balcony covered in gold brocade, and she had the pleasure of seeing her knights win the evil cause for her. Gracieuse, who was behind her, attracted a thousand gazes; Grognon, foolish and vain, believed that everyone only had eyes for her.

There was almost no one any longer who dared to dispute Grognon's beauty when a young knight was seen to arrive, who was carrying a portrait in a diamond locket. He said that he sustained that Grognon was the ugliest of all women and that the one who was painted in his locket was the most beautiful of all young women. At the same time he ran against the six knights, whom he unhorsed. Six more presented themselves, and so on until twenty-four, and he felled them all. Then he opened his locket and told them that in order to console them he would show them the beautiful portrait. Everyone recognized it as that of Princess Gracieuse; he made her a profound reverence and withdrew without having wanted to declare his name, but she had no doubt that it was Percinet.

Anger almost suffocated Grognon; her throat swelled; she could not pronounce a word. She made a sign that it was

Gracieuse with whom she was angry, and when she was able to explain herself she set out to make life desperate.

"How dare you dispute the prize for beauty with me?" she said. "To make my knights receive such an insult! No, I can't bear it. It's necessary that I avenge myself or die."

"Madame," said the princess, "I protest that I had no part in what just happened. I will sign in my blood, if you wish, a statement that you are the most beautiful person in the world and that I'm a monster of ugliness."

"Oh, you can joke, my little darling," replied Grognon, "but I'll have my turn before long."

Someone went to tell the king about his wife's fury, and that the princess was dying of fear, that she begged him to have pity on her, because if he abandoned her to the queen, she would do her a thousand injuries. He was unmoved, and only replied: "I've given her to her stepmother; she can do with her what she pleases."

The malevolent Grognon waited impatiently for nightfall. As soon as it had arrived, she had horses fitted to her carriage. Gracieuse was obliged to climb into it, and under a large escort she was taken a hundred leagues away, into a great forest through which no one dared to pass because it was full off lions, bears, tigers and wolves. When they had penetrated to the heart of that horrible forest, they made her get down and abandoned her, no matter what pleas she could make them to have pity on her.

"I don't ask you for life," she said to them, "I only ask for a quick death. Kill me, in order to spare me all the evils that are about to befall me."

It was like talking to the deaf; they did not even bother to reply, and drew away from her at great speed, leaving the beautiful and unfortunate young woman all alone.

She walked for some time without knowing where she was going, sometimes bumping into a tree, sometimes falling, sometimes getting tangled in bushes. Finally, overwhelmed by dolor, she threw herself on the ground, without having the strength to get up again.

"Percinet!" she shouted, sometimes. "Percinet, where are you? Is it possible that you've abandoned me?"

As she spoke, she suddenly saw the most beautiful and the most surprising thing in the world: it was an illumination so magnificent that there was not a tree in the forest in which there were not several chandeliers full of candles, and in the depths of a pathway she perceived a palace entirely made of crystal, which was shining like the sun. She began to believe that Percinet had something to do with that new enchantment; she felt a joy mingled with dread.

"I'm alone," she said. "That prince is young, lovable and amorous; I owe him my life. Oh, it's too much! Let's get away from him! It's better to die than to love."

As she spoke she stood up, in spite of her lassitude and her weakness, and without looking in the direction of the beautiful castle, she marched in another direction, so troubled and so confused in the different thoughts that were agitating her that she did not know what she was doing.

At that moment she heard a noise behind her. Fear gripped her; she thought that it was some ferocious beast that was about to devour her. She looked, trembling, and she saw Prince Percinet, as handsome as Amour is depicted.

"You're fleeing me, my princess," he said. "You fear me, when I adore you. Is it possible that you are so little instructed of my respect that you believe me capable of lacking it for you? Come, come without alarm into the Palace of Faerie; I won't enter it if you forbid me to. You'll find the queen, my mother, there, and my sisters, who already love you tenderly on the basis of what I've told them about you."

Gracieuse, charmed by the submissive and engaging manner in which her young lover spoke, could not refuse to enter with him into a small painted and gilded sleigh, which two red deer drew at a prodigious speed, with the result that in very little time it took her through a thousand places in the forest that seemed admirable to her. One could see clearly everywhere; there were shepherds and shepherdesses, elegantly dressed, who were dancing to the sound of flutes and bagpipes. In other places, on the banks of springs, she saw villagers with their mistresses, who were eating and singing joyfully.

"I thought," she said, "that this forest was uninhabited, but it seems to be populated everywhere, and joyful."

"Since you have been here, my princess," Percinet replied, "there is no longer anything in this somber solitude but pleasures and agreeable amusements; amours accompany you, flowers are born under your footfalls."

Gracieuse did not dare to reply; she did not want to embark on those sorts of conversations, and she begged the prince to take her to the queen, his mother.

Immediately, he told his deer to go to the Palace of Faerie. As she arrived there she heard an admirable music, and the queen, with two of her daughters, who were both charming, came to meet her, embraced her and took her into a great hall, the walls of which were rock crystal. She remarked with great astonishment that her history, up to that day, was engraved there, even the excursion she had just made in the sleigh with the prince; but it was sculpted so finely that Phidias and all the ancient Greeks we praise would not have been able to approach it.

"You have very diligent workmen," said Gracieuse to Percinet. "As soon as I do something or make a gesture, I see it engraved."

"That's because I don't want to lose anything if what relates to you, my princess," he replied. "Alas, nowhere am I happy or content."

She made no reply, and thanked the queen for the manner in which she had welcomed her. A great meal was served, at which Gracieuse ate with a good appetite, for she was delighted to have found Percinet in the forest instead of the bears and lions she had feared. Although she was very tired, he engaged her to pass into a drawing room brilliant with gold and paintings, in which an opera was performed; it was the amours of Psyche and Cupid, mingled with dances and little songs. A young shepherd came to sing these words:

You are loved, Gracieuse, and the god of love himself
Could not love you to the extent that you are loved.
Imitate, at least, the tigers and the bears,
Which let themselves be tamed by the smallest amours.
The proudest animals, savage by nature,
Are gentled by the pleasures in which amour engages them;
All speak of amour and let themselves be charmed thereby;
You alone are surly and refuse to love.

She blushed to hear herself named thus before the queen and the princesses; she told Percinet that she it caused her some pain that everyone shared their secrets.

"I remember a maxim in that regard," she continued, "which pleased me greatly:

Do not make confidences
And be sure that silence
Has powerful charms for me;
The world has strange maxims;
The most innocent pleasures
Sometimes pass for crimes.

He begged her pardon for having done something that had displeased her. The opera finished and the queen had the two princesses conduct her to her apartment. Nothing has ever been more magnificent than the furniture, nor as elegant as the bed and the chamber in which she was to sleep. She was served by twenty-four young women dressed as nymphs; the oldest was twenty-eight, and each of them seemed a miracle of beauty. When she had been put to bed they commenced making a delightful music in order to lull her to sleep, but she was so surprised that she could not close her eyes.

"Everything that I have seen," she said, "is an enchantment. How redoubtable a prince is who is so amiable and so clever! I can't get away from this place soon enough."

The thought of that separation troubled her greatly. To quit such a magnificent palace in order to put herself in the hands of the barbaric Grognon was such a great difference that one was bound to hesitate. However, she found Percinet so engaging that she did not want to remain in a palace of which he was the master.

When she got up, she was presented with dresses of all colors, decorations of all manner of precious stones, lace, ribbons, gloves and silk stockings, all marvelously tasteful; nothing was lacking. She was placed at a dressing-table of sculpted gold; she had never been so well adorned and had never appeared so beautiful.

Percinet came into her room clad in gold and green—for gold was his color, since Gracieuse loved it. Everything that can be imagined of the best-made and most lovable could not approach that young prince. Gracieuse told him that she had not been able to sleep, that the memory of her misfortunes tormented her, and that she could not help being apprehensive of their consequences.

"What is there that can alarm you, Madame?" he said to her. "You are a sovereign here, and you are adored; would you want to abandon me for your cruel enemy?"

"If I were the mistress of my destiny," she told him, "the course of action that you propose to me would be the one I would accept, but I am accountable for my actions to my father, the king. It is better to suffer than to fail in my duty."

Percinet said everything there was to be said to persuade her to marry him, but she did not want to consent to it; it was almost in spite of herself that he retained her there for a week, during which he imagined a thousand new pleasures to amuse her.

She often said to the prince: "I would like to know what is happening in Grognon's court, and how she has explained what she has done to me."

Percinet told her that he would send his squire, who was an intelligent fellow. She replied that she was convinced that he had no need of anyone to be informed of what was happening, and that he was thus able to tell her.

"Come with me into the high tower, then," he said to her, "and you can see for yourself."

With that he took her to the top of a prodigiously high tower, which was all made of rock crystal, like the rest of the castle. He told her to put her foot on his and her little finger in her mouth, and then to look in the direction of the city.

Immediately, she perceived the vile Grognon with the king. She was saying to him: "That wretched princess has hanged herself in the cellar. I've just seen her, she's a horrific sight; it's necessary to bury her quickly and console yourself for such a small loss."

The king started to weep at the death of his daughter. Grognon turned her back on him and retired to her room, had someone take a log, fit a nun's head-dress to it, wrap it up well and put it in a coffin. Then by order of the king, there was a grand burial, at which everyone was present, weeping, and cursing the stepmother whom they accused of that death. Everyone put on full mourning; she heard the regrets caused by her death, which were whispered.

"What a pity that such a young and beautiful princess should perish by the cruelties of such an evil creature!"

"It was necessary to chop her up and make mincemeat of her."

The king, unable to eat or drink, wept wholeheartedly.

Seeing her father so afflicted, Gracieuse said: "Oh, Percinet, I can't bear to let my father believe that I'm dead any longer. If you love me, take me back."

Whatever he could say, it was necessary to obey, albeit with an extreme reluctance.

"My princess," he said to her, "you'll regret the Palace of Faerie more than once; as for myself, I dare not believe that you'll regret me; you're more inhumane to me than Grognon is to you."

No matter what he said, she was obstinate in departing; she took her leave of the prince's mother and sisters. He climbed into the sleigh with her, and the deer set off at a run. As she emerged from the palace she heard a loud noise and looked behind her; it was the entire edifice shattering into a thousand pierces behind her.

"What do I see?" she cried. "There's no more palace!"

"No," replied Percinet. "My palace will be among the dead; you'll only enter it after your burial."

"You're angry," Gracieuse said to him, trying to soothe him. "But fundamentally, don't I have more to lament than you?"

When they arrived, Percinet made the princess, himself and the sleigh invisible. She went up to the king's room and threw herself at his feet. When he saw her he was afraid and tried to flee, mistaking her for a phantom. She retained him, and told him that she was not dead, that Grognon had had her taken into the savage forest; that she had climbed a tree where she had lived on fruits; that a log had been buried in her stead and that she asked him the favor of sending her to one of his castles in which she would no longer be exposed to the fury of her stepmother.

The king, uncertain as to whether she was telling the truth, had the log disinterred, and was very astonished by Grognon's malice. Anyone but him would have had her put in the same place, but he was a poor, weak man who did not have the courage to become entirely disagreeable. He caressed his daughter a great deal and had supper with her,

When Grognon's creatures went to tell her about the return of the princess, and that she was having supper with the king, she entered into a frenzy, and ran to his room. She told him that there was no room for hesitation, that it was necessary to abandon the little wretch to her or to see her depart that instant, never to return as long as she lived; that it was a supposition to think that she was Princess Gracieuse; that the truth was that she resembled her slightly but that Gracieuse had hanged herself; that she had seen it with her own eyes; and that if anyone believed in this imposture of this one they would be would lacking in consideration and confidence for her.

Without saying a word, the king abandoned the unfortunate princess to her, believing, or pretending to believe, that she was not his daughter.

Grognon, transported by joy, dragged her, with the help of her women, into a dungeon, where she had her undressed. Her rich garments were taken away and she was clad in poor rags of coarse cloth, with clogs on her feet and a hood on her head. She was only given a little straw for a bed and some brown bread.

In that distress she started weeping bitterly, and regretting the Palace of Faerie, but she dared not appeal to Percinet to help her, thinking that she had treated him too badly, and not being able to promise herself that he loved her enough to help her again.

Meanwhile, the wicked Grognon sent someone in quest of a fay who was no less malicious than her.

"I'm holding a little rogue here," she said to her, "of whom I have reason to complain. I want to make her suffer and always to give her difficult tasks, which she cannot complete, in order to be able to thrash her without her having any grounds for complaint. Help me to find new punishments every day."

The fay replied that she would think about it, and would come back the next day.

She did not fail to do so; she brought a bundle of thread as stout as four people, so delicate that the thread broke if one blew on it and so intricately entangled that it was screwed up in a ball with no beginning or end.

Delighted, Grognon sent for the beautiful prisoner and said to her: "Here, my good woman, "get your thick paws ready to wind this thread, and be sure that if you break the slightest wisp, you'll be doomed, because I'll flay you myself.

Begin when you like, but I want it wound by sunset." Then she locked her in a room, with three keys.

The princess was no sooner there than, looking at the huge tangle, turning it over and over, breaking a thousand threads rather than one, she remained so nonplused that she did not even want to attempt to wind it and threw it into the middle of the room.

"Go, fatal thread," she said. "You'll cause my death. Oh, Percinet, Percinet, if my rigors have not repelled you too much, I don't ask that you come to my aid, but at least come to receive my last adieu."

With that she started to weep so bitterly that someone far less sensible than a lover would have been touched by it.

Percinet opened the door with the same facility as if he had kept the key in his pocket. "Here I am, my princess," he said, "ever ready to serve you; I'm not capable of abandoning you, although you recognize my passion so poorly."

He tapped the bundle three times with his wand; the threads immediately joined up with one another, and after two further taps, it was all wound with a surprising neatness. He asked whether she wanted anything more of him, and whether she would only ever appeal to him in her distress."

"Don't reproach me, handsome Percinet," she said. "I'm unhappy enough already."

"But my princess, it only depends on you to liberate yourself from the tyranny of which you are the victim. Come with me; let us make our common felicity. What do you fear?"

"That you might not love me enough," she replied. "I want time to confirm your sentiments."

Percinet, outraged by those suspicions, took his leave of her and left.

The sun was on the point of setting; Grognon was awaiting the moment with a thousandfold impatience. Finally, she anticipated it and came with her four Furies, who accompanied her everywhere. She put the three keys into the three locks and as she opened the door she said: "I'll wager that that beautiful idler won't have done the work of her ten fingers;

she'll have preferred to sleep in order to have a fresh complexion."

When she had entered, Gracieuse presented her with the
ball of thread, in which nothing was lacking. She had nothing
else to say except that it was dirty, that she was a slut, and for
that she gave her two slaps, which turned her white and pink
cheeks blue and yellow. The unfortunate Gracieuse suffered
patiently an insult to which she was not in a state to respond.
She was taken back to her dungeon, where she was securely
imprisoned.

Grognon, chagrined at not having succeeded with the
tangle of thread, went to the fay and charged her with reproaches. "Find something less easy," she said to her, in order
that she can't complete it."

The fay went away, and the following day she brought a
huge barrel full of feathers. They were from all sorts of birds:
nightingales, canaries, siskins, goldfinches, linnets, warblers,
parrots, owls, sparrows, doves, ostriches, bustards, peacocks,
skylarks and grouse; I would never end if I wanted to name
them all. Those feathers were all mixed together; even the
birds would not have been able to recognize them.

"Here," said the fay, speaking to Grognon, "is what will
test the skill and patience of your prisoner. Tell her to sort out
these feathers, to put the peacock feathers in one place, the
nightingale feathers in another, and so on, and to make a heap
of each kind: a fay would find it difficult enough."

Grognon swooned with joy on imagining the embarrassment of the unfortunate princess; she sent for her, made her
the usual threats, and shut her with the barrel in the room with
three locks, ordering her to have all the work done by sunset.

Gracieuse picked up a few feathers, but it was impossible
for her to tell them apart and she threw them back in the barrel. She picked them up again; she tried several times, but,
seeing that she was attempting something impossible, she said,
in a despairing tone and manner: "Let's die. It's my death that
is wanted; that will put an end to my woes. It's necessary not

to call Percinet to my aid any longer; if he loved me, he'd already be here."

"I am here, my princess," cried Percinet, emerging from the bottom of the barrel, where he was hiding. "I'm here to get you out of the difficult you're in; have no doubt, after so many proofs of my attention, that I love you more than my life."

Immediately, he tapped his wand three times, and the feathers emerged from the barrel in thousands and arranged themselves of their own accord in little piles all around the room.

"What do I not owe you?" Gracieuse said to him. "Without you I was about to succumb; be certain of all my gratitude."

The prince did not neglect anything to persuade her to make a firm resolution in his favor; she asked him for more time, and whatever violence he felt, he accorded her what she wished.

Grognon came; she remained so surprised by what she saw that she no longer knew what to imagine in order to desolate Gracieuse. She beat her anyway, saying that the piles were poorly arranged.

She sent for the fay and was horribly angry with her. The fay did not know how to respond; she remained confounded. Finally, she said that she would employ all her industry to make a box that would certainly embarrass her prisoner if she attempted to open it.

A few days later she brought her a fairly large box "Here," she said to Grognon. "Send your slave to take this somewhere; forbid her strictly to open it; she won't be able to help herself, and you'll be content."

Grognon did not fail to do it. "Take this box," she said, "to my rich castle and put it on the table in the cabinet. But I forbid you, on pain of death, to look inside it."

Gracious departed in her clogs, her cotton dress and her woolen hood. The people who encountered her said: "That's some goddess in disguise," for she had a marvelous beauty nevertheless.

She did not walk far without getting very weary. As she went through a little wood that was bordered by a pleasant meadow she sat down in order to catch her breath. She was holding the box on her knees, and the desire suddenly took her to open it.

"What can happen to me?" she said. "I won't take anything from it, but at least I'll see what's inside."

She did not reflect further on the consequences; she opened it, and immediately, a great many tiny men and women emerged, with violins and other instruments, little tables, little cooks and little dishes; the giant of the troop was as tall as a finger. They leapt down into the meadow, separated into small groups and commenced the jolliest ball that has ever been seen; some danced, others cooked and others ate; the little violins played marvelously.

At first Gracieuse took some pleasure in seeing something so extraordinary, but when she was no longer weary and wanted to oblige them to go back into the box, not one wanted to do so; the little ladies and gentlemen fled, and the violins, and the cooks too, with their cooking-pots on their heads and their skewers over their shoulders. They went into the wood when she came into the meadow, and went into the meadow when she came into the wood.

"Excessively indiscreet curiosity," said Gracieuse, weeping, "you'll be favorable to my enemy. The only misfortune from which I could have protected myself will occur by my own fault. No, I can't reproach myself enough. Percinet," she cried, "Percinet, if it's possible that you still love a princess so imprudent, come to aid me in the most deplorable situation of my life!"

Percinet did not have to be called three times; she perceived him with this rich green coat.

"Without the malevolent Grognon, beautiful princess," he said, "you'd never give me a thought."

"Oh, judge my sentiments better," she said. "I'm not insensible to merit, nor ingrate to benefits. It's true that I've tested your constancy, but that's in order to crown it when I'm convinced of it."

Percinet, more convinced than he had ever been, tapped his wand three times on the box. Immediately the little men, women, musicians, cooks and equipment were all replaced, as if they had never budged.

Percinet had left his chariot in the wood; he begged the princess to make use of it in order to go to the rich castle; she had need of that vehicle, in the state she was in; with the consequence that, rendering himself invisible, he took her personally, and had the pleasure of keeping her company: a pleasure to which my chronicle says that she was not indifferent in the depths of her heart, although she hid her sentiments carefully.

She arrived at the rich castle, and when she asked, on the part of Grognon, that the cabinet be opened for her, the governor burst out laughing.

"What!" he said. "You think that on leaving your sheep you can enter such a fine place? Go back where you came from; clogs were never made for such a floor."

Gracieuse begged him to write a word for her regarding what he had refused her. He agreed to that, and when she emerged from the rich castle she found the amiable Percinet waiting for her, who took her back to the palace. It would be difficult to write everything tender and respectful said to her on the way in order to persuade her to put an end to his woes. She replied that if Grognon did her yet another bad turn she would consent to it.

When the stepmother saw her coming back she threw herself on the fay, whom she had retained; she scratched her, and would have strangled her if a fay could be strangled. Gracieuse presented her with the note from the governor and the box; she threw both of them in the fire without deigning to open them, and if she had followed her inclination she would have thrown the princess on it too, but she did not defer her torture for long.

She had a great hole dug in the garden, as deep as a well; a large stone was placed on top of it. She went for a walk and said to Gracieuse and all those accompanying her: "Here's a stone, under which I'm told there's a treasure; come on, lift it up promptly. Everyone lent a hand to that, Gracieuse like the others. That was what was wanted; as soon as she was on the edge, Grognon pushed her rudely into the well, and the stone that sealed it was allowed to fall back.

For that coup there was no longer any hope; how would Percinet be able to find her in the depths of the earth? She understood the difficulties very well, and repented of having waited so long to marry him.

"How terrible my destiny is!" she cried "I'm buried alive! That kind of death is more frightful than any other. You're avenged for my procrastinations, Percinet, but I feared that you might have the light humor of other men, who change when they're certain of being loved. I wanted, in sum, to be sure of your heart; my unjust suspicions are the cause of the state in which I find myself. Still," she continued, "if I could hope that you would suffer regrets at my doom, it seems that it would be less sensible to me."

She was speaking thus in order to soothe her dolor when she felt a little door open that she had not remarked in the obscurity. At the same time she perceived daylight and a garden filled with flowers, fruits, fountains, grottoes, statues, boscages and arbors. She did not hesitate to go into it. She advanced along a broad pathway, dreaming in her mind as to what the end of this commencement of an adventure might be. At the same time, she discovered the Palace of Faerie; she had no difficulty recognizing it, apart from the fact that it was entirely made of rock crystal and she could see new adventures engraved therein.

Percinet appeared, with the queen, his mother, and his sisters. "Don't forbid yourself any longer, beautiful princess," the queen said to Gracieuse. "It's time to render my son happy and get you out of the deplorable state in which you're living under the tyranny of Grognon."

The grateful princess threw herself at her knees and told her that she could order her destiny, that she would obey her in everything; that she had not forgotten Percinet's prophecy when she left the Palace of Faerie, when he had told her that the same palace would be among the dead, and that she would only enter it after having been buried; that she saw his knowledge with admiration: that she had no less for his merit; and that she accepted him, therefore, as a husband.

The prince threw himself at her feet in his turn; at the same time the palace resounded with voices and instruments, and the wedding was celebrated with the utmost magnificence. All the fays for a thousand leagues around came with sumptuous equipages; some arrived in chariots drawn by swans, others by dragons, others on clouds and others in globes of fire.

Among them appeared the fay who had helped Grognon to torment her; when she recognized her, no one had ever been more surprised; she begged her to forget what had happened and told her that she would seek means to repair the evils that she had caused her to suffer. What is true is that she did not want to remain at the feast, and, climbing back into her chariot, harnessed to two terrible serpents, she flew to the king's palace; there she sought out Grognon, and wrung her neck, without her guards or her women being able to prevent it.

> *It's you, bleak and deadly envy*
> *That causes human woes,*
> *And who, of the most beautiful life,*
> *Troubles the most serene days.*
> *It's you, who against Gracieuse*
> *Animated the wrath of the unworthy Grognon*
> *It's you who guided the blows*
> *That rendered her unhappy.*
> *Alas, what would her fate have been*
> *If the amorous constancy of her Percinet*
> *Had not snatched from death so many times?*
> *He merited the recompense*
> *That his ardor finally received.*
> *When one loves with constancy,*
> *Sooner or later, one finds perfect happiness.*

THE GOLDEN-HAIRED BEAUTY

There was once a king's daughter so beautiful that there was nothing in the world more beautiful, and because she was so beautiful, she was called the Golden-Haired Beauty, for her hair was finer than gold and marvelously blond, all curly, and fell all the way to her feet. She always went abroad covered by her blonde hair, with a crown of flowers in her hair and clothes embroidered with diamonds and pearls, so that no one could see her without loving her.

There was a young king among her neighbors; he was not married, although he was well made and very rich. When he heard everything that was being said about the Golden-Haired Beauty, even though he had not yet seen her, he began to love her so forcefully that he was unable to eat or drink, and he resolved to send an ambassador to ask for her in marriage. He had a magnificent carriage made for his ambassador; he gave him more than a hundred horses and a hundred lackeys, and commanded him to bring the princess back with him.

When the ambassador had taken his leave of the king and set forth, the whole court did not talk about anything else; the king, having no doubt that the Golden-Haired Beauty would consent to what her wished, was already having fine dresses made for her, and admirable furniture.

While the workers were toiling away, the ambassador arrived at the court of the Golden-Haired Beauty and delivered his little message; but either because she was not in a good mood that day, or the compliment did not seem to be to her taste, she responded to the ambassador that she thanked the king, but that she had no desire to marry.

The ambassador left the princess's court, very sad not to be taking her with him; he took back all the presents that he had brought on the king's behalf, for she was very sage, and knew full well that it was necessary for young women not to receive anything from young men; so she did not want to accept the beautiful diamonds and the rest, and in order not to discontent the king, she only took a quarter-pound of English pins.

When the ambassador arrived in the king's capital city, where he was awaited so impatiently, everyone was afflicted that he had not brought the Golden-Haired Beauty, and the king began to weep like a child; people consoled him, but to no avail.

There was a youth at the court who was as handsome as the sun and the best made person in the realm; because of his grace and intelligence, he was known as Avenant. Everyone loved him, except for the envious, who were annoyed that the king favored him so much and confided his affairs to him every day.

Avenant found himself with people who were talking about the ambassador's return, and said that there was nothing to be done about it. Without thinking about it overmuch, he said: "If the king had sent me to the Golden-Haired Beauty, I'm certain that she would have come with me."

Immediately, malevolent people went to say to the king: "Sire, do you know what Avenant is saying? That if you had sent him to the Golden-Haired Beauty, he would have brought her back. Consider his malice: he is claiming to be more handsome than you, and that she would have loved him so much that she would have followed him anywhere."

That made the king angry, so angry that he was beside himself. "Ha ha!" he said. "That pretty lad is making fun of my misfortune, and he values himself more highly than me; go on, have him put in my stout tower and let him die of hunger there."

The king's guards went to Avenant's home; he was no longer thinking about what he had said. They dragged him to the prison and gave him a thousand woes. The poor youth only had a little straw on which to sleep, and he would have died but for a little spring that ran at the foot of the tower, from which he drank a little in order to refresh himself, for hunger had dried out his mouth considerably.

One day, when he could do no more, he said with a sigh: "What complaint does the king have? He has no subject more faithful than me; I've never offended him."

The king chanced to be passing the tower, and when he heard the voice of the person he had liked so much, he stopped to listen in spite of those who were with him, who hated Avenant, and who said to the king: "What is amusing you, Sire? Don't you now that he's a rogue?"

"Leave me alone," said the king. "I want to listen." Having heard his laments, tears came to his eyes; he opened the door of the tower and called to him.

Avenant came sadly to knee before him, and kissed his feet. "What have I done to you, Sire," he said, "for you to treat me s harshly?"

"You made fun of me and my ambassador," said the king. "You said that if I'd sent you to the Golden-Haired Beauty, you would have brought her back."

"It's true, Sire," Avenant replied, "that I would have made her so aware of your great qualities that I'm convinced that she would not have been able to forbid herself; in that I haven't said anything that ought to be disagreeable to you."

The king found that, in fact, he had not done anything wrong. He looked askance at the people who had spoken evil of his favorite, and took Avenant with him, repenting of the harm he had done him.

After having given him a marvelous supper, he summoned him to his cabinet and said to him: "Avenant, I still love the Golden-Haired Beauty; her refusal has not put me off, but I don't know what to do to make her want to marry me; I have a yen to send you, to see if you can succeed."

Avenant replied that he was disposed to obey him in all things, and that he would depart the next day.

"Ho!" said the king. "I want to give you a great equipage."

"That's not necessary, Sire," he replied. "I only need a good horse, and letters on your part."

The king embraced him, for he was delighted to find him so ready.

It was a Monday morning when he took his leave of the king and his friends in order to undertake his embassy on his own, without any pomp or noise. He only thought about means of engaging the Golden-Haired Beauty to marry the king. He had a writing-pad in his pocket, and when some beautiful thought occurred to him to put into his speech he got down from his horse and went to sit down under the trees in order to write, so that he would not forget anything.

One morning, when he had set forth at daybreak, as he was passing through a large meadow, a very pretty thought came to him; he dismounted and went to lean on the willows and poplars that were planted along a little stream that ran on the edge of the meadow. After he had written it down he looked around, charmed to find himself in such a beautiful spot.

He perceived a large golden carp on the grass that was gasping, and which could do no more, for, having tried to catch little midges, she had leapt so high out of the water that she had landed in the grass, where she was about to die. Avenant took pity on her, and even though it was a lean day[6] and he had not been able to being anything with him for his dinner, he picked the fish up and put her back into the stream, gently.

As soon as the carp feet the freshness of the water she began to rejoice, and let herself sink to the bottom; then, returning boldly to the edge of the stream, she said: "Thank you,

---

[6] i.e., a day on which one is not supposed to eat meat—Friday in the Roman Church—and on which it therefore became conventional to eat fish in Western Europe, although it is odd to find such a convention in a world where there is no trace of the Christian Church.

Avenant, for the pleasure you have just given me; without you I'd be dead, and you're saved me. I'll pay you back."

After that little compliment, she dived into the water, and Avenant remained very surprised by the intelligence and the great civility of the carp.

On another day, as he continued his journey, he saw a crow in great difficulty. The poor bird had been pursued by a large eagle, a great eater of crows; it was about to be caught, and would have been swallowed like a lentil if Avenant had not had compassion for the bird's misfortune. "That," he said, "is how the stronger oppress the weaker; what reason does the eagle have to eat the crow?" He took his bow, which he always carried, and an arrow; then, taking aim at the eagle, *snap*, he unleashed the arrow into its body and pierced it all the way through; it fell dead, and the delighted crow came to perch in a tree.

"Avenant," he said to him, "you're very generous to have helped me, being only a wretched crow; but I won't be ingrate; I'll pay you back."

Avenant admired the good intelligence of the crow, and continued on his way.

As he went into a large wood, so early that he could hardly see to guide himself, he heard an owl screech desperately.

"Yes," he said, "that's a very afflicted owl; it must have let itself get caught in some net."

He searched in all directions, and finally found nets that bird-catchers had spread by night in order to trap little birds.

"What a pity!" he said "Men are only made to torment one another, or to persecute poor animals, which do them no harm or damage."

He took out his knife and cut the cords. The owl took flight, but he came back with a flick of his wings. "Avenant," he said, "it isn't necessary to make you a long speech to make you understand the obligation I have to you; it speaks for itself. The hunters would have come; I was caught; I'd have died without your help. I have a grateful heart; I'll pay you back."

Those were the three most considerable adventures that happened to Avenant during his journey; he was in such a hurry to arrive that he did not delay in going to the palace of the Golden-Haired Beauty. Everything there was admirable; diamonds were seen there heaped up like stones; fine clothes, bonbons and money; there were marvelous things, and he thought to himself that if she quit all that to go to the home of the king, his master, he would be very lucky.

He put on a brocade coat and red and white plumes; he combed his hair, washed and powdered is face; he put a rich embroidered scarf around his neck, and a little basket with a lovely little dog inside, which he had bought while passing through Boulogne. Avenant was so well made, so amiable, and did everything with so much grace that when he presented himself at the palace gate, all the guards bowed deeply to him, and someone ran to tell the Golden-Haired Beauty that Avenant, the ambassador of the king, her nearest neighbor, was asking to speak to her.

At the name Avenant, the princess said: "That name brings me a good signification; I'll wager that he's pretty and that he pleases everyone."

"Truly, yes, Madame, said all her maids of honor. "We saw him from the grain loft where we were sorting out your flax, and as long as he remained under the windows we weren't able to do anything."

"That's fine thing," replied the Golden-Haired Beauty, "amusing yourselves looking at young men. Someone fetch me my robe of embroidered blue satin, and scatter my blonde hair over it well; fetch me garlands of fresh flowers and give me my high-heeled shoes and my fan. Have my chamber and my throne swept, for I want him to say everywhere that I really am the Golden-Haired Beauty."

All the women hastened to adorn her like a queen; they were in so much haste that they bumped into one another and scarcely made any progress. Finally, the princess went into the gallery with the large mirrors to see if anything was lacking; then she mounted her throne of old, ivory and ebony, which smelled like balm, and she ordered her young women to take up instruments and sing very softly, in order not to deafen anyone.

Avenant was taken to the audience hall; he was so transported by admiration that he said many times thereafter that he was almost incapable of speaking; nevertheless, he gathered his courage and made a marvelous speech; he begged the princess to give him the pleasure of not returning without her.

"Genteel Avenant," she said to him, "all the reasons that you've just given me are very good, and I assure you that I'd be very glad to favor you rather than another, but it's necessary that you know that I went for an excursion on the river a month ago with all my women, and, as a collation was being served, while taking off my glove, I pulled a ring of my finger, which unfortunately fell into the river. I cherished it more than my realm; I leave you to judge by what affliction that loss was followed. I swore an oath never to listen to any proposals for my marriage unless the ambassador who was proposing a spouse to me brought back my ring. See now what you have to do in that regard, for even if you talked to me for fifteen days and fifteen nights in succession, you wouldn't persuade me to change my sentiment."

Avenant was very astonished by that response. He made her a profound reverence and begged her to receive the little dog, the basket and the scarf; but she replied that she did not want any presents and that he should think about what she had just said.

When he had returned to his lodgings he went to bed without supper, and his little dog, whose name was Cabriolle, not wanting any supper either, came to lie down beside him. All night long, Avenant did not cease to sigh.

"How can I recover a ring fallen into a great river a months ago?" he said. "It's folly to attempt it. The princess only told me that to put me in the impossibility of obeying her." He sighed, and was very afflicted.

Cabriolle, who was listening, said to him: "I beg you, my dear master, don't despair of your good fortune. You're too amiable to be unfortunate. Let's go to the river bank at day-break."

Avenant patted him twice, and made no reply; over-whelmed by sadness, he went to sleep.

As soon as he saw the daylight, Cabriolle capered so much that he woke him up, and said to him: "Get dressed, my master and let's go."

Avenant did as he was bid; he got up, got dressed and went down into the garden, and from the garden, he went in-sensibly to the river's edge, where he was walking with his hat pulled down over his eyes and his arms folded, only thinking about his departure, when all of a sudden he heard someone calling: "Avenant! Avenant!"

He looked in all directions and did not see anyone; he thought he was dreaming. He continued walking, but he was called again: "Avenant! Avenant!"

"Who's calling me?" he said.

Cabriolle, who was very small and was looking closely into the water, replied: "Never believe me, if it's not a golden carp that I can see."

Immediately, the large carp appeared, and said to him: "you saved my life in the meadow of service trees, where I would have remained but for you. Here, dear Avenant, is the Golden-Haired Beauty's ring."

He bent down, and took it from the mouth of the carp, whom he thanked a thousand times.

Instead of returning to his lodgings he went straight to the palace with little Cabriolle, who was very glad to have made his master come to the river bank.

Someone went to tell the princess that he wanted to see her. "Alas," she said, "the poor boy has come to take his leave of me; he's considered that what I want is impossible and he's going to tell that to his master."

Avenant was shown in; he presented the ring to her and said: "Madame la Princesse, that's your command executed; will you please receive my master the king for your husband?"

When she saw her ring, in which nothing was lacking, she was so astonished that she thought she was dreaming. "Truly, gracious Avenant," she said, "it's necessary that you're favored by some fay, for naturally, this isn't possible."

"Madame," he said, "I don't know any, but I had a strong desire to obey you."

"Since you have such good will," she said, "It's necessary that you render me another service, without which I shall never marry. There is a prince, not far from here, named Galifron, who got it into his head to marry me. He had his design declared with frightful threats that if I refused he would desolate my realm. But judge whether I could accept: he's a giant taller than a high tower; he eats a man as a monkey eats a chestnut. When he goes on campaign he carries small cannons in his pockets, which he uses instead of pistols, and when he speaks loudly, those who are nearby are deafened. I told him that I didn't want to marry, and asked him to excuse me, but he has never wearied of persecuting me. He kills all my subjects, and before anything else, it's necessary for you to fight him and bring me his head."

Avenant was slightly stunned by that proposition. He thought about it for some time, and then he said: "Well, Madame, I'll fight Galifron. I believe that I'll be defeated, but I'll die a brave man."

She said a thousand things to prevent him from undertaking that enterprise, but it was futile. He withdrew in order to go in search of weapons, and everything he needed.

When he had everything he wanted, he put little Cabriolle back into his basket, mounted his beautiful horse, and went into Galifron's land. He asked for news of him of the people he encountered, and everyone told him that he was a true demon, whom no one dared approach. The more he heard that said, the more afraid he was.

Cabriolle reassured him and said to him: "My dear master, while you fight, I'll go to bite his legs; he'll lower his head in order to chase me away, and you'll be able to kill him."

Avenant admired the spirit of the little dog, but he knew that his help would not be sufficient.

Finally, he arrived near Galifron's castle. All the roads were covered with the bones and the carcasses of men he had between or torn into pieces.

He did not have to wait for long before he saw him coming through a wood. His head surpassed the tallest trees, and he was singing in a frightful voice:

Where are the little children
That I crunch with fine teeth when
I need so many, having such a penchant,
That the world is not sufficient.

Immediately, Avenant began to sing, to the same tune:

Approach, here's Avenant
Who will pull your teeth out;
He isn't very tall, no doubt,
But to beat you he's sufficient.

The rhymes were not very regular, but he had made the song very quickly, and it was even a miracle that it wasn't any worse, for he was horribly afraid.

When Galifron heard his words he looked in all directions, and he perceived Avenant, sword in hand, who improvised two or three insults in order to irritate him. He did not need so many; they put him in a frightful wrath, and, raising an iron club, he would have felled the genteel Avenant with the first blow but for a crow, who flew at him at head height and pecked him so accurately in the eyes that he punctured them; his blood ran down his face; he was desperately striking in all directions, Avenant evaded the club and dealt him great thrusts with his sword, which went in all the way to the hilt, and inflicted a thousand wounds on him, from which he lost so much blood that he collapsed.

Immediately, Avenant cut off his head, delighted to have been so fortunate, and the crow, which came to perch in a tree, said to him: "I haven't forgotten the service you rendered me by killing the eagle that was pursuing me; I promised to acquit myself; I believe I've done it today."

"It's me who owes you everything, Messire Crow," replied Avenant, "And I remain your servant."

He mounted his horse right away, charged with Galifron's terrible head.

When he arrived in the city everyone followed him, crying: "There goes the brave Avenant, who had just killed the monster," with the consequence that the princess, who heard the noise and was trembling that someone might come to bring her news of Avenant's death, dared not asked what had happened. She saw Avenant come in, however, with the head of the giant, which scared her, even though there was no longer anything to fear.

"Madame," he said to her, "your enemy is dead; I hope that you will no longer refuse the king, my master."

"Oh, yes indeed," said the Golden-Haired Beauty, "I shall refuse him, if you don't find the means, before my departure, to bring me water from the tenebrous grotto. Near here there is a profound grotto that is a full six leagues around. At the entrance there are two dragons that prevent anyone from entering; they have fire in their mouths and in their eyes; and then, when one is in the grotto, one finds a vast hole into which it is necessary to descend; it is full of toads and snakes. At the bottom of the hole there is a dismal cave, in which the fountain of beauty and health flows; it is that water that I absolutely must have. Everything that is washed in it becomes marvelous; if one is beautiful one always remains beautiful; if one is young, one becomes young. You can imagine, Avenant, that I won't quit my realm without taking some with me."

"Madame," he said, "you are so beautiful that the water in question is quite unnecessary to you; but I am an unfortunate ambassador whose death you want. I will go in search of the water you desire, with the certainty of not returning."

The Golden-Haired Beauty did not change her design, and Avenant departed with the little dog Cabriolle to go to the tenebrous grotto in search of the water of beauty. All those who encountered him on the way said: "It's a pity to see such a likeable fellow going to his doom with a cheerful heart; he's going alone to the grotto, and even if there were a hundred more with him, he wouldn't reach the end. Why does the princess only want impossible things?"

He continued to march and did not say a word, but he was very sad.

He arrived near the top of a mountain, where he stopped to rest for a while. He let his horse graze and Cabriolle run after flies. He knew that the tenebrous grotto was not far away; he looked to see whether it might be visible. Finally, he perceived an ugly rock as black as ink, from which thick smoke was emerging, and, a moment later, one of the dragons that projected fire from its eyes and mouth; it had a yellow and green body, claws and a long tail that coiled around more than a hundred times Cabriolle saw all that, and did not know where to hide, he was so frightened.

Avenant, resolved to die, drew his sword and went downhill with a phial that the Golden-Haired Beauty had given him to fill with the water of beauty. "I'm done for!" he said to his little dog, Cabriolle. "I'll never be able to get that water, which is guarded by the dragons. When I'm dead, fill the phial with my blood and take it to the princess so that she can see what she cost me, and then go to find the king, my master and tell him about my misfortune."

As he was speaking thus, he heard someone calling: "Avenant! Avenant!"

"Who's calling me?" he said; and he saw an owl in a hole in a old tree, who said to him: "You took me out of the hunters' net in which I was caught and you saved my life; I promised you I'd repay you; the time has come. Give me your phial; I know all the routes to the tenebrous grotto, I'll go in quest of the water of beauty for you. Who'll be glad? I leave you to imagine."

Avenant gave him the phial, quickly, and the owl flew into the grotto without hindrance. In less than a quarter of an hour he came back, bringing the bottle, well sealed. Avenant was delighted; he thanked him with all his heart and, going back up the mountain, he took the road to the city, full of joy.

He went straight to the palace; he presented the phial to the Golden-Haired Beauty, who had nothing more to say. She thanked Avenant, and gave orders to everyone that it was necessary to depart; then she set forth on the journey with him. She found him very likeable and she said to him sometimes: "If you had wanted I would have made you king; we wouldn't have left my realm."

But he replied: "I would not want to give my master such a great displeasure for all the kingdoms in the world, although I find you more beautiful than the sun."

Finally, they arrived in the king's capital city. Knowing that the Golden-Haired Beauty was coming, he came to meet her and gave her the finest presents in the world. He married her with so much rejoicing that no one talked about anything else; but the Golden-Haired Beauty, who loved Avenant in the depths of her heart, was only glad when she saw him, and always praised him.

"I wouldn't have come without Avenant," she told the king. "It was necessary for him to do impossible things in my service; you ought to be obliged to him; he has given me the water of beauty; I shall never grow old and I shall always be beautiful."

The envious individuals who listened to the queen said to the king: "You aren't jealous, and you have reason to be; the queen loves Avenant so much that she's neglecting to eat and drink; she talks about nothing but him and the obligations you have to him, as if any other envoy you'd sent wouldn't have done as much."

The king said: "Truly, I think so; let him be put in the tower with irons on his feet and hands."

Avenant was seized, and his recompense for having served the king so well was to be locked in the tower with irons on his hands and feet. He did not see anyone but the jailer, who threw him a piece of black bread through a hole, and water in an earthenware bowl. His little dog Cabriolle did not quit him, though; he consoled him, and came to tell him all the news.

When the Golden-Haired Beauty heard about his disgrace she threw herself at the king's feet and, in tears, begged him to let Avenant out of prison. But the more she begged the irritated he became, thinking: *It's because she loves him*; and he did not want to do anything. She did not mention it again, and she was very sad.

The king thought that perhaps she did not think him handsome enough; he wanted to rub his face with the water of beauty, in order that the queen would love him more than she did. That water was in the phial on the mantelpiece of the queen's chamber; she had put it there in order to look at it more often; but one of the chambermaids, trying to kill a spider with a broom, unfortunately knocked the phial to the floor, where it broke, and all the water was lost. She swept rapidly, not knowing what to do, but she remembered having seen an exactly similar phial in the king's cabinet full of water as clear as the water of beauty. She took it adroitly, without saying anything, and took it to the queen's mantelpiece.

The water that was in the king's cabinet served to kill princes and great lords when they were criminal, instead of cutting of their heads or hanging them, their faces were rubbed with the liquid; they went to sleep and did not wake up again. One evening, therefore, the king took the phial and rubbed his face with it; then he went to sleep and died.

The little dog Cabriolle was one of the first to know, and did not fail to go and tell the Golden-Haired Beauty, and to remind her about the poor prisoner. Cabriolle slipped gently through the crowd, for there was a great tumult in the court because of the death of the king. He said to the queen: "Madame, don't forget poor Avenant."

She remembered immediately the pains he had suffered because of her and his great fidelity. She went out without speaking to anyone, went straight to the tower and removed the irons from Avenant's hands and feet personally. Putting a golden crown on his head, she said to him: "Come noble Avenant; I'm making you a king and taking you for my husband."

He threw himself at her feet and thanked her.

Everyone was delighted to have him for a master; he had the most beautiful wedding in the world, and the Golden-Haired Beauty lived for a long time with the handsome Avenant, both happy and satisfied.

If by chance an unfortunate
Asks for your assistance,
Do not refuse a generous help
A benefit is recompensed sooner or later.
When Avenant, with so much kindness,
Served the carp and the crow, and even the owl
Without being put off by its ugliness
He conserved liberty;
Would one ever have thought
That those animals, one day,
Would take him to the summit of glory
When he wanted to serve the king with amour?
In spite of the attractions of a charming beauty,
Who commenced to feel desires for him,
He conserved for his master, stifling his sighs,
A constant fidelity.
Nevertheless, he was accused without reason;
But when there seemed most hindrance to his happiness;
Heaven owed him a miracle
That heaven never refuses to virtue.

THE BLUE BIRD

There was once a king rich in land and money; his wife died, and he was inconsolable. He locked himself in his little cabinet for a week, where he banged his head against the walls, so afflicted was he. It was feared that he might kill himself; mattresses where placed between the tapestries and the wall, with the consequence that he could keep banging but did not do himself any more harm.

All his subjects resolved between them to go and see him and to tell him what they could that was most appropriate to soothe his sorrow. Some prepared grave and serious speeches, others agreeable ones, and even joyful ones, but that did not make any impression on his mind, and he scarcely heard what was said to him. Finally, a woman presented herself before him so covered in black crepe, veils, mantles and long mourning clothes, who wept and sobbed so long and loudly, that he was surprised by it.

She told him that she would not attempt, like the others, to diminish his dolor, that she had come to augment it, because nothing was more just than to weep for a good wife; as for her, who had had the best of all husbands, she expected to weep on his account for as long as she had eyes in her head. With that she redoubled her cries, and the king, following her example, started howling.

He received her better than the others; he talked to her about the fine qualities of his dear departed; they talked so much that they no longer knew what to say about their grief. When the delicate widow saw the material almost exhausted, she lifted her veils slightly, and the afflicted king diverted his sight in gazing at that poor afflicted woman, which turned back and forth very appropriately two large blue eyes edged by long black lashes; her complexion was rather florid. The king considered her very attentively; gradually, he talked less about his wife, and then he no longer talked at all.

The widow said that she always wanted to weep for her husband; the king begged her not to immortalize her chagrin. By way of a conclusion, everyone was astonished that he married her, and that the black was exchanged into green and the color of rose; it is often sufficient to know the weakness of people to enter into their heart and make what one wants of it.

The king had only had one daughter during his first marriage, who passed for the eighth wonder of the world; she was named Florine because she resembled Flora, she was so fresh, young and beautiful. She was hardly ever seen in magnificent clothes; she like loose taffeta dresses with a few clasps of precious stones and garlands of flowers, which had an admirable effect when they were placed in her beautiful hair. She was only fifteen years old when the king remarried.

The new queen sent for her own daughter, who had been nursed in the home of her godmother, the fay Soussio,[7] but she was no more gracious and no more beautiful for that. Soussio had tried to work on it, but had gained nothing. She nevertheless loved her dearly; her name was Truitonne, for her face had as many red patches as a trout. Her black hair was so greasy and dirty that no one could touch it, and her yellow skin distilled oil. The queen loved her madly anyway; she only talked about the charming Truitonne, and as Florine had all sorts of advantages over her, the queen was in despair; she sought all possible means of doing her harm in regard to the king. Not a day went by when the queen and Truitonne did not play some trick on Florine. The princess, who was mild and intelligent, tried to rise above that bad behavior.

One day, the king said to the queen that Florine and Truitonne were old enough to be married, and that it was necessary to make an effort to give one of the two to the first

---

[7] Some modern versions of this tale, in both French and English, render the name of the fay as Souffio, the long *s* and the letter *f* bring indistinguishable in the eighteenth century texts.

prince who came to the court. "I intend my daughter to be the first one established," said the queen. "She's older than yours, and as she's a thousand times more lovable there can be no hesitation about that." The king, who did not like disputes, said that he approved of that, and made her the mistress of it.

Sometime after that it was learned that King Charming was to arrive. No prince had ever taken gallantry and magnificence so far; his mind and his person had nothing that did not respond to his name. When the queen heard the news she employed all the embroiderers, all the tailors and all the dressmakers in making garments for Truitonne. She asked the king that Florine should have nothing new, and having bribed her chambermaids, she had all her garments, all her coiffures and all her gems stolen on the very day that Charming arrived, with the result that when she wanted to adorn herself she did not find a single ribbon. She understood to whom she owed that favor; she send to the merchants for cloth, but they replied that the queen had forbidden that she be given any. She remained, therefore with a very dirty short dress, and her shame was so great that he put herself in a corner of the room when Charming arrived.

The queen received him with great ceremonies; she introduced her daughter to him, more brilliant that the sun and uglier by virtue of her adornments than she usually was. The king turned his eyes away from her, and the queen tried to persuade herself that she pleased him too much and he feared engaging himself, with the result that she always put her in front of him.

He asked whether there was not another princess, named Florine.

"Yes," said Truitonne, pointing a finger at her. "There she is, hiding, because she isn't brave."

Florine blushed, and became so beautiful, so very beautiful that King Charming was as if dazzled. He got up immediately and made a profound reverence to the princess. "Madame," he said to her, "your incomparable beauty ornaments you too much for you to have need of any foreign assistance."

"Sire," she said, "I confess to you that I am not accustomed to wear a costume as dirty as this one, and you would have given me pleasure by not perceiving me."

"It would be impossible," exclaimed Charming, "for such a marvelous princess to be in such a place and for one to have eyes for anyone but her."

"Oh," said the irritated queen, "I'm spending my time well listening to you. Believe me, Sire, Florine is already enough of a coquette, she has no need of anyone to say such gallantries to her."

King Charming immediately deduced the motives that were making the queen speak thus, but as he was not in a position to constrain her, he allowed all his admiration for Florine to show and conversed with her for three hours in succession.

The queen, in despair, and Truitonne, inconsolable at not having preference over the princess, made great complaints to the king, and obliged him to consent that during King Charming's sojourn, Florine would be locked in a tower where they would not see one another.

In fact, as soon as she had returned to her room, four masked men took her to the top of the tower, and left her there in the utmost desolation, for she saw clearly that she was only being thus treated in order to prevent her from pleasing the king, who already pleased her greatly, and whom she would have liked very much for a husband.

As he was unaware of the violence that had just been done to the princess, he waited for the hour to see her again with great impatience; he wanted to talk about her to the people that the king had put with him in order to do him more honor, but on the queen's orders they spoke as badly of her as they could, saying that she was a coquette, fickle, and ill-tempered; that she tormented her friends and her servants; that one could not be any dirtier; and that she pushed avarice so far that she would rather dress like a little shepherdess than buy rich clothes with the money that her father gave her. At every detail, Charming suffered, and felt stirrings of anger that he had difficulty moderating

No, he said to himself, *it's impossible that Heaven has put such an ill-made soul into that masterpiece of nature; I agree that she wasn't properly dressed when I saw her, but the shame she had in that proves sufficiently that she isn't accustomed to seeing herself thus. What! Could she be nasty with that air of modesty and mildness that is enchanting? That's not something that makes sense to me; it's easier for me to believe that it's the queen who decries her thus; one isn't a stepmother for nothing, and Princess Truitonne is such an ugly beast that it wouldn't be extraordinary if she was envious of the most perfect of all creatures.*

While he was reasoning thus, the courtiers who surrounded him divined from his attitude that they had not pleased him by speaking ill of Florine. One of them, who was more adroit than the others, changing his tone and his language in order to determine the prince's sentiments, started to say marvelous things about the princess. At those words he woke up, as if from a profound sleep, and entered into the conversation, with joy spread over his face.

Amour, amour, how difficult it is to hide you! You appear everywhere, on a lover's lips, in his eyes, in the sound of his voice; when one is in love, silence or conversation, joy or sadness all speak of what one feels.

The queen, impatient to know whether King Charming was touched, sent for those she had put in his confidence and spent the rest of the night questioning them; everything they told her only served to confirm the opinion she had that the king loved Florine.

But what can I tell you about the melancholy of the poor princess? She was lying on the floor at the top of that terrible tower, to which the masked men had taken her.

I would have less to lament, she thought, *if I had been put here before I had seen that lovable king; the idea that I conserve of him can only serve to augment my pain. I can't doubt that it's in order to prevent me from seeing him again*

that the queen is treating me so cruelly. Alas that the scant beauty with which Heaven has provided me should cost my repose so dear!

She wept so bitterly, so very bitterly, afterwards that her worst enemy would have had pity on her if she had been witness to her dolor.

It was thus that she spent the night. The queen, who wanted to engage King Charming by means of all the testimony she could give him of her attention, sent him clothes of an unparalleled richness and magnificence, made in the fashion of the land, and the Order of the Chevaliers of Amour, which she had obliged the king to institute on the day of their wedding. It was a golden heart enameled in flame-red, surrounded by several arrows and pierced by one, with the words: *Only one wounds me.* The queen had had a ruby as large as a ostrich egg cut for Charming; each arrow was a single diamond as long as a finger; and the chain that held the heart was made of pearl, the smallest of which weighed a pound. In sum, since the world has been the world, nothing like it had been seen.

At that sight the king was so surprised that he was rendered speechless for some time; he was presented at the same time with a book, the pages of which were vellum, with admirable miniatures and the binding was gold studded with precious stones; the statutes of the Order of the Chevaliers of Amour were written therein, in a very tender and very gallant style. The king was told that the princess he had seen begged him to be her knight and that she had sent him that present.

At those words he dared to flatter himself that it was the one he loved. "What!" he exclaimed. "The beautiful Princess Florine is thinking about me in such a generous and engaging manner?"

"Sire," someone said, "You're mistaking the name; we've come on behalf of the lovely Truitonne."

"It's Truitonne who wants me for her knight?" said the king, with a cold and serious expression. "I'm sorry to be unable to accept that honor, but a sovereign is not the master of himself to make the engagements he wishes. I know those of a knight; I would like to fulfill them all, and I would rather not receive the favor she offers me than to render myself unworthy of it." He immediately put the heart, the chain and the book in the same basket; then he sent them all to the queen, who nearly choked with rage, along with her daughter, at the scornful manner in which the foreign king had received such a particular favor.

When he was able to go and see the king and the queen, he went to their apartment; he hoped that Florine would be there; he looked everywhere for her. As soon as he heard someone enter the room he turned his head abruptly toward the door; he appeared anxious and chagrined.

The malicious queen divined easily enough what was on his mind, but she did not let it show. She only talked about pleasure parties; he responded haphazardly; finally, he asked where Princes Florine was.

"Sire," said the queen, proudly, "the king, her father, has forbidden her to leave her room until my daughter is married."

"And what reason can there be," replied the king, "for keeping that beautiful person prisoner?"

"I don't know," said the queen, "and if I did know, I could dispense with telling you."

The king felt an inconceivable anger; he looked askance at Truitonne and thought internally that it was because of that little monster that he was being denied the pleasure of seeing the princess. He quit the queen promptly; her presence was causing him too much pain.

When he had returned to his room he told a young prince who had accompanied him and whom he liked a great deal, to give anything necessary to bribe one of the princess's women, in order that he could talk to her for a moment. The prince easily found ladies of the palace who entered into confidence; one of them assured him that that very evening Florine would be at a low window that overlooked the garden, and that he could talk to her there, provided that he took great precautions in order that no one knew, "because," she added, "the king and queen are so severe that they would put me to death of they discovered that I had aided Charming's passion."

The prince, delighted to have taken the affair to that point, promised her everything she wished, and ran to pay his court to the king, after telling her the hour of the rendezvous. But the false confidante did not fail to go and warn the queen of what was happening and receive her order.

Immediately, she thought that it was necessary to send her daughter to the little window; she instructed her well, and Truitonne did not fail in anything, although she was naturally very stupid.

The night was so dark that it would have been impossible for the king to perceive the deceit that was being perpetrated on him even if he had not been as prejudiced as he was; thus, he approached the window with transports of inexpressible joy. He said to Truitonne everything that he would have said to Florine to persuade her of his passion.

Truitonne, profiting from the circumstance, told him that she was the most unfortunate person in the world in having such a cruel stepmother and that she would always have to suffer until her sister was married.

The king assured her that if she wanted him for her husband he would be delighted to share his crown and his heart with her; with that he took his ring off his finger and put it on Truitonne's, as a sign that it was an eternal pledge of his faith and that she only had to take the opportunity to depart with diligence.

Truitonne replied as best she could to his urgency; he perceived that she did not say anything definite, and that would have caused him pain if he had not been convinced that fear of being surprised by the queen was taking away her liberty of thought. He only quit her on condition of coming back the next day at the same hour, which she promised him with all her heart.

The queen, having learned of the fortunate outcome of that conversation, promised herself everything in consequence. And in fact, the day having been agreed, the king came to take her in a flying chaise drawn by winged frogs; one of his friends, an enchanter, had made him a present of it. The night was very dark; Truitonne emerged mysteriously through a small door, and the king, who was waiting for her received her in his arms and swore her an eternal fidelity a hundred times over. As he was not in a humor to fly for a long time in the airborne chaise without espousing the princes he loved, he asked her where she wanted the marriage to take place.

She told him that she had a godmother who was a fay, named Soussio, who was very famous; she wanted to go to her castle. Although the king did not know the way, he only had to tell his large frogs to take him there; they knew the general map of the world, and in very little time they took the king and Truitonne to Soussio's abode.

The castle was so well illuminated that on arrival the king would have discovered his error of the princess had not carefully lowered hr veil. She asked for her godmother; she talked to her in private and told her how she had trapped Charming and begged her to appease him.

"Well, my daughter," said the fay, "it won't be easy; he loves Florine too much; I'm certain that he'll make us despair."

Meanwhile, the king was waiting for them in a room, the walls of which were diamonds so clear and transparent that he saw Soussio and Truitonne through them, conferring together. He thought he was dreaming.

What! he said to himself. *Have I been betrayed? Have the demons brought that enemy of our repose here? Has she come to trouble my marriage? My dear Florine won't appear! Perhaps her father has followed her!*

He thought a thousand things that began to desolate him. But it was much worse when they came into the room and Soussio said to him in an absolute tone: "King Charming, this is Princess Truitonne, to whom you have pledged your faith; she is my goddaughter and I want you to marry her immediately."

"Me!" he cried. "Me, marry this little monster! You must believe me to be of a very docile nature if you make me such propositions. Know that I have promised her nothing. If she says otherwise, she is a..."

"Don't finish," Soussio interrupted, "and never be bold enough to lack respect for me."

"I consent to respect you as much as a fay is respectable, provided that you return my princess to me."

"Am I not her, perjurer?" said Truitonne, showing him his ring. "To whom have you given this ring as a pledge of your faith? To whom have you spoken at the little widow, if not to me?"

"Well then," he said, "I've been deceived and tricked. No, no, I won't be a dupe. Let's go, let's go, my frogs. I want to leave right away."

"Ho! That isn't in your power unless I consent to it," said Soussio. She touched him, and his feet were attached to the floor as if they had been nailed to it.

"Even if you stone me," said the king, "even if you flay me, I shall not belong to anyone but Florine; I am resolved in that, and you can use your power as you wish."

Soussio employed persuasion, threats, promises and prayers. Truitonne wept, cried, moaned, became irritated and calmed down. The king did not say a word, and, looking at them both with the most indignant expression in the world, he made no reply to their verbiage.

He spent twenty days and twenty nights in that fashion, without them ceasing to talk, without eating, without sleeping and without sitting down. Finally, Soussio, exhausted and fatigued, said to the king: "Ho! You're a stubborn one, who won't listen to reason. Choose; either seven years of penitence for having given your word without keeping it, or marry my goddaughter."

The king, who had maintained a profound silence, suddenly cried: "Do what you want with me, provided that I'm delivered from that loathsome person!"

"Loathsome yourself," said Truitonne, angrily. "You're a fine petty king, with your marshy equipage, to come into my country to insult me and break your word. If you had four sous worth of honor, would you behave thus?"

"There are touching reproaches!" said the king, in a mocking tone. "Can you see that one is wrong not to take such a beautiful person for one's wife?"

"No, no, she won't be," cried Soussio, angrily. "You have only to fly out of that window, if you wish, for you'll be a Blue Bird for seven years."

At the same time, the king changes form; his arms are covered in feathers and form wings; his legs and feet become black and thin; he feels his fingernails becoming hooked, his body shrinking; he is garnished all over with long fine plumes mingled with celestial blue; his eyes are rounded and shine like suns; his nose is no more than an ivory beak; a white crest of feathers rises up on his head, which form a crown; he sings delightfully, and speaks in the same way. In that state, he utters a dolorous cry on seeing himself thus metamorphosed, and flies away at top speed to flee Soussio's deadly palace

In the melancholy that overwhelms him, he flutters from branch to branch, only choosing the trees consecrated to amour or sadness, sometimes on myrtles and sometimes on cypresses; he sings plaintive songs, in which he deplores his ill fortune and that of Florine.

In what place have her enemies hidden her? he wondered. *What has become of that beautiful victim? Has the queen's barbarity allowed her to continue breathing? Where shall I search for her? Am I condemned to spend seven years without her? Perhaps, during that time, she'll be married, and I'll lose forever the hope that sustains my life.*

Those different thoughts afflicted the Blue Bird to such a point that he wanted to let himself die.

On the other hand, the fay Soussio sent Truitonne back to the queen, who was very anxious to know how the wedding had gone. When she saw her daughter, however, and she had told her everything that had happened, she flew into a terrible anger, the repercussion of which fell upon poor Florine.

"It's necessary," she said, "that she repents more than once of having been able to please Charming."

She went up into the tower with Truitonne, whom she had dressed in her richest clothes; she wore a crown of diamonds on her head and three daughters of the richest barons in the state carried the train of her royal mantle. She had King Charming's ring on her thumb, which Florine had noticed on the day when they conversed together. She was strangely surprised to see Truitonne in such pompous apparel

"Here is my daughter, who has come to bring you presents from her wedding," said the queen. "King Charming has married her; he loves her madly; there have never been people more satisfied." Immediately, gold and silver cloth, precious stones, lace and ribbons were set before the princess in large baskets of gold filigree. In presenting her with all those things, Truitonne did not fail to make the king's ring sparkle, with the consequence that Florine could no longer doubt her misfortune. She cried, desperately, for all those baleful presents to be taken away, that she no longer wanted to wear anything but black; or, rather, she wanted presently to die.

She fainted, and the cruel queen, delighted to have succeeded so well, did not permit anyone to help her. She left her alone in the most deplorable state in the world, and told the king maliciously that his daughter was so transported with tenderness that nothing equaled the extravagances she made; that it was necessary to make sure that she was not allowed to emerge from the tower. The king told her that she could govern the affair as she wished, and that he would always be satisfied with that.

When the princess recovered consciousness and reflected on the conduct that had been employed in her regard, the ill-treatment she had received from her unworthy stepmother and the hope she had lost forever of marrying King Charming, her dolor became so sharp that she wept all night. In that state she went to her window, where she expressed very tender and very touching regrets. When daylight approached, she closed it, and continued weeping.

The following night she opened the window, she uttered profound sighs and sobs, she shed a torrent of tears; when daylight came she hid herself in her room.

Meanwhile, King Charming—or, to put it better, the beautiful Blue Bird—never ceased fluttering around the palace; he judged that his dear princess was imprisoned there; and if she uttered sad plaints, his were no less sad. He approached the windows as closely as he could in order to look into the rooms, but the fear that Truitonne might perceive him and suspect that it was him prevented him from doing what he would have wished.

It will cost me my life, he said to himself, *if those evil princesses discover where I am; they will want to avenge themselves. It's necessary that I keep my distance, or I'll be exposed to the worst dangers.*

Those reasons obliged him to take great precautions; ordinarily, he only sang by night.

Facing the window to which Florine went there was a prodigiously tall cypress. The Blue Bird came to perch in it. He was scarcely there when he heard someone lamenting.

"Will I suffer much longer?" she said. "Will death not come to my aid? Those who fear it see it only too closely; I desire it, and it flees me cruelly. Oh, barbaric queen, what have I done to you to be retained in such a frightful captivity? Have you not enough other ways to desolate me? You have only to render me witness to the happiness your unworthy daughter is savoring with King Charming."

The Blue Bird had not missed a word of that lament; he remained very surprised by it, and waited for daybreak with the utmost impatience in order to see the afflicted lady, but before it arrived she had closed the window and gone back inside.

The curious bird did not fail to come back the following night; the moonlight was bright; he saw a young woman at the window of the tower, who commenced her regrets.

"Fortune," she said, "you who flattered me with reigning, you who rendered amour to my father, what have I done for you to plunge me suddenly into the most bitter dolors? Is it at an age as tender as mine that one ought to commence suffering your inconstancy? Come back, barbarian, come back, if it is possible: the only favor I ask of you is to terminate my fatal destiny."

The Blue Bird listened, and the more he listened, the more convinced he was that it was his lovely princess who was lamenting. He said to her: "Adorable Florine, marvel of our days, why do you want to finish yours so promptly? Your woes are not without remedy."

"Eh? Who is speaking to me in such a consoling manner?" she exclaimed.

"An unfortunate king," said the bird, "who loves you, and will never love anyone but you."

"A king who loves me!" she added. "Is this a trap that my enemy is extending for me? But then, what would she gain by it? If she's seeking to discover my sentiments, I'm ready to make her a confession of them."

"No, my princess," he replied, "the lover who is speaking to you is incapable of betraying you." As he finished speaking he flew to the window.

At first, Florine was very frightened by such an extraordinary bird, which spoke with as much intelligence as if it were human, although it conserved the tiny voice of a nightingale, but the beauty of its plumage reassured her.

"Is it permitted to me to see you again, my princess!" he cried. "Can I savor a happiness so perfect without dying of joy? But alas, how that joy is troubled by your captivity, and the state to which the wicked Soussio has reduced me for seven years."

"And who are you, charming bird?" said the princess, caressing him.

"You have said my name," the king added, "and you're pretending not to know me."

"What! The greatest king on the world!" said the princess. "King Charming is the little bird I see?"

"Alas, beautiful Florine, it is only too true," she said, "and if anything can console me, it is that I preferred this punishment to that of renouncing the passion that I have for you."

"For me?" said Florine. "Oh, don't seek to deceive me! I know that you have married Truitonne; I recognized your ring on her finger, and I saw her all brilliant with diamonds that you have given her. She came to insult me in my sad prison, charged with a rich crown and a royal mantle, which she had from your hand while I as laden with chains and irons."

"You have seen Truitonne in that apparel?" interjected the king. "She and her mother have dared to tell you that those jewels came from me? O Heaven, is it possible that I am hearing such frightful lies and that I cannot avenge myself as soon as I wish? Know that they wanted to deceive me by abusing your name; they engaged me to abduct the ugly Truitonne, but as soon as I discovered my error, I wanted to abandon her, and I chose in the end to be a Blue Bird for seven consecutive years rather than fail in the fidelity that I had vowed to you."

Florine had a pleasure so sensible in hearing her amiable lover speak that she no longer remembered the woes of her prison. What did she not say to him to console him for his sad adventure and to persuade him that she would do no less for him than he had done for her.

Daylight appeared; the majority of the servants had already got up, while the Blue Bird and the princess were still talking; they separated with a thousand difficulties, after having promised one another that they would converse in the same fashion every night.

The joy of having found one another was so extreme that there are no terms capable of expressing it; each of them thanked fortune on their own behalf. However, Florine was anxious for the Blue Bird. *Who will protect him from hunters,* she said to herself, *or the sharp claw of some eagle or fam-*

ished vulture, who would eat him with as much appetite as if he were not a great king? O Heaven, what would become of me if his light and fine feathers, impelled by the wind, came into my prison to announce the demise that I dread?

That thought prevented the poor princess from closing her eyes, for when one is in love, illusions appear to be verities, and what one would believe to be impossible at another time seems easy then. The result was that she spent the day weeping until the time came to come to stand at her window.

The charming bird, hidden in the hollow of a tree, had spent all day thinking about his beautiful princess. *How content I am*, he said, *to have found her again! How engaging she is! How keenly I feel the generosity she testifies to me!* The tender lover counted to the slightest moments the penitence that prevented him from marrying her, and he had never desired the end of it with so much passion.

As he wanted to make Florine all the gallantries of which he was capable, he flew all the way to the capital city of his kingdom; he went to his palace and entered his cabinet through a broken window. He picked up diamond ear-rings so perfect and so beautiful that nothing in the world approached them; in the evening he brought them to Florine and begged her to put them on.

"I would consent to that," she said, "If you saw me by day, but since I only talk to you by night, I won't put them on."

The bird promised her to pick his time so well that he would come to the tower at any hour she wished. Immediately, she put the ear-rings on, and the night was spent talking, as the other had been.

The next day the Blue Bird returned to his kingdom. He went to his palace; he went into his cabinet through the broken window and he took away the richest bracelets that had ever been seen; they were made of a single emerald, cut into facts, hollowed out in the middle in order to pass the hand and arm through.

"Do you think," the princess said to him, "that my sentiments for you need to be cultivated by presents? Oh, how little
you know me!"

"No, Madame," he replied, "I don't believe that the
bagatelles I offer you are necessary for me to conserve your
tenderness, but mine would be wounded if I neglected any
opportunity to mark my attention to you, and when you do not
see me, these little jewels will recall me to your memory."

Florine said a thousand obliging things to him in that regard, to which he responded with a thousand others, which
were no less obliging.

The following night, the amorous bird did not fail to
bring his beauty a watch of reasonable grandeur, which was in
a pearl; the excellence of the workmanship surpassed that of
the material.

"It's futile to regale me with a watch," she said. "When
you're away from me, the hours seem endless; when you're
with me, they pass as in a dream, so I can't measure them accurately."

"Alas, my princess," the Blue Bird exclaimed, "I have
the same opinion as you, and I'm convinced that I go further
in the matter of delicacy."

"After what you have suffered in order to conserve your
heart for me," she replied, "I'm able to believe that you have
taken amity and esteem as far as they can go."

As soon as daylight appeared, the bird flew into the
depths of his tree, where fruits served as his nourishment.
Sometimes he also sang beautiful songs; his voice delighted
passers-by; they heard him but could not see anyone, so they
concluded that it was spirits. That opinion became so common
that no one dared go into the wood; a thousand fabulous adventures were related that had happened there, and the general
terror assisted the particular security of the Blue Bird.

Not a day passed when he did not bring a present to
Florine, sometimes a pearl necklace, or the rings of the greatest brilliance and the finest workmanship, diamond brooches,
pins, clusters of stones that imitated the color of flowers,

agreeable books or lockets; in the end she had an accumulation of marvelous riches; she only ever put them on at night in order to please the king, and by day, having nowhere to put them, she hid them carefully in her mattress.

Two years went by thus without Florine complaining once about her captivity. And why would she have complained? She had the satisfaction of speaking every night to the person she loved and who loved her. He had never said so many pretty things. Although she did not see anyone, and the Blue Bird spent every day in the hollow of a tree, they had a thousand new things to tell one another; the material was inexhaustible; their hearts and minds furnished sufficiently abundant topics of conversation.

Meanwhile, the malicious queen who was keeping her in prison so cruelly made futile efforts to marry Truitonne. She sent ambassadors to propose her to all the princes whose names she knew; as soon as they arrived they were dismissed abruptly.

"If it were a matter of Princes Florine, you'd be welcomed with joy," they were told, "but as for Truitonne, she can remain vestal without anyone opposing it."

At this news, the mother and daughter were transported by anger against the innocent princess that they were persecuting. "What!" they said. "In spite of her captivity, that arrogant hussy is thwarting us? What means are there of pardoning the bad turns that she's doing us? She must have secret correspondence with foreign countries; that's at least a crime against the state; let's treat her on that footing and seek all possible means of convicting her."

They finished their conference so late that it was nearly midnight when they decided to go up into the tower to interrogate her. She was with the Blue Bird at the window, adorned with her jewels and coiffed by her beautiful hair with a care that is natural to afflicted people. Her room and her bed were strewn with flowers, and a few Spanish pastilles that she had just burned were spreading an excellent odor.[8]

The queen listened at the door; she thought she could hear a song in two parts being sung; for Florine had an almost celestial voice. Here are the words, which appeared to her to be tender:

> *How deplorable our fate is,*
> *And that we suffer torments*
> *For having loved too constantly.*
> *But it's in vain that they oppress us;*
> *In spite of our cruel enemies,*
> *Our hearts will always be united.*

A few sighs finished the little concert.

"Oh, my Truitonne, we're betrayed!" cried the queen, opening the door abruptly and hurling herself into the room.

What became of Florine at that sight? She closed her little window promptly, in order to give the royal bird time to fly away. She was much more occupied with his conservation than her own; but he did not have the strength to go away. His piercing eyes had discovered the peril to which the princess was exposed. He had seen the queen and Truitonne; what an affliction not to be in a state to defend his mistress!

They approached her like Furies who wanted to devour her.

"You're making conspiracies against the state!" cried the queen. "Don't think that your rank will save you from the punishment you merit."

"And with whom, Madame?" relied the princess. "Have you not been my jailer for two years? Have I seen any other people than those you've sent to me?"

---

[8] "Spanish pastilles" were fuel for perfume burners, usually compounded out of ambergris and musk bound with sugar.

While she was speaking, the queen and her daughter examined her with an unparalleled surprise; her admirable beauty and her extraordinary adornment dazzled them.

"And where, Madame," said the queen, "did you get those gems that shine more brightly than the sun? "Do you expect us to believe that there are mines in this tower?"

"I found them here," Florine replied. "That's all I know about them."

The queen looked at her attentively, in order to penetrate the depths of her heart, and what was happening there. "We're not your dupes," she said. "You think we'll believe that, princess, but we know what you do from morning until evening. Someone has given you those jewels with the sole intention of obliging you to sell your father's kingdom."

"I'd be in a fine state to deliver it," she replied, with a disdainful smile. "An unfortunate princess who has been languishing in irons for such a long time can do a great deal in a plot of that nature."

"And for whom, then," said the queen, "have you coiffed yourself like a little coquette, your chamber full of odors and your person so magnificent that you'd be less well adorned in the midst of the court?"

"I have enough leisure," said the princess. "It's not extraordinary that I devote a few moments to dressing myself; I spend so many others lamenting my woes that I shouldn't be reproached for those."

"Yes, yes," said the queen. "Let's see whether this innocent person has made some treaty with the enemies."

She searched everywhere, personally, and when she came to the mattress she had it emptied, and found such a large quantity of diamonds, pearls, rubies, emeralds and topazes that she had no idea where it came from. She had resolved to put papers in some place in order to doom the princess; while she was not looking she hid them in the chimney, but fortunately, the Blue Bird was perched up above, who could see better than a lynx, and who was listening to everything.

"Look out, Florine!" he cried. "Your enemy is trying to commit a treason against you."

That voice, so unexpected, frightened the queen to such a point that she dared not do what she had meditated.

"You see, Madame," said the princess, "that the spirits that fly in the air are favorable to me."

"I believe," said the queen, beside herself with rage, "that the demons are interested in you; but in spite of them, your father will be able to give you justice."

"I wish to Heaven," cried Florine, "that I had nothing to fear but my father's fury! But yours, Madame, is more terrible."

The queen quit her, troubled by what she had just seen and heard. She held council as to what she ought to do against the princess; she was told that if some fay or enchanter had taken her under their protection, the true secret to irritate them would be to cause her further pains, and that it would be better to try to discover her intrigue.

The queen approved of that idea; she sent a young woman to sleep in her room who pretended to be an innocent; she had orders to tell her if anyone came to the princess to serve her. But what appearance could such a crude snare give? The princess regarded her as a spy; a more violent dolor then hers could not be felt.

What! she said. *I shall no longer to be able to talk to the bird who is so dear to me. He aided me to support my misfortunes; I soothed his; our tenderness was sufficient for us. What will he do? What shall I do myself?* In thinking those things she shed streams of tears.

She no longer dared go to her little window, although she heard him fluttering around it. She was dying of the desire to open it to him, but she feared risking the life of her dear lover. She spent an entire month without appearing. The Blue Bird became desperate; what plaints did he not make? How could he live without seeing his princess? He had never felt the woes of absence and those of his metamorphosis so keenly; he searched in vain for remedies to either, but after having racked his brains he found nothing to soothe him.

The princess's spy, who had been watching night and day for a month, felt so overwhelmed by the need to sleep that she finally fell into a profound slumber. Florine perceived that; she opened the window and said:

> *Blue Bird, color of the sky*
> *Come to me promptly, fly.*

Those were her own words, none of which have been changed. The bird heard them so clearly that he came to the window promptly. What a joy to see one another again! How many things they had to say! Amities and protestations of fidelity were renewed a thousand times; the princess having been unable to help shedding tears, her lover became very tender and did his best to console her.

Finally, the time to part having come without the jailer waking up, they bid one another the most touching adieu in the world.

The next day, the spy went to sleep again. The princess went to the window diligently, and then said, as she had before:

> *Blue Bird, color of the sky*
> *Come to me promptly, fly.*

Immediately, the bird came; the night passed like the other, without noise or alarm, by which the lovers were delighted. They flattered themselves that the watcher would obtain so much pleasure from sleeping that she would do it every night.

In fact, the third passed very happily, but on the one that followed, the sleeper having heard a noise, she listened without giving any semblance of it; then she looked as best she could and saw in the moonlight the most beautiful bird in the world, which was talking to the princess, caressing her with its foot and pecking her gently. Finally, she heard a few items of their conversation, and was very astonished, for the bird spoke like a lover and the beautiful Florine responded to it tenderly.

Daylight appeared; they bid one another adieu; as if they had a presentiment of their imminent disgrace, they quit one another with an extreme difficulty. The princess threw herself on her bed, bathed with her tears, and the king returned to the hollow of his tree.

The jailer ran to the queen and told her everything that she had seen and heard. The queen sent for Truitonne and her confidantes; they held a long discussion, and concluded that the Blue Bird was King Charming.

"What an affront!" cried the queen. "What an affront, my Truitonne! That insolent princess, whom I thought so afflicted, is enjoying agreeable conversations with our ingrate, in repose. Oh, I shall avenge myself in a manner so bloody that it will be legendary. Truitonne begged her not to waste a moment, and as she believed herself to be more interested in the affair than the queen, she was dying of joy when she thought of everything that would be done to desolate the lover and the mistress.

The queen sent the spy back to the tower; she ordered her to give no evidence of any suspicion or curiosity, and to appear more deeply asleep than usual.

She went to bed early and snored as loudly as she could, and the poor deceived princess, opening the little window, cried:

Blue Bird, color of the sky
Come to me promptly, fly.

But she called all night in vain; he did not appear, because the malevolent queen had had swords, knives, razors and daggers attached to the cypress, and when he came with a flutter of wings to land there, those murderous weapons cut his feet; he fell upon others, which cut his wings, and finally, pierced all over, he escaped with a thousand difficulties as far as his tree, leaving a long trail of blood.

If only you were there, beautiful princess, to soothe that royal bird! But she would have died if she had seen him on that deplorable state. He no longer wanted to take any care of his life, convinced that it was Florine who had played that nasty trick on him.

"Oh, barbarian," he said, dolorously, "is it thus that you repay the purest and most tender passion there ever was? If you wanted my death, you only had to ask me yourself; it would have been dear to you from your hand. I came to find you with so much amour and confidence! I suffered for you and I suffered without complaint. What! You have sacrificed me to the cruelest of women! She was our common enemy; you have just made peace with her at our expense. It's you, Florine, it's you who have stabbed me. You have borrowed Truitonne's hand and have guided it to my breast."

Those fatal ideas overwhelmed him to such a degree that he resolved to die.

However, his friend the enchanter, who had seen the flying frogs return to his abode with the chariot, but without the king appearing, had taken so much trouble to discover what might have happened to him that he had gone around the world eight times searching for him without being able to find him. He was making his ninth tour when he passed over the wood where he was, and, in accordance with the rules that he had prescribed himself, he sounded his horn for a long time and then shouted five times, with all his might: "King Charming, King Charming, where are you?"

The king recognized the voice of his best friend.

"Approach," he said from that tree, "and see the wretched king that you cherish, drowned in his own blood."

The enchanter, very surprised, looked in all directions without seeing anyone.

"I'm the Blue Bird," said the king, in a weak and languid voice.

At those words the enchanter found him without difficulty in his little nest. Another would have been more astonished than he was, but he was not unaware of any trick of the necromantic art. It only cost him a few words to stem the blood that was still flowing, and with herbs that he found in the woods, over which he recited a few magic words, he cured the king so perfectly that it was as if he had not been wounded.

He begged him then to tell him by virtue of what adventure he had become a bird, and who had wounded him so cruelly. The king satisfied his curiosity; he told him that it was Florine who had revealed the secret of the amorous visits he made to her, and that, in order to make her peace with the queen she had consented to allow the cypress to be garnished with daggers and razors, by which he had almost been sliced up. He protested a thousand times against the infidelity of the princess, and said that he would esteem himself fortunate to have died before having known that wicked heart.

The magician raged against her and against all women, and advised the king to forget her.

"How unfortunate you would be," he said to him, "if you were capable of loving that ingrate any longer. After what she has just done to you, everything ought to be feared."

The Blue Bird could not agree with him. He still loved Florine too dearly, and the enchanter, who knew his sentiments, in spite of the care he took to hide them, said to him in an agreeable manner:

> *Overwhelmed by cruel misfortune*
> *One speaks and reasons in vain;*
> *One only listens to one's dolor*
> *And not the advice we are given.*
> *It is necessary to leave it time*
> *Everything has its viewpoint,*
> *And when the time has not come,*
> *One torments oneself in vain.*

The royal bird agreed with him, and asked his friend to take him to his abode and put him in a cage, where he would be shielded from the cat's paw and every murderous weapon.

"But are you going to stay in that deplorable state, so unsuited to your dignity, for another five years?" the enchanter said to him. "For in sum, you have enemies who sustain that you are dead; they want to invade your kingdom; I fear that you will have lost it before recovering your original form."

"Could I not go to my palace," he replied, and govern everything as I ordinarily did?"

"Oh, that's difficult!" cried his friend. "Someone who wants to obey a man doesn't want to obey a parrot; someone who fears you as a king, surrounded by grandeur and luxury, would pluck out all your feathers on seeing you as a little bird."

"Oh, human weakness, externally brilliant," exclaimed the king, "you signify nothing regarding merit and virtue; you have deceptive places, that one can hardly defend! Oh well," he continued, "let's be philosophical, let's scorn what we cannot obtain, our decision won't be the worst."

"I don't give in so soon," said the magician. "I hope to find some good expedient."

Meanwhile, Florine, the sad Florine, desperate at no longer seeing the king, spent days and nights at her window, incessantly repeating:

> *Blue Bird, color of the sky*
> *Come to me promptly, fly.*

The presence of her spy did not prevent her from doing so; her despair was such that she no longer ate anything.

"What has become of you, King Charming?" she cried. "Have our common enemies made you feel the dire effects of their rage? Have you been sacrificed to their fury? Alas, alas, are you no more? Shall I never see you again? Or, fatigued by my misfortunes, have you abandoned me to the harshness of my fate?"

How many tears, how many sobs, followed her tender laments! How long the hours became in the absence of such a dear and amiable lover! The princess, defeated, ill, thin and changed, could scarcely sustain herself; she was convinced that everything there was of the most catastrophic had happened to the king.

The queen and Truitonne were triumphant; the vengeance gave them more pleasure than the offense had caused them pain. And fundamentally, what was the offense? King Charming had not wanted to marry a little monster, whom he had a thousand reasons to hate.

Meanwhile, Florine's father fell ill and died. The fortune of the malevolent queen and her daughter changed its aspect. They were regarded as favorites who had abused their favor. The mutinous people ran to the palace to demand Princess Florine, recognizing her as their sovereign. The queen, irritated, wanted to treat the affair arrogantly; she appeared on a balcony and threatened the mutineers. In the meantime, the sedition became general; the doors of her apartment were forced, it was pillaged and she was felled by thrown stones.

Truitonne fled to the abode of her godmother, the fay Soussio; she was in no less danger than her mother.

The noblemen of the realm assembled promptly, and went up to the tower, where the princess was very ill. She was unaware of her father's death and the execution of her enemy. When she heard so much noise she had no doubt that someone was coming to put her to death; she was not frightened by that. Life had been odious to her since she had lost the Blue Bird. But her subjects, throwing themselves at her feet, informed her of the change that had just occurred in her fortune. She was unmoved by it. They carried her to her palace, and crowned her.

The infinite care that was taken of her health, and the desire that she had to go in search of the Blue Bird contributed a great deal to her recovery, and soon gave her enough strength to appoint a council, in order to take care of her realm in her absence. Then she took precious stones worth a thousand million and departed one night on her own, without anyone knowing where she was going.

The enchanter, who was taking care of King Charming's affairs, not having enough power to undo what Soussio had done, decided to go and find her and to propose some accommodation, in favor of which she would return the king to his original form. He took the frogs and flew to the fay's abode; she was chatting at that moment to Truitonne.

Between an enchanter and a fay there is only a handspan; they had known one another for five or six hundred years, and in that space of time they had been on good terms and at odds a thousand times over. She received him very agreeably.

"What does my colleague want?" she asked him—that was how they addressed one another. "Is there something for his service that depends on me?"

"Yes, my colleague," said the magician, "you can do everything for my satisfaction; it's a matter of the best of my friends, a king whom you have rendered unfortunate."

"Ha ha, I understand you, colleague," Soussio cried. "I'm sorry, but there's no mercy to hope for in his case, if he doesn't want to marry my goddaughter; here she is, beautiful and pretty, as you see. Let m think about it."

The enchanter almost remained mute, so ugly did he find her, but he could not resolve to go away without settling something with her, because the king had run a thousand risks since he had been in the cage. The nail on which it was hooked hand broken; the cage had fallen; His feathery Majesty had had suffered a great deal from that fall; the cat, which had been in the room when the accident happened, had dealt him a claw-thrust in the eye, of which he nearly remained one-eyed. Another time, they had forgotten to give him anything to drink; he was a long way toward dying of thirst when a few drops of water saved him. A little rogue of a monkey had escaped, grabbed his plumes through the bars of the cage, and spared so few that he might have made a jay or a blackbird. The worst thing of all was that he was on the point of losing his kingdom; his heirs were perpetrating new knaveries every day in order to prove that he was dead.

Finally, the enchanter agreed with Soussio that he would take Truitonne to King Charming's palace, where she would remain for a few months, during which he could make the resolution to marry her and she would restore his form, but he would resume that of a bird if he did not want to marry her.

The fay gave Truitonne gold and silver garments; then she set her behind her on a dragon and they went to Charming's kingdom, who had just arrived there with his faithful friend the enchanter. With three strokes of a wand, he saw himself as he had been before: handsome, amiable, witty and magnificent, but he bought very dear the time that diminished his penitence; the mere thought of marrying Truitonne made him shiver. The enchanter gave him the best reasons he could; they only made a mediocre impression on his mind, and he was les occupied with the conduct of his kingdom than means of prolonging the term that Soussio had given him to marry Truitonne

Meanwhile, Queen Florine, disguised in the costume of a peasant woman, with her hair scattered and tangled, which hid her face, a straw hat on her head and a canvas sack over her shoulder, commenced her voyage, sometimes on foot, sometimes on horseback, sometimes by sea and sometimes on land. She made all possible diligence, but, not knowing where to direct her steps, she always feared going one way while her lovable king was going in the other.

One day, when she arrived at the edge of a spring, the silvery water of which was bounding over little pebbles, she had a desire to wash her feet. She sat down on the grass, put up her blonde hair with a ribbon and dipped her feet in the stream. She resembled Diana bathing on returning from a hunt.

A little old woman, very stooped, leaning on a stout staff passed by; she stopped and said: "What are you doing here, my beauty? Are you all alone?"

"My good mother," said the queen, "I'm in great company nevertheless, for I have my chagrins, anxieties and displeasures with me." At those words her eyes were covered with tears.

"What! So young, you're weeping!" said the good woman. "Oh, my daughter, don't afflict yourself. Tell me what's wrong sincerely, and I hope to soothe you."

The queen was glad to do that; she told her about her enemies, the conduct that the fay Soussio had adopted in the affair, and finally, how she was searching for the Blue Bird.

The little old lady straightened up, pulled herself together, suddenly changed face, and appeared beautiful, young and superbly dressed. Looking at the queen with a gracious smile, she said: "Incomparable Florine, the king you are seeking is no longer a bird; my sister Soussio has returned his original form; he is in his kingdom. Don't be afflicted; you will arrive there, and you will achieve the objective of your design. Here are four eggs; beak them in your pressing need, and you'll find the help that will be useful to you."

As she finished speaking, she disappeared.

Florine felt greatly consoled by what she had just heard; she put the eggs in her sack and directed her steps toward Charming's kingdom.

After having walked for eight days and nights without stopping, she arrived at the foot of a mountain prodigious in its height, all made of ivory, and so steep that ne could not even set foot on it without falling. She made a thousand futile attempts; she slipped; she became fatigued. In despair at such an insurmountable obstacle she lay down at the foot of the mountain, resolved to let herself die, when she remembered the eggs that the fay had given her. She took one.

"Let's see," she said, "whether she was making fun of me, in promising me the help that I need."

As soon as she had broken it, she found little golden crampons inside, which she put on her feet and hands. When she had them she climbed the ivory mountain without any difficulty, for the crampons entered to it and prevented her from slipping.

When she was at the top she had further difficulties descending; the entire valley was a single mirror. More than sixty thousand women were gathered around it, looking at themselves with extreme pleasure, for the mirror was two leagues wide and six high. Everyone saw herself within it as she wanted to be; redheads appeared blonde therein, brunettes had black hair; the old believed themselves to be young, the young did not age; in sum, all defects were well hidden there, so people came from all four corners of the world. It was enough to make one die laughing to see the grimaces and simpers that the majority of the coquettes were making. That circumstance attracted men no less; the mirror pleased them too. It made some appear with beautiful hair, others with taller stature, and better build, a martial air and a better face. The women of whom they were making fun, made fun of them no less, with the result that the mountain was known by a thousand different names. No one had ever reached the summit, and when they saw Florine there, the women uttered long cries of despair.

"Where is that ill-advised person going?" they said. "Doubtless she has enough wit to walk on our mirror; at the first step she'll break everything." They were making a frightful racket.

The queen did not know what to do, for she saw great peril in descending that way. She broke another egg, from which two pigeons and a chariot emerged, which became large enough at the same time for her to place herself in it comfortably. Then the pigeons descended lightly with the queen, without anything unfortunate happening.

She said to them: "My little friends, if you would like to take me all the way to the place where King Charming is holding his court, you won't be obliging an ingrate."

The civil and obedient pigeons did not stop by day or night until they had arrived at the gates of the city. Florine got down, and gave each of them a soft kiss, more estimable than a crown.

Oh, how fast her heart was beating as she went in! She smeared mud on her face in order not to be recognized. She asked passers-by where she might see the king. Some of them started laughing. "See the king?" they said. "What do you want with him, you little slattern?[9] Go and clean yourself up; you don't have eyes good enough to see such a monarch."

The queen made no reply; she drew away quietly and asked again of those she encountered where she could go to see the king. "It's necessary for him to come to the temple tomorrow with Princess Truitonne," someone said, "for he's finally consented to marry her."

Heaven, what news! Truitonne, the unworthy Truitonne, on the point of marrying the king! Florine nearly died; she no longer had the strength to speak or walk. She sat down on stones in a doorway, well hidden by her hair and straw hat.

Unfortunate that I am, she said, *I've come here to augment the triumph of my rival and render myself witness to her satisfaction. So it's for that reason that the Blue Bird ceased to come and see me! It's for that little monster that he was committing the cruelest of his infidelities, while plunged in dolor, I was anxious for the conservation of his life! The traitor has changed, and remembering me less than if he'd never seen me, he left me in the care of afflicting myself with his overly long absence, without caring about mine.*

When one has a great chagrin, it is rare to have a good appetite. The queen looked for lodgings and went to bed without supper. She got up with the dawn and ran to the temple; she only got in after being endured a thousand rebuffs from guards and soldiers. She saw the king's throne and that of Truitonne, who was already regarded as the queen. What ago-

---

[9] The phrase I have translated as "you little slattern," in order to convey its intended meaning, is rendered in the original as *ma mie souillon*, which is why Florine subsequently adopts the pseudonym Mie-Souillon.

ny for a person as tender and as delicate as Florine! She approached her rival's throne; she stood upright, leaning against a marble pillar.

The king came first, more handsome and more lovable than he had ever been in his life. Truitonne appeared then, richly clad, and so ugly that she made one afraid. She looked at the queen and frowned.

"Who are you," she said to her, "to dare to approach my excellent figure, so close to my golden throne?"

"My name is Mie-Souillon," she replied. "I've come a long way to sell you rarities. She immediately rummaged in her canvas sack and took out the emerald bracelets that King Charming had given her.

"Ho ho," said Truitonne, "those are pretty glassware. Would you like a five-sol piece?"

"Show them to connoisseurs, Madame, and then we'll make our bargain."

Truitonne, who loved the king more tenderly that such a stupid person ought to be capable of loving, delighted to find an opportunity to speak to him, advanced as far as his throne and showed him the bracelets, asking him to tell her what he thought.

At the sight of the bracelets, he remembered those he had given to Florine. He went pale; he sighed, and did not reply for a long time. Finally, fearing that the state to which his different thoughts had reduced him might be perceived, he made an effort and replied: "Those bracelets are worth, I think, as much as my kingdom. I thought there was only one pair in the world, but here are similar ones."

Truitonne returned to her throne, where she had a face like a scaly oyster-shell. She asked the queen how much she wanted for the bracelets.

"You'd have too much difficulty paying me for them, Madame," she said. "It's better to propose another bargain to you; if you can enable me to sleep for one night in the cabinet of echoes that is in the king's palace, I'll give you my emeralds."

"I agree," said Truitonne, laughing like a lunatic and showing teeth as long as a boar's tusks.

The king did not ask where the bracelets came from, less out of indifference for the person who presented them—although she was scarcely inappropriate to give rise to curiosity—than the invincible repulsion he felt for Truitonne.

Now, it is necessary to know that while the king was the Blue Bird, he had told the princess that there was a cabinet in his apartment known as the cabinet of echoes, which was so ingeniously made that everything that was whispered there could be heard by the king while he was lying in his bedroom, and as Florine wanted to reproach him for his infidelity she had been unable to imagine a better means.

She was taken to the cabinet on Truitonne's order; she commenced her plaints and regrets.

"The misfortune that I wanted to doubt is only too certain, cruel Blue Bird," she said. "You have forgotten me, you love my unworthy rival! The bracelets that I received from your disloyal hand have not been able to recall me to your memory, so distant am I from it." Then sobs interrupted her words, and when she had enough strength to speak, she lamented again, and continued until dawn. The valets de chambre had heard her moaning and sighing all night long; they told Truitonne, who asked her what racket she had made. The queen told her that she slept so well that she usually dreamed, and often spoke aloud.

As for the king, he had not heard anything, by virtue of a strange fatality. It was because, since he had loved Florine, he could no longer sleep, and when he went to bed to obtain some repose, he was given opium.

The queen spent part of the day in a strange anxiety. *If he heard me*, she said to herself, *can there be a crueler indifference? If he didn't hear me, what can I do to make myself heard?* He no longer found rarities extraordinary, for precious stones are always beautiful; it required something that would pique Truitonne's appetite. She had recourse to her eggs.

She broke one; immediately, a little coach of polished steel emerged, garnished with gold. It was harnessed to six green mice and driven by a pink rat; the postillion, who was also of the rodent family, was flax-gray. In the coach there were four marionettes, smarter and wittier that all those that appear at the Saint-Germain and the Saint-Laurent fairs. They did surprising things, especially two little gypsy women who, for dancing the saraband and the passepied, who would not have ceded anything to Leance.[10]

The queen was delighted by that new masterpiece of the necromantic art; she did not say a word until the evening, which was the time when Truitonne went for her walk. She placed herself in a pathway, and made the mice drawing the coach, the rats and the marionettes gallop. That novelty astonished Truitonne so much that she shouted two or three times: "Mie-Souillon, Mie-Souillon, would you like five sols for the coach and its mousy team?"

"Ask the men of letters and the doctors of the real, what such a marvel might be worth," said Florine. "I'll refer to the most savant estimation."

Truitonne, who was absolute in everything, replied: "Without importuning me any further with your filthy presence, tell me the price?"

"To sleep again in the cabinet of echoes," she said, "is all that I ask."

"Well, poor fool," replied Truitonne, "you won't be refused." Turning to her ladies, she said: "There's a stupid creature, to obtain so little for her rarities."

Night fell. Florine said everything she could of the most tender, and said it as pointlessly as she had done before, because the king never failed to take his opium.

The valets de chambre said to one another: "Doubtless that peasant woman is mad. What is she arguing about all night?"

---

[10] Leance is a character in Mademoiselle de Scudéry's eight-volume romance *Alamahide, ou l'esclave reine* (1660).

"Apart from that," said the others, "there's nevertheless intelligence and passion in what she says."

She waited impatiently for daylight, to see what effect her speech had produced.

What! That barbarian has become deaf to my voice, she said. *He can no longer hear his dear Florine! What weakness still to love him! How I merit the marks of scorn he has given me.* But she thought that in vain; she could not cure herself of her tenderness.

There was only one egg left in her sack from which she could hope for aid. She broke it, and a pie of six birds emerged from it, which were larded, cooked and ready to eat; in spite that, they sang marvelously well, told fortunes and knew medicine better than Aesculapius. The queen was charmed by such an admirable thing. She went with her talking pie to Truitonne's antechamber.

As she was waiting for her to pass through, one of the king's valets de chambre approached her and said: "Mie-Souillon, do you know that if the king didn't take opium to sleep you'd surely deafen him, for you jabber at night in a surprising manner."

Florine was no longer astonished that he had not heard; she rummaged in her sack and said to him: "I fear so little interrupting the king's sleep that if you would care not to give him opium this evening, in the case that I sleep in the same cabinet, all these pearls and diamonds will be for you. The valet de chambre consented to that, and gave her his word.

A few moments later, Truitonne came; she perceived the queen with her pie, who pretended to be about to eat it.

"What are you doing there, Mie-Souillon?" she asked her.

"I'm eating astrologers, musicians and physicians, Madame," Florine replied. At the same time, all the birds started to sing more melodiously than sirens. Then they cried: "Give us a silver coin and we'll tell your fortune. One duck, which was domineering, said more loudly than the others: "Quack, quack,

quack, I'm a doctor and I cure all ills and all sorts of madness, except for that of amour."

More surprised by so many marvels than she had ever been in her life, Truitonne swore: "By the holy cabbage, that's an excellent pie. I want to have it. Now, now, Mie-Souillon, what can I give you for it?"

"The ordinary price," she said, "to sleep in the cabinet of echoes and nothing more."

"Here," said Truitonne generously—for she was in a good mod by virtue of the acquisition of such a pie—"you can have a pistole as well."

Florine, more content than she had been, because she hoped that the king would hear her, withdrew, thanking her.

As soon as night fell, she had herself taken to the cabinet, hoping ardently that the valet de chambre had kept his word, and that instead of giving him opium he had presented him with something else that could keep him awake. When she thought that everyone was asleep she commenced her ordinary laments.

"To how many perils have I exposed myself," she said, "in order to search for you, while you were fleeing me, and you wanted to marry Truitonne? What have I done to you, cruel man, for you to forget your oaths? Do you remember your metamorphosis, my shames, our tender conversations?" She repeated almost all of them, with a memory that proved sufficiently that nothing was dearer to her than the memories in question.

The king was not asleep, and he heard Florine's voice so distinctly, and all her words, that he could not understand where they were coming from; but his heart, penetrated by tenderness, recalled so vividly the idea of his incomparable princess, that he felt his separation with the same dolor as at the moment when the knives had wounded him in the cypress. He started to speak, on his part, as the queen had done on hers. "Oh, Princess," he said, "too cruel for a lover who adored you! Is it possible that you have sacrificed me to our common enemies?"

Florine heard what he was saying, and did not fail to reproach him, and to tell him that if he wanted to listen to Mie-Souillon he would be enlightened regarding all the mysteries that he had not been able to penetrate thus far."

At those words the impatient king called one of his valets de chambre and asked him whether he could find Mie-Souillon and bring her. The valet de chambre replied that nothing was easier, since she was sleeping in the cabinet of echoes.

The king did not know what to think. What means were there of believing that a great queen like Florine was disguised as Mie-Souillon? At what means were there of believing that Mie-Souillon had the voice of the queen, and knew secrets so particular, unless she was the same person? In that uncertainty he got up, and, dressing precipitately, he went down a hidden stairway to the cabinet of echoes. The queen had taken away the key, but the king had one that opened all the doors n the palace,

He found her with a light white taffeta dress, which she wore under her dirty clothes; her beautiful hair covered her shoulders; she was lying on a bed with a lamp a short distance away that only rendered a dim light. The king entered suddenly and his amour prevailed over his resentment; as soon as he recognized her he came to throw himself at her feet, he moistened her hands with his tears and thought he would die of joy, dolor and a thousand different thoughts that were passing through his head at the same time.

The queen was no less troubled; her heart was constricted; she could scarcely sigh; she stared at the king without saying anything, and when she had the strength to speak to him, it was not a matter of making him reproaches. The pleasure of seeing him again made her forget for some time the complaints that she thought she had. Finally, they enlightened one another; they justified themselves; their tenderness reawakened, and the only thing that embarrassed them was the fay Soussio.

At that moment, however, the enchanter that loved the king arrived with a famous fay; it was the same one who had given Florine the four eggs. After the initial compliments, the enchanter and the fay declared that, their power now being combined in favor of the king and the queen, Soussio could do nothing against them, and thus, their marriage would not be subject to any delay.

It is easy to imagine the joy of the two young lovers. As soon as day dawned, it was published throughout the palace, and everyone was delighted to see Florine.

The news reached as far as Truitonne; she ran to the king's apartment. What a surprise to find her beautiful rival there! As soon as she tried to open her mouth to heap them with insults, the enchanter and the fay appeared, who metamorphosed her into a trout, in order that she could retain at least a part of her name and her surly nature; she fled, still grumbling, toward the farmyard, where the long bursts of laughter that were uttered in her regard completed her despair.

King Charming and Queen Florine, delivered from such an odious person, were no longer thinking of anything but their wedding celebration; gallantry and magnificence appeared therein equally, and it is easy to judge their felicity after such long misfortunes.

When Truitonne hoped to marry Charming
Without having been able to please him,
She wanted to form a sad engagement
That death alone could undo
How imprudent she was! Alas,
Doubtless she did not know that such a marriage
Becomes a disastrous slavery
If it is not formed by amour.
I find that Charming was sage
In my view it is far better
To be a blue bird, a crow or even an owl
Than to experience the extreme pain
Of having the person one hates always before one's eyes.

In those sorts of marriages our century is fertile;
Marriages would be much happier
If a clever enchanter could still be found
Who wanted to oppose those culpable knots,
And never to suffer that marriage unite
By interest or caprice
Two unfortunate hearts, if both do not love.

THE SPRITE PRINCE

There was once a king and a queen, who only had one son, whom they loved passionately although he was very ill-made. He was as fat as the fattest man, and as short as the smallest dwarf; but the ugliness of his face and the deformity of his body were nothing compared to the malice of his mind; he was a stubborn brute who desolated everyone. Since his earliest childhood the king had seen that clearly, but the queen was mad about him; she contributed further to spoiling him with her excessive complaisance, which made him aware of the power he had over her, and in order to pay court to that princess, it was necessary to tell her that her son was handsome and intelligent. She wanted to give him a name that would inspire respect and dread; after searching for a long time, she called him Furibon.

When he was of an age to have a tutor, the king chose a prince who had ancient rights to the crown, which he would have sustained, as a man of courage, if his affairs had been in a better state; but for a long time he had not thought about it any longer; all his application was to bringing up his only son well. There had never been anyone more naturally handsome, or possessed of a livelier and more penetrating, docile and submissive mind, than his son. Everything he said had a fortunate turn and a particular grace; his person was quite perfect.

The king had chosen that great lord to guide Furibon's youth; he commanded him to be very obedient, but he was a rebel who could be whipped a hundred times without correcting anything. His tutor's son was named Leandre; everyone loved him. The ladies looked at him very favorably; but he did not attach himself to any; they called him the handsome indifferent. They made war on him without changing his attitude.

He almost never quit Furibon; that companion only served to make the latter seem more hideous. He only approached ladies to say harsh things to them, sometimes that they were badly dressed, at other times that they had a provincial appearance; he accused them before everyone of wearing make-up. He only wanted to know their intrigues in order to talk about them to the queen, who scolded them and made them fast in order to punish them. All that caused Furibon to be hated mortally. He saw that clearly, and almost always took it out on young Leandre.

"You're very lucky," he said to him, looking at him askance. "The ladies praise you and applaud you; they don't do the same for me."

"Sire, he replied modestly, "the respect that they have for you prevents them from being familiar."

"They know that very well," he said, "for I beat them like plaster to teach them their duty."

One day, when ambassadors from far away arrived, the prince, accompanied by Leandre, stayed in a gallery in order to see them go by. As soon as the ambassadors perceived Leandre they advanced and bowed profoundly to him, testifying their admiration in gestures. Then, looking at Furibon, they believed that he was his dwarf; they took him by the arm and made him turn back and forth, to his chagrin.

Leandre was in despair; he made every effort to tell them that Furibon was the king's son, but they did not understand him; unfortunately, the interpreter had gone to wait in the king's apartment. Leandre, knowing that they had not understood any of his signs, humiliated himself even more before Furibon, but the ambassadors, as well as their retinue, believing that it was a joke, laughed until they became ill, and tried to pull and flick his nose in the fashion of their homeland.

The desperate prince drew his sword, which was no longer than a fan; he would have done some violence if the king had not come to meet the ambassadors, who were very surprised by that fit of temper. He asked them to excuse him, for he knew their language; they replied that it was of no consequence, that they had perceived that the frightful little dwarf was in a bad mood. The king was very afflicted that his son's bad appearance and his extravagances had caused him to be unrecognized.

When Furibon no longer saw them, he seized Leandre by the hair and tore out two or three handfuls; he would have strangled him if he could; he forbade him to appear before him. Leandre's father, offended by Furibon's behavior, sent his son to a castle he had in the country. He was not idle there; he liked hunting, fishing and walking; he could paint well, read beautifully, and played several instruments. He deemed himself fortunate no longer to have to pay court to his eccentric prince, and in spite of the solitude, he was not bored for a moment.

One day, when he had walked for a long time in the gardens, as the heat increased, he went into a little wood, the trees of which were so tall and leafy that he was agreeably shaded. He had begun to play the flute in order to amuse himself, when he felt something coil around his leg several times and squeeze it very forcefully. He looked to see what it was and as surprised to see a large snake. He took his handkerchief and caught it by the head. He was about to kill it, but it wound around the rest of his body, and around his arms; looking at him fixedly, it seemed to be asking him for mercy.

One of the gardeners arrived then; he had no sooner perceived the snake than he shouted to his master: "Hold it well, Sire; I've been pursuing it or an hour in order to kill it; it's the wiliest beast in the world; it desolates our flower beds."

Leandre cast his eyes over the snake again, which was speckled with a thousand extraordinary colors, and which, still staring at him, did not move to defend itself.

"Since you want to kill it," he said to his gardener, "and it has come to seek refuge with me, I forbid you to do it any harm. I want to nourish it, and when it has shed its beautiful skin, I'll let it go."

He returned home; he put it in a large room, of which he kept the key; he had it brought bran, milk, flowers and herbs, to nourish it and to cheer it up: that was a very fortunate snake! He went to see it sometimes; as soon as it perceived him it came to meet him, crawling and making all the little expressions and graceful mannerisms of which a snake is capable. The prince was surprised by that, but he did not pay any great attention to it.

All the ladies of the court were afflicted by his absence; there was no talk of anything but him and the desire for his return. "Alas," they said, "There's no more pleasure at court since Leandre has left it; the malevolent Furibon is the cause. Is it possible that he wishes him harm for being more amiable and more loved than him? Is it necessary, in order to please him, that one disfigures one's stature and face? Is it necessary that, in order to resemble him, one dislocates one's bones, splits one's mouth all the way to the ears, narrows one's eyes and tears away one's nose? That's a very unjust little ape! He'll never have any joy in his life, for he won't find anyone who isn't better looking than him."
However malevolent princes are, they always have flatterers, and the malevolent ones even have more than others. Furibon had his; his power over the queen's mind made him feared. He was told what the ladies were saying; he flew into a fit of anger that went as far as fury. He entered thus into the queen's chamber and told her that he was going to kill himself before her eyes if she did not find a way to make Leandre perish. The queen, who hated Leandre because he was more handsome than her ape of a son, replied that she had regarded him as a traitor for a long time, and that she would gladly lend a hand to his death. It was necessary that he go hunting with a few confidants, that Leandre should join in, and that he be shown the consequences of make himself loved by everyone.
Furibon therefore went hunting. When Leandre heard the dogs and the horns in his woods he mounted up and went to see who it was. He was very surprised to encounter the prince unexpectedly; he dismounted and saluted him respectfully. The prince received him better than he expected, told him to follow him, and then immediately turned away, making a sign to the assassins not to miss their coup.

The prince was drawing away very rapidly when a lion of prodigious size emerged from the depths of a cavern, hurled itself upon him and threw him to the ground. Those accompanying him took flight; Leandre alone remained to battle the furious animal. He drew his sword, risked being devoured, and by means of his valor and skill he saved his cruelest enemy.

Furibon had fainted from fear; Leandre helped him with marvelous cares, and when he had recovered somewhat, presented his horse to him in order for him to mount. Anyone but an ingrate would have felt obligations so keen and so recent in the depths of his heart, and would not have failed to do and say marvelous things, but not at all; he did not even look at Leandre, and only made use of his horse to go in search of the assassins, whom he ordered to kill him.

They surrounded Leandre, and would infallibly have killed him if he had had less courage. He backed up against a tree in order not to be attacked from behind, and did not spare any of his enemies, fighting like a desperate man.

Furibon, believing him to be dead, hastened to come in order to give himself the pleasure of seeing him, but it was another spectacle than the one he expected; all the scoundrels were rendering their last sighs.

When Leandre saw him he advanced and said to him: "Sire, if it is by your order that I was to be assassinated, I'm sorry to have defended myself."

"You're insolent," replied the prince, angrily. "If you ever appear before me again, I'll have you put to death."

Leandre made no reply. He went home very sadly and spent the night thinking about what he should do, for there was no possibility of standing up to the king's son. He resolved to travel through the world. As he was ready to leave, however, he remembered the snake. He took it some milk and fruit.

As he opened the door, he perceived an extraordinary light shining in one of the corners of the room. He looked in that direction and was surprised by the presence of a lady, whose noble and majestic air did not allow any doubt about the grandeur of her birth. His garment was amaranth satin embroidered with diamonds and pearls.

She advanced toward him graciously and said to him: "Young prince, don't look for the snake that you brought here; she is no longer here. You've found me in her place, in order to repay you what she owes you, but it's necessary to speak to you more intelligibly. Know that I am the fay Gentille, famous because of the turns of gaiety and flexibility that I can make. We live for a hundred years without aging, without diseases, without chagrins and without difficulties. When that term expires we become snakes for a week; it is that time alone that is fatal to us, for then we cannot foresee or prevent our misfortunes, and if we are killed, we cannot be resuscitated. When the week has finished, we resume our ordinary form, with our beauty, our power and our treasures. You know now, Sire, the obligations that I have to you, and it is just that I acquit them. Think how I can be useful to you, and count on me."

The young prince, who had not had commerce with the fays until then, was so surprised that he could not speak for some time, but, bowing profoundly, he said: "Madame," he said, "after the honor I have had of serving you, it seems to me that I have nothing to desire of fortune."

"I shall be greatly chagrined," she replied, "if you do not give me an opportunity to be useful to you. Consider that I can make you a great king, prolong your life, render you more lovable, give you diamond mines and houses full of gold; I can make you an excellent orator, musician and painter; I can make ladies love you or augment your intelligence. I can make you an aerial, aquatic and terrestrial sprite..."[11]

---

[11] The French word *lutin*, here translated as "sprite," refers to entities that are similar to a species of English elves or "fairies" whose most famous literary member is Shakespeare's Puck; Irish leprechauns belong to the same genus, as do various Breton entities, notably *follets*, which are occasionally cited in *contes de fées*. Madame d'Aulnoy here makes a very clear distinction between that genus and fays, and specifies a

Leandre interrupted her at that point. "Permit me to ask you, Madame," he said, "what I could do if I were a sprite?"

"A thousand useful and agreeable things," replied the fay. "You can be invisible whenever it pleases you, you can travel the vast space of the universe in an instant; you can rise into the air without having wings; you can go into the depths of the earth without being dead; you can penetrate the abysms of the sea without drowning; you can enter everywhere, locked doors and windows notwithstanding; and as soon you judge it appropriate, you can allow yourself to be seen in your natural form."

"Oh, Madame," he cried. "I choose to be a sprite; I'm on the point of voyaging; I imagine infinite pleasures in that personage, and I prefer it to all the other choices that you have just offered me so generously."

"Be a sprite," Gentille replied, passing her hand three times over his eyes and face. "Be a beloved sprite, be an amiable sprite, be a mischievous sprite." Then she kissed him and gave him a little red hat garnished with two parrot feathers. "When you put on this hat," she continued, "you will be invisible; when you take it off, people will see you."

Leandre, delighted, stuck the little red hat on his head and wished to go into the forest to pick some wild roses that he had remarked there. At the same time, his body became as light as thought; he transported himself into the forest, passing through the window, and fluttering like a bird. He was afraid nevertheless when he found himself so high, and was apprehensive as he crossed the river that he might fall into it and that the fay might not have the power to protect him from it. But he reached the foot of the rose-bush safely; he picked three roses and returned immediately to the room where the fay was waiting. He presented them to her, delighted that his little trial had succeeded so well.

---

relationship between them taken for granted by her fellow core contributors to the nascent genre of *contes de fées*.

She told him to keep the roses, that one of them would furnish him with all the money he needed, that by putting another over his mistress's breasts he would know whether she was faithful, and that the last would prevent him from ever falling ill. Then, without waiting to be thanked, she wished him a fortunate voyage and disappeared.

He rejoiced infinitely at the fine gift he had just obtained. *Could I ever have thought*, he said to himself, *that for having saved a poor snake from my gardener's hands, I would receive such rare and great advantages? Oh, how I shall enjoy myself, how many agreeable moments I shall have, how many things I shall know! Becoming invisible, I shall be informed of the most secret adventures.*

He also thought that there would be a sensible pleasure in taking some vengeance on Furibon. He quickly put his affairs in order, and mounted the most beautiful horse in his stable, called Flax-Gray, followed by some of his domestics dressed in livery, in order that the rumor of his return would spread more rapidly.

It is necessary to know that Furibon, who was a great liar, had said that, but for his courage, Leandre would have assassinated him during the hunt; that he had killed all his men and that he wanted him to be justly punished. The king, importuned by the queen, gave orders that he be arrested, with the result that when he came in such a resolute fashion, Furibon was alerted. He was too timid to go in search him himself; he ran to his mother's room and told her the Leandre had just arrived and asked her to have him arrested.

The queen, diligent in everything that her ape of a son might desire, did not fail to go and find the king, and the prince, impatient to know what would be resolved, followed her without saying a word. He stopped at the door, put his ear to it and lifted up his hair in order to hear better.

Leandre came into the great hall of the palace with the little red hat on his head, having become invisible. As soon as he perceived Furibon listening, he picked up a hammer and a nail and attached his ear rudely to the door.

Furibon, desperate and enraged, knocked on the door like a madman, uttering loud cries. At that voice the queen ran to open it, and finished tearing away her son's ear. He bled as if his throat had been cut, and made an ugly grimace. The inconsolable queen got down on her knees, picked up the ear, kissed it and refitted it. The sprite seized a handful of switches, with which the king's little dogs were beaten, and commenced delivering several strokes to the queen's hands and her son's snout. She screamed for someone to kill him, to get rid of him.

The king looked on, people came running, but, not seeing anyone, they said in whispers that the queen was mad and that it was caused by the dolor of seeing Furibon's ear torn off. The king was the first to believe it; he evaded her when she tried to approach him; that scene was very funny.

Finally, the good sprite gave Furibon a thousand further strokes; then he left the room, went through the garden and rendered himself visible. He went boldly to pick cherries, apricots, strawberries and flowers from the queen's flower-garden. She was the only one who watered it; it was at the risk of life that anyone touched it. The gardeners, very surprised, went to tell Their Majesties that Prince Leandre was stripping the trees of fruits and he garden of flowers.

"What insolence!" cried the queen. "My little Furibon! My darling baby! Forget your bad ear for a moment and run after that scoundrel; take our guards, our musketeers, our men-at-arms and our courtiers; put yourself at their head, catch him and beat him to a pulp."

Animated by his mother and followed by a thousand well-armed men, Furibon went into the garden and saw Leandre under a tree, who threw a stone at him, which broke his arm, and more than a hundred oranges at the rest of the troop. They tried to run toward Leandre, but at the same time, they no longer saw him.

He slipped behind Furibon, who was already hurt; he passed a cord around his legs and made him fall on his nose. He was picked up and carried to his bed, very ill.

Satisfied with that vengeance, Leandre returned to where his servants were waiting; he gave them money and sent them back to his castle, not wanting to take anyone with him who might discover the secrets of the little red cap and the roses.

He had not decided where he wanted to go; he mounted his beautiful horse, called Flax-Gray, and let it wander at will. He traversed countless woods, plains, hills and valleys, without paying attention to them. He rested from time to time, ate and slept, without encountering anything worthy of remark. Finally, he arrived in a forest where he stopped in order to be in the shade, for it was very hot.

After a moment, he heard sighing and sobbing; he looked around, and perceived a man who was running, stopping, crying out, then shutting up, tearing out his hair and hitting himself. He had no doubt that it was some unfortunate madman. He seemed to be well made and young; his clothes had been magnificent but they were all torn.

Touched by compassion, the prince approached him.

"I see you in such a pitiful state," he said to him, "that I can't help asking you the reason for it and offering you my services."

"Oh, Sire," the young man replied, "there's no remedy for my woes; it's today that my dear mistress will be sacrificed to a jealous old man who has a great deal of wealth but who will render her the most unfortunate person in the world."

"She loves you, then?" said Leandre.

"I can flatter myself that she does," he replied.

"Where is she?" the prince continued.

"In a castle on the edge of this forest," the lover replied.

"Well, wait for me here," said Leandre. "I'll bring you good news before long." At the same time, he put on the little red cap and wished to be in the castle. He was not yet there when he heard an agreeable music; when he arrived, everything was resonant with the sound of violins and instruments. He went into a large hall filled with relatives and friends of the old man and the young damsel. Nothing was lovelier than her, but the pallor of her complexion, the melancholy that appeared in her features and the tears that covered her eyes from time to time marked her trouble well enough.

Leandre was then a sprite. He stayed in a corner in order to indentify some of those who were present. He saw the father and mother of the pretty girl, who scolded her in low voices for the bad appearance she was putting on; then they returned to their places. The sprite put himself behind the mother and, approaching her ear, he aid to her: "Since you're constraining your daughter to give her hand to that old ape, be assured that within a week you'll be punished by your death."

Frightened by hearing a voice and not seeing anyone, and even more so by the threat it had made, the woman uttered a loud scream and collapsed. Her husband asked her what was wrong. She cried that she was a dead woman if her daughter's marriage was completed, that she would not suffer it for all the treasures in the world. The husband tried to mock her, saying that she was deluded, but the sprite approached him and said to him: "Incredulous old man, if you don't believe your wife it will cost you your life; stop your daughter's wedding and give her promptly to the man she loves."

Those words produced an admirable effect; the groom was dismissed immediately; he was told that they were breaking the engagement on orders from on high. He wanted to argue and quibble, for he was a Norman, but the sprite made such a terrible *hoo! hoo!* in his ear that he thought he was going deaf, and stamped on his gouty feet so hard that he crushed them.

Then people ran to fetch the lover from the wood, where he was still despairing. The spite waited for him with great impatience, and there was only the young mistress who could have had more. The lover and the mistress were on the point of dying of joy; the feast that had been prepare for the old man's wedding served for that of the happy lovers, and the sprite, de-spiriting himself, suddenly appeared at the door of the hall, like a stranger who had been attracted by the noise of the fête. As soon as the husband perceived him, he ran to throw himself at his feet, calling him by all the names that gratitude could furnish him.

He spent two days n the castle, and if he had wanted, they would have been ruined for they offered him all their wealth. He only quit such good company with regret.

He continued his voyage and went to a great city, where there was a queen who took pleasure in swelling her court with the most beautiful women in her realm.

When he arrived, Leandre made himself the greatest equipage that had ever been seen, but he only had to shake his rose and he had no lack of money. It is easy to judge that, being handsome, young, witty and, above all, magnificent, the queen and all the princesses received him with a thousand testimonies of esteem and consideration.

That court was one of the most gallant; not to be in love there was to give oneself to ridicule. He tried to follow the custom, and thought that he would make a game of amour, that in going along he would leave his passion like a wake. He cast his eyes on one of the queen's maids of honor, who was known as the Beautiful Blondine. She was a very accomplished person, but so cold and serious that he did not know what to do to please her.

He gave her enchanted fêtes, a ball or a play every evening; he brought her rarities from all over the world; all of that could not touch her, and the more indifferent she appeared, the more obstinate he became in trying to please her. What engaged him most is that he thought that she had never loved. In order to be more certain he desired to test his rose. In jest, he put it over Blondine's breasts; at the same time, having been fresh and blooming, it became dry and faded. It required no more to inform Leandre that he had a beloved rival. He felt that keenly, and in order to be surer, he wished himself into Blondine's room that evening.

He saw a musician enter, with the nastiest face possible; he howled three or four couplets that he had made for her, the words and music of which were detestable, but she received them as if they were the most beautiful things she had ever heard in her life. He made the grimaces of a man possessed, which she praised, so mad about him was she, and finally permitted the filthy individual to kiss her hand for his trouble. Beside himself, the sprite threw himself upon the impertinent musician and, shoving him rudely on to a balcony, he threw him into the garden, where he broke what remained of his teeth.

If lightning had struck Blondine she could not have been more surprised; she thought that it was a spirit. The sprite left the room without allowing himself to be seen, and immediately returned to his own, where he wrote to Blondine all the reproaches that she merited. He departed without waiting for a reply, leaving his equipage to his squires and gentlemen; he recompensed the rest of his servants. He took the faithful Flax-Gray and mounted up, firmly resolved not to love again after such an experience.

Leandre drew away with extreme speed. He was chagrined for a long time, but reason and absence cured him. He went to another city, where he learned on arrival that there was to be a great ceremony that day for a young woman who was about to be put among the vestals, although she did not want to enter their ranks. The prince was touched by that; it seemed to him that his little red cap only ought to be used to repair public wrongs and to console the afflicted.

He ran to the temple; the child was crowned with flowers, dressed in white, covered by her hair; two of her brothers were leading her by the hand and her mother was following her with a large troop of men and women. The oldest of the vestals was waiting at the door of the temple.

At the top of his voice, the sprite shouted: "Stop, stop, bad brothers, inconsiderate mother! Heaven opposes this unjust ceremony. If you go on, you will be crushed like frogs."

Everyone looked around without being able to see where those terrible threats were coming from. The brothers said that it was their sister's lover, who had hidden in the depths of some hole in order to play the oracle, but the angry sprite took a long staff and gave them a hundred blows. The staff could be seen being raised over their shoulders and coming down, like a hammer striking an anvil; there was no longer any means of saying that the blows were not real. Fear seized the vestals; they fled; everyone else did the same.

The sprite stayed with the young victim, promptly removed his cap, and asked her how he might serve her. She said, with more boldness than might have been expected of a girl of her age, that there was a cavalier who was not indifferent to her, but who lacked wealth. He shook the fay Gentille's rose so much that he left them ten millions; they were married, and lived very happily.

The last adventure that he had was the most agreeable. As he entered a great forest he heard the plaintive cries of a young woman; he did not doubt that some violence was being done to her. He looked around and finally saw four well-armed men who were taking away a young woman, who appeared to be thirteen or fourteen years old.

He approached rapidly and shouted to them: "What has that young woman done to be treated like a slave?"

"Oho, my young lord," said the most apparent of the troop, "why are you interfering?"

"I order you to let her go immediately," Leandre added.

"Yes, yes, we won't fail to do that," they cried, laughing.

Angrily, the prince jumped to the ground and put on the red cap, for he did not think it excessive, in order to attack four men who were strong enough to beat a dozen.

When he had his little cap on and could no longer be seen, the abductors said: "He's fled; it isn't worth the trouble of looking for him; let's simply catch his horse."

One of them remained with the young woman to guard her while the others ran after Flax-Gray, who gave them plenty of exercise. The little girl continued to cry out and lament: "Alas, my beautiful princess, how happy I was in your palace! How can I live far away from you? If you knew of my sad adventure you would send your amazons after poor Abricotine."

Leandre listened, and without delay he seized the arms of the kidnapper who was holding her and attached him to a tree, without him having the time or the strength to defend himself, for he could not even see the person who tied him up. At the cries he uttered, one of his comrades arrived, out of breath and asked him who had tied him up.

"I don't know," he said. "I didn't see anyone."

"That's to excuse yourself," said the other, "but I've known for a long time that you're nothing but a poltroon; I'm going to treat you as you merit." He gave him twenty lashes with his stirrup-leathers.

The spite was very amused to see him crying out; then, approaching the second thief, he took his arms and tied him up facing his companion. Then he did not fail to say to him: "Well, brave man, who has just tied you up? Are you not a great poltroon to have suffered it?"

The other did not say a word, and lowered his head in shame, unable to imagine by what means he had been tied up without having seen anyone.

Meanwhile, Abricotine had taken advantage of the moment to run away, without even knowing where she was going. Leandre, no longer able to see her, called Flax-Gray three times, who hastened to go and find his master, ridding himself with two kicks of the two thieves who had pursued him; he fractured the skull of one, and three of the other's ribs.

It was only a question any longer of catching up with Abricotine, for she had appeared very pretty to the sprite. He wished to be where the young woman was. Immediately, he was there. He found her so weary, so very weary that she was supporting herself on the trees no longer able to sustain herself. When she perceived Flax-Gray she cried; "Good, good, here's a pretty horse that will take Abricotine back to the Palace of Pleasures."

The spite could hear her, but she could not see him. He drew nearer; Flax-Gray stopped and she tried to mount him. The sprite took her in his arms and set her in front of him gently.

How frightened Abricotine was to feel someone without being able to see anyone! She dared not budge; she closed her ears or fear of perceiving a spirit; she did not say a single word.

The prince, who still had the best sugared almonds in the world in his pocket, tried to put one of them in her mouth, but she clenched her teeth and lips.

Finally, he took off his little cap and said to her: "Well, Abricotine, you're very timid to fear me so much; it's me who took you out of the hands of the thieves."

She opened her eyes and recognized him. "Oh, Sire," she said, "I owe you everything! It's true that I was very afraid to be with an invisible man."

"I'm not invisible," he replied, "but apparently you had something wrong with your eyes that prevented you from seeing me."

Abricotine believed him, although she was very intelligent. After having talked for some time about indifferent things, Leandre begged her to tell him her age, her country and by what hazard she had fallen into the hands of thieves.

"I have too much obligation to you," she said, "not to satisfy your curiosity, but Sire, I beg you to think less about listening to me than advancing in your journey.

"A fay whose knowledge has no equal became so infatuated with a certain prince that, although she was the first fay who had ever had the weakness to love, she married him, in spite of all the others, who represented to her incessantly the wrong she was doing to the order of Faerie. They no longer wanted her to live with them, and all that she could do was to build herself a grand palace in the vicinity of their realm.

"The prince she had married wearied of her, however; he was in despair because she knew everything that he did. As soon as he had the slightest penchant for another, she seized her unceremoniously, and rendered the prettiest person in the world frighteningly ugly. The prince, finding himself hampered by the excess of such an inconvenient tenderness, departed one day with a fast horse, and went far, far away to bury himself in a great hole in the depths of a mountain, in order that she could not find him.

"That did not succeed; she followed him, and told him that she was pregnant, that she implored him to return to her palace, that she would give him money, horses, dog, arms, a tennis court and a sheltered walk to divert him. All that could not persuade him; he was naturally stubborn and libertine. He said a hundred harsh things to her; he called her an old fay and a werewolf. 'You're very fortunate,' she said, 'that my sagacity is greater than your insanity, for if I wanted, I could turn you into a cat mewling eternally in the gutters, or an owl; but the greatest harm I can do you is to abandon you to your extravagance. Stay in your hole, in your dark cave, with the bears; appeal to the neighboring shepherdesses; you'll know with time what a difference there is between slatterns and peasant girls and a fay like me, who can render herself as charming as she wishes.

"She immediately entered her flying carriage and went away, more rapidly than a bird. As soon as she returned she transported her palace to an island, expelled the guards and officers therefrom, took women of the amazon race and set them around her island to mount an exact guard there, in order that no man could enter it. She named that place the Isle of Tranquil Pleasures; she always said that one could not have any veritable ones if one had any society with men.

"She raised her daughter in that opinion. There never was a more beautiful person. She is the princess I serve, and as the pleasures reign with her, no one grows old in her palace. Such as you see me, I'm more than two hundred years old. When my mistress was grown up, her mother the fay left her the island; she gave her excellent lessons to live happily. She returned to the realm of Faerie, and the Princess of Tranquil Pleasures governed her estate in an admirable manner.

"I don't remember, since I came into the world, having seen any other men than the thieves who abducted me and you, Sire. Those men told me that they had been sent by a certain ugly and ill-made person named Furibon, who loves my mistress, but has only ever seen her portrait. They prowled around the island without daring to set foot on it; our amazons are too vigilant to let anyone enter. But while I was looking after the princess's birds I let a beautiful parrot fly away, and in the fear of being scolded, I left the island imprudently to go in search of it. They caught me and would have taken me with them, without your help."

"If you are sensible to gratitude," Leandre said, "may I not hope, beautiful Abricotine, that you can enable me to enter the Isle of Tranquil Pleasures and see this marvelous princess who does not grow old?"

"Oh, Sire," she said, "we would be doomed, you and I, if we attempted such an enterprise. It ought to be easy for you to do without something that you do not know; you have never been in the palace, imagine that there is nothing there."

"It's not as easy as you think," the prince relied, "to rid one's memory of things that have been placed there so agreeably; and I don't agree with you that it's a reliable means to have tranquil pleasures to banish our sex absolutely."

"Sire," she said, "it doesn't belong to me to decide that matter. I'll even confess to you that if all men resembled you, I'd be content for the princess to make other laws, but since, having only seen five of them, I've found four so malevolent, I conclude that the number of bad ones is superior to that of the good, and that it's better to banish them all."

While talking in that fashion thy reached the bank of a great river. Abricotine leapt lightly to the ground. "Adieu, Sire," she said to the prince, bowing to him profoundly. "I wish you every good fortune, and that the entire world might be an isle of pleasures for you. Retire promptly, for fear that our amazons might perceive you."

"And I, beautiful Abricotine, wish you a sensible heart, in order sometimes to have a part in your memories."

He drew away thereafter, and went into the thickest part of a wood that he saw near the river. He removed Flax-Gray's saddle and bridle so that he could move around and graze the grass. He put on the little red cap and wished himself on the Isle of Tranquil Pleasures. His wish was immediately granted, and he found himself in the most beautiful and least vulgar place in the world.

The palace was made of pure gold. Above it rose figures of crystal and gems, which represented the zodiac and all the marvels of nature, the sciences and the arts, the elements, the sea and its fish, the earth and its animals, the hunts of Diana with her nymphs, the noble exercises of the amazons, the amusements of rural life, the flocks of shepherds and their dogs, the cares of rustic life, agriculture, crops, gardens, flowers and bees; and among so many different things no men or boys appeared, not one poor little Amour. The fay had been too angered by her fickle husband to show mercy to his infidel sex.

Abricotine hasn't deceived me, the prince said to himself. *The very idea of men has been banished from this place. Let's see whether they have lost very much.* He went into the palace, and encountered such marvelous things at every step that it required an extreme violence to draw away from them. Gold and diamonds were less rare by virtue of their qualities than the manner in which they were employed. On all sides he saw young women of mild, innocent cheerful appearance, as beautiful as a fine day.

He traversed a large number of vast apartments. Some of them were filled with the most beautiful pieces of china, the odor of which, combines with the eccentricity of colors and forms, was infinitely pleasing; others had porcelain so fine that that one could see daylight through walls that were made of it; others were made of engraved rock crystal; there were some of amber and coral, lapis, agate and cornelian; that of the princess was entirely composed of huge mirrors, for one could not multiply such a charming object too much.

Her throne was made of a single pearl hollowed out into a shell, in which she could sit down very comfortably; it was surrounded by girandoles garnished with rubies and diamonds; but that was less than nothing next to the incomparable beauty of the princess. Her child-like air had all the graces of the youngest girls with all the manners of those already formed. Nothing equaled the mildness and vivacity of her eyes. It was impossible to find a flaw in her. She smiled graciously at her maids of honor, who had dressed as nymphs that day in order to amuse her.

As she did not see Abricotine, she asked them where she was. The nymphs replied that they had searched for her fruitlessly, and that she had not appeared. The sprite, dying of the desire to talk, adopted the tone of voice of a parrot—for there were several of them in the room—and said: "Charming Princess, Abricotine will return soon; she would have been in great danger of being abducted, but for a prince she found."

The princess was surprised by what the parrot said to her, for it had replied very accurately.

"You're very pretty, little parrot," she said, "but you seem to be mistaken, and when Abricotine arrives she'll whip you."

"I won't be whipped," said the sprite, still mimicking the parrot, "and she'll tell you about the desire that stranger had to be able to come to this palace, in order to destroy in your mind the false ideas that you've adopted against his sex."

"In truth, parrot," the princess exclaimed, "it's a pity that you aren't as amiable every day. I'd love you dearly."

"Oh, if it were only necessary to talk in order to please you," the sprite replied, "I wouldn't cease talking for a moment."

"But wouldn't you swear that that this parrot is a sorcerer?" said the princess

"He's more amorous than a sorcerer," he said.

At that moment, Abricotine came in, and came to throw herself at the feet of her beautiful mistress. She told her about her adventure, and depicted the prince in vivid and very advantageous colors.

"I would have hated all men," she added, "if I had not seen that one. Oh, Madame, how charming he is! His appearance and all his manners have something so noble and intelligent about them, and as everything he said pleased me infinitely, I believe that I've done well not to bring him."

The princess did not say anything in reply to that, but she continued to question Abricotine about the prince, as to whether she knew his name, his country, his birth, where he came from, where he was going. Afterwards she fell into a profound reverie.

The sprite examined everything and continued talking as he had commenced: "Abricotine is an ingrate, Madame," he said. "That poor stranger will die of chagrin if he does not see you."

"Well, parrot. Let him die," the princess replied, sighing, "and since you're dabbling in reasoning like an intelligent person, and not a little bird, I forbid you to mention that stranger to me again."

Leandre was delighted to see that Abricotine's story and the parrot's speech had made such an impression on the princess. He looked at her with a pleasure that made him forget his oath not to live again as long as he lived; there was so little comparison to be made between her and the coquettish Blondine. *Is it possible*, he said to himself, *that this masterpiece of nature, this miracle of our days, should remain eternally on an island, without any mortal daring to approach it. But*, he continued, *what does it matter to me that all the others are banished from it, since I have the good fortune of being here, since I can see her, and hear her, and admire her, and I already love her recklessly.*

It was late; the princes went into a room of marble and porphyry, where several spraying fountains maintained an agreeable freshness. As soon as she went in, the symphony commenced, and a sumptuous supper was served. In the longer side walls of the room there were aviaries full of rare birds, of which Abricotine took care.

Leandre had learned during his travels to sing like them; he mimicked them even better than them. The princess listened, marveling, left the table and drew nearer. The sprite chirped even more loudly, and, taking the voice of a canary, he spoke the following words, for which he improvised a tune:

> *The most beautiful days of life*
> *Go by without pleasure;*
> *If amour has no part in them*
> *One passes them sadly;*
> *Love, love tenderly.*
> *Everything here befits it;*
> *Make the choice of a lover,*
> *Amour himself begs you to do so.*

Even more surprised, the princess summoned Abricotine and asked her whether she had taught one of her canaries to sing. She said no, but that she believed that canaries had as much intelligence as parrots. The princess smiled, and imagined that Abricotine had given lessons to the bird population. She sat down at the table again to finish her supper.

Leandre had traveled far enough to have a good appetite; he approached the great repast, the odor which alone gave him joy. The princess had a very fashionable blue cat, of which she was very fond. One of her maids of honor was holding it in her arms. She said: "I must warn you that Bluet is hungry, Madame." He was put on the table with a little golden plate, above a neatly folded lace napkin on top of it. It had a little golden bell with a pearl collar and it began to eat in a raminagrobis manner.[12]

Oho, the sprite said, silently, *a fat blue cat that has probably never caught a mouse, and is surely not from better family than me, has the honor of eating with my beautiful princess! I'd like to know whether he loves her as much as I*

---

[12] The trivial noun raminagrobis, which refers to a large tomcat, is derived from a proper noun often given as a name to literary cats, notably by Jean de La Fontaine in several of his fables, although it was probably coined by Rabelais, who attributed it to a scruffy poet.

do, and whether it's just that I only swallow smoke while he crunches fine morsels. He removed the blue cat very gently, sat down in the armchair, and put it on top of him. Nobody saw the sprite. How could they? He had the little red cap on.

The princess put grouse, quail and pheasant on Bluet's golden plate; the grouse, the quail and the pheasant disappeared in a moment. The entire court said: "No cat has ever eaten with a greater appetite." There were excellent stews; the sprite took a fork and, holding the cat's paw, he sampled the stews. He sometimes took a little too much.

Bluet did not understand the joke; he mewled and tried to scratch like a desperate cat. The princess said: "Someone move that torte and the fricassee closer to poor Bluet; look how he's crying to have some."

Leandre laughed quietly at such a pleasant venture, but he was very thirsty. Not being accustomed to take such long meals without drinking. He trapped a large melon with the cat's paw, which slaked his thirst a little, and when the supper had almost finished he ran to the sideboard and took two bottles of a delicious nectar.

The princess went into her cabinet; she told Abricotine to follow her and to close the door. The spite walked on her heels and made a third party without being seen.

The princes said to her confidante: "Admit that you exaggerated in making a portrait of that stranger; it isn't possible, it seems to me, that he could be so amiable."

"I protest to you, Madame, that if I failed in anything it was in not having said enough."

The princess sighed, and fell silent momentarily, then resumed speaking: "I owe you thanks," she said, "for refusing to bring him with you."

"But Madame," replied Abricotine—who was a clever girl, and who had already penetrated her mistress's thinking— "if he had come to admire the marvels of his beautiful place, what harm could have befallen you? Do you want to be eternally unknown in a corner of the world, hidden from the rest of mortals? What purpose does so much grandeur, pomp and magnificence serve, if no one sees it?"

"Shut up, shut up, little chatterbox," said the princess. "Don't trouble the happy repose that I've enjoyed for six hundred years. Do you think that if I'd led an anxious and turbulent l would have lived for such a great number of years? It's only innocent and tranquil pleasures that can produce such effects. Have we not read in the most beautiful histories the revolutions of the greatest states, the unexpected coups of an inconstant fortune, the extraordinary disorders of amour, the pains of absence or jealousy? What is it that produces all those alarms and afflictions? Solely the commerce that humans have with one another. Thanks to my mother's cares, I'm exempt from all those defects; I know nether the bitterness of the heart, nor futile desire, envy, amour and hatred. Oh, let us live, let us always live, with the same indifference!"

Abricotine dared not respond; the princess waited for some time and then asked her whether she had nothing to say. She replied that she thought that it was quite unnecessary to have sent her portraits to several courts, where it would only serve to sow misery; that everyone would desire to see her, and, not being able to succeed, would despair.

"I confess to you, in spite of that," said the princess, "that I would like my portrait to fall into the hands of that stranger whose name I do not know."

"Oh, Madame," she replied, "does he not already have a violent enough desire to see you? Would you want to augment it?"

"Yes!" cried the princess. "A certain impulse of vanity that had been unknown to me until present had given birth in me to that desire."

The sprite listened to everything without missing a word; there were several that gave him flattering hope, and a few others that destroyed them absolutely.

It was late and the princess went into her bedroom to go to bed. The sprite would have liked to follow her in her toilette, but even though he could have done, the respect that he had for her prevented him from doing it. It seemed to him that he ought only to take the liberties that she would have been prepared to grant him; and his passion was so delicate and so ingenuous that he tormented himself over the smallest things.

He went into a cabinet next to the princess's bedroom in order at least to have the pleasure of hearing her speak. At that moment she asked Abricotine whether she had seen anything extraordinary during her little journey.

"I passed through a forest, Madame," she said, "where I saw animals that resemble children; they leapt and danced in the trees like squirrels."

"Oh, I'd like to have some of them," said the princess. "If they weren't so nimble, they could be caught."

The sprite, who had passed through the forest, had no doubt that they were monkeys. Immediately, he wished to be there; he captured a dozen, large and small, of several different colors, put them, with great difficulty, in a big sack, and then wished himself in Paris, where, he had heard it said, one could get anything one wanted for money. He bought a little golden coach from Dautel, a dealer in curios, and hitched six green monkeys to it with little flame-colored leather harnesses trimmed with gold. Then he went to see Brioché, a famous operator of marionettes;[13] he found two meritorious monkeys there, the more intelligent called Briscambille and the other Perceforest, who were very gallant and well-educated. He dressed Briscambille as a king and out him in the coach;

---

[13] Brioché was the stage name of a family of seventeenth-century puppeteers, whose actual surname was Datelin; one of them played for three months for the Dauphin, at Saint-Germain-de-Laye, apparently accompanied by a monkey named Fagotin—reputedly killed by Cyrano de Bergerac—whose name was also handed down to subsequent performing monkeys. Briscambille is a card game and *Perceforest* one of the most elaborate of the late (i.e., fourteenth century) Arthurian romances.

Perceforest served as a coachman; the other monkeys were dressed as pages. Nothing had ever been more gracious. He put the coach and the booted monkeys in the same sack

When the princess had not yet gone to bed, she heard the sound of the little coach in her gallery, and her nymphs came to tell her about the arrival of the King of the Dwarfs. At the same time, the coach entered her bedroom with its simian cortege, and the country monkeys did not fail to do tricks that were worth as much as those of Briscambille and Perceforest. To tell the truth, the sprite managed the whole performance. He pulled the strings of the ape in the little golden coach, who was holding a box covered in diamonds, which he presented to the princess with a very god grace. She opened it promptly and found a note inside, where she read these lines:

How much beauty! How many charms!
Delightful palace, how charming you are!
But you are not yet as charming
As the one I adore.
Blissful tranquility,
Which reigns in that rural spot,
I am losing my liberty in you,
Without daring to speak or reveal myself.

It is easy to imagine her surprise. Briscambille made a sign to Perceforest to come and dance with him; all the most renowned marionettes had nothing approaching the skill of those. The anxious princess, however, not being able to divine where those verses came from, dismissed the players sooner than she might have done, although they were amusing her infinitely and she had laughed loudly enough to begin to make her feel ill. Eventually, she abandoned herself entirely to her reflections, without being able to solve such an opaque mystery.

Leandre, content with the attention with which she had listened to those lines and the pleasure the princess had obtained from seeing the monkeys, was only thinking about taking a little repose, for he had a great need of it; but he feared choosing an apartment occupied by one of the princess's nymphs. He stayed for some time in the main gallery of the palace, and then went downstairs. He found an open door, and went into a ground-floor apartment without making a noise.

It was the most beautiful and agreeable that had ever been seen; there was a bed of green and gold gauze lifted in festoons with pearl cords and ruby and emerald tassels. There was already enough daylight to enable him to admire the extraordinary magnificence of that furniture. After having closed the door, he went to sleep, but the memory of the princess woke him up several times, and he could not help uttering amorous sighs in her direction.

He got up so early that he had time to become impatient while awaiting the moment when he would be able to see her again. Looking in all directions, he perceived a prepared canvas and colors; he remembered then what his princess had said to Abricotine about his portrait, and without wasting a moment—for he painted better than the most excellent masters—he sat in front of a large mirror and made his portrait. In an oval he painted that of the princess, having her so vividly in his imagination that he had no need to see her in order to make that first sketch. He perfected the study of her later without her perceiving it, and as it was the desire to please her that made him work, no portrait was ever better-finished. He painted himself with one knee on the ground, supporting the portrait of the princess in one hand and a scroll in the other, on which was written: *She is better in my heart.*

When she came into her cabinet she was astonished to have the portrait of a man there; she attached her gaze to it with a surprise all the greater because she also recognized her own, and the words written on the scroll gave her ample material for curiosity and reverie. She was alone at that moment; she could only judge such an adventure extraordinary, but she convinced herself that it was Abricotine who had perpetrated that gallantry; it only remained for her to know whether the portrait of the cavalier was the effect of her imagination or whether it had an original. She got up abruptly and ran to summon Abricotine.

The sprite was already in the cabinet, wearing the little red cap, curious to hear what was about to happen.

The princess told Abricotine to cast her eyes on the painting and tell her what she though. As soon as she had looked at it, she cried: "I protest to you, Madame, that that is the portrait of the generous stranger to whom I owe my life. Yes, it's him, I can't doubt it; those are his features, his stature, his hair and his expression."

"You're feigning surprise," said the princess, smiling, "but it's you who put it here."

"Me, Madame!" said Abricotine. "I swear to you that I have never seen that painting in my life. Would I be bold enough to hide anything from you that would interest you? And by what miracle would it have entered my hands? I can't paint; no man has ever entered this place. There he is, however, painted with you."

"I'm gripped by fear," said the princess. Some demon must have brought it."

"Madame," said Abricotine, "might it not have been Amour? If you believe that, as I do, I dare to give you some advice: let's burn it right away."

"What a pity," said the princess, sighing. "It seems to me that my cabinet couldn't be better ornamented than by that painting." She was looking at it as she spoke, but Abricotine was obstinate in sustaining that she ought to burn an object that could only have arrived there by virtue of a magical power.

"And these words: *She is better in my heart*," said the princess, "must we burn those too?"

"It's necessary not to give mercy to anything," replied Abricotine, "not even your portrait."

She ran immediately in quest of fire. The princess approached a window, no longer able to look at a portrait that had made such an impression on her heart. The sprite, not wanting it to be burned, took advantage of that moment to take it and to escape without being perceived.

He had scarcely left the cabinet than the princess turned round in order to look again at the enchanting portrait that had pleased her so much. How surprised she was no longer to find it! She searched everywhere. Abricotine returned; she asked her whether it was her who had just taken it. She assured her that it was not, and that last adventure completed frightening them.

The sprite hid the portrait and immediately retraced his steps. He had an extreme pleasure in hearing and seeing the beautiful princess so often. He ate every day at the table with the blue cat, which had never had better cheer; however, the sprite's satisfaction lacked a great deal, since he did not dare speak nor allow himself to be seen, and it is rare for a invisible person to make himself loved.

The princess had a universal liking for beautiful things; in the situation that her heart was in, she needed amusement. When she was with all her nymphs one day, she told them that it would give her great pleasure to know how ladies were dressed in the different courts in the universe, in order to dress herself in the most gallant manner.

It required no more to determine the sprite to travel the world. He stuck on his little red cap and wished himself in China; he bought the finest fabrics and took a model costume. He flew to Siam, where he did the same. He traveled all four continents of the world in three days; as he accumulated material he returned to the Palace of Tranquil Pleasures to hide everything that he bought in a room. When he had assembled a number of infinite rarities—for money cost him nothing, and his rose furnished it incessantly—he bought five or six dozen dolls, which he had dressed in Paris, as that is the place in the world where fashions are most up-to-date; they were of all kinds and of an unparalleled magnificence. The sprite arranged them in the princess's cabinet.

When she came in, no one had ever been so agreeably surprised. Each one was holding a present: there were watches, bracelets, diamond buttons and necklaces. The most apparent had a locket. The princess opened it and found Leandre's portrait. The idea she retained of the first allowed her to recognize the second. She uttered a loud scream; then, looking at Abricotine, she said to her: "I don't understand at all what has been happening in this palace for some time. My birds are full of intelligence; it seems that I only have to form wishes for them to be granted; twice I've seen the portrait of the man who saved you from the hands of thieves; here are fabrics, diamonds, embroiders, lace and infinite rarities. What, then, is the fay, or the demon, which takes care to render me such agreeable services?"

Leandre, hearing her speak, wrote these words in his notepad and threw it at the feet of the princess:

No, I am neither demon nor fay;
I am an unfortunate lover
Who dare not appear to your eyes;
At least lament my destiny.
The Sprite Prince

The notepad was so brilliant with gold and precious stones that she perceived it immediately; she opened it and read what the sprite had written with the utmost astonishment.

"This invisible person is a monster, then," she said, "since he dare not show himself. But if it is true that he has some attachment to me, he would scarcely have the delicacy to present me with such a touching portrait. It's necessary that he doesn't love me, to expose my heart to this ordeal, or that he has a good enough opinion of himself to believe himself more lovable."

"I've heard it said," said Abricotine, "that sprites are composed of air and fire, that they have no body, and that it's only their mind and will that can act."

"I'm very glad," replied the princess. "Such a lover can scarcely trouble the repose of my life."

Leandre was delighted to hear her and see her so occupied with his portrait. He remembered that in a grotto to which she often went there was a pedestal on which a Diana was to stand, which was not yet finished. He placed himself there with an extraordinary costume, crowned with laurels and holding a lyre in his hand, which he played better than Apollo. He waited impatiently for the princess to go there, as she did every day.

It was the place where she went to dream about the stranger. What Abricotine had said about him, combined with the pleasure she had in gazing at the portrait of Leandre, scarcely gave her any repose. She loved solitude, and her cheerful humor had changed so much that her nymphs scarcely recognized her any longer.

When she went into the grotto she made a sign that no one was to follow her. Her nymphs drew away, into different paths. She threw herself down on a bed of grass; she sighed; she shed a few tears; she even spoke, but in such a low voice that the sprite could not hear it. He had put the little red cap on so that she would not see him immediately; then he took it off.

She perceived him, with an extreme surprise. She imagined that he was a statue, for he affected not to emerge from the attitude he had chosen. She looked at him with a joy mingled with dread. That unexpected vision astonished her, but deep down, the pleasure expelled the fear, and she had become accustomed to seeing a figure so proximal to nature when the prince harmonizing his lyre with his voice, sang these words:

How dangerous this abode is!
The most indifferent become sensible here.
In vain I pretended no longer to be amorous,
I lost hope of that here; it is impossible!
Why do they say that this palace
Is the place of tranquil pleasures?
I lost my liberty as soon as I was here,
And my efforts to protect myself were futile
I surrender to my ardent amour,

And would like to be here until my last day.

Charming as Leandre's voice was, the princess could not resist the fear that gripped her. She suddenly went pale, and fell in a faint. The sprite, alarmed, leapt from the pedestal to the ground and put his little red cap on again in order not to be seen by anyone. He took the princess in his arms; he helped her with an unparalleled zeal and ardor.

She opened her beautiful eyes; she looked all around as if searching for him. She could not see anyone, but she felt someone next to her who was holding her hands, who was kissing them and moistening them with tears. She did not dare to speak for a long time; her agitated mind was suspended between dread and hope; she feared the sprite but she loved him when he took on the face of the stranger.

Finally, she cried: "Sprite, gallant sprite, are you not the man for whom I wish?"

At those words, the spite was about to declare himself, but he still did not dare. *If I frighten the object of my adoration,* he said to himself, *if she fears me, she won't want to love me.* Those considerations made him keep quiet, and obliged him to withdraw to a corner of the grotto.

The princess, thinking that she was alone, called Abricotine and told her about the marvel of the animate statue, that its voice was celestial, and that in her faint, the sprite had helped her.

"What a pity," she said, "that the sprite is deformed and frightful, for can there be more gracious and amiable manners than his?"

"And what tells you, Madame that he is as you imagine him? Did not Psyche think that Amour was a serpent? Your adventure has something similar to hers, and you are no less beautiful. If it were Cupid who loved you, would you not love him?"

"If Cupid and the unknown were the same thing," said the princess, blushing, "I would like to love Cupid, alas! But how far I am from such good fortune! I'm attached to a chimera, and that fatal portrait of the stranger, combined with what you have told me about him, throws me into dispositions so opposed to the precepts I've received from my mother that I have too much dread of being punished for them."

"Well, Madame," said Abricotine, interrupting, "Have you not already had punishments? Why foresee misfortunes that might never arrive?"

It is easy to imagine all the pleasure that conversation gave Leandre.

Meanwhile, little Furibon, who was still in love with the princess without having seen her, was waiting impatiently for the return of the four men that he had sent to the Isle of Tranquil Pleasures. Only one returned, who rendered him an account of everything. He told him that it was defended by amazons, and that unless he took a large army, he would never enter the island.

His father, the king, had just died, and he found himself master of everything. He assembled more than four hundred thousand men and departed at their head. He was some general; Briscambille or Perceforest would have done better than him; his battle-horse as only half an aune high.

When the amazons perceived that great army, they came to give the princess the news; she did not fail to send the faithful Abricotine to the realm of the fays to beg her mother to tell her what she ought to do to drive Furibon back to his estates. But Abricotine found the fay very angry.

"I'm not unaware of anything my daughter does," she said. "Prince Leandre is in her palace; he loves her, and is loved. All my cares have been unable to protect her from the tyranny of Amour; now she is under his fatal empire. Alas, the cruel god is not content with the harm he has done me; now he is exercising his power over the person I loved more than my life! Such are the decrees of destiny; I cannot oppose them. Go away, Abricotine; I no longer want to hear mention of that daughter, whose sentiments cause me so much chagrin!"

Abricotine came to give the princess that bad news; it would not have taken much to drive her to despair. The sprite was with her without her seeing him; he knew with an extreme pain the excess of her dolor. He dared not speak to her at that moment, but he remembered that Furibon was very avaricious and that if he were given a great deal of money, perhaps he would withdraw.

He dressed as an amazon and wished himself in the forest in order to recover his horse. As soon as he had called Flax-Gray, Flax-Gray came to him, leaping and bounding, for he was very bored, having been parted from is dear master for such a long time. When he saw him dressed as a woman, however, he no longer recognized him, and feared being mistaken.

Leandre arrived in Furibon's camp; everyone took him for an amazon, he was so handsome. The king was told that a young lady wanted to speak to him on behalf of the Princess of Tranquil Pleasures. He promptly donned his royal mantle and put himself on his throne. One might have thought that he was a huge toad that was mimicking the king.

Leandre spoke to him and told him that the princess, preferring a mild and peaceful life to the turmoil of war, had sent him to offer him as much money as he wanted to leave her in peace, but that in truth, if he refused that proposition, she would neglect nothing to defend herself. Furibon replied that he would be delighted to have pity on her, that he would accord her the honor of his protection, and that she only had to send him a hundred thousand thousand thousand millions of pistoles and he would immediately return to his kingdom. Leandre said that it would take too long to count out a hundred thousand thousand thousand millions of pistoles, that he had only to say how many chambers he wanted filled and that the princess was generous and enough and powerful enough not to look it so closely.

Furibon was very astonished that instead of trying to beat down the sum he was being offered an augmentation. He thought secretly that it was necessary to get all the money he could, and then arrest the amazon and kill her, in order that she could not return to her mistress.

He told Leandre that he wanted thirty very large chambers entirely filled with gold coins, and that he gave his royal word that he would return. Leandre was taken to the chambers that he had to fill with gold. He took the rose, shook it, and shook it, so much that pistoles, quadruples, louis, gold écus, rose nobles, sovereigns, guineas and sequins all fell out like heavy rain; there was nothing in the world prettier.

Furibon was delighted, ecstatic, and the more gold he saw, the more desire he had to take the amazon and capture the princess. As soon as the thirty chambers were full he shouted to his guards: "Arrest her, arrest that slut; its fake money that she's brought me."

All the guards threw themselves upon the amazon, but at the same time the little red cap was put on and the sprite disappeared. They thought he had gone out and ran after him, leaving Furibon alone. At that moment, the sprite took him by the hair and cut off his head like a pullet, without the wretched little king seeing the hand that cut his throat.

When the sprite had the head he wished himself in the Palace of Pleasures. The princess was walking, thinking sadly about what her mother had said, and means of repelling Furibon, which she imagined would be difficult, being alone with a small number of amazons, who could not defend her against four hundred thousand men. She suddenly saw a head in the air without anyone holding it.

That prodigy astonished her so much that she did not know what to think. It was worse when the head was placed at her feet without her seeing the hand that was holding it. Immediately, she heard a voice, which said: "Have no fear, charming princess, Furibon will never do you any harm."

Abricotine recognized Leandre's voice, and cried: "I protest to you, Madame, that the invisible person who is speaking is the stranger who rescued me."

The princess seemed astonished and delighted. "Ah!" she said. "If it is true that the sprite and the stranger are one and the same, I confess that I would have more pleasure in testifying my gratitude to him."

The sprite replied: "I want to work again in order to merit it."

Indeed, he returned to Furibon's army, where the news of his death had just spread. As soon as he appeared there in his ordinary clothes, everyone came to him; the captains and the soldiers surrounded him, uttering loud cries of joy. They recognized him as their king, and that the crown belonged to him. He gave them liberally, to divide between them, the thirty chambers full of gold, so that the members of the army were rich forever. After a few ceremonies that assured Leandre of the faith of his soldiers, he ordered his army to return to their homeland at daybreak, and returned to the princess again.

The princess was in bed, and the profound respect that the prince had for her prevented him from entering her room. He retired to his own, for he had always slept on the ground floor. He was sufficiently fatigued to need repose; that caused him to neglect to close his door as carefully as he usually did.

The princess was dying of heat and anxiety, and went downstairs, undressed, into her ground-floor apartment. What a surprise she had on finding Leandre there asleep on a bed! She had all the time necessary to look at him without being seen, and to convince herself that he was the person whose portrait she had in the diamond locket. *It isn't possible*, she said to herself, *that this is the sprite. Do sprites sleep? Is that a body of air and fire that does not occupy any space, as Abricotine says?*

She touched his hair gently, she listened to him breathing; she could not tear herself away from him, so delighted was she to have found him, and so alarmed was she.

While she was at her most attentive, her mother the fay came in, making a noise so frightful that Leandre woke up with a start. What a surprise and what affliction it was for him to see his princess in the utmost despair. Her mother was dragging her away, charging her with a thousand reproaches.

What dolor for the young lovers! They found themselves on the point of being separated forever. The princess dared not say anything to the terrible fay; she cast her eyes upon Leandre, as if to ask for his help.

He judged, rightly, that he could not retain her against the will of such a powerful person, but he sought in his eloquence for the means to touch that irritated mother. He ran after her and threw himself at her feet; he implored her to have pity on a young king who would never change for her daughter, and who would find his sovereign felicity in rendering her happy. The princess, encouraged by his example, immediately embraced her mother's knees and said to her that without the king she could not be content, and that she had great obligations to him.

"You don't know the disgraces of amour," cried the fay, "and the treasons of which these amiable deceivers are capable. They only enchant us in order to poison us; I've experienced it. Do you want a destiny similar to mine?"

"Oh, Madame," replied the princess, "is there no exception? Do not the assurances that the king has given you, and which appear so sincere, seem to protect me from what you dread?"

The stubborn fay let them sigh at her feet; they moistened her hands with their tears in vain; she appeared to be insensible to them, and doubtless would not have pardoned them, if the amiable fay Gentille had not appeared in the room, brighter than the sun. The Graces accompanied her and she was followed by a troop of Amours, Games and Pleasures, who sang a thousand agreeable and novel songs as they frolicked like children.

She embraced the old fay. "My dear sister," she said to her, "I'm convinced that you have not forgotten the good offices that I rendered you when you wanted to return to our realm; but for me, you would never have been received, and since that time I have not asked you for any service, but the time has finally come for you to render me an essential one. Pardon this beautiful princess, consent that this young king marries her, and I will answer to you for the fact that he will not change for her. Their days will be woven in gold and silk; this alliance will fill you with satisfaction, and I shall never forget the pleasure you will have given me."

"I consent to everything you wish, charming Gentille," cried the fay. "Come, my children, come into my arms; receive the assurance of my amity."

With those words she embraced the princess and her lover. The fay Gentille was rapturous with joy, and the entire troop commenced the hymns of marriage. The sweetness of that symphony having awakened all the nymphs in the palace, they ran in light gauze robes to see what was happening.

What an agreeable surprise for Abricotine! She had scarcely cast her eyes on Leandre that she recognized him, and, seeing him holding the hand of the princess, she had no doubt of their common happiness. That was confirmed for her when the mother fay said that she wanted to transport the Isle of Tranquil Pleasures, the castle and all the marvels it contained to Leandre's kingdom; that she would live with them and would make them even greater benefits.

"Whatever your generosity inspires, Madame," the king said to her, "it is impossible that you can make me a present that equals the one I have received today; you have rendered me the happiest of men, and I feel that I am also the most grateful."

That small compliment pleased the fay very much; she was from the old days, when people made compliments all day long on a beauty spot.

As Gentille thought of everything she had transported, by means of the virtue of magic, the general and the captains of Furibon's army to the princess's palace, in order that they could witness the gallant fête that was about to take place. She did indeed take care of that, and five or six volumes would not be sufficient to describe the comedies, the operas, the ring races, the music, the gladiatorial combats, the hunts and other magnificent things there were in celebration of that charming wedding.

The most singular aspect of the adventure is that each the nymphs found, among the brave men that Gentille had attracted, a husband as passionate as if they had been seeing them for ten years. It was, in fact, an acquaintance of twenty-four hours at the most; but the little wand produces effects even more extraordinary.

What has become of those happy times.
When, by the power of a fay,
Innocence was delivered
From the most evident perils?
By the powerful aid of a cap and a rose
Many metamorphoses were seen.
Seeing all without being seen,
A mortal traveled the world,
And found in the air an unknown route.
Leandre possessed a fecund rose,
Which poured into his hand at the whim of his desire
The precious metal from which pleasures are born.
By the power of a second,
He savored the sweetness of perfect health;
The third, in my view was less desirable;
Of an object he loved he discovered the heart;
And knew whether it burned with a veritable ardor,
Or whether it was deceptive fire,
Alas, in the matter of mistresses,
Happy is the man who can be unaware,
That the one who heaps you with caresses
Only has an apparent amour.

PRINCESS SPRINGTIME

There was once a king and a queen who had several children, but they all died, and the king and queen were so sorry, so very sorry, that nothing could make up for it; for they had wealth to spare, they lacked nothing except children. It was five years since the queen had had one; everyone believed that she would not have another, because she was too afflicted when she thought of all the pretty little princes who had died.

Finally, the queen became pregnant; she only thought night and day how she could conserve the life of the little creature that she was going to have, the name that it would be given, the clothes, the dolls and the toys that she would give it.

The trumpets had been sounded and posters put up at every crossroads instructing the best nurses to present themselves before the queen, because she wanted to choose one for her child. They came from the four corners of the world; there was nothing but nurses with their babies.

One day, when the queen was taking the air in a large wood, she sat down and said to the king: "Sire, have all our nurses come; let's choose one, for our cows don't have enough milk to furnish pap to so many little children."

"Gladly, my dear," said the king. "Let's go, summon the nurses."

So they all came, one after another, making beautiful reverences to the king and the queen; then they formed a line, each against a tree. Once they were arranged, and their fresh complexions, beautiful teeth and breasts full of milk had been admired, an ugly woman was seen coming in a wheelbarrow pushed by two wretched little dwarfs; her feet were mismatched, her knees were under her chin, she had a big hump, squinting eyes and a skin blacker than ink; she was holding in her arms a little ape, to which she was giving suck and she spoke a jargon that no one understood.

She came in her turn to offer herself but the queen rejected her. "Go away, vile creature," she said. "You're nothing but an idiot, to come before me made as you are; if you stay any longer I'll have you removed." The surly individual passed on, grumbling loudly and dragged by her frightful dwarfs. She had herself lodged in the hollow of a large tree, from which she could see everything.

The queen, who was no longer thinking about her, chose a beautiful nurse, but as soon as they had named her a horrible snake that was hidden in the grass bit her in the foot and she fell as if dead. Much chagrined by that accident, the queen cast her eyes on another; immediately, an eagle flying overhead, which was holding a tortoise, dropped it on the head of the poor nurse, which shattered like a glass. Even more afflicted, the queen summoned a third nurse, who, wanting to advance more rapidly, stumbled into a bush full of long thorns and punctured an eye.

"Oh!" cried the queen, "There's a great deal of misfortune in my affair today. It isn't possible for me to choose a nurse with bring her bad luck! I'll leave the concern to my physician."

As she got up in order to return to the palace she heard full-throated laughter. She looked, and saw the malevolent hunchback behind her, like a she-monkey with her simian baby, in her wheelbarrow. She was mocking the entire company, particularly the queen. The princess was in such great annoyance that she wanted to go to her in order to beat her, suspecting that she was the cause of the nurses' misfortunes; but the hunchback tapped her wand three times; the dwarfs changed into winged griffins and the wheelbarrow into a fiery chariot, and they all flew away through the air, uttering threats and loud cries.

"Alas, my dear, we're doomed," said the king. "That's the fay Carabosse; the evil woman has hated me since I was a little boy, because of a trick I played on her with sulfur in her soup; since then she's always sought to avenge herself."

The queen started weeping. "If I'd been able to divine her name," she said, "I would have tried to make her a friend; I believe I'd like to be dead."

When the king saw her so afflicted he said: "My love, let's hold a council to see what we can do." He took her under his arm, for she was still trembling from the fear that Carabosse had caused.

When the king and the queen were in the chamber they summoned their counselors; the doors and windows were firmly closed so that they would not be overheard, and they made the resolution to invite all the fays for a thousand leagues around to the child's birth. Couriers departed immediately, and very civil letters were written to the fays begging them to take the trouble to come to the queen's childbed and to keep the affair secret, for they trembled with fear that Carabosse might be informed of it and come to cause a squabble. To recompense them for their trouble they were promised a blue velvet overskirt, an amaranth velvet skirt, crimson satin slit slippers, small gilded scissors and a case full of fine needles.

As soon as the couriers had left the queen began working with her damsels and maidservants on everything that she had promised the fays. They knew several, but only five of them came. They arrived at the moment when the queen had just given birth to a little princess. They shut themselves away quickly in order to endow her. The first endowed her with perfect beauty, the second with infinite intelligence, the third with a marvelous singing voice, the fourth with the ability to produce works in prose and verse.

As the fifth was opening her mouth to speak a noise was heard in the chimney, like a large stone falling from the height of a bell-tower, and Carabosse appeared, heavily smeared with soot, crying at the top of her voice: "I endow the little creature with constant bad luck until the age of twenty years."

At those words, the queen, who was in her bed, stated weeping, and imploring Carabosse to have pity on the little princess. All the fays said to her: "Alas, my sister, reverse her ill-luck, what has she done to you?" But the ugly fay snorted and made no reply, with the consequence that the fifth, who had not spoken, tried to repair the matter by endowing her with a long life full of happiness after the time of the malediction had passed. Carabosse only laughed, and started to sing twenty ironic songs, while climbing up by the way she had come.

All the fays remained in great consternation, and the queen even more so. She nevertheless gave them what she had promised; she even added ribbons, which they liked very much. They were given a good meal, and the oldest one said as she left that her opinion was that the princess should be put, until the age of twenty, in some place where she would not see anyone except the maidservants she was given, and that she should be securely locked in.

For that, the king had a covered tower built in which there were no windows; one could only see clearly therein by candlelight. One arrived there via a vault that extended for a league underground; it was by that route that the nurses and governesses were brought everything they needed. There were thick doors every twenty paces, that were locked, and guards everywhere.

The young princes was named Springtime, because she had a complexion of lilies and roses, fresher and more flowery than spring. She rendered herself admirable in everything she said or did; she learned the most difficult sciences as readily as the easiest, and grew so tall and so beautiful that the king and queen never saw her without weeping with joy. She sometimes begged them to stay with her or to take her with them, for she was bored without knowing why, but they always declined.

Her nurse, who had not quit her, and who did not lack intelligence, sometimes told her what the world was like, and she understood it immediately, with as much facility as if she had seen it.

The king often said to the queen: "My dear, Carabosse will be the dupe; we're much cleverer than she is; our Springtime will be happy in spite of her prediction; and the queen laughed until she shed tears thinking about the chagrin of the malevolent fay. They had Springtime painted and sent her portrait all over the world, for the time to bring her out of the tower was approaching and they wanted to marry her.

Only four days remained to complete the twenty years; the court was in great joy at the imminent liberty of the princess, and it was augmented by the news that King Merlin wanted to have her hand, on behalf of his son, and was sending his ambassador Fanfarinet to make the request.

The nurse, who told the princess everything, told her all that, and that there was nothing in the world finer than the entrance of Fanfarinet.

"Oh, how unfortunate I am," she exclaimed. "I'm retained in this somber tower as if I had committed some great crime. I've never seen the sky, the sun and the stars, of which so many marvelous things are said. I've never seen a horse, a monkey or a lion except in paintings. The king and queen say that they'll take me out of here when I'm twenty years old, but they want to amuse me to make me be patient, and I know full well that they want to make me perish, without me having offended them in any way."

With that she stated to weep and weep, so much that her eyes were as big as fists, and the nurse, her foster-sister, the and the other nursery-maids, who all loved her passionately also began to weep, so much that nothing could be heard but sobs and sighs. They thought they would choke; it was a great desolation.

When the princess saw them in such great affliction she took a knife and said: "Well, I've resolved to kill myself right away if you don't find a means of letting me see the fine entrance of Fanfarinet. The king and the queen will never know. Confer together as to whether you'd rather I cut my own throat here than give me that satisfaction."

At those words, the nurse and the others recommenced weeping even harder, and they all resolved to enable her to see Fanfarinet or to die trying. They spent the rest of the night proposing expedients without finding one, and Springtime, who was in despair, said incessantly: "Don't tell me anymore that you love me; if you loved me, you'd find better means. I've read that love and amity can succeed in anything."

Finally, they concluded that it was necessary to make a hole in the tower on the side of the city, by which Fanfarinet ought to come. They moved the princess's bed and they all set to work incessantly, day and night. By dint of scraping they removed all the plaster, and then the small stones. They removed so many that they made a hole, thorough which a needle could pass, with great difficulty.

It was through that hole that Springtime saw daylight for the first time; she was dazzled by it; and as she looked through the little hole incessantly she saw Fanfarinet appear at the head of his entre troop. He was mounted on a white horse, which danced to the sound of trumpets and jumped marvelously. Six flute-players came before him, playing the finest opera arias, and six oboes responded with echoes; then the trumpets and drums made a great din. Fanfarinet had a coat embroidered with pearls, golden bots, scarlet plumes, ribbons everywhere, and so many diamonds—for King Merlin had rooms full of them—that the sun shone less brightly than him.

At that sight, Springtime felt so beside herself that she could not take any more, and, after having thought for a while, she swore that she would not have any other husband than the handsome Fanfarinet; that there was no appearance that his master would be as lovable; that she did not know ambition; that since she had lived well in a tower she could live well, if necessary, in some country house with him; that it seemed to her that bread and water with him was better than pullets and bonbons with another. In sum, she said so much that her women were in great difficulty when she had told them a quarter of it. When they tried to remind her of her rank, and the wrong she was doing, she told them to shut up, without deigning to listen to them.

As soon as Fanfarinet had arrived in the king's palace, the queen came in quest of her daughter. All the streets were carpeted and the ladies were at the windows; some were holding baskets full of flowers, others full of pearls, or, even better, excellent sugared almonds, to throw at her as she passed by.

They were commencing to dress her when a dwarf mounted on an elephant arrived at the tower; he came on the part of the five good fays who had endowed her on the day of her birth. They sent her a crown, a scepter, a gold brocade robe and a butterfly-wing skirt of marvelous workmanship, with a casket even more marvelous so full was it of gemstones that were said to be priceless; so many riches had never been seen together. At that sight the queen was swooning with admiration. As for the princess, she looked at all of it indifferently, because she was only thinking about Fanfarinet.

The dwarf was thanked; he received a pistole for a tip, and more than a thousand aunes of nonpareil ribbon of all colors, with which he made beautiful gaiters, and knots for his cravat and his hat. The dwarf was so small that when he had all the ribbons he could no longer be seen. The queen said that she would search for something beautiful to send to the fays, and the princess, who was very generous, made them a present of several German spinning-wheels, with cedar-wood distaffs.

Everything than the dwarf had brought of ornamentation was put on the princess; she appeared to everyone to be such great beauty that the sun hid in chagrin and the moon, which is not overly shameful, dared not appear while she was en route. She went on foot along the streets, walking over rich carpets; the people, assembled in crowds, cried around h: "Oh, how beautiful she is! Oh, how beautiful she is!"

As she went forth in that pompous apparel, between the queen and four or five dozen princesses of the blood, not to mention more than ten dozen who had come from neighboring states to attend the fête, the sky began to darken, thunder rumbled and rain, mixed with hail, began to fall in torrents.

The queen put her royal mantle over her head; all the ladies put their skirts over theirs. Springtime was about to do the same when more than a thousand crows, owls, ravens and other birds of sinister augury were heard in the air, the croaking of which announced nothing good. At the same time, a horrible owl of prodigious size swooped down at high speed, holding in its beak a cobweb scarf. It dropped that scarf over Springtime's shoulder, and long bursts of laughter were heard, which signified well enough that it was a nasty joke on the part of Carabosse.

At that lugubrious vision, everyone stated to weep, and the queen, more afflicted than anyone else, tried to tear away the black scarf, but it seemed to be stuck to her daughter's shoulders.

"Oh," she said, "this is one of our enemy's tricks; nothing can appease her. I've sent her in vain more than fifty pounds of jam, as much royal sugar and two Mayence hams; she hasn't taken any account of it."

While she was lamenting, everyone was soaked to the skin. Springtime, infatuated with the ambassador, was still making headway, and without saying a single word. She thought that, provided that she could please him, she did not care about Carabosse or her sash of ill omen. She was secretly astonished that he had not come to meet her, when she suddenly saw him appear beside the king. Immediately, the trumpets, drums and violins made an agreeable noise; the cries of the people redoubled; in sum, the joy appeared extraordinary.

Fanfarinet had a great deal of intelligence, but when he saw the beautiful Springtime with so much grace and majesty he was so rapturous that, instead of speaking, he could do no more than stammer; one might have thought that he was drunk, although he had certainly only taken a cup of chocolate. He was in despair at having forgotten, in the blink of an eye, a speech that he had been repeating every day for months, and knew well enough to be able to recite it in his sleep.

While he put his memory to the question in order to recover it, he made profound reverences to the princess, who, for her part, made half a dozen without any reflection. Finally, she broke the silence, and in order to get him out of the embarrassment that she saw him in, she said: "Sire Fanfarinet, I have no difficulty knowing that everything you are thinking is charming, I thank you for having so much intelligence, but let us hasten to reach the palace; the rain is pouring down; it's the malevolent Carabosse who is inundating us; when we're under cover she'll be the dupe."

He replied gallantly that the fay had sagely foreseen the fire that her beautiful eyes were about to ignite, and was spreading deluges of water in order to temper it. After those few words he extended his hand, in order to help her to walk.

In a low voice she said to him: "I have sentiments for you that you would never divine if I did not explain them myself; that will be difficult for me, nevertheless, but shame upon whoever thinks evil. Know then, Messire Ambassador that when I saw you with admiration mounted on your fine dancing horse, I regretted that you were coming on behalf of another rather than yourself. We will find a remedy for that, if you have as much courage as me; instead of marrying you on your master's behalf, I will marry you on your own. I know that you are not a prince, but you please me as much as if you were. We will run away together to some corner of the world. There will be talk at first, and then someone else will do what I have done, or worse, and I shall be left in repose in order for them to talk about her, and I shall have the pleasure of living with you."

Fanfarinet thought he was dreaming, for Springtime was such a marvelous princess that, save for some strange caprice, he could never have hoped for that honor; he did not even have the strength to reply. If they had been alone he would have thrown himself at her feet, but he took the liberty of squeezing her hand so forcefully that he hurt her little finger badly, without her crying out, so madly in love was she.

When she entered the palace a thousand kinds of musical instruments resounded, with which near-celestial voices joined in so precisely that no one dared breathe for fear of making too much noise.

After the king had kissed his daughter on the forehead and both cheeks, he said to her: "My little ewe-lamb"—for he gave her all sorts of pet names—"would you not like to marry the son of the great King Merlin? Here is Lord Fanfarinet, who will perform the ceremony for him and who will take you to the most beautiful kingdom in the world."

"Yes, my father," she said, making a profound reverence. "I want to do everything that will please you, provided that my good Maman consents to it."

"I consent to it, my darling," said the queen, embracing her. "Let's go; let the tables be laid."

That was done with diligence. There were a hundred of them in a great gallery, and no one in human memory ate so much, except for Springtime and Fanfarinet, who were only thinking about looking at one another, and dreaming so much that they forgot everything.

After the meal there was a ball, a ballet and a play, but it was already so late that, no matter what they did, everyone was asleep on their feet. The king and the queen, gripped by slumber, threw themselves on to a sofa; the majority of the ladies and cavaliers were snoring, the musicians went out of tune and the actors did not know what they were saying; only the lovers were awake, like mice, and making a hundred little faces at one another.

Seeing that there was nothing to fear, and that the guards, lying on their mattresses, were asleep in their turn, the princess said to Fanfarinet: "Believe me, let's profit from such a favorable opportunity, for if I wait for the marriage ceremony, the king will give me ladies to serve me and a prince to accompany me to the home of your King Merlin. It's better if we go now, as quickly as we can."

She got up, took the king's dagger, which was full of diamonds, and the tiara that the queen had taken off in order to sleep more at her ease. She gave her white hand to Fanfarinet in order to leave; he took it, and put one knee on the floor. "I swear to Your Highness," he said, "an eternal fidelity and obedience. Great princess, you are doing so much for me, what would I not do for you?"

They left the palace; the ambassador was carrying a hooded lantern. They went through the muddy streets to the port; they got into a small boat where there was a poor old boatman who was asleep. They woke him up, and when he saw Princes Springtime, so beautiful and brave, with so many diamonds and her cobweb scarf, he took her for the goddess of the night and knelt before her. As it was necessary not to waste time, however, she ordered him to depart.

It was very hazardous, for the moon and the stars were invisible; the weather was still overcast with the rain that Carabosse had excited. It is true that there was a carbuncle in the queen's head-dress that shone more than fifty lighted torches and Fanfarinet—it is said—could have done without his hooded lantern; it also had a stone that rendered invisibility.

Fanfarinet asked the princess where she wanted to go. "Alas," she said, "I want to go with you; that is all I have in mind."

"But Madame," he said, "I dare not take you to the abode of King Merlin; I'd surely be hanged there."

"Well," she replied, let's go to the desert Isle of Squirrels. It's far enough away for no one to follow us there." She commanded the mariner to depart, and although he only had a little boat, he obeyed.

As daylight approached, the king, the queen and everyone else, having shaken their ears and rubbed their eyes, were only thinking about concluding the marriage of the princess. The queen, in haste, asked for her rich tiara in order to be coiffed. They searched for it from the cabinets to the saucepans, but the tiara was not there. Anxiously, the queen ran downstairs and upstairs, to the cellars and the grain-lofts; it could not be found.

In his turn, the king wanted to put on his beautiful dagger; in the same way, people began searching for it everywhere; coffers and caskets were opened the keys of which had been lost a hundred years ago. A thousand rarities were found—dolls that moved their heads and eyes, golden ewes with their little lambs, fine lemon-peel marmalades and walnut conserves, but that could not console the king. His despair was so great that he tore out his beard. The queen, to keep him company, tore out her hair; for in truth, the tiara and the dagger were worth more than ten cities as big as Madrid.

When the king saw that there was no hope of finding anything, he said to the queen: "My love, let us have courage and hasten to conclude the ceremony that has already cost us so dear."

He asked where the princess was. Her nurse came forward and said: "My lord, I assure you that I have been searching for her for two hours without being able to find her."

Those words brought the dolor of the king and the queen to a peak. She started to screech like an eagle whose chicks have been stolen and fell in a faint. No one had ever been in such a pitiful state. More than two bucketfuls of the Queen of Hungary's water were thrown over Her Majesty's face before it was possible to bring her round. The ladies and damsels were weeping and all the valets were saying: "What! The queen's daughter is lost?"

The king, seeing that the princess was no longer present, said to his senior page: "Go fetch Fanfarinet, who's asleep in some corner, in order that he can come and be afflicted with us."

The page went everywhere, and found no more trace of him than had been found of Springtime, the tiara and the dagger. That was a further surplus of affliction, which completed Their Majesties' desolation.

The king summoned all his counselors and men-at-arms. He went with the queen into a great hall that had been promptly hung in black; they had taken off their beautiful garments and had each put on a long mourning robe girded by a rope.

When they were seen in that state there was no heart so hard that it was not ready to break; the hall resounded with sobs and sighs; streams of tears flowed over the floorboards.

As the king had had not time to prepare his speech, he did not say anything for three hours; finally, he commenced thus:

"Now listen, great and small; I have lost my dear daughter Springtime; I don't know whether she has melted or whether she has been stolen from me. The queen's tiara and my dagger, which are worth their weight in gold, have also disappeared with her, and what is worse, Ambassador Fanfarinet is no longer here. I fear that the king, his master, not hearing any news of him, will come to search for him among us, and might accuse us of having chopped him up like mincemeat. I could still be patient if I had money, but I confess to you that the expenses of the wedding have ruined me. Advise me, then, my dear subjects, of what I can do to recover my daughter, Fanfarinet and the rest."

Everyone admired the king's fine speech; he had never made one so eloquent. Lord Gambille, the chancellor of the realm, took the floor and said: "Sire, we are all very sorry about your misfortune, and would have given even our wives and children, for you not to have had such a great subject of annoyance, but apparently, it's a trick of the fay Carabosse. The princess's twenty years were not yet accomplished, and since it's necessary to say everything, I remarked that she looked constantly at Fanfarinet, and that he also looked at her. Perhaps Amour has also played some trick of his métier."

At those words the queen was very quick to interrupt him. "Beware of what you're suggesting. Lord Gambille; know that the princess was not in a humor to become smitten with Fanfarinet; I've brought her up too well."

With that, the nurse, who was listening to everything, came to kneel before the king and the queen. "I have come," she said, "to confess to you what has happened. The princess desired to see Fanfarinet or die; we made a little hole through which she perceived him, and immediately swore that she would never have any other than him."

At that news everyone was afflicted, and knew full well that Chancellor Gambille had a great deal of penetration. The queen, utterly chagrined, scolded the nurse, the foster-sister and all the other nursemaids so much that little more would have had to be said to choke them

Admiral Pointed-Hat interrupted the queen, saying: "Come on, let's go after Fanfarinet; there's no doubt about it, that good-for-nothing has abducted our princess."

Everyone clapped their hands and replied: "Let's go."

Some put to sea and others went from kingdom to kingdom beating the drum and sounding the trumpet; when crowds gathered around them they cried: "Whoever wants to obtain a beautiful doll, dry and liquid jams, little scissors, a golden robe, and a fine satin bonnet has only to tell us where Fanfarinet has taken Princess Springtime."

Everyone replied: "Go elsewhere; we haven't seen them."

Those who were pursuing the princess by sea were more fortunate; one night, after a long navigation, they perceived something shining in front of them like a great fire. They dared not approach it, not knowing what it might be, but the light suddenly stopped on the desert Isle of Squirrels; for it was, indeed, the princess and her lover, with the shining carbuncle.

They landed, and after having given a hundred gold écus to the fellow who had brought them, they bid him adieu and forbade him, on the eyes in his head, to speak to anyone about anything.

The first thing he encountered was the king's ships, which he had no sooner recognized than be tried to evade; but the admiral, having seen him, sent a boat after him, and the fellow was so old and so weak that he did not have enough strength to row. They caught up with him and took him to the admiral, who had him searched; they found the hundred brand new gold écus, for new money had been minted for the wedding of the princess. The admiral questioned him, and in order not to be obliged to respond he pretended to be deaf and dumb.

"Someone attach this mute to the mainmast," said the admiral, "and give him the lash. There's nothing better for mutes."

When the old man saw that it was all up he confessed that a young woman more celestial than human and a genteel cavalier had commanded him to take them to the desert Isle of Squirrels. At those words the admiral deduced that it was the princess, and advanced his fleet to surround the island.

Meanwhile, Springtime, fatigued by the sea, having found a patch of green grass, had lain down on it and gone meekly to sleep; but Fanfarinet, who was more hungry than amorous, did not let her repose for long. "Do you think, Madame," he asked, "that I can stay her much longer? I can't see anything to eat. Even if you were more beautiful than the dawn, that wouldn't be sufficient for me; I need something to eat; I have long teeth and an empty stomach."

"What, Fanfarinet!" she replied. "Is it possible that the marks of my amity do not take the place of everything for you? Is it possible that you are not occupied with your good fortune?"

"I'm more so with my ill fortune," he cried. "I wish to heaven that you were still in your black tower!"

"Handsome knight," she said to him, graciously, "I beg you not to get annoyed; I'll search everywhere; perhaps I'll find some fruits."

"May you find a wolf that will eat you," he said.

Afflicted, the princess ran into the wood, tearing her beautiful garments on the brambles and her white skin on the thorns. She was scratched as if she had been playing with cats. That is what it is to love a young man; it brings one nothing but pains.

After having been everywhere, she returned to Fanfarinet very sadly and told him that she had not found anything. He turned his back on her and drew away, muttering between his teeth.

They searched the next day, as fruitlessly, with the consequence that they went for three days without eating anything except leaves and a few cockchafers. The princess did not complain, although she was much more delicate.

"I would be content," she said to him, "if I were suffering alone, and I would not career about dying of hunger, provided that you had something to eat."

"It would be indifferent to me," he replied, "if you died, as long as I had what I needed."

"Is it possible," she added, "that you would be so little touched by my death? Are those the oaths that you have made me?"

"There is a great difference," he said, "between a man at his ease, who is neither hungry nor thirsty, and an unfortunate ready to expire on a desert island."

"I'm in the same danger," she continued, "and I'm not complaining."

"You're very kind," he replied abruptly. "You wanted to quit your father and mother to go gadding about. Now we're at our ease!"

"But it's for love of you," she said, holding out her hand to him."

"I could do without that," he said, and turned his back on her.

The beautiful princess, overwhelmed by dolor, started weeping, so much that she would have softened the heart of a rock. She sat down at the foot of a bush charged with white and red roses. After having looked at them for some time she said to them: "How fortunate you are, young flowers. The zephyrs caress you; the dew moistens you; the sun embellishes you; the bees cherish you; your thorns defend you; everyone admires you. Alas, is it necessary that you are more tranquil than me?"

That reflection caused her to shed such a great abundance of tears that the foot of the rose-bush was moist with them. Then, to her great astonishment, she saw that the bush was agitating and the roses blossoming, and the most beautiful of them said to her: "If you had not fallen in love your fate would be as enviable as mine; whoever falls in love exposes themselves to the utmost misfortune. Poor princess! Take a honeycomb from the hollow of that tree, but don't be so simple as to give it to Fanfarinet."

She ran to the tree, not knowing whether she was dreaming or whether she was wide awake. She found the honey, and as soon as she had it she took it to her ingrate lover. "Here," she said, "is a honeycomb; I could have eaten it on my own, but I prefer to share it with you."

Without thanking her or looking at her, he snatched it from her and ate it in its entirety, refusing to give her even a small piece. He even added mockery to brutality; he told her that it was too sweet, that she would spoil her teeth, and a hundred similar impertinences.

Springtime, more afflicted than she had been before, sat down under an oak tree and paid it a compliment very similar to the one she had paid the rose-bush. The oak, moved to compassion, lowered some of its branches toward her and said to her: "It would be a pity if you ceased to live, beautiful Springtime; take that pitcher of milk and drink, without giving a drop to your ingrate lover."

The princess, utterly astonished, looked behind her. Immediately, she saw a large pitcher of milk. She only remembered then the thirst that Fanfarinet might have after having eaten more than five pounds of honey. She ran to him, carrying her pitcher.

"Slake your thirst, handsome Fanfarinet," she said, "and remember to keep some for me, for I'm dying of hunger and thirst."

He took the pitcher rudely, and drank all the milk in a single draught. Then, throwing it down on stones, he broke it into pieces, saying with a malign smile: "When one hasn't eaten, one isn't thirsty."

The princess put her hands together and raised her beautiful eyes to the heavens. "Oh," she cried, "I have merited his; this is a just punishment for having quit the king and the queen, for having loved so inconsiderately a man I did not know, for having fled with him, without remembering my rank, or the misfortunes by which I was threatened by Carabosse."

Then she began to weep more bitterly than she had ever done in her life. Plunging into the densest part of the wood, she collapsed of weakness at the foot of an elm tree, in which a nightingale was perched, which was singing marvelously. It sang these words while flapping its wings, as if it were only singing them for Springtime; it had learned them expressly from Ovid:

> *Amour is malevolent; the little traitor never*
> *Does you favors without being master of them,*
> *And, beneath the charms of his false mildness,*
> *His envenomed features poison hearts.*

"Who can know that better than me?" she cried, interrupting the bird. "Alas, I know only too well the cruelty of his features and that of my fate."

"Have courage, "the amorous nightingale said to her, "And search in that bush; you'll find sugared almonds there and tartlets from Chez le Coq. But don't be imprudent enough to give any to Fanfarinet."

The princess had no need of that prohibition to keep them to herself; she had not yet forgotten the last two bad turns that he had done her, and she also had such a great need to eat that she crunched the sugared almonds and the tartlets all alone.

The greedy Fanfarinet, having perceived her eating without him, became so angry that he ran to her with his eyes sparkling with rage and his sword in his hand, in order to kill her.

She immediately uncovered the stone in the tiara that rendered invisibility, and, drawing away from him, she reproached him for his ingratitude in terms that made him know that she could not hate him yet.

Meanwhile, Admiral Pointed-Hat had dispatched the bumpkin Jean Caquet, the usual courier of the cabinet, to go and tell the king that the princess and Fanfarinet had landed on the Isle of Squirrels; but that, not knowing the country, he feared ambushes.

At that news, which gave Their Majesties much joy, the king had a huge book brought to him, each page of which was eight aunes long; it was the masterpiece of a savant fay, in which there as a description of the entire earth. He discovered immediately that the Isle of Squirrels was uninhabited. "Go back," he said to Jean Caquet. "Order the admiral, on my part, to land immediately; he'll regret, and so will I, leaving my daughter for such a long time with Fanfarinet."

As soon as Jean Caquet had arrived at the fleet, the admiral had all the drums beaten and the trumpets sounded; the oboes, flutes, violins hurdy-gurdies, organs and guitars were played; there was a desperate racket, for all those instruments of war and peace could be heard all over the island.

At that noise, the alarmed princess ran to her lover to offer him her help. He was not brave; the common peril reconciled them very rapidly. "Stay behind me," she said. "I'll uncover the stone of invisibility and I'll take my father's dagger to kill the enemies while you kill them with your sword."

The invisible princess advanced among the armed men; she and Fanfarinet killed them all without being seen. Nothing was heard but cries of "I'm dead!" and "I'm dying." The soldiers fired in vain; they did not hit anything, for the princess and her lover ducked down and the shots passed over their heads. Finally, the admiral, afflicted by losing so many men in such an extraordinary manner, without them knowing who was attacking them or how to defend themselves, sounded the retreat and return to the ships to hold council.

The night was already well advanced. The princess and Fanfarinet went to take refuge in the densest part of the wood. She was so tired that she lay down on the grass and as falling asleep when she heard a tiny voice saying: "Save yourself, Springtime, for Fanfarinet wants to kill you and eat you."

Opening her eyes quickly, she perceived by the light of her carbuncle that the evil Fanfarinet had his arm raised, ready to pierce her breast with his sword; for, seeing her so plump and so pale, and having a good appetite, he wanted to kill her in order to eat her.

She did not deliberate as to what she ought to do; she drew her dagger, which she had kept since the battle, and she dealt him such a furious blow in the eye that he died instantly.

"There, ingrate," she cried, "receive that last favor as the one you merited most; serve in future as an example to perfidious lovers, and may your disloyal heart enjoy no repose."

When the first impulses of anger had passed and she thought about the situation she was in, she was almost as dead as the man she had just killed. "What will become of me?" she cried, weeping. "I'm alone on this island; the wild beasts will devour me or I'll die of hunger." She almost regretted not having allowed Fanfarinet to eat her. She sat down tremulously, waiting for daylight, for which she wished ardently, for she feared the spirits, especially the nightmare.

As she was leaning against a tree, she looked up in the air and saw a beautiful golden chariot drawn by six large crested chickens; a cock served as coachman and a fatted pullet as postillion. In the chariot there was woman so beautiful, so very beautiful, that she resembled the sun; her robe was embroidered all over with golden spangles and silver streaks. She saw another chariot harnessed to six bats; a crow served as coachman and a snail as postillion. There was a frightful little she-ape in it, whose coat was made of snakeskin, and she had a huge toad on her head that served as a fontange.[14]

Never—absolutely never—has anyone been as astonished as the young princess was. As she considered those marvels, she suddenly saw the chariots advancing toward one another, the beautiful lady holding a gilded lance and the ugly one a rusty pike; they commenced a rude combat, which lasted more than a quarter of an hour. Finally, the beauty was victorious; the ugly one fled with her bats. At the same time the beauty descended to the ground and addressed Springtime.

"Have no fear, amiable princess," she said, "I have only come to this place to oblige you; the battle I have fought against Carabosse was only for love of you. She wanted to have the authority to give you the whip, because you emerged from the tower four days before the twenty years, but you've seen that I took your side and chased her away. Enjoy the good fortune that I have acquired for you."

The grateful princess prostrated herself before her. "Great queen of fays," she said, "your generosity delights me; I don't know how to thank you, but I feel that I do not have a single drop of the blood that you have just conserved that is not at your service."

The fay kissed her three times and rendered her even more beautiful than she was, if that were possible. She ordered her cocks to go to the king's ships and to tell the admiral to come ashore without fear; and she sent the fatted pullet to her palace in quest of the most beautiful clothes in the world for Springtime.

At the news that the cocks gave him, the admiral was so delighted that he nearly fell ill. He came to the island promptly, with all his men, even Jean Caquet, who, seeing the precipitation with which everyone was descending from the ships,

---

[14] A fontange was a kind of elevated head-dress allegedly named after one of Louis XIV's mistresses, which became popular in the latter days of his court.

hastened like the rest and put a skewer over his shoulder charged with game.

Scarcely had Admiral Pointed-Hat covered a league when he saw the chicken-chariot in a broad pathway through the wood and the two ladies walking there. He recognized the princess and came to put himself at her feet, but she told him that all the honors were due to the generous fay who had protected her from the claws of Carabosse, with the consequence that he kissed the hem of her robe and paid her the most beautiful compliment ever pronounced on such an occasion.

While he was speaking the fay interrupted him and exclaimed: "I swear that I can smell a roast."

"Yes, Madame," replied Jean Caquet, showing the skewer charged with excellent piglets, "Your Highness is welcome to sample them."

"Very willingly," she said, "less for love of myself than love of the princess, who is in need of a good meal."

At the same time, someone went to the ships in quest of all the necessary things, and the joy of having recovered the princess, combined with the good cheer, left nothing to be desired.

The meal having finished and the fat pullet having returned, the fay dressed Springtime in a gold and green brocade robe sewn with rubies and pearls; she knotted her beautiful blonde hair with strings of diamonds and emeralds, crowned her with flowers and invited her to climb into her chariot. All the stars that saw her pass by believed that she was Aurora, who had not yet retired, and they said to her as she went past: "Good day, Aurora."

After great adieux on the part of the fay and that of the princess, the latter said to the former: "By the way, Madame, may I not tell my mother, the queen, who has done me so much good?"

"Beautiful princess" she replied, "kiss her for me, and tell her that I am the fifth fay who endowed you at your birth."

When the princess was on the ship all the cannons were fired, and more than a thousand rockets. She arrived in port safely and found the king and the queen waiting for her with so much good will that they did not give her time to ask their pardon for her past extravagances, although she would have thrown herself at their feet as soon as she saw them if paternal tenderness had not prevented it. Everything was blamed on old Carabosse.

In the meantime, the son of the great King Merlin arrived, anxious at having received no news of his ambassador. He had a thousand horses and thirty lackeys well-dressed in red with rich golden braid. He was a hundred times more amiable than the ingrate Fanfarinet.

They refrained carefully from telling him the story of the abduction, which might have given him a few suspicions. He was told very sincerely that his ambassador, being thirsty and trying to draw water to drink, had fallen into a well and had drowned there. He believed it without difficulty, and the wedding was celebrated, in which the joy was so great that it effaced all past chagrins.

Whatever Amour might subject us to
We must not emerge from the rules of duty,
And in spite of the penchant that often draws us,
I want reason always to be sovereign,
So that, always mistress of the heart
It regulates our wishes and ardors at will.

PRINCESS ROSETTE

There was once a king and a queen who had two beautiful boys. They grew like the day, so well were they nourished. The queen never had children without inviting the fays to their birth; she always begged them to tell her what would happen to them.

She became pregnant and had a beautiful little girl, who was so pretty that one could not see her without loving her. The queen, having regaled well all the fays who had come to see her, said to them when they were ready to go: "Don't forget your good custom, and tell me what will happen to Rosette"—that was what the little princes had been named.

The fays told her that they had left their grimoire at home, and that they would come back and see her another time.

"Oh," said the queen, "that doesn't announce anything good to me; you don't want to afflict me with a bad prediction, but I beg you to let me know everything; don't hide anything from me."

They excused themselves very insistently, and the queen had even more desire to know what the reason was.

Finally, the principal one said to her; "We fear, Madame, that Rosette will cause a great misfortune to her brothers, that they might die in some affair for her. That is all that we can divine regarding that beautiful little girl. We're very sorry not to have better news to give you."

They left, and the queen was so sad, so very sad, that the king read it in her face. He asked her what was wrong. She replied that she had got too close to the fire and had burned all the flax that was on her distaff.

"Is that all?" said the king. He went up to the grain-loft and brought her more flax than she could have spun in a hundred years.

The queen continued to be sad; he asked her what was wrong. She told him that when she was on the river bank she had dropped her green satin slipper into the water.

"Is that all?" said the king. He sent for all the shoemakers in his realm, and brought her ten thousand green satin slippers.

She continued to be sad. He asked her what was wrong. She said that while eating with too good an appetite she had swallowed her wedding ring, which was on her finger. The king knew that she was lying because he had put her ring away. "You're lying, my dear wife," he said. "Here's your ring, which I had put in my purse."

She was very upset to be caught in a lie—for it is the ugliest thing in the world—and she saw that the king was offended; that is why she told him what they fays had predicted for little Rosette, and that if he knew of any good remedy, he should say so.

The king was very sad, to the extent that he said one day to the queen: "I can't see any other way of saving our two sons than making the little one die while she's still in swaddling clothes." But the queen exclaimed that she would sooner die herself, that she would not consent to such a great cruelty, and that he should think of something else.

While the king and queen had nothing but that on their minds, someone told the queen that there was an old hermit in a large wood near the city, who slept in a tree trunk, where people went to consult him about everything. She said to herself: *It's necessary that I go there too; the fays have told me about the harm, but have neglected to tell me the remedy.*

Early in the morning she mounted a lovely little white mule, clad in gold, with two of her damsels, each of whom had a pretty horse. When they were near the wood the queen and her damsels dismounted out of respect and went to the tree where the hermit lived. He did not like to see women, but when he saw that it was the queen he said to her: "Be welcome; what do you want with me?" She told him what the fays had said about Rosette and asked him for advice. He told her that it was necessary to put the princess in a tower, without her ever coming out.

The queen thanked him, gave him generous alms, and returned to tell the king everything.

When the king heard the news he had a large tower built rapidly. He put his daughter in it, and in order that she would not be bored the king, the queen and the two brothers went to see the princess every day.

The elder brother was known as the big prince, the younger as the little prince. They loved their sister passionately, for she was the most beautiful and the most gracious person that had ever been seen, and the slightest of her gazes was worth more than a hundred pistoles. When she was fifteen, the big prince said to the king: "Papa, my sister is old enough to be married; aren't we going to have a wedding soon?" The little prince said the same to the queen, and Their Majesties amused them, without making any response regarding the marriage.

Eventually, the king and the queen fell very ill and died almost on the same day. Everyone was very sad, and dressed in black; the bells were rung everywhere. Rosette was inconsolable at the death of her good Mama.

When the king and the queen were buried, the marquises and the dukes of the kingdom had the big prince mount a throne of gold and diamonds, with a beautiful crown on his head and garment of violet velvet decorated with suns and moons. Then the court shouted "Long live the king," three times, and people only thought of rejoicing.

The king and his brother had a discussion. "Now we're the masters, it's necessary to take our sister out of the tower, where she has been bored for a long time." It was only necessary to traverse the garden to go to the tower, which had been built in a corner, as high as possible, for the late king and queen had wanted her to stay there forever.

Rosette was embroidering a beautiful dress on a work-frame that was in front of her, but when she saw her brothers she stood up and went to take the king's hand, saying: "Good day, Sire; you're the king now, and I'm your little servant. I beg you to take me out of the tower, where I'm very bored." And with that, she began to weep.

The king kissed her and told her not to cry, that he had come to take her out of the tower and take her to a beautiful castle.

The prince had his pockets full of sugared almonds, which he gave to Rosette. "Come on," he said, "let's get out of this wretched tower. Don't be upset; the king will find you a husband soon.

When Rosette saw the beautiful garden full of flowers, fruits and fountains she was so astonished that she could not say a word, for she had never seen anything before. She looked in all direction, she walked, she said down, she picked fruits, and flowers from the flower-bed. Her little dog, named Fretillon, who was as green as a parrot, only had one ear and danced delightfully, ran in front of her, going *yap, yap, yap*, with a thousand leaps and capers.

Fretillon amused the company greatly. He suddenly started running into a little wood. The princess followed him, and no one has ever marveled as much as she did when she saw a large peacock in the wood displaying its tail, and which seemed to her to be so beautiful, so very, very beautiful, that she could not take her eyes off it. The king and the prince arrived soon after her and asked her what had amused her. She showed them the peacock and asked them what it was. They told her that it was a bird that was sometimes eaten.

"What!" she said "People dare to kill such a beautiful bird and eat it? I declare to you that I will only ever marry the King of Peacocks, and when I'm the queen, I shall prevent anyone from eating them."

"But my sister," they said, "where do you expect us to find the King of Peacocks?"

"Wherever you please, Sire, but I won't marry anyone but him."

After having made that resolution, the two brothers took her to their castle, where it was necessary to bring the peacock and put it in her room, for she was very fond of it.

All the ladies who had not seen Rosette ran to salute her and pay court to her; some brought her jam, others sugar, others golden dresses, beautiful ribbons, dolls, embroidered slippers, pearls and diamonds. She was regaled everywhere, and she was so well-mannered, so civil, kissing hands, curtseying when she was given something nice, that there was no lady or gentleman who did not go away content.

While she was conversing with good company, the king and the prince thought about finding the King of Peacocks, if there were any such thing in the world. They decided that it was necessary to have a portrait made of Princess Rosette, and they had one made that was so beautiful that it lacked nothing but speech. They said to her: "Since you don't want to marry anyone but the King of Peacocks, we're going to depart and search for him all over the world. If we find him, we'll be very glad. Take care of our kingdom until we came back."

Rosette thanked them for the trouble they were taking; she told them that she would govern their kingdom well, and that during their absence, her only pleasures would be looking at the beautiful peacock and making Fretillon dance. They could not help weeping in bidding one another adieu.

So the two princes departed and asked everyone: "Do you know the King of Peacocks."

Everyone said: "No, no,"

They passed on, and went further. They went so far, so very far, that no one had ever been so far before.

They arrived in the realm of the cockchafers; they had never seen so many; they made such a loud buzz that the king was afraid of going deaf. He asked the one that seemed the most reasonable whether he knew where he might find the King of Peacocks.

"Sire," said the cockchafer, "his kingdom is thirty thousand leagues from here; you've taken the longest way to go there."

"How do you know that?" asked the king.

"It's because we know you well," said the cockchafer, "and we go every year to spend two or three months in your garden."

So, the king and his brother embraced the cockchafer, arm in arm; they formed a great amity and dined together; they saw, with admiration, all the curiosities of the county, where the smallest leaf on a tree is worth a pistole. After that they departed to finish their journey, and as they knew the way it did not take them long to arrive. They saw all the trees charged with peacocks, and everywhere was so full of them that their cries could be heard or two leagues around.

The king said to his brother: "If the King of the Peacocks is a peacock himself, how does our sister intend to marry him? It would be necessary to be mad to consent to it. Look at the fine alliance we'd be making, with little peachicks for nephews.

The prince was in no less difficulty. "That," he said, "is an unfortunate whim that has come into her mind. I don't know how she was able to divine that there is a King of Peacocks in the world."

When they arrived in the capital city, they saw that it was full of men and women, but they had garments made from peacock plumes and put them everywhere was a thing of great beauty. They encountered the king, who was riding in a beautiful coach of gold and diamonds, which twelve peacocks were pulling.

The King of Peacocks was handsome, so handsome that the king and the prince were charmed by him. He had long curly blond hair, a white face and a peacock-tail crown. When he saw them he judged that, since they were dressed in a fashion other than that of the people of the country, they must be foreigners, and in order to make sure he stopped his carriage and called to them.

The king and the prince went to him. Having bowed, they said: "Sire, we have come from far away to show you a beautiful portrait. They took the large portrait of Rosette out of their valise. When the King of Peacocks had looked at it close-ly he said: "I can't believe that there is such a beautiful young woman in the world."

"She is a hundred times more beautiful," said the king."

"Oh. you're joking," replied the King of Peacocks

"Sire," said the prince, "This is my brother, who is a king like you; he is called the king, and I am called the prince; our sister, whose portrait this is, is Princess Rosette. We have come to ask whether you would like to marry her; she is beau-tiful and very sage, and we will give her a bushel of gold écus."

"Yes," said the king, "I'll marry her with a good heart; she won't lack anything with me; I'll love her very much, but I assure you that I want her to be as beautiful as her portrait, and if she lacks the slightest little thing, I'll have you put to death."

"Well, we consent to that," said Rosette's two brothers.

"You consent to that?" added the king. "Go to prison, then, and stay there until the princess has arrived."

"The princes did that without difficulty, for they were quite certain that Rosette was more beautiful than her portrait.

When they were in prison the king sent them marvelous service; he went to see them often, and he had Rosette's por-trait in his castle; he was so madly in love with her that he did not sleep by day or night. As the king and his brother were in prison they wrote to the princess by post to pack her bags quickly and come diligently because the King of Peacocks was waiting for her. They did not mention that they were prisoners, for fear of making her too anxious.

When Rosette received the letter, she was so transported that she nearly died. She told everyone that the King of Pea-cocks had been found and that he wanted to marry her. Joyful fireworks were lit, the cannons were fired and people ate sug-ared almonds and sugar everywhere. All those who came to see the princess for three days were given jam, butter, honeyed waffles and hypocras.

After she had made so many liberalities she gave her beautiful dolls to her good friends and her brother's kingdom in the hands of the wisest elders of the city. She recommended them to take care of everything, not to spend much, and to amass money for the return of the king; she begged them to conserve her peacock and only wanted to take her nurse and foster-sister with her, with the little green dog Fretillon.

They put to sea in a boat. They took with them a bushel of gold écus and enough clothes for ten years, changing them twice a day. They did nothing but laugh and sing.

The nurse asked the boatman: "Are we getting close, close to the kingdom of peacocks?"

"No, no," he told her.

Another time she asked: "Are we getting close, close?"

"Soon, soon," he told her.

Another time she asked: "Are we getting close, close?"

"Yes, yes," he replied. And when he said that, she went to the end of the boat, sat down next to him and said: "Do you want to be rich forever?"

"I'd like that very much," he replied.

"Do you want to earn a great many pistoles?"

"I'd like nothing better," he replied.

"Well," she said, "it's necessary that tonight, when the princess is asleep, you help me to throw her into the sea. After she has drowned, I'll dress my daughter in her beautiful clothes, and we'll take her to the King of Peacocks, who will be very glad to marry her, and for your recompense, we'll give you a whole necklace of diamonds."

The boatman was astonished by what the nurse proposed to him. He told her that it was a pity to drown such a beautiful princess, that she made him feel pity; but she took a bottle of wine and made him drink so much that he was no longer able to refuse.

Night having fallen, the princess went to bed as usual; her little Fretillon was lying nicely at the bottom of the bed, without moving his paws. Rosette was deeply asleep when the evil nurse, who was not asleep, went in quest of the boatman.

She made him enter the princess's cabin; then, without waking her, they picked her up with her feather bed, her mattress, her sheets and her blankets; the foster sister helped them with all her might. They threw all that into the sea, and the princess was sleeping so soundly that she did not wake up.

What was fortunate, however, is that her feather bed was made of phoenix feathers, which are very rare, and which have the property of never sinking to the bottom in water, with the consequence that she floated in her bed as if she had been in a boat. The water gradually wet the feathers, though, and then the mattress, and Rosette feeling the water, was afraid that she might have wet her bed and might be scolded.

As she turned over, Fretillon woke up. He had an excellent nose; he sensed sole and cod so close by that he began to yap, and yapped so much that he woke all the other fish. They started swimming; the big fish bumped their heads against the princess's bed; not paying any attention to it, she turned over and over, like a pirouette.

She was quite astonished. *Is our boat dancing on the water?* she wondered. *I'm not accustomed to being so ill-at-ease as I am tonight.* And Fretillon was still yapping, as if in despair of life.

The evil nurse and the boatman heard him in the distance and said: "That's that funny little dog drinking to our health with his mistress; let's make haste to arrive."

They were directly outside the city of the King of Peacocks.

He had sent a hundred coaches to the edge of the sea, pulled by all sorts of rare beasts; there were lions, bears. red deer, wolves, horses, oxen, donkeys, eagles and peacocks; and the coach in which Princess Rosette was to travel was drawn by six blue monkeys, which leapt and danced on a tightrope, and performed a thousand agreeable tricks; they had beautiful harness of crimson velvet with golden plaques. Sixty young damsels were seen, whom the king had chosen to amuse her, dressed in all sorts of colors, of which gold and silver were the least.

The nurse had taken great care to adorn her daughter; she had put Rosette's diamonds on her head and everywhere. But with all her attire she was as ugly as a she-monkey; She had greasy black hair; she was cross-eyed; her limbs were twisted; she had a large hump in the middle of her back; she had a nasty and surly humor, always grumbling.

When all the servants of the King of Peacocks saw her coming out of the boat, they were so surprised that they could not speak.

"What's this?" she said. "Are you asleep? Come on, come on, bring me something to eat. You're a fine rabble and I'll have you all hanged."

At that news they said to one another: "What a vile beast! She's as nasty as she is ugly! That's our king well married! I'm not astonished; it wasn't worth the trouble of going to the ends of the earth."

She was still playing the mistress, handing out slaps and punches to everyone for less than nothing.

As her equipage was very large, it went slowly; she settled comfortably, like a queen, in her coach; but all the peacocks that had put themselves in the trees in order to salute her in passing, and had resolved to cry: "Long live Queen Rosette," when they saw that she was so horrible, cried: "Fie, fie, how ugly she is!"

She was enraged by chagrin and said to her guards: "Kill those villainous peacocks who are singing insults at me."

The peacocks flew away very quickly, mocking her.

The rogue of a boatman, who saw all that, whispered to the nurse: "Mother, we're not doing well; your daughter ought to be prettier."

She replied: "Shut up, idiot, you'll bring us bad luck."

Someone went to inform the king that the princess was approaching.

"Well," he said, "have her brothers told me the truth? Is she more beautiful than her portrait?"

"Sire," they said, "it's quite enough if she's as beautiful."

"Yes," said the king. "I'll be well content. Let's go see her." He could hear by the noise that was being made in the courtyard that she was arriving, but he could not make out what was being said, except for: "Fie, fie, how ugly she is!" He thought they were talking about some dwarf or some beast that she had perhaps brought with her, for it could not enter his head that it was, in fact, her.

The portrait of Rosette was carried at the end of a long pole, uncovered, and the king marched gravely after it, with all his barons and all his peacocks, and then the ambassadors of neighboring kingdoms. The King of Peacocks was very impatient to see his dear Rosette; but, when he saw her, it would not have taken much or him to die on the spot. He flew into the greatest anger in the world; he tore his clothes; he did not want to go near her; she frightened him.

"What!" he said. "Those two scoundrels that I have in my prison have a great deal of boldness to make fun of me, and to have proposed that I marry an ape like that. I'll have them put to death. Let's go; have that foul woman locked up immediately, with her nurse and the man who has brought them. Put them in the depths of my great tower."

On the other hand, the king and his brother, who were prisoners, and who knew that their sister was due to arrive, had made themselves worthy to receive her. Instead of coming to open the prison and set them free, as they had hoped, the jailer came with soldiers and took them down into an utterly dark cellar full of vile beasts, where they had water up to the neck. No one has ever been more astonished or sadder. "Alas," they said to one another, "this is a sad wedding for us! What can have procured us such a great misfortune?" They had no idea what to think, except that they were going to die, and were utterly dejected by it.

Three days passed without them hearing anything. After three days the King of Peacock came to shout insults at them through a hole. "You have taken the titles of king and prince to ensnare me," he cried, "and to engage me to marry your sister, but you're nothing but vagabonds who aren't worth the water you drink. I'm going to give you judges who will try you very rapidly. The rope with which I shall have you hanged in already being woven."

"King of Peacocks," replied the king, angrily, "don't go so quickly in this affair, for you might repent of it. I am a king like you; I have a beautiful kingdom, clothes, crowns and good coinage; I will eat my shirt on that. Ha ha, how you joke about having us hanged. Is it because we have stolen something?"

When the king heard him speak so resolutely he did not know where he was up to, and had some desire to let them go, with their sister, without putting them to death; but his confidant, who was a true flatterer, encouraged him, saying that if he did not avenge himself, everyone would mock him for being taken for a four-denier petty king. He swore not to pardon them and commanded that their trial be held.

That did not last long; it was only necessary to see the portrait of the veritable Princess Rosette next to the one who had come and who claimed to be her, with the result that they were condemned to have their necks severed, as liars, since they had promised the king a beautiful princess and had only given him a ugly peasant woman.

Someone came to the prison in grand apparel to read that sentence to them; and they cried that that they had not lied; that their sister was a princess and more beautiful than the day; that there was something underneath this that they did not understand, and that they asked for seven days before being put to death; that perhaps in that time their innocence would be recognized. The King of the Peacocks, who was very angry, had great difficulty in granting them that favor, but in the end he consented.

*

While all these things were happening at the court, it is necessary to say something about poor Princess Rosette. As soon as it was daylight she was very astonished, and Fretillon too, to see that they were in the open sea with neither a boat or any help. She started to weep, to weep so much that she moved all the fish to pity. She did not know what to do, not what would become of her.

Assuredly, she said to herself, *I've been thrown into the sea by order of the King of Peacocks; he has repented of marrying me, and to get rid of me honestly he has made me drown! What a strange man!* she continued. *I would have loved him so much! We would have made such a good household!* With that she wept harder, for she could not help loving him.

She remained floating for two days on the sea, drifting in one direction and the other, wet to the bone, with a mortal chill, and almost paralyzed. If it had not been for little Fretillon, who warmed her heart a little, she would have died a hundred times. She was terribly hungry. She lived on oysters; she caught as many as she liked and ate them; Fretillon did not like them much, but it was necessary nevertheless that he nourish himself on them. When night came, great fear gripped Rosette and she said to her dog: "Keep yapping, Fretillon, for fear that the soles might eat us."

He had yapped all night, and the princess's bed was not far from the water's edge. In that place there was a worthy old man who lived alone in a little cottage, where no one ever went. He was very poor, and did not care about worldly wealth. When he heard Fretillon yapping, he was very astonished, for few dogs passed that way; he thought some travelers had gone astray, and he went out charitably, in order to put them on the right path.

Suddenly he perceived the princess and Fretillon, who were floating on the sea. The princess, seeing him, held out her arms and cried to him: "Good old man, save me, for I shall perish here; I've been languishing for two days."

When he heard her speak so sadly, he felt great compassion, and went back into his house to get a long hook. He advanced into the water up to the neck, and thought two or three times that he would drown, but in the end he pulled so hard that he brought the bed to the shore.

Rosette and Fretillon were very glad to be on land; they thanked the fellow abundantly and took his blanket, with which she wrapped herself. Then, entirely barefoot, she went into the cottage, where he lit a little fire of dry straw and took from his trunk his late wife's most beautiful clothes, with stockings and shoes, which the princess put on. Dressed thus as a peasant, she was as beautiful as the day, and Fretillon danced around her to divert her.

The old man could see clearly that Rosette was some great lady, for the covers of her bed were all gold and silver and her mattress was satin. He begged her to tell him her story, and said that he would not say a word if she wished. She told him everything, from beginning to end, weeping abundantly, for she still believed that it was the King of Peacocks who had made her drown.

"What shall we do, my girl?" the old man said to her. "You're such a great princess, accustomed to eating fine morsels, and I only have black bread and beets; you'll have poor fare. If you believe me, I'll go and tell the King of Peacocks that you're here; if he had seen you he'd certainly have married you."

"Oh, he's wicked," said Rosette. "He'd put me to death. But if you have a little basket, it's necessary to attach it to my dog's neck, and he'll be very unfortunate if he doesn't bring me provisions."

The old man gave the princess a basket; she attached it to Fretillon's neck and said to him: "Go to the best cooking-pot in the city and bring me back what's inside it."

Fretillon ran to the city, and as there was no cooking-pot better than the king's he went into his kitchen, discovered the pot, cleverly removed everything inside it, and returned to the house. Rosette said to him: "Go back to the pantry and take the best of what it contains."

Fretillon went back to the pantry and took white bread, muscat wine, all sorts of fruits, and jam; he was so heavily loaded that he could not carry any more.

When the King of Peacocks wanted to have his midday meal, there was nothing in his pot or in his pantry. Everyone looked at one another, and the king was horribly angry. "Oh well," he said, "so I won't eat anything; but this evening, put the spit over the fire and I'll have good roast meat."

When evening came, the princess said to Fretillon: "Go to the city, go into the best kitchen and bring me some good roast meat."

Fretillon did as his mistress had commanded, and, knowing no better kitchen that the king's, he went in very quietly, while the cooks had their backs turned; he took all the roast meat there was on the spit; it had an excellent appearance, and merely looking at it gave one an appetite. He took his full basket back to the princess; she immediately sent him back to the pantry and he brought back all the king's compotes and sugared almonds.

The king, who had not had a midday meal, being very hungry, wanted to have supper early, but there was nothing there; he flew into a fearful rage, and went to bed without supper.

The next day, at the midday meal and supper, the same thing happened, with the consequence that the king went three days without eating or drinking, because whenever he went to table, it was found that everything had been taken.

His confidant, who was worried, fearing that the king might die, hid in a little corner of the kitchen and always had his eyes of the boiling pot. He was very astonished to see a little green dog that only had one ear enter very quietly, uncover the pot and put all the meat into its basket. He followed it in order to see where it went.

He saw it leave the city. Still following it, he went all the way to the old man's cottage. Then he came back to tell the king everything: that it was to the home of an old peasant that his stew and his roast went every morning and evening.

The king was astonished; he said that someone must make enquiries. In order to pay his court, the confidant decided to go himself, and took archers. They found the old man dining with the princess, and that they were eating the king's broth. He had them taken and bound with stout cords, and Fretillon too.

When they had arrived, someone went to tell the king, who replied: "Tomorrow is the seventh day that I granted to the affronters. I'll put them to death with the thieves of my dinner." Then he went into the hall of justice. The old man fell to his knees and said that he would tell him everything.

While he was speaking, the king looked at the beautiful princess, and felt compassion on seeing her weep; then, when the old man had declared that her name was Princess Rosette, and that she had been thrown into the sea, in spite of the weakness he was suffering from not having eaten for such a long time, the king immediately made three jumps and ran to embrace her, and detached the cords by which she was bound, telling her that he loved her with all his heart.

At the same time, someone went in quest of the princes, who believed that it was to put them to death, and who came very sadly, with bowed heads. Someone also went in search of the nurse and her daughter. When they saw one another, they all recognized one another.

Rosette threw her arms around her brothers; the nurse, her daughter and the boatman threw themselves to their knees and asked for mercy. The joy was so great that the king and the princess pardoned them and the worthy old man was recompensed generously; he always stayed in the palace.

Finally, the King of Peacocks gave all sorts of satisfactions to the king, testifying his sorrow for having maltreated them. The nurse returned the beautiful clothes and bushel of gold écus to Rosette, and the wedding celebrations lasted a fortnight. Everyone was content, including Fretillon, who no longer ate anything but grouse wings.

Heaven watches over us, and when innocence

Finds itself in pressing danger.
It embraces its defense,
Delivers it and avenges it.
On seeing the timid Rosette,
Like a halcyon in its little cradle,
Floating at the mercy of the winds,
One feels a secret pity in her favor,
One dreads that she might meet a tragic end,
Sinking in the midst of the waves,
And that she might make a light meal
For some hungry whale.
Without the aid of heaven she would doubtless have per-
ished.
Fretillon played his role
Against the cod and the sole;
And when he acted thus
To nourish his dear mistress,
It is surely in these times
That one would like to encounter dogs of his species!
Rosette, escaped from shipwreck,
Granted pardon to the authors of her woes.
You, who suffer outrage,
And who want a reckoning,
Learn that it is good to pardon the offense
After the enemy has been vanquished.
And that one can obtain a just vengeance,
Is what our century admires in Louis.

THE GOLDEN BRANCH

There was once a king whose austere humor and chagrin inspired dread rather than love. He rarely allowed himself to be seen, and had his subjects put to death on the slightest suspicions. He was known as King Brun, because he was always frowning.

King Brun had a son who did not resemble him at all. His intelligence, mildness, magnificence and capability were unequaled; but he had twisted legs, a hump higher that his head, he was cross-eyed and his mouth was askew; never had such a beautiful soul animated such an ill-made body. By a singular charm, however, he made people he wanted to please love him to the point of folly; his mind was so superior to all others that he could not be heard indifferently

His mother, the queen, wanted him to be called Torticoli, either because she liked the name or because, being in fact all awry, she thought she had found the one that suited him most.

King Brun, who thought more about his grandeur than his son's satisfaction, cast his eyes on the daughter of a powerful king who was his neighbor and whose estates, combined with his own, could render him redoubtable throughout the world. He thought that the princess in question would be very appropriate for Prince Torticoli, because she would have no reason to reproach him for his deformity or his ugliness, since she was at least as ugly and deformed as him. She always went out in a bowl, her legs being broken. She was known as Trognon. She was the most amiable creature in the world mentally; it seemed that Heaven had wanted to compensate her for the wrong that nature had done her.

Having requested and obtained a portrait of Princess Trognon, King Brun had it placed in a great hall under an awning and he sent for Prince Torticoli, whom he commanded to look at the portrait with tenderness, since it was that of

Trognon, who was destined for him. Torticoli cast his eyes upon it and turned them away immediately with a disdainful expression that offended his father.

"Are you not content?" the king said to him, in a bitter and vexed tone.

"No, Sire," he replied. "I shall never be content to marry a cripple."

"It ill behooves you," said King Brun, "to find fault with that princess, being a little monster yourself who frightens people."

"It's for that reason," added the prince, "that I don't want to ally myself with another monster; I have enough difficulty suffering myself; what would I be if I had such a companion?"

"You fear perpetuating a race of apes," replied the king, in an offensive manner, "but your fears are vain; you'll marry her. It's sufficient that I order it to be obeyed."

Torticoli made no reply. He bowed profoundly and withdrew.

King Brun was not accustomed to find the slightest resistance; his son's put him in a terrible anger. He had him locked in a tower that had been built expressly for rebel princes, but none had been found for two hundred years, with the result that everything therein was in rather poor order. The apartments and the furniture appeared to be of a surprising antiquity.

The prince liked reading. He asked for books; he was permitted to take some from the tower bookcase. At first he thought that permission sufficient, but when he tried to read them, he found the language so ancient that he could not understand it. He put them aside, and then picked them up again, trying to understand something, or at least to pass the time.

King Brun, convinced that Torticoli would weary of his prison, acted as if he had consented to marry Trognon. He sent ambassadors to the king, his neighbor, to ask for his daughter, to whom he promised a perfect felicity. Trognon's father was delighted to find such an advantageous opportunity to marry her, for not everyone has a humor to take on the burden of a cripple. He accepted King Brun's proposal, although, to tell the truth, the portrait of Prince Torticoli that had been brought to him did not appear to him to be very touching. In his turn, he had it placed in a magnificent gallery; Trognon was brought there.

When she perceived it, she lowered her eyes and started to weep. Her father, indignant at the repugnance she testified, picked up a mirror. Putting it in front of her, he said: "You're weeping, my daughter. Well, look at yourself and agree afterwards that it isn't permissible for you to weep."

"If I had any urgency to be married, Sire," she said to him, "perhaps I would be wrong to be so delicate, but I can cherish my disgraces if I suffer them alone. I don't want to share with anyone else the ennui of seeing me. If I remain all my life the unfortunate Princes Trognon, I shall be content, or at least, I shall not complain."

However good her reasons were, the king did not listen to them; it was necessary for her to depart with the ambassadors who had come to ask for her.

While she makes her journey in a litter, like a tree-stump, it is necessary to return to the tower and see what the prince is doing.

None of his guards dared speak to him. They had orders to allow him to become bored, not to give him much to eat and to wear him out with all sorts of ill-treatment. King Brun knew that he would be obeyed, if not for love, at least out of dread; but the affection people had for the prince caused them to lessen his punishments as much as they could.

One day, when he was walking in a long gallery, thinking sadly about his destiny, which had led him to be born so ugly and frightful and to encounter a princess even more disgraced. He glanced at the stained-glass windows, which were painted in colors so bright, with designs so well-expressed, that, having a particular liking for beautiful workmanship, his gaze was attached to them. He did not understand them at all, however, for they were histories that had happened several centuries before.

It is true that what struck him most was seeing a man who resembled him so strongly that it appeared to be his own portrait. The man was in the topmost room of the tower, searching in the wall, where he found a slender golden rod with a hook on the end, with which he opened a cabinet. There were many other things there that struck his imagination, and in most of the stained-glass windows he saw his portrait again.

By what adventure, he said to himself, *do I feature as a character here, having not yet been born? And by what fatal idea did the painter amuse himself depicting a man like me?*

He saw in those windows a beautiful woman whose features were so regular and her physiognomy so spiritual that he could not take his eyes off her. In sum, there were a thousand different objects, and all the passions were so well expressed there that he thought he was seeing something happen that was not only represented by the mixture of colors.

He only left the gallery when there was insufficient daylight left to distinguish the paintings. When he had returned to his room he picked up an old manuscript, which was the first one that came to hand. The pages were vellum, painted all around, and the binding gold, enameled with blue, which formed figures. He was very surprised to see there the same things that were on the windows of the gallery. He tried to read what was written, but could not do so.

Suddenly, however, he saw that on one of the pages where musicians were represented, they began to sing; and on another leaf, where there were players of bassette and tric-trac, the cards and dice going back and forth. He turned the page; there was a ball in which people were dancing; all the ladies were adorned, and of marvelous beauty. He turned the page again; she smelled the odor of an excellent repast; there were little figures eating. The tallest was not a quarter high. There was one who turned toward the prince. "To your health, Torticoli," she said to him. "Think about returning our queen to us; if you do that, you will come out of it well; if you fail, things will go badly for you."

At those words, the prince was seized by such a violent fear—because he had already begun to tremble some time before—that he dropped the book in one direction, and fell in the other like a dead man.

At the sound of his fall his guards came running; they loved him dearly and did not neglect anything to bring him round from his faint. When he was in a state to talk they asked him what was wrong. He told them that he was so poorly nourished that he had been unable to resist it, and that, having his head full of imaginations, he had thought he saw and heard such surprising things in the book that he had been gripped by fear. His guards, afflicted, gave him something to eat in spite of all King Brun's prohibitions.

When he had eaten, he picked up the book again in front of them, and no longer found anything of what he had seen; that convinced him that he had been mistaken.

The following day he returned to the gallery. Again he saw the paintings on the stained glass, of people moving, walking in pathways, hunting deer and hares, fishing or building little houses—for they were very tiny miniatures—and his portrait was everywhere. The person depicted had a costume similar to his own; he went up into the top of the tower and he found the golden hook.

As the prince had eaten well, he no longer had any reason to believe the visions entered into the affair. *This is too mysterious*, he said to himself, *for me to neglect means of knowing more. Perhaps I'll learn them at the top of the tower.*

He went up there, and when he rapped on the wall, it seemed to him that there was a hollow place. He took a hammer, chipped away the plaster at that place and found a golden hook, very neatly formed. He did not know yet what usage it might have, when he saw in a corner of the attic a cupboard of rotten wood.

He wanted to open it, but he could not find a lock; no matter which way he turned it, it was wasted effort. Finally, he saw a small hole, and, suspecting that the hooked rod might be useful he inserted it. Then, tugging forcefully, he opened the cupboard.

As old and ugly as it was outside, it was beautiful and marvelous inside. All the drawers were made of engraved rock crystal, amber or precious stones; when one was pulled out, smaller ones were found at the sides, above and below, and in the bottom; they were separated by mother-of-pearl. The nacre was pulled, and then the drawers; each one was filled with the most beautiful weapons in the world, rich crowns and admirable portraits.

Prince Torticoli was charmed; he kept pulling, without wearying. Finally, he found a little key made of a single emerald, with which he opened a small golden door at the back; he was dazzled by a brilliant carbuncle, which formed a drawer. He pulled it promptly, but what became of him when he found it full of blood, and a man's hand that had been severed! It was still holding a portrait-locket.

At that sight Torticoli shivered; his hair stood on end; his unsteady legs could scarcely sustain him. He sat down on the floor, still holding the drawer, turning his eyes away from such a baleful object. He had a strong desire to put it back where he had found it, but he thought that everything that had happened thus far had not arrived without greater mysteries. He remembered what the little figure in the book had said to him: that in accordance with how he acted, he would come out of it well or badly. He feared the future as much as the present.

Coming to reproach himself for a timidity unworthy of such a great mind, he made an effort to pull himself together. Then, attaching his eyes to the hand, he said: "Unfortunate hand, can you not, by means of a few signs, inform me of your sad adventure? If I am in a position to serve you, be sure of the generosity of my heart."

At those words, the hand appeared agitated, and the fingers moved. It made signs to him, which he understood as well as speech, as if an intelligent mouth were speaking to him.

"Learn," said the hand, "that you can do everything for the man from whom the barbarity of a jealous individual has separated me. You see in this portrait the adorable beauty who is the cause of my misfortune. Go without delay into the gallery; take account of the place where the sun darts its most ardent rays, search, and you will find my treasure."

The hand stopped moving then. The prince asked it several questions, to which it did not reply.

"Where shall I put you?" he asked.

It made further signs; he understood that it was necessary to put it back into the cupboard; he did not fail to do so. Everything was closed again; he put the hooked rod back in the same wall from which he had taken it, and, somewhat battle-hardened with regard to prodigies, he went down into the gallery.

When he arrived, the stained-glass window began to make an extraordinary rattling and trembling. He looked to see where the sun's rays went; he saw that it was to the portrait of a young adolescent, so handsome and with such a noble air that he was charmed.

When he lifted away the picture he found an ebony panel with gold threads, as in all the rest of the gallery. He did not know how to remove it, or whether he ought to remove it. He looked at the windows and knew that the panel lifted up, he did so, and found himself in a vestibule of porphyry, ornamented with statues.

He went up a broad agate stairway, the rail of which was gold. He went into a lapis room, and traversed countless apartments, where he was delighted by the excellence of the paintings and the richness of the furniture.

He finally arrived in a small room, all of the ornaments of which were turquoise, and he saw a lady, who seemed to be asleep, on a bed of blue and gold gauze. She was incomparably beautiful. Her hair, blacker than ebony, heightened the whiteness of her complexion. She seemed anxious in her sleep; her face had something despondent about it, as if she were ill.

Fearing to wake her, the prince approached slowly; he heard her speaking, and, paying great attention to her words, he heard a few of them punctuated by sighs.

"Do you think, traitor, that I can love you, after having separated me from my lovable Trasimene? What! Before my eyes you dared to sever a hand so dear from an arm that must still be redoubtable to you? Is it thus that you intend to prove your respect and amour to me? Oh, Trasimene, my dear lover, will I ever see you again?"

The prince remarked that tears were seeking a passage between her closed eyelids, and that, running down her cheeks, they resembled the tears of the dawn.

He remained at the foot of the bed, as if immobilized, not knowing whether he ought to wake her or leave her any longer in a slumber so sad. He understood already that Trasimene was her lover, and that he had found his hand in the room at the top of the tower.

He was rolling a thousand confused thoughts on so many different things when he heard a charming music; it was composed by nightingales and canaries, which were harmonizing their songs so well that they surpassed the most agreeable voices. Immediately, an eagle of extraordinary grandeur entered; it was flying slowly, and holding in its claws a golden branch charged with rubies, which formed cherries. It attached its eyes fixedly to the sleeping beauty; it seemed to be seeing its sun; and, deploying its great wings, it glided before her, sometimes rising up and sometimes descending as far as her feet.

After a few moments it turned toward the prince and approached him in order to put the golden cherry-branch in his hand; the singing birds then uttered tones that pierced the vaults of the palace.

The prince applied his mind so well to the different things that were succeeding one another that he judged that the lady was enchanted and that the honor of an adventure so glorious was reserved for him.

He advanced toward her, put one knee on the floor, touched her with the branch and said to her: "Beautiful and charming person, sleeping by virtue of a power that is unknown to me, I implore you in the name of Trasimene to reenter into all the functions of life, which you seem to have lost."

The lady opened her eyes, perceived the eagle, and cried: "Stop, dear lover, stop!" But the royal bird uttered a cry as shrill as it was dolorous and flew away with its little feathered musicians.

At the same time the lady turned toward Torticoli. "I have listened to my heart rather than my gratitude," she said to him. "I know that I owe you everything, and that you have recalled me to the light, which I lost two hundred years ago. The enchanter who loves me, and who made me suffer so many misfortunes, had reserved that great adventure for you. I have the power to serve you, and a passionate desire to do so. Decide what you want; I will employ the art of Faerie, which I possess sovereignly, to render you happy."

"Madame," the prince replied, "if your science enables you to penetrate as far as the sentiments of the heart, it is easy for you to know that, in spite of the disgraces by which I am overwhelmed, I have less to lament than another.

"That is the effect of your good mind," added the fay, "but after all, do not leave me the shame of being ingrate in your regard. What do you wish? I can do anything; ask."

"I wish," Torticoli replied, "to render to you the handsome Trasimene, who costs you such frequent sighs."

"You are too generous," she told him, "in preferring my interests to yours; that great affair will be accomplished by another person. I cannot explain myself further. Only know that she is not indifferent to you. But don't refuse me any longer the pleasure of obliging you. What do you desire?"

"Madame," said the prince, throwing himself at her feet, "you see my frightful form; people call me Torticoli by virtue of derision. Render me less ridiculous.

"There, Prince," the fay said to him, touching him three times with the golden branch; "there, you will be so accomplished and so perfect that no man before or after you will ever be your equal. Name yourself Peerless; you will wear that name with just title.

The grateful prince embraced her knees, and by means of a silence that expressed his joy, he allowed her to divine what was happening in his soul. She obliged him to get up; he looked at himself in the mirrors that ornamented the room, and Peerless no longer recognized Torticoli. He had grown three feet; he had hair that fell in long curls over his shoulders, an attitude full of grandeur and grace, regular features and intelligent eyes; in sum, he was the worthy work of a benevolent and sensitive fay.

"If only it were permitted to me," she said to him, "to inform you of your destiny, to instruct you as to the reefs that fortune will place in your path and the means of avoiding them, how much satisfaction I would obtain from combining that good office with the one I have just rendered you! But I would offend the superior genius that guides you. Go, prince; flee this tower and remember that the fay Benigne will always be your friend."

With those words, she disappeared, along with the palace and the marvels that the prince had seen, and he found himself in a dense forest, more than a hundred leagues from the tower where King Brun had put him.

Let us leave him to recover from his just astonishment, and let us see two things: firstly, what is happening among the guards that his father had given him; and secondly, what is happening to Princess Trognon.

Those poor guards, surprised that their prince was not asking for any supper, went into his room, and not having found him there, they searched everywhere, with an extreme dread that he might have escaped. Their efforts were futile, and they were almost in despair, for they feared that King Brun, who was so terrible, might put them to death. After having discussed all the means appropriate to appease him, they concluded that it was necessary for one of them to get into the bed and not allow himself be seen; that they would say that the prince was very ill; that shortly afterwards they would feign his death, and that a log, shrouded and buried, would get them out of trouble.

That remedy appeared to them to be infallible; they put it into practice immediately. They made a large hump for the smallest of the guards, and he lay down in the bed. Word was sent to the king that his son was very ill; he believed that it was to soften his heart, and did not want to relax his severity at all. That was exactly what the timid guards wanted, and the more urgency they showed, the more King Brun marked his indifference.

As for Princess Trognon, she arrived in a small machine that was only a cubit high, and the machine was in a litter. King Brun went to meet her. When he saw her so deformed, wedged in a bowl, her skin as scaly as a cod, her eyebrows joined, her nose flat and broad and her mouth approaching her ears, he could not help saying to her: "In truth, Princess Trognon, you're gracious to scorn my Torticoli. Know that he's very ugly, but without lying, he's less so than you."

"Sire," she said to him, "I do not have enough self-esteem to be offended by the disagreeable things you say to me; I do not know whether you believe that to be a sure means of persuading me to love your charming Torticoli, but I declare to you, in spite of my miserable bowl and the defects with which I am filled, that I do not want to marry him and that I prefer the title of Princess Trognon to that of Queen Torticoli."

King Brun was greatly angered by that response. "I assure you," he said, "that I will not be belied. The king, your father, ought to be your master; I shall become so, since he has put you in my hands."

"There are matters," she said, "in which we have no choice. It is against my will that I was brought here, I warn you, and I shall regard you as my most mortal enemy if you do me any violence."

The king quit her, even more irritated, and gave her an apartment in his palace, with ladies who had orders to persuade her that the best thing for her to do was to marry the prince.

Meanwhile, the guards, who feared being discovered and that the king might discover that his son had escaped, hastened to go and tell him that he was dead. At that news, he felt a dolor of which one would have thought him incapable. He cried, he howled, and, taking out the loss he had just suffered on Trognon, he sent her to the tower instead of the dear departed.

The poor princess was as sad as she was astonished to find herself a prisoner. She had courage, and she said what she thought of a procedure so harsh. She thought that someone would tell the king, but no one dared to talk to him. She also thought that she could write to her father about the ill-treatment she was suffering, and that he would me to deliver her. Her projects in that direction were futile; her letters were intercepted and they were given to King Brun.

As she was living in that hope, she was less afflicted, and she went every day to the gallery to look at the paintings on the stained glass. Nothing seemed to her to be as extraordinary as the number of different things that were represented there, and to see herself there in her bowl.

Since I have arrived in this country, she said to herself, *the painters have taken a strange pleasure in painting me; are there not enough ridiculous forms without mine? Or do they want by means of opposition to make the beauty of that young shepherdess, who seems to me to be charming, stand out more?*

Then she gazed at the portrait of a shepherd, which she could not praise enough.

How lamentable it is, she thought, *to be disgraced by nature to the extent that I am! Oh, how fortunate one is when one is beautiful!*

As she formed those words she had tears in her eyes; then, seeing herself in a mirror, she turned away abruptly. She was very astonished to find behind her a little old woman coiffed in a hood, who was uglier than her by half, and the bowl that she was trailing had more than twenty holes, so worn out was it.

"Princess," said the old woman, "you can choose between virtue and beauty. Your regrets are so touching that I have heard them. If you want to be beautiful, you will be a coquette, vainglorious and very gallant; if you want to remain as you are, you will be sage, esteemed and very humble."

Trognon looked at the person who was talking to her, and asked her whether beauty was incompatible with goodness.

"No," said the good woman, "but in your regard is it determined that you can only have one of the two.

"Well then," exclaimed Trognon, in a firm manner, "I prefer my ugliness to beauty."

"What! You'd prefer to frighten those who see you?" said the old woman.

"Yes, Madame," said the princess. "I'd rather choose all misfortunes put together than to lack virtue."

"I've brought my yellow and white muff expressly," said the fay. "By blowing on the yellow side, you'll become similar to that admirable shepherdess who appeared to you to be so charming, and you'll be loved by a shepherd whose portrait has arrested your gaze more than once. By blowing on the white side, you can affirm yourself on the path of virtue, into which you've entered to courageously."

"Well, Madame," said the princess, "Don't refuse me that favor; it will console me for all the scorn that people have for me."

The little old woman gave her the muff of virtue and beauty. Trognon did not scorn it; she blew on the white side and thanked the fay, who disappeared immediately.

She was delighted by the good choice she had made, and whatever reason she had to envy the incomparable beauty of the shepherdess painted on the windows, she thought, to console herself, that beauty passes like a dream, while virtue is an eternal treasure and an inalterable beauty, which lasts longer than life.

She still hoped that the king, her father, would put himself at the head of a large army and would come to take her out of the tower. She waited for the moment when he would appear with great impatience, and was dying of the desire to go up into the top of the tower to see whether the help she was expecting was arriving; but how could she climb so high? She went into her bedroom less rapidly than a tortoise, and when she went upstairs, it was her women who carried her.

However, she found a rather particular means of doing it. She knew that the clock was in the top of the tower; she removed the weights and put herself in their place. When the clock was wound she was hoisted up to the top. Promptly, she looked out of the window that overlooked the countryside, but she could not see anyone coming and she withdrew in order to rest for a while.

As she leaned against the wall that Torticoli—or, to put it better, Prince Peerless—had dismantled and reassembled rather poorly, the plaster fell away along with the golden hook, which made a metallic sound next to Trognon. She perceived it, and after having picked it up, looked round to see what purpose it might serve. As she had more intelligence than others, she deduced very rapidly that it was for opening the cupboard, where there was no lock.

She did that, and was no less delighted than the prince had been by everything rare and elegant she encountered therein. There were four thousand drawers, all filled with antique and modern jewels.

Eventually, she found the golden door, the carbuncle box and the hand floating in blood. She shivered, and wanted to throw it away, but it was not in her power to let go of it; a secret power prevented her from doing so.

"Alas, what have I done?" she said, sadly. "I'd rather die than stay any longer with this severed hand."

At that moment she heard a soft and agreeable voice, which said to her: "Have courage, Princess; your felicity depends on this adventure."

"Eh! What can I do?" she replied, trembling.

"It's necessary," the voice said to her, "To take this hand to your room and hide it under your bed; and when you see an eagle, to give the hand to it without wasting a moment."

Frightened as the princess was, the voice had something so persuasive about it that she did not hesitate to obey. She replaced the drawers and the rarities as she had found them, without taking anything.

Her guards, who feared that she might escape them in her turn, having not seen her in her room, searched for her and were surprised to find her in a place to which, they thought, she could only have mounted by enchantment

She did not see anything for three days; she dared not open the carbuncle box, because the severed hand frightened her too much.

Finally, one night, she heard a noise outside her window. She opened her curtain and perceived by moonlight an eagle hovering. She got up as best she could, dragged herself across the room, and opened the window. The eagle came in, making a loud noise with its wings as a sign of rejoicing. She did not delay presenting it with the hand, which it took with its claws, and a moment later, she no longer saw it.

In its place there was a young man, the most handsome and best made that she had ever seen. His forehead was circled by a diadem and his coat was covered in precious stones. He was holding a portrait in his hand, and, breaking the silence first, he said to Trognon:

"For two hundred years a perfidious enchanter has retained me in this place. We both loved the admirable fay Benigne; I was tolerated; he was jealous. His art surpassed mine, and, wanting to prevail in order to doom me he told me in an absolute fashion that he forbade me to see her again. Such a prohibition did not suit either my amour or the rank I held; I threatened him, and the beauty I adore was so offended by the enchanter's conduct that she forbade him in her turn ever to approach her. That cruel individual resolved to punish us both.

"One day, when I was with her, charmed by a portrait that she had given me and at which I was gazing, finding it a thousand times less beautiful than the original, he appeared, and with a blow of a saber he severed my hand from my arm. The fay Benigne—who was my queen—felt more dolorously than I did the grief of that accident; she fell in a faint on her bed, and immediately, I felt myself covered in feathers; I was metamorphosed into an eagle. It was permitted to me to come every day to see the queen, without being able to approach her or to awaken her, but I had the consolation of hearing her incessantly uttering tender sighs and talking in her dream about her dear Trasimene.

"I also knew that at the end of two hundred years, a prince would recall Benigne to the light, and that a princess, by returning my severed hand to me, would render my original form to me. A fay who is interested in your glory, wanted it to be thus; she was the one who enclosed my hand carefully in the cupboard at the top of the tower; she was the one who gave me the power that will mark my gratitude to you today. Wish, princess. for whatever can give you the most pleasure, and you shall obtain it immediately."

"Great king," replied Trognon, after a few moments of silence, "if I have not replied to you immediately, it is not that I am hesitant, but I confess to you that I am not accustomed to adventures as surprising as this one, and I imagine that it is a dream rather than a verity."

"No, Madame," Trasimene replied, "this is not an illusion; you will feel its effects as soon as you want to tell me what gift you desire."

"If I asked for all those I would need to be perfect," she said, "whatever power you have, it would be difficult to satisfy them, but I shall restrict myself to the most essential: render my soul as beautiful as my body is ugly and deformed."

"Oh, Princess," cried King Trasimene, "you charm me by such a just and elevated choice, but whoever is capable of making it has already accomplished it; your body will therefore become as beautiful as your soul and your mind."

He touched the princess with the portrait of the fay.

She heard a *crick, crack* in all her bones; they were elongated and reset; she stood up; she was tall, beautiful and upright; she had a complexion whiter than milk; all her features were regular; she had a majestic and modest air, and a fine and agreeable physiognomy.

"What a prodigy!" she cried. "Is this me? Is such a thing possible?"

"Yes, Madame," said Trasimene, "it's you. The sage choice you made of virtue has attracted to you the fortunate change you have experienced. What a pleasure it is for me, after what I owe you, to have been destined to contribute to it. But quit forever the name of Trognon; take that of Brillante, which you merit by your enlightenment and your charms."

At that moment, he disappeared, and the princess, without knowing by what vehicle she had been conveyed, found herself on the bank of a stream, in a place shaded by trees, the mot agreeable in the world.

She had not yet seen herself; the water of the stream was so clear that she knew with an extreme surprise that she was the same shepherdess whose portrait she had admired so much in the stained-glass windows of the gallery. Like her, in fact, she was wearing a white dress garnished with fine lace, cleaner than any shepherdess had ever been seen to wear; her belt was made of little roses and jasmines, her hair ornamented with flowers; she found a painted and gilded crook beside her, with a flock of sheep that were grazing along the bank, and which heard her voice, as well as the flock's dog; it seemed to know her, and caressed her.

What reflections did she not make of such novel prodigies! She had been born and had lived until then as the ugliest of all creatures, but she had been a princess; she was no longer anything but a shepherdess, and the loss of her rank was inevitably sensible to her.

Those different thoughts agitated her until she fell asleep. She had been awake all night, as I said, and the journey she had made without perceiving it was of a hundred leagues, with the result that she found that she was rather tired. Her sheep and her dog, assembled at her sides, seemed to be guarding her and giving her the care that they owed her.

The sun could not inconvenience her although it was shining with its full force; the leafy trees protected her from it, and the fresh, fine grass on to which she had let herself fall appeared to be proud of such a beautiful charge. It was there

> *That one saw the violets*
> *To the envy of other flowers,*
> *Rising over the short grass*
> *To spread their odors.*

The birds there were performing soft concerts, and the zephyrs held their breath, afraid of waking her.

A shepherd, fatigued by the ardor of the sun, having remarked the spot from a distance, went there diligently, but when he saw the young Brillante, he was so surprised that, but for a tree against which he was leaning, he would have fallen full length.

In fact, he recognized her as the same person whose beauty he had admired in the stained glass of the gallery and in the vellum book, for the reader will not have doubted that the shepherd in question was Prince Peerless. An unknown power had arrested him in that locale; he was made to be admired by all those who saw him there. His skill in all things, his good looks and his intelligence, distinguished him no less from the other shepherds than his birth would have distinguished him elsewhere.

He attached his gaze to Brillante with an attention and a pleasure that he had not previously felt. He knelt down beside her. He examined the assemblage of beauty that rendered her quite perfect, and his heart was the first to pay the tribute that no other would henceforth dare to refuse her.

While he was dreaming profoundly, Brillante woke up, and, seeing Peerless next to her with the extremely gallant costume of a pastor, she gazed at him and immediately remembered her idea, because she had seen his portrait in the tower.

"Lovely shepherdess," he said to her, "What fortunate destiny brings you here? You have doubtless come to receive our incense and our prayers. Oh, I sense already that I shall be the most urgent to render you my homage."

"No, shepherd," she said, "I have no intention of demanding honors that are not due to me; I want to remain a simple shepherdess; I love my flock and my dog. Solitude has charms for me; that is all I seek."

"What, young shepherdess! In arriving in this place you have brought the design of hiding yourself from the mortals that live here? Is it possible," he continued, "that you wish us so much harm? All except me, at least, since I am the first who has offered you his services."

"No," said Brillante, "I don't want to see you more frequently than the others, although I already sense a particular esteem for you. But inform me as to some sage shepherdess, into whose home I might retire, for, being a stranger here, and at an age when one cannot live alone, I would very glad to place myself under her conduct."

Peerless was delighted by that commission. He took her to a very clean cabin, which had a thousand charms in its simplicity. There was a little old woman there who rarely went out, because she could hardly walk any longer. "Look, my good mother," said Peerless, presenting Brillante to her, "here is an incomparable young woman, whose presence alone will rejuvenate you."

The old woman embraced her and said in an affable manner that she was welcome; that it pained her to lodge her so poorly, but at least she would lodge her very well in her heart.

"I did not think," Brillante said, "that I would find such a favorable welcome here, and so much politeness. I sure you, my good mother, that I am delighted to be in your company." Addressing the shepherd, she continued: "Do not refuse to tell me your name, in order that I know to whom I am obliged for such a service."

"My name is Peerless," the prince replied, "but at present I want no other name than that of your slave."

"And I," said the little old woman, "also desire to know what to call the shepherdess for whom I am exercising hospitality."

The princess told her that her name was Brillante. The old woman seemed charmed by such an admirable name and Peerless made a hundred pretty remarks about it

The old shepherdess, afraid that Brillante might be hungry, presented her with a very proper terrine and sweet milk, with brown bread, fresh eggs, newly churned butter and cream cheese. Peerless ran to his cabin; he brought back strawberries, hazelnuts, cherries and other fruits, all surrounded by flowers; and in order to have a reason to remain with Brillante for longer, he asked for permission to eat with her. Alas, how difficult it would have been to refuse him that. She saw him with an extreme pleasure, and whatever coldness she affected, she felt strongly that his presence would not be indifferent to her. When he had gone, she continued thinking about him for a long time, as he did about her.

He saw her every day; he conducted his flock to the place where she was grazing hers; he sang passionate words in her presence; he played the flute and the bagpipe to enable her to dance, and she acquitted herself with a grace and accuracy that he could not admire sufficiently. Both of them, each on their own account, reflected on the surprising series of adventures that had happened to them, and, and both commenced to become anxious. Peerless sought her out carefully everywhere,

In the end, every time he found her alone, he spoke to her so amorously; he depicted his fire and his passion so well, and that which makes the sweet union of two hearts, that she recognized in her soul that the little I-know-not-what that she felt for him, without knowing why, was an amorous flame. Then, knowing the danger to which, by virtue of her scant experience, her innocence was exposed, she carefully avoided the lovable shepherd; but that was a cruel penalty for her! And often her heart, sighing in secret reproached her for fleeing a lover so discreet.

Peerless, who could not understand what had caused that cruel change, sought everywhere for a opportunity to learn, but he sought in vain. Brillante no longer wanted to approach him or to hear him. She avoided him with care, and reproached herself incessantly for what she felt for him.

What! she said to herself. *I have the misfortune to be in love, and in love with an unfortunate shepherd! What destiny is mine? I preferred virtue to beauty; it seems that Heaven, to recompense me for that choice, wanted to render me beautiful, but that I esteem myself unfortunate for having become so! Without these unnecessary attractions, the shepherd I am fleeing would not have attached himself to pleasing me and I would not have the shame of blushing with shame at the sentiments I have for him.*

Her tears always ended such dolorous reflections, and her trouble was augmented by the state to which she reduced her lovable shepherd.

For his part, he was overwhelmed by sadness. He had a desire to reveal to Brillante the grandeur of his birth, thinking that she might perhaps be pricked by a sentiment of vanity and that she would listen to him more favorably, but he convinced himself afterwards that she would not believe him, and that if she asked him for some proof of what he was saying, he would be unable to give her any.

How cruel my fate is! he exclaimed. *Although I was frightful, I would have succeeded my father. A great kingdom repairs many faults. It would be futile now or me to present myself to him or his subjects; none of them could recognize me, and all the good that the fay Benigne has done me in taking away my name and my ugliness, consists of rendering me a shepherd and delivering me to the charms of an inexorable shepherdess who cannot tolerate me. Barbaric star*, he added, sighing, *become more propitious to me or render me my deformity with my initial indifference.*

Those were the sad egrets that the lover and the mistress had without knowing it. But as Brillante was applying herself to flee Peerless, one day when he had resolved to speak to her, in order to find a pretext that would not offend her, he took a little lamb, which he decorated with ribbons and flowers; he put a collar of painted straw on it, so neatly wrought that it was a masterpiece of sorts. He had a pink taffeta coat covered in English lace, a crook decked with ribbons and a scrip. In that state, all the Celadons in the world would not have dared appear before him.

He found Brillante sitting on the edge of a stream, which was flowing slowly through the densest part of the wood; her scattered sheep were grazing there. The profound sadness of the shepherdess did not permit her to give them her cares. Peerless approached in a timid fashion; he presented the little lamb to her and looked at her tenderly.

"What have I done to you then, beautiful shepherdess," he said to her, "to attract such terrible marks of your aversion? Your eyes reproach me with the slightest of their gazes, and you flee me. Does my passion seem so offensive to you? Can you want one purer and more faithful? Have my words not always been full of respect and ardor? Doubtless you love someone else; your heart is prejudiced for another."

She replied immediately: "Shepherd, when I avoid you, should you be alarmed? It is evident enough by my flight, that I fear loving you too much. I would flee with less difficulty if hatred made me flee; but when reason draws me away, amour seeks to retain me. Everything alarms me; at this very moment, I sense your gaze enfeebling my heart. I stay nevertheless; when amour is extreme, Shepherd, how full of rigor duty seems! And how slowly one flees, when one is fleeing the person one loves! Adieu; if you love me, alas, refrain from following me; my repose depends on it. Perhaps, without you, I can no longer live, but nevertheless, shepherd, do not follow me."

As she finished speaking, Brillante drew away. The amorous and desperate prince wanted to follow her, but his dolor became so intense that he fell unconscious at the foot of a tree.

Ah, severe and excessively grim virtue, why do you fear a man who has cherished you since his earliest childhood? He is incapable of misunderstanding you, and his passion is entirely innocent. But the princess mistrusted herself as much as him; she could not help rendering justice to that charming shepherd, and she knew full well that it is necessary to avoid that which appears too lovable to us.

No one has ever taken so much upon herself as she took at that moment; she was tearing herself away from the most tender and the most dearly loved object that she had seen in her life. She could not help turning her head several times to see whether he was following her; she saw him fall half-dead. She loved him, but she refused herself the consolation of helping him.

When she was in the plain she raised her eyes pitiably and put her hands together. "O virtue! O glory! O grandeur!" she cried, "I am sacrificing my repose to you. O destiny! O Trasimene! I renounce my fatal beauty; render me my ugliness, or render me without my being able to blush at it, the lover that I am abandoning!"

She stopped at those words, uncertain as to whether she ought to continue to flee or to retrace her steps. Her heart wanted her to go back into the woods where she had left Peerless, but her virtue triumphed over her tenderness. She made the generous resolution not to see him again.

Since she had been transported into this place, she had heard mention of a celebrated enchanter, who lived in a castle that he had built with his sister in the confines of the island.

People talked about nothing but his knowledge; there were new prodigies every day. She thought that it would require nothing less than a magical power to efface the image of the shepherd from her heart; and without saying anything to her charitable hostess, who had received her and treated her like her daughter, she set forth, so occupied with her displeasures that she did not make any reflection on the peril she was running, being young and beautiful and traveling all alone.

She did not stop by day or by night; she did not eat or drink, so much did she desire to arrive at the castle in order to cure her tenderness. As she passed through a wood, however, she heard someone singing; she thought that she heard her name pronounced, and recognized the voice of one of her companions. She stopped to listen, and heard these words:

Peerless, in his hamlet,
The best made and most handsome,
Loved the shepherdess Brillante;
Lovable, young and beautiful, utterly charming,
By a thousand petty cares, that shepherd, every day
Declared what he felt for her;
But the young rebel
Did not know what love is.
Her heart, full of sadness
Sighed nonetheless far from the absent shepherd;
Which proves that tenderness
Is not made for someone indifferent.
It is true that to our shepherdess
Such chagrins scarcely arrived;
For her lover followed her everywhere.
She asked for nothing better.
Often, lying on the grass,
He sang her verses in his fashion;
The beauty listened with pleasure to the bagpipe,
And even learned the song.

"Oh, that's too much," she said, shedding tears. "Indiscreet shepherd, you have boasted about the innocent favors I have accorded you! You have dared to presume that my feeble heart is more sensible to your passion than to my duty! You have made the confidence of your unjust desires and you have caused people to sing about me in the woods and in the plain!"

She conceived a chagrin so violent in consequence that she was in a state to see him with indifference, and perhaps with hatred,

"There is no need," she continued, "for me to go any further to seek remedies for my trouble; I have nothing to fear from a shepherd in whom I find such little merit. I'll return to the hamlet with the shepherdess that I've just heard."

She called out to her with all her might, without anyone replying to her, and yet she heard singing from time to time, close at hand. Anxiety and fear gripped her. In fact, that wood belonged to the enchanter, and no one passed through it without having some adventure.

More uncertain than ever, Brillante hastened to emerge from the wood. "Has the shepherd I fear," she said, "become so scantly redoubtable to me that I ought to risk seeing him again? Is not my heart, in intelligence with him, rather seeking to deceive me? Oh, let's flee, let's flee; that's the best course for an unfortunate princess like me."

She continued her route toward the enchanter's castle; she reached it, and entered it without any obstacle. She traversed several large courtyards, in which the grass and the brambles were so high that it seemed that no one had walked there for a hundred years; she parted them with her hands, which she scratched in more than one place. She went into a room that daylight only entered through a little hole; it was carpeted with bats' wings.

There were a dozen cats suspended from the ceiling that served as chandeliers, which were mewling to test the patience, and on a long table, a dozen mice attached by the tail, each of which had a lump of lard before it, which it could not reach—with the consequence that the cats could see the mice without being able to eat them, while the mice feared the cats, and were each perishing of hunger near a fine lump of lard.

The princess was considering the torture of those animals when she saw the enchanter enter, in a long black robe. He had a crocodile on his head, which served as a bonnet, and there had never been a coiffure so frightening. The old man was wearing spectacles, and had a whip in his hand made of twenty long snakes, all alive.

Oh, how afraid the princess was! How she regretted her shepherd, her sheep and her dog at that moment! She only thought of fleeing, and not saying a word to that terrible man; she ran toward the door, but it was covered with spider-webs. She lifted one, and found another, which she also lifted, and when a third one succeeded it and she lifted that one, another appeared, which was before another. In sum, those vile cob-web door-curtains were innumerable.

Overtaken by lassitude, the poor princess could do no more; her arms did not have the strength to sustain the webs. She tried to sit down on the ground in order to repose for a while, but she felt long thorns penetrating her. She soon got up again and tried once again to pass through, but one web always appeared after another.

The malevolent old man, who was watching her, was gripped by bursts of choking laughter. In the end, he called to her and said: "You could spend the rest of your life without getting through. You seem young to me, and more beautiful than all that I have seen of the most beautiful. If you wish, I'll marry you. I'll give you these twelve cats that you see suspended from the ceiling, to do with whatever you wish, and these twelve mice on this table will be yours too.

"The cats are as many princes and the mice as many princesses. The hussies had the honor of pleasing me at various times—for I've always been amiable and gallant—but none of them wanted to love me. Those princes were my rivals, and more fortunate than me. Jealousy took hold of me; I found the means of drawing them here, and as I trapped them, I metamorphosed them into cats and mice. What's pleasant is that they hate one another as much as they loved one another, and one can't find a vengeance more complete."

"Oh, Sire," cried Brillante, "make me a mouse; I merit it no less than those poor princesses."

"What, little shepherdess," said the magician, "you don't want to love me?"

"I've resolved never to love," she said.

"Oh, how simple you are," he continued. "I'll nourish you marvelously, I'll tell you tales, I'll give you the most beautiful clothes in the world; you'll only go out in a coach or a litter, you'll be called Madame."

"I've resolved never to love," replied the princess, again.

"Oh well, excessively indifferent creature," he said, touching her, "since you don't want to love, you ought to be a particular species; in future, therefore, you shall be neither fish nor fowl, you'll have neither blood nor bone, you'll be green, because you're still in your green youth; you'll be light and frisky; you'll live in the meadows, as you lived; people will call you a grasshopper."

At the same moment, Brillante became the prettiest grasshopper in the world, and, enjoying her liberty, she returned promptly to the garden.

As soon as she was in a state to lament, she cried dolorously: "Oh, my bowl, my dear bowl, what has become of you? This, then, is the effect of your promises, Trasimene? This, then, is what was kept in store for me so carefully for two hundred years? A beauty as little durable as the flowers of spring, and by way of conclusion, a coat of green crepe, a singular little form that is neither flesh not fowl, which has neither bone not blood. I'm very unfortunate, alas! A crown would have covered all my defects; I would have found a spouse worthy of me; and if I had remained a shepherdess, the amiable Peerless only wanted the possession of my heart; he is only too well avenged or my unjust disdain. Now I'm a grasshopper, destined to sing day and night, while my heart, full of bitterness, invites me to weep!"

That was how the grasshopper spoke, hidden in the slender grass that bordered a stream.

But what was Prince Peerless doing, in the absence of his adorable shepherdess? The harshness with which she had quit him penetrated him so sharply that he had not had the strength to follow her. Before he would have caught up with her, he had fainted, and he remained unconscious or a long time at the foot of the tree where Brillante had se him fall.

Finally, the freshness of the earth or some unknown power brought him round. He dared not go to her house that day, and, passing through his mind the last lines that she had said to him, he thought: *To flee a lover, tender, young and confident, one scarcely takes more trouble than when one does so out of hatred*; he formed sufficiently fattening hopes, and he promised himself, from time and his cares, a little relief.

But what became of him when, having been to the house of the old shepherdess, to which Brillante had retired, he learned that she had not reappeared since the previous day? He nearly died of anxiety. He drew away, overwhelmed by a thousand different thoughts. He sat down sadly on the bank of the river; he was ready a hundred times over to throw himself in and seek in the end of his life that of his woes. Finally, he picked up a metal point and engraved the following lines in the bark of a service tree:

Beautiful spring, clear stream,
Delightful valleys and fertile plains.
Abode I found so beautiful,
You augment my pains, alas!
The tender object of my amour
From which you borrowed all your charms,
To flee an unfortunate, has quit you without return.
You will no longer see me, except shedding tears.
When Aurora comes to mortals to announce the day,
She sees me plunged in my profound dolor;
The sun is witness at every moment to my tears,

And when it is hidden in the waves
I do not interrupt my dolors.
O tender tree, forgive the wounds
That I dare inflict in your bosom to grave my woes;
They are light depictions
Of what that inhumane object has done to mine.
The point of this iron does not take away your life,
With the letters of her name you seem more beautiful.
But alas, my dearest desire,
Having lost Brillante, is to enter the tomb.

He could not write any more, because he was approached
by a little old woman, who had a strawberry birthmark on her
neck, a farthingale, a cape under her white hair and a velvet
hood, and her antiquity had something venerable.

"My son," she said, "you're uttering very bitter regrets; I
beg you to tell me the reason."

"Alas, my good mother," Peerless said to her, "I'm deploring the loss of a lovely shepherdess who is fleeing me.
I've resolved to search for her all over the world until I've
found her."

"Go that way, my son," she said to him, showing him the
path to the castle where poor Brillante had become a grasshopper. "I have a presentiment that you won't search for
long."

Peerless thanked her, and begged Amour to be favorable
to him.

The prince had no encounter on the route worthy of making him pause, but when he arrived in the wood near the castle
of the magician and his sister, he thought he saw his shepherdess; she drew away. "Brillante," he cried, "Brillante, who I
adore, stop a while, deign to hear me."

The phantom fled even faster, and the rest of the day
passed in that exercise. When night fell, he saw a great many
lights in the castle; he flattered himself that the shepherdess
might be there. He ran there, and entered without any impedi-
ment.

He went upstairs, and found, in a magnificent drawing room, a tall and aged fay who was horribly thin. Her eyes resembled two extinct lamps; daylight could be seen through her cheeks. Her arms were like laths, her fingers like spindles; a black goatskin covered her skeleton; in spite of that she had rouge, beauty spots and green and pink ribbons, a mantle of silver brocade, a crown of diamonds on her head and gemstones everywhere.

"Finally, Prince," she said, "you've arrived in a place where I've wanted you for a long time. Don't think any longer about your little shepherdess; a passion so disproportionate ought to make you blush. I'm the Queen of Meteors; I wish you well, and I can do you an infinite amount of good if you love me."

"Love you!" cried the prince, looking at her with an indignant eye. "Love you, Madame! Am I the master of my heart? No, I won't consent to an infidelity, and I even sense that if I changed the object of my amour, it wouldn't be you that would become its object. Choose from among your meteors some influence that suits you; love the air, love the winds, and leave mortals in peace."

The fay was proud and angry; with two strokes of her wand she filled the gallery with frightful monsters, against which it was necessary for the young prince to exercise his skill and valor. Some appeared with several hands and several arms; others had the form of a centaur or a siren; there were several lions with human faces, sphinxes and flying dragons. Peerless only had his crook and a small spike, with which he had armed himself when he commenced his voyage.

The tall fay caused the battle to cease from time to time, and asked him whether he wanted to love her. He always said that he was sworn to faithful amour, and could not change.

Weary of his firmness, she finally made Brillante appear. "Well," she said, "you see your mistress in the depths of that gallery; think about what you should do. If you refuse to marry me, she'll be torn apart and rent into pieces before your eyes by tigers."

"Oh, Madame!" cried the prince, throwing himself at her feet, "I'll willingly sacrifice myself to death to save my dear mistress; spare her days while abridging mine."

"It's not a question of your death, traitor," replied the fay, "it's a question of your heart and your hand."

While they were talking, the prince heard the voice of his shepherdess, who seemed to be lamenting. "Do you want to let me be devoured?" she said to him. "If you love me, determine to do what the queen orders you to do,"

The poor prince hesitated

"What!" he cried. "Have you abandoned me, then, Benigne, after so many promises? Come, come to our aid."

Those words had scarcely been pronounced when he heard a voice in the air, which pronounced these words: "Let destiny act, but be faithful, and seek the golden branch."

The tall fay, who had thought herself victorious by virtue of the aid of so many different illusions, almost despaired on finding an obstacle in her path as powerful as the protection of Benigne.

"Flee my presence, unfortunate and obstinate prince!" she cried. "Since your heart is filled with so many flames, you'll be a cricket, a friend of warmth and fire."

Immediately, the handsome and marvelous Prince Peerless became a little black cricket, who would have been burned alive in the first hearth or the first oven if he had not remembered the favorable voice that had reassured him.

It's necessary, he said to himself, *to seek the golden branch; perhaps it will decricketize me. Oh, if I could find my shepherdess, what would my felicity lack?*

The cricket hastened to get out of the fatal palace, and without knowing where he was going, he recommended himself to the care of the beautiful fay Benigne, and then departed without equipage and without noise, for a cricket fears neither thieves nor evil encounters.

At the first shelter, which was in a hole in a tree, he found a very sad grasshopper; she was not singing. Having no suspicion that it was a person full of intelligence and reason, the cricket said to her: "Where are you going, Mother Grasshopper?"

She replied immediately: "And you, Colleague Cricket, where are you going?"

That reply surprised the amorous cricket strangely. "What! You can talk!" he cried.

"Well, you can talk well!" she retorted. "Do you think that a grasshopper has privileges less extensive than a cricket?"

"I can talk well," said the cricket, "because I'm a man."

"And by the same rule," said the grasshopper, "I ought to be able to talk even better than you, since I'm a young woman."

"You've experienced a fate similar to mine, then," said the cricket.

"Undoubtedly," said the grasshopper. "But again, where are you going?"

A voice that is unknown to me," he replied, "became audible in the air; it said: 'Let destiny act, and seek the golden branch.' It seemed that it could only have been said to me. Without hesitation, I set forth, although I don't know where I ought to go. I'd be delighted," the cricket added, "if we were together for a long time."

Their conversation was interrupted by two mice, which were running as fast as they could, and which, having seen a hole at the foot of the tree, threw themselves into it head first and nearly stifled Colleague Cricket and Mother Grasshopper. They arranged themselves as best they could in a little corner.

"Oh, Madame," said the larger mouse, "I've got a stitch in my side from having run so much; how is Your Highness?"

"I've torn off my tail," replied the younger mouse, "for otherwise I'd still be pinned to that old sorcerer's table. But did you see how he chased us? How lucky we are to be out his infernal palace!"

"I still fear the cats and the rat-traps, my princess," continued the fat mouse, "and I'm making ardent prayers to arrive soon at the golden branch."

"You know the way there, then?" said the mousy Highness.

"Yes, I know it, Madame! Like that to my house," replied the other. "That branch is marvelous; a single one of its leaves is sufficient to be rich forever; it furnishes money; it disenchants; its renders beautiful; it conserves youth. It's necessary that we set out on campaign before daylight."

"We'll have the honor of accompanying you, this honest cricket and myself, if you don't mind, Mesdames," said the grasshopper, "for like you, we are pilgrims of the golden branch."

Compliments were made then on either part; the mice were princesses whom the evil enchanter had fastened to the table; as for the cricket and the grasshopper, they had a politeness that was never belied.

They all awoke very early; the company departed very quietly, for they feared that hunters lying in ambush, on hearing hear them speak, might catch them in order to put them in a cage.

They arrived thus at the golden branch. It was planted in the middle of a marvelous garden; instead of sand, the paths were filled with little oriental pearls rounder than peas; the roses were pink diamonds and the leaves emeralds; the pomegranate flowers were garnets and the marigolds topazes; the jonquils were yellow diamonds, the violets sapphires, the cornflowers turquoises, the tulips amethysts, opals and diamonds; in sum, the quantity and diversity of those beautiful flowers shone more brightly than the sun.

So, as I have said, the golden branch was there: the same one that Prince Peerless had received from the eagle and with which he had touched the fay Benigne when she was enchanted. It had become as tall as the tallest trees, and was entirely laden with rubies, which formed cherries. As soon as the cricket, the grasshopper and the two mice were close to it, they resumed their natural form.

What joy! What transports did the amorous prince not feel at the sight of his beautiful shepherdess? He threw himself at her feet; he was about to tell her everything that such an agreeable and so unexpected surprise made him feel when Queen Benigne and King Trasimene appeared in an unparalleled pomp; for everything responded to the magnificence of the garden. Four Amours armed from head to toe, bows at their sides and quivers over their shoulders, were sustaining with their arrows a little tent of gold and blue brocade beneath which appeared two rich crowns.

"Come, amiable lovers," cried the queen, extending her arms to them. "Come and receive from our hands the crowns that your virtue, your birth and your fidelity merit; your travails will change into pleasures. Princess Brillante," she continued, "this shepherd, so terrible to your heart, is the prince for whom you were destined by your father and his. He did not die in the tower. Receive him for your husband, and leave the care of your repose and your happiness to me."

The delighted princess threw her arms around Benigne, and let her see the tears that were flowing from her eyes. The fay knew by her silence that the excess of her joy had taken away the usage of speech. Peerless had put himself at the knees of the generous fay; he kissed her hands respectfully and said a thousand things without order or consequence.

While Trasimene was making his great caresses, Benigne told them, in a few words, that she had hardly ever quit them; that it was her who had proposed to Brillante to blow on the yellow and white muff; that she had taken on the form of an old shepherdess in order to lodge the princess in her home; and that it was also her who had told the prince in which direction to follow his shepherdess.

"In truth," she continued, "you had difficulties that you would have avoided, if I had been the mistress of them, but in the end, the pleasures of amour are worth being bought.

A sweet symphony was immediately heard, which resounded on all sides. The amours hastened to crown the young lovers. The marriage was made, and during the ceremony the two princesses who had just quit the form of mice implored the fay to use her power to deliver the despairing mice and casts from the enchanter's castle.

"This day is too famous," she said, "to refuse you anything." At the same time, she tapped the golden branch three times, and all those who had been retained in the castle appeared; each prince, in his natural form, recovered his mistress there. The liberal fay, wanting everyone to share the celebration, gave them the cupboard from the tower to share between them. That present was worth more than ten kingdoms in those days. It is easy to imagine their satisfaction and their gratitude.

Benigne and Trasimene completed that great work with a generosity that surpassed everything they had done thus far, declaring that the palace and the garden of the golden branch would belong in future to King Peerless and Queen Brillante; a hundred other kings would be tributaries to them, and a hundred kingdoms would depend on them.

> *When a fay offered her aid to Brillante*
> *Who was not very brilliant the time,*
> *She was able, with, charming beauty,*
> *To ask for rare treasures;*
> *It is a very tempting thing!*
> *I can only take for witnesses*
> *The embarrassments and cares*
> *By which the sex torments itself to conserve it.*
> *But Brillante did not listen*
> *To the seductive desire to obtain charms;*
> *She preferred to have negligence and a noble soul;*
> *The roses and lilies of a charming face,*
> *Like other flowers, pass in a moment;*
> *But the soul remains immortal.*

THE ORANGE TREE AND THE BEE

There was once a king and queen who lacked nothing in order to be happy except for having children. The queen was already old, and no longer hopeful, when she became pregnant, and brought into the world the most beautiful little girl that has ever been seen. The joy was extreme in the royal household. Everyone strove to find a name for the princess that expressed how people felt about her. Finally she was called Aimée.

The queen had the name *Aimée, daughter of the King of the Fortunate Isle*, engraved on a turquoise heart. She attached it around the princess's neck, believing that the turquoise would bring her luck, but that rule was a blatant lie, for one day, in order to divert her nurse, she was taken for an excursion at sea, in the most beautiful summer weather; a frightful tempest suddenly blew up. It was impossible to reach land, and as she was in a small boat that only served for trips along the coast, it was soon smashed to pieces. The nurse and all the sailors perished.

The little princess, who was asleep in her cradle, remained afloat on the water. Eventually, the sea cast her up in a rather agreeable country, but one that had been almost uninhabited since the ogre Ravagio and his wife Tourmentine had come to live there. They ate everyone. Ogres are terrible individuals; since they have eaten fresh flesh—that is what they call humans—they are almost unable to eat anything else.

Tourmentine always found the secret of making someone come along, for she was half-fay. She scented the poor little princess from a league away; she ran to the shore to look for her before Ravagio found her. They were as greedy as one another. Such hideous faces had never been seen, with one squinting eye placed in the middle of the forehead, a mouth as large as an oven, a long, flat nose, long donkey's ears, bristling hair and humps before and behind.

However, when she saw Aimée in her rich cradle, wrapped in golden brocade, who was playing with her tiny hands, her cheeks like white roses mingled with pink, and her red mouth half open, laughing, seemingly smiling at the loathsome monster that was about to devour her, Tourmentine was touched by a pity of which she would never have been thought capable; she resolved to nourish her, and, if she had to eat her, not to eat her right away.

She took her in her arms; she tied the cradle to her back, and with that equipage returned to her cabin.

"Look, Ravagio," he said to her husband, "here's some fresh flesh, very plump, very soft, but by my head, you won't crunch it with a single tooth. It's a lovely little girl. I want to nourish her; we'll marry her to our little ogrelet, and they'll make ogrichons of an extraordinary form; that will rejoice us in our old age.

"That's a good idea," Ravagio replied. "You have more intelligence than when you were pregnant. Let me look at the child; it seems to me to be marvelously beautiful."

"Don't eat it," said Tourmentine, putting the child into his huge claws.

"No, no," he said. "I'd rather die of hunger."

So, Ravagio, Tourmentine and the ogrelet started caressing Aimée in a manner so humane that it was a kind of miracle. But the poor child, who only saw those deformed apes around her, and who could not perceive her nurse's teat, commenced puling faces, and then started screaming with all her might; Ravagio's cavern resounded with it.

Fearing that it might annoy him, Tourmentine took the child and carried it into the woods, to which her ogrelets followed her. She had six of them, all as frightful as one another. As I said, she was half-fay; her science consisted of holding her ivory wand and wishing for something. She took the wand, therefore, and said: "I wish in the name of the royal fay Trufio, that the most beautiful hind in our forest will soon come along, meek and placid, who will leave her fawn and nourish this little creature that fortune has given me."

At the same time, the hind appeared; the ogrelets welcomed her. She approached and suckled the princess. Then Tourmentine took her back to her grotto. The hind ran after them, leaping and gamboling; the child gazed at her and caressed her. When she was in her cradle and she cried, the hind had milk ready, and the ogrichons rocked her.

It was thus that the king's daughter was brought up, while he wept for her night and day, and, believing her to be at the bottom of the sea, thought about choosing an heir. He mentioned it to the queen, who told him to do whatever he thought appropriate; that her dear Aimée was dead and she could not hope to have any more children; that that he had waited long enough, and that since fifteen years had passed since she had had the misfortune of losing her, it would be extravagant to hope to see her again.

The king deliberated, therefore, and to whether he should ask his brother to choose whichever of his sons he believed to be the most worthy to reign and to send him to him diligently.

The ambassadors, having received their dispatches and all the necessary instructions, departed. They had a long way to go; they embarked on a good ship; the wind was favorable, and they eventually arrived in the lands of king's brother, who possessed a large realm.

He received them very well, and when they asked him for one of his sons, in order to take him with them in order to succeed their master, he started weeping with joy. He told them that since his brother had left the choice to him, he would send the one he would have taken himself. That was the second of his sons, whose inclinations responded so well to the grandeur of his birth that he had never wished for anything in him that he had not found in the utmost perfection.

Someone went in quest of Prince Aimé—that was his name—and although the ambassadors had been warned, when they saw him, they were very surprised. He was eighteen years old. Amour, tender Amour himself, had less beauty, but it was not a beauty that diminished in any way the noble and martial air that inspired respect and affection. He was told of his uncle's urgency have him with him, and his father's intention of sending him diligently. His equipage was prepared; he made his adieux, embarked and headed out to sea.

Let us leave him there and let fortune guide him.

Meanwhile, let us return to Ravagio to see what is occupying our young princess. She had grown in beauty as well as age, and once could well say of her that Amour, the Graces and all the goddesses put together had never had as many charms. When she was in that profound cavern with Ravagio, Tourmentine and the ogrelets, it seemed that the sun, the stars and the skies had descended thereinto.

The cruelty that she saw in those monsters rendered her milder, and since she had known their inclination for fresh flesh she had only been occupied in saving the unfortunates who fell into her hands, with the consequence that, in order to protect their victims, she often exposed herself to all their fury. She would have experienced them in the end, if the ogrelet had not cherished her like his eye.

What can a strong passion not achieve? That little monster had acquired a mild character by virtue of seeing and loving the beautiful princess. Alas, though, what was her dolor when she thought that it would be necessary to marry that detestable lover? Although she knew nothing of her birth, she had judged by the richness of her swaddling-clothes, the golden chain and the turquoise, that she came from a good place, and she judged it even better by the sentiments of her heart. She did not know how to read or write, or any languages; she spoke the jargon of ogrelie and she lived in a perfect ignorance of all matters of society, but she had nevertheless principles of virtue, mildness and congeniality as good as if she had been raised in the most polite court in the world.

She had made herself a garment out of tiger-skin. Her arms were semi-naked. She wore a quiver and arrows over her shoulder and a bow at her waist. Her blonde hair was only tied with a cord of sea-rush and floated at the whim of the wind over her breast and her black. She had brodequins of the same rush. In that outfit she traversed the woods like a second Diana, and she would not have known that she was beautiful if the crystal of springs had not offered her innocent mirrors, to which her eyes were attached without rendering her vain or prejudicing her in her favor. The sun had the same effect on her complexion as it produced on wax, whitening it, and the sea air could not darken it.

She only ever ate what she obtained by hunting and fishing, and on that pretext she often drew away from the horrible cavern in order to avoid the sight of the most deformed objects in nature. "Heaven," she said, shedding tears, "what have I done to you to have been destined for that cruel ogrelet? Why did you not let me perish at sea? Why have you preserved a life for me that I must pass in such a deplorable manner? Will you not have some compassion on my dolor?" She addressed the gods in that fashion, and requested their help.

When the weather was bad and she thought that the sea might have cast up unfortunates on to the shore, she went there dutifully in order to help them, and to do so in such a manner that they did not end up in the ogres' cave.

One night, there was a terrible wind; she got up as soon as there was daylight and ran toward the sea.

She perceived a man who was holding a plank in his arms, and who was trying to reach the shore in spite of the violence of the waves that were pushing him back. the princess would have liked to help him; she made signs to him to indicate the easiest places, but he neither saw nor heard her. He sometimes got so close that he seemed have nothing more to do, but then a wave covered him and he did not appear again.

Eventually, he was driven on to the sand, and remained lying there, without any movement. Aimée approached him, and, in spite of the pallor that made her fear that he was dead, she gave him all the help she could. She brought him certain herbs, the odor of which was so strong that it brought people round from the longest faints. She crushed them in her hands and rubbed his lips and temples with them.

He opened his eyes and was so surprised by the beauty and attire of the princess that he was unable to determine whether she was a dream or a reality. He spoke to her first; she spoke to him in her turn; they had as little understanding as one another, and looked at one another with an attention mingled with astonishment and pleasure.

The princess had only seen a few poor fishermen whom the ogres had captured and whom she had saved, as I said. What could she think, then, when she saw the best made and most magnificently clad man in the world? For, in sum, it was Prince Aimé, her first cousin, whose fleet, battered by a furious tempest, had broken up on reefs, and everyone, driven at the whim of the wind, had perished or arrived on some beach, for the most part unknown.

For his part, the young prince was amazed that, in such primitive clothing and in a country that seemed to be deserted, it was possible to find such a marvelous person. The recent idea of princesses and ladies that he had seen only served to convince him that the one he saw at present could not be equaled by any other.

In that mutual surprise they continued to talk to one another without being heard. Their eyes and a few gestures served as interpreters of their thoughts The princess passed a few minutes thus, but, suddenly reflecting on the peril to which the stranger was about to be exposed, she fell into a melancholy and a dejection that immediately appeared on her face.

The prince, fearing that she might be ill, hastened to move closer and tried to take her hands. She pushed him away and showed him, as best she could, that he should go away. She started running in front of him, came back, and made him a sign to do the same. He fled, and came back.

When he came back she was annoyed; she took one of her arrows and placed it over her heart, to signify to him that he might be killed. He thought she wanted to kill him; he put one knee on the ground and awaited the blow. When she saw that, she no longer knew what to do, nor how to express herself. Looking at him tenderly, she said: "What! You're going to be the victim of my frightful hosts, then? With the same eyes with which I have the pleasure of gazing at you, I shall see you torn to pieces and devoured, mercilessly? She wept, and the prince, nonplussed, could not understand what she was doing at all.

However, she succeeded in making him understand that she did not want him to follow her. She took him by the hand, and let him to a rock that had an opening overlooking the sea. She often went there to bewail her disgrace, and sometimes slept here when the sun was too ardent to return to the cavern. As she was very tidy and clever, she had furnished it with a fabric of butterfly-wings of various colors extended over interwoven canes, which formed a kind of bed. She had laid down a carpet of se-rushes. She had put flowering branches in large and profound seashells, which served as vases that she filled with water in order to conserve her bouquets. There were a thousand pretty things that she contrived, sometimes with fish-bones and shells, sometimes with sea-rush and canes; and those little works, in spite of their simplicity, had such delicacy that it was easy to judge therefrom the skill and good taste of the princess.

The prince was surprised by so much neatness; he thought that it was where she slept, and was delighted to find himself there with her. Although he was not fortunate enough to be able to make her understand the sentiments of admiration that she inspired in him, it already seemed that he would prefer seeing her and living with her to all the crowns to which his birth and the will of his relatives called him.

She obliged him to sit down and in order to indicate to him that she wanted him to stay there until she had bought him something to eat, she unfastened the cord that held a part of her hair, attached it to the prince's arm, tied him to the bed and then went away. He was dying of the desire to follow her, but he feared displeasing her and he began to abandon himself to the reflections from which the presence of the princess had distracted him.

Where am I? he thought. *To what land has fortune brought me? My ships have perished, my men have drowned; I lack everything. Instead of the crown that I was offered I find a sad rock in which I am seeking a retreat. What will become of me here? What people will I find here? If I can judge by the person who helped me, they are divinities, but the fear she had that I might follow her, the harsh and barbaric language that sounds so poorly in her beautiful mouth, lead me to dread some adventure even more catastrophic than the one that has already happened to me.*

Then he applied all his application to passing through his mind again the incomparable beauties of the young savage. His heart warmed; he became impatient at not seeing her return, and her absence seemed to him to be the worst of all his woes.

She came back with all possible urgency; she had not ceased to think about the prince, and tender sentiments were so new to her that she had no protection against those he inspired in her, She thanked heaven for having saved him from the perils of the sea, and implored it to preserve him from those he was risking in proximity with the ogres. She was so heavily laden and she had walked so rapidly that when she arrived she felt uncomfortable in the coarse tiger-skin that served her as a mantle.

She sat down; the prince set himself at her feet, troubled because she was suffering, although he was certainly more ill than she was. Finally, she recovered from her weakness; immediately, she showed him all the tidbits she had brought him, including four parrots and six squirrels cooked in the sun, strawberries, cherries, raspberries and other fruits. The plates were made of cedar-wood and carambola, the knife of stone, the napkins of large, soft and manipulable leaves; there was a seashell from which to drink, and fresh water in another.

The prince expressed his gratitude by means of all the signs of his head and hand that he could make, and she let him know, with a soft smile, that everything he did was agreeable to her. But, the time to separate having come, she enabled him to understand that she was going away so well that they both started sighing and hiding their tears. She stood up and tried to leave; the prince uttered a loud cry and threw himself at her feet, imploring her to stay; she saw clearly what he wanted, but she pushed him away, adopting a severe expression. He knew that it was necessary to accustom himself quickly to obeying her.

It is necessary to tell the truth: he passed a terrible night; the princess's was no less sad. When she arrived at the cavern and found herself in the midst of the ogres and ogrichons, when she looked at the frightful ogrelet as the monster who would be her husband, and when she thought about the charms of the stranger she had just quit, she was on the point of going to throw herself head first into the sea. It is necessary to add to that the fear that Ravagio or Tourmentine might scent fresh flesh and go straight to the rock to devour Prince Aimé.

Those various alarms kept her awake all night; she got up with the dawn and took the path to the shore. She ran there, or flew, laden with parrots, monkeys and a bustard, fruit, milk and everything that she was able to believe might be the best.

The prince had not undressed; he had suffered so much fatigue on the sea and had slept so little that he fell into a light slumber at daybreak.

"What!" she said to him, when she woke him up. "I've been thinking about you since I quit you and I haven't even closed my eyes, and you're capable of sleeping?"

The prince looked at her and listened to her without understanding her. He spoke in his turn. "What joy, my dear child," he said to her, kissing her hands, "What joy to see you again. It seems to me that it has been a century since you departed from this rock." He talked for a long time without reflecting that she did not understand him; when he remembered that, he sighed sadly and fell silent.

She spoke again and told him that she had cruel anxieties; that Ravagio and Tourmentine might discover him; that she dared not hope that he would be safe for long in this rock, that his going away might be death of her, but that she would consent to that rather than expose him to the risk of being devoured; that she implored him to flee. At that point her eyes were covered with tears; she put her hands together before her in a supplicant fashion.

He did not understand what she wanted; he was in despair and threw himself at her feet. Finally, she showed him the way so often that he understood a part of her signs, and made her understand in her turn that he would die rather than abandon her. She sensed that evidence of the prince's amity so keenly that, in order to show the degree to which she was touched by it; she took from her arm the golden chain and the turquoise heart that her mother had attached to her neck, and attached it to the prince's arm in the most gracious fashion in the world.

Transported as he was by that favor, he nevertheless perceived the characters engraved on the turquoise; he looked at them attentively and read: *Aimée, daughter of the King of the Fortunate Isle.*

There has never been an astonishment similar to his. He knew that the little princess who had perished had been named Aimée; he had no doubt that the heart had been hers, but he still did not know whether the beautiful savage was the princess, or whether the sea had washed the jewel up on the sand. He looked at Aimée with an extraordinary attention, and the more he looked at her, the more he seemed to discover a sort of family resemblance in her features, and particularly movements of tenderness in his soul, which assured him that the savage was his cousin.

She examined the actions he performed with surprise: raising his eyes to the heavens as if to render them thanks, looking at her and weeping, taking her hands and kissing them wholeheartedly. He thanked her for the liberality she had just shown him, and, replacing the heart on her arm, he made her understand that he would rather have a lock of her hair, which he requested, and had no difficulty obtaining.

Four days passed thus; every morning the princess brought him all that he needed for his nourishment; she remained with him as long as she could, and the hours went by very rapidly, even though they did not have the pleasure of conversation.

One evening, when she came back rather late and she feared that she might be scolded by the terrible Tourmentine, she was very surprised to receive a favorable welcome and to find a table fully laden with fruits. She asked for permission to take some. Ravagio said that they were for her; that his ogrelet had gone in search of them; that the time had finally come to render him happy; and that he wanted her to marry him in three days' time.

What news! Could there be anything in the world more catastrophic for that amiable princess? She thought she would die of fear ad dolor, but, hiding her affliction, she replied that she would obey them without reluctance, provided that they would prolong the prescribed time a little.

Ravagio became irritated and cried: "Why don't I eat you instead?" The poor princess fainted from fear between the claws of Tourmentine and the ogrelet, who loved her very much, and who begged Ravagio so much that he calmed down.

Aimée did not sleep for a moment. She waited for daylight impatiently; as soon as it appeared she went to the rock, and when she saw the prince she uttered dolorous cries and shed a stream of tears. He remained almost mobile; his passion for the beautiful Aimée had made more progress in four days than ordinary passions make in four years; he strove desperately to ask her what was wrong. She knew that he did not understand but did not know how to make him understand. Finally, she let down her long hair; she put a crown of flowers on her head and, touching Aimé's with her hand, to which she made a sign that she would do the same with another, he understood the misfortune by which she was menaced, and that she was about to be married.

He was on the point of expiring at her feet; he did not know the routes, not the means of saving her; she did not know them either. They wept; they looked at one another, and indicated to one another mutually that it would be better to die together than to be separated. She remained with him until the evening, but as the night arrived sooner than they expected, and, being very pensive, she did not pay attention to the route she was following, she advanced into a path through a wood that as little frequented, where a long thorn entered into her foot that went all the way through. Fortunately for her, it was not far from there to the cavern; she had a great deal of difficulty getting there, her foot covered in blood.

Ravagio, Tourmentine and the ogrelet helped her; she suffered great pain when it as necessary to extract the thorn. They crushed herbs and put them on her foot, and she went to bed with an understandable anxiety for her prince.

Alas, she thought, *I won't be able to walk tomorrow. What will he think when he doesn't see me? I've made him understand that I'm to be married; he'll believe that I couldn't prevent it. Who will nourish him? One way or another, he's going to die. If he comes to look for me, he's doomed; if I send an ogrelet to him, Ravagio will find out.*

She dissolved in tears, she sighed. She tried to get up early in the morning, but it was impossible for her to walk; her injury was too bad. Tourmentine, who saw her going out, stopped her and told her that if she took another step she would be eaten.

Meanwhile, the prince, who saw the hour pass when she was accustomed to come, commenced to be afflicted and to dread; the more time passed, the more his alarm was augmented; all the tortures in the world would have seemed less terrible to him than the anxieties to which amour delivered him; he exercised he utmost violence on himself to wait, but the longer he waited, the less hope he had. Finally, he sacrificed himself to death and set forth resolutely to look for his lovely princess.

He walked without knowing where he was going; he followed a beaten path that he found at the entrance to the wood. After having walked for an hour, he heard a noise; he perceived a cavern from which thick smoke as emerging. He thought he might obtain some news there. He went in, and had scarcely advanced when he saw Ravagio, who, suddenly seizing him with frightful strength, would have devoured him if the cries he uttered while struggling had not reached the ears of his dear lover.

At that voice, she felt that nothing could stop her any longer; she emerged from her hole, went into the one in which Ravagio was holding the poor prince; she was as pale and tremulous as if he wanted to eat her. She threw himself to her knees before him and implored him to keep that fresh flesh for the day of her wedding to the ogrelet, on which she promised that she would eat him.

Ravagio was so content in thinking that the princess wanted to adopt his customs that he released the prince and shut him in the hole in which the ogrichons slept. Aimée asked for permission to nourish him well in order that he would not get thin and that he would do honor to the repast; the ogre consented to that. She took the prince all the best things she could find.

When he saw her come in he felt a joy that diminished his displeasure, but when she showed him the wound in her foot his dolor took on new force. They wept for a long time; the prince could not eat, and his dear mistress cut little morsels with her delicate hands, which she presented to him with such a good grace that it was not possible for him to refuse them.

She had the ogrichons bring fresh moss, which she covered with a carpet of feathers and made the prince understand that it was his bed. Tourmentine called her; she could not bid him any other adieu than that of holding out her hand. He kissed it with indescribable transports of tenderness. She left her eyes the care of expressing what she thought.

Ravagio, Tourmentine and the princess slept in one of the concavities of the cavern; the ogrelet and five ogrichons slept in another, where the prince also slept. Now, it is the custom in Ogrichonia that every evening an ogre, an ogress and their ogrichons put beautiful golden crowns on their head, in which they sleep; that is their only magnificence, but they would rather be hanged and strangled than do without it.

When everyone was asleep, the princess, who was thinking about her amiable lover, made the reflection that, in spite of the promise at Ravagio and Tourmentine had given her not to eat him, if they felt hungry during the night—which almost always happened when they had fresh flesh—he would be done for. The anxiety that she had about that began to deliver her to such rude assaults that she nearly died of fright. After having thought about it for some time she got up, covered herself hastily with her tiger skin and, feeling her way without making a sound, she went into the cave where the ogrichons slept. She took the crown of the first one she found and placed it on the head of the prince, who was wide awake but who dared not make a sound, not knowing who was performing the ceremony. Afterwards, the princess returned to her little bed.

She had scarcely tucked herself in than Ravagio, thinking about the good meal that the prince had had, his appetite augmenting the more he thought about it, got up in his turn and went into the hole where the ogrichons were asleep. As he could not see clearly, for fear of making a mistake, he groped with his hand, and, throwing himself on the individual who had no crown, he wolfed him down like a pullet. The poor princess, who heard the sound of the crunching bones of the unfortunate individual that he was eating, fainted, dying of the fear that it might be her lover.

For his part, the prince, being much closer, felt all the alarm that one can have on such an occasion.

Daylight extracted the princess from a terrible anxiety. She hastened to go in search of the prince, and made him aware by signs of her dread and her impatience to see him safe from the murderous teeth of the monsters. She made him amities, and he would have made her a thousand in his turn but for the ogress coming to see her children. She perceived the blood with which the cavern was full and found that the smallest ogrichon had been eaten.

Ravagio understood well enough the error he had made, but the harm was without remedy. He told her in a whisper that, having been hungry, he had mistaken his choice and thought that he was eating the fresh flesh. Tourmentine pretended to calm down, for Ravagio was cruel, and if she had not taken his excuses in good part he might have eaten her too.

Alas, though, what strange anxieties the beautiful princess was suffering! She never ceased imagining means to save the prince. And what was he not thinking on his part about the frightful place in which the lovely girl lived? He could not resolve to go away so long as she was there; death would have appeared milder to him than that separation. He made her understand that when, by means of reiterated signs, she urged him to flee and to save his life. They wept together, they held hands; each of them swore, in a different language, a reciprocal faith and an eternal amour.

She could not resist showing him the linen in which she had been wrapped when Tourmentine found her, and the cradle she had had. The prince recognized the arms and the motto of the King of the Fortunate Isle. That sight delighted him, and he gave signs of his joy to the princess, who realized that the sight of the cradle had informed him of something important. She was dying to know what it was, but no matter what trouble he took, how could he make her understand that she was the daughter of a king, and the relationship there was between them? All that penetrated her was that she had some reason to be glad.

The hour came to retire, and everyone went to bed as they had previous night. The princess, who had the same anxieties, got up without making a noise, went into the cabin where the prince was, removed the crown from the head of an ogrelette and put it on her lover's. He dared not stop her; no matter how much he desired to do so, the respect he had for her and the fear of displeasing her prevented him.

The princess had never been better inspired than to put the crown on Aimé's head. Without that precaution he would have been done for. The barbaric Tourmentine woke up with a start, and, thinking about the prince, whom she had thought as handsome as the day and very appetizing, she was gripped by a great fear that Ravagio might eat him on his own, and decided that the best thing was to anticipate him. She slipped into the ogrichons' hole without saying a word, touched gently those who had crowns—the prince was one of them—and one of the ogrelettes disappeared in three mouthfuls.

Aimé and his mistress heard everything, and were trembling with fear, but having made that expedition, Tourmentine asked no more than to go to sleep, and they were safe for the rest of the night.

Heaven help us! said the princess, silently. *Inspire me with what we ought to do in such a pressing extremity.* The prince was praying with no less ardor. Sometimes, he had a desire to attack the two monsters and fight them, but what hope was there that he might have any advantage over them? They were as tall as giants and their skin was proof against pistol shots, with the consequence that he thought very prudently that only cleverness could get him out of that frightful place.

As soon as it was daylight and Tourmentine had found the bones of her ogrelette, she filled the air with frightful howls. Ravagio appeared to be no less desperate. They were ready a hundred times over to hurl themselves upon the prince and the princess and murder them mercilessly; they had hidden in a dark corner, but the flesh-eaters knew only too well where they were, and of all the perils they had run, the present one appeared the most evident.

Aimée, thinking hard and racking her brains, suddenly remembered that the ivory wand of which Tourmentine made use produced prodigies of a sort, which she could not explain herself.

If such surprising things happen in spite of her ignorance, she said to herself, *why shouldn't my words have as much virtue?* Filled with that idea, she ran to the cavern where Tourmentine slept, searched for the wand, which was hidden at the bottom of a hole. When she had it she cried: "I wish in the name of the royal fay Trufio to speak the language that the man I love speaks."

She would have made other wishes, but Ravagio came in; the princess shut up and replaced the wand. She went to the prince very quietly.

"Dear stranger," she said to him, "your troubles touch me more sensibly than my own."

At those words the prince was astonished and confused. "I understand you, adorable princess," he said. "You are speaking my language, and I can hope that you understand in your turn that I am suffering less for myself than for you; that you are dearer to me than my life, than light, and everything lovable there is in nature."

"My expressions are simpler," said the princess, "but they are no less sincere. I feel that I would give everything that I have on this rock in the sea, my sheep and my lambs—in sum, everything I possess—solely for the pleasure of seeing you."

The prince gave her a thousand thanks for her generosity and implored her to tell him how she had learned, in such a short time, all the terms and all the delicacies of a language previously unknown to her. She told him about the power of the enchanted wand, and he informed her of her birth and their relationship. The princess was transported by joy; because she had a naturally marvelous mind, she said things so fine and so well-expressed that the prince felt a violent increase in his passion.

They had no time to lose in order to regulate their affairs. It was a question of fleeing irritated monsters, and promptly seeking a refuge for their innocent amour. They promised to love one another eternally and to unite their destinies as soon as they were able to marry. The princess told her lover that when she saw that Ravagio and Tourmentine were asleep, she would go in quest of their large camel, which they would mount in order to go wherever it pleased Heaven to conduct them. The prince was so glad that he could not contain his joy, and whatever reason they still had for great fear, the charming idea of the future effaced a part of the woes of the present.

The night so much desired arrived; the princess took some flour and kneaded a pancake with her white hands into which she put a bean; then, holding the ivory wand, she said: "O bean, little bean, I wish in the name of the royal fay Trufio that you speak, if necessary, until you are cooked. She put the pancake under the warm ashes, and went to get the prince, who was waiting for her very impatiently in the ogrichons' wretched lodgings.

"Let's go," she said. "The camel is tethered in the wood.

"May amour and fortune guide us," whispered the young prince. "Let's go, Aimée, let's go and seek a happy and tranquil abode."

The moon was shining; she had seized the helpful ivory wand. They found the camel and set forth, without knowing where they were going.

Meanwhile, Tourmentine, whose head was full of chagrin, was tossing and turning without being able to sleep. She reached out her arm to see whether the princess was already in the little bed, and not finding her, she cried in a thunderous voice: "Where are you, girl?"

"I'm next to the fire," replied the bean.

"Would you care to to bed?" said Tourmentine.

"In a little while," replied the bean. "Go to sleep, go to sleep."

Tourmentine, afraid of waking Ravagio, did not say any more, but two hours later she felt Aimée's little bed again, and cried: "What, little gallows-bird, you don't want to go to bed, then?"

"I'm warming myself as much as I can," replied the bean.

"I wish you were in the middle of the fire, for your trouble," added the ogress.

"That's where I am," said the bean, "and I've never been warmed so closely."

They exchanged a few other remarks, which the bean sustained like a very clever bean.

The conclusion was that toward dawn, Tourmentine called out to the princess again, but the bean, which was cooked, made no reply. That silence made her anxious. She got up, very worried, looked, spoke, became alarmed, and searched everywhere. No princess, no prince, and no little wand. She screeched with such force that the woods and valleys resounded. "Wake up, my lad, wake up, handsome Ravagio; your Tourmentine is betrayed, our fresh flesh has run away."

Ravagio opened his eye, and leapt into the middle of the cavern like a lion; he roared, he bellowed, he howled, he foamed at the mouth. Let's go, let's go," he said. "My seven-league boots, my seven-league boots, so that I can pursue our fugitives. I'll have a good hunt and reason to gloat before long."

He put on his boots, with which he could advance seven leagues in a single stride. Alas, what means are there of going quickly enough to be safe from such a runner? It might be thought astonishing that with the ivory wand they did not go quicker than him, but the princess was a complete novice in the art of faerie; she did not know everything that one might do with such a wand, and only great extremities can produce sudden enlightenments.

Flattered by the pleasure of being together, that of being able to understand one another, and the hope of not being pursued, they were making progress when the princess, who was the first to perceive the terrible Ravagio, cried: "Prince, we're doomed! See that frightful monster who is coming toward us like lightning!"

"What are we going to do?" said the prince "What will become of us? Oh, if I were alone, I wouldn't regret my life, but yours, my dear mistress, is at risk."

"I'm without consolation, if the wand doesn't protect us," said Aimée, weeping. "It's necessary to resolve ourselves to death. I wish," she added, "in the name of the royal fay Trufio, that our camel becomes a pond, that the prince might be a boat, and me an old boatwoman who can guide it."

At the same time, the pond, the boat and the boatwoman were formed. Ravagio arrived on the edge. "Hola," he shouted, "Ho, eternal old mother, have you seen a camel, a young man and a young woman go past?"

The boatwoman, who was in the middle of the pond, put her spectacles on her nose, and, looking at Ravagio, she made a sign that she had seen them, and that they had gone on into the meadowland. The ogre believed it; he turned left. The princess wished to return to her natural form. She tapped three times with her wand, striking the boat and the pool. She became young and beautiful again, as did the prince. They mounted the camel and turned right, in order not to encounter their enemy.

While they were advancing diligently, wishing that they could find someone of whom to ask about the way to the Fortunate Isle, they lived on the fruits of the countryside, drank the water of springs and slept under trees, very anxious that wild beasts might find them and devour them. But the princess had her bow and arrows, with which she would have tried to defend herself. The peril did not frighten them so much that they did not feel keenly the pleasure of having escaped the cavern and finding themselves together. Since they had understood one another they had said the nicest things the world to one another; amour ordinarily provides intelligence. For themselves, they had no need of that assistance, having a thousand natural charms, and always having new thoughts.

The prince expressed to the princess the extreme impatience he had to arrive soon in the abode of the king, his father, or hers, since she had promised him that, with their consent, she would receive him as a husband. What is only believable with difficulty is that while awaiting that happy day he lived with her in the woods, in solitude and master of proposing anything he wanted, in a manner so respectful and sage. So much passion and so much virtue have never been found in combination.

After Ravagio had traveled the mountains, the forests and the plains, he returned to his cavern, where Tourmentine and the ogrichons were waiting for him impatiently. He was laden with five or six people who had fallen misfortunately into his claws.

"Well?" shouted Tourmentine. "Have you found them and eaten them, those fugitives, those thieves, that fresh flesh? Haven't you kept me any feet or hands?"

"I believe they've flown," replied Ravagio. "I ran like a wolf in all directions without encountering them. I only saw an old woman in a boat on a pond, who gave me news of them."

"And what did she say?" replied the impatient Tourmentine.

"That they'd turned left," said Ravagio.

"By my head," she said, "You're the dupe! I have it in my head that you were talking to them. Go back, and if you catch them, don't give them a minute's quarter."

Ravagio greased his seven-league boots and departed like a desperate man. Our young lovers came out of a wood where they had spent the night. When they perceived him they were equally frightened.

"My Aimée," said the prince, "here comes our enemy. I feel enough courage to fight him; will you not have enough to flee all alone?"

"No," she cried, "I won't abandon you. Cruel man, do you doubt my tenderness, then? But let's not waste a moment; perhaps the wand will be a great help to us. I wish," she said, "in the name of the royal fay Trufio, that the prince might be metamorphosed into a portrait, the camel into a pillar and me into a dwarf.

The change was made, and the dwarf began to sound a horn. Ravagio, who was advancing with great strides, said to him: "Tell me, little abortion of nature, whether you have seen a handsome lad, a young woman and a camel pass this way?"

"I'll tell you," replied the dwarf.[15] "So you're in quest of a genteel damsel, a marvelable lady and their mount? I saw them yesterday at this time, strutting, all cooing and rejoicing; the genteel knight received the spoils of jousts and tournaments that would given in honor or Merlusine, whom you see here, painted in all her resemblance; many proud gentlemen and fine knights broke lances, halberds, helmets and armor there; the conflict was rude and the prize a fine gold clasp accoutered with pearls and diamonds. On departure the unknown lady said to me: 'Dwarf, my friend, without longer parley, I request a gift of you in the name of your most tender friend.' 'If it's to oblige you' I said, 'I'll grant you that on condition that it's in my power.' 'In case you see a great and uncommon giant, who carries an eye in the middle of his forehead, beg him please to go in peace and let us be.' Then she spurred her palfrey and they drew away."

"Which way," said Ravagio.

"As far as that verdant meadowland on the edge of the wood," said the dwarf.

"If you're lying," replied the ogre, "Be assured, filthy midget, that I'll eat you, your pillar and your portrait of Merluche."

"No villainy or fallacy is there in me," said the dwarf, "my mouth is no liar; no living man can find me in fraud; but go quickly if you want to catch them before sunset."

The ogre drew away; the dwarf resumed her own form and touched the portrait and the pillar, which became what they ought to be.

What joy for the lover and his mistress!

"No," said the prince, "I've never felt such sharp alarms, my dear Aimée. As my passion for you takes on new force constantly, my anxieties augment when you're in peril."

---

[15] The dwarf speaks in a bizarre jargon that parodies the language and style of Medieval Romance, with a certain amount of pure gibberish thrown in; I have approximated the meaning, without attempting a similar feat in fake Chaucerian English.

"For myself," she said, "it seems to me that I had little to fear, because Ravagio doesn't eat paintings; I alone was exposed to his fury; my figure was scarcely appetizing, and in any case, I would give my life to conserve yours."

Ravagio ran fruitlessly; he did not find the lover or his mistress; he was dog-tired and he resumed the path to the cavern.

"What! You're coming back without our prisoners!" cried Tourmentine, tearing out her bristly hair. "Don't come near me or I'll strangle you."

"I only encountered," he said, "a dwarf, a pillar and a painting."

"By my head," she continued, "that was them! I'm very foolish to confide the care of my vengeance to you, as if I were too small to take it myself. Well, I'll go get it. I want to boot myself in my turn, and I won't go with less diligence than you."

She put on the seven-league boots and departed.

What means did the prince and princess have of going fast enough to escape those monsters with their accursed seven-league boots? They saw Tourmentine coming, clad in snakeskin whose variegated colors were surprising. She was carrying an iron club of terrible weight over her shoulder, and as she as looking carefully in all directions she would have perceived the prince and princess if they had not been in the heart of a wood.

"The affair is irremediable," said Aimée, weeping. "Here comes the cruel Tourmentine, the sight of whom chills my blood. She's cleverer than Ravagio. If one of the two of us speaks to her, she'll recognize us and commence our trial by eating us. It'll soon be over, as you can believe."

"Amour, Amour," cried the prince, "don't abandon us! Are there under your empire hearts more tender than ours, and fires purer? Oh, my dear Aimée," he continued, taking her hands and kissing them ardently. Are you destined to perish in such a barbaric manner?"

"No," she said, "no; I sense certain stirrings of courage and firmness that reassure me; let's go, little wand, do your duty. I wish in the name of the royal fay Trufio that the camel be a tub, that my dear prince becomes an orange tree therein and that, metamorphosed into a bee, I can fly around him."

As usual, she tapped each of them with three strokes of the wand, and the change was effected soon enough that Tourmentine, who arrived in the place, did not perceive it.

The frightful Megaera was out of breath; she sat down under the orange tree. The bee princess gave herself the pleasure of stinging her in a thousand places; hard as her skin was, she penetrated it, and caused her to cry out. To see her rolling and writhing in the grass, she resembled a bull or a young lion assailed by flies, for the bee as worth a hundred of them. The orange tree prince was dying of the fear that she might be caught and killed.

Eventually, Tourmentine drew away, all bloody, and the princess was about to resume her original form when, unfortunately, travelers passing through the wood, having perceived the ivory wand, which was very characteristic, picked it up and carried it away.

It was hard to imagine a contretemps more disastrous than that one. The prince and the princess had not lost the usage of speech, but that was a feeble aid in the situation in which they found themselves. The prince, overwhelmed by dolor, uttered regrets that sensibly augmented the displeasure of his dear Aimée.

He sometimes cried: "I was approaching the moment when my dear princess was to crown my tenderness; that sweet hope enchanted all my senses. Amour, who works so many marvels, and whose arrows are so powerful, conserve my dear Bee; ensure that her heart does not change, and in spite of the metamorphosis that our misfortune has caused, let her love me until death.

"How unfortunate I am," he continued. "I find myself confined within the bark of a tree; I'm an orange tree; I have no movement; what would become of me if you abandoned me, my dear little bee? But why are you drawing away from me?" he added. "You'll find an agreeable dew in my flowers, and a liquid sweeter than honey; you can nourish yourself on it. My leaves will serve you as a bed of repose, in which you will have nothing to fear from the malice of spiders."

As soon as the orange tree finished its laments, the bee replied to it: "Have no fear that I will ever quit you, Prince; nothing can shake my heart; let nothing agitate you, except the sweet memory of being the victor." She added to that: "Have no fear that I shall ever leave you; neither the lilies, nor the jasmines, nor the roses, nor all the flowers in the most charming flower-bed could make me commit such an infidelity; you will see me flying around you incessantly, and you will know that the orange tree is no less dear to the bee than Prince Aimé was to Princess Aimée."

In fact, she settled into one of the largest flowers, as if in a palace, and the veritable tenderness that finds resources everywhere did not fail to have its own in that union.

The wood in which the orange tree stood served as a promenade for a princess who lived in a magnificent palace; she had youth, beauty and intelligence; her name was Linda. She did not want to marry, because she feared not always being loved by the man she chose as a husband; and as she had great wealth, she had a sumptuous castle built, where she only received ladies and old men, more philosophical than gallant, without permitting any cavaliers to approach her.

The heat of the day having confined her in her apartment for longer than she would have liked, she went out in the evening with all her ladies and went for a walk in the wood. The odor of the orange tree surprised her; she had never seen it before and was charmed to have found it. No one could understand by what hazard they had encountered it in a place like that; it was quickly surrounded by the whole company. Linda forbade anyone to pick a single flower, and it was carried to her garden, to which the faithful bee followed it.

Linda, delighted with its excellent odor, sat beneath it. On the point of going back into the palace she was about to take a few flowers when the vigilant bee emerged, buzzing, from beneath the leaves where she was standing sentinel, and stung the princess with such force that she nearly fainted. There was no further question of despoiling the orange tree of its flowers. Linda returned home very ill.

When the prince could speak freely to Aimée, he said: "What chagrin has gripped you, my dear bee, against young Linda? You stung her cruelly."

"Can you ask me such a question?" she replied. "Are you not sufficiently delicate to understand that you ought only to have sweet things for me; that everything that is you belongs to me, and that I am defending my property when I defend your flowers?"

"But you see them fall without pain," he said. "Isn't it irrelevant to you if the princess adorns herself with them, whether she puts them in her hair or on her bosom?"

"No," said the bee, in a rather bitter tone, "it isn't irrelevant to me. I know ingrate, that you're more touched by her than by me. There's such a great difference between a polite person, richly dressed, who holds a considerable rank, and unfortunate princess that you've seen clad in a tiger-skin in the midst of several monsters, who have only given her harsh and barbaric manners, and whose beauty is too mediocre to arrest you."

She wept at that point, to the extent that a bee is capable of producing tears; a few flowers of the amorous orange tree were moistened by them, and his displeasure at having caused his princess chagrin went so far that some of his leaves turned yellow, several branches dried out and he nearly died of it.

"What have I done, beautiful Bee?" he cried. "What have I done to attract your anger to me? Oh, you doubtless want to abandon me; you are already weary of being attached to an unfortunate like me!"

The night passed in reproaches, but at daybreak an obliging zephyr, who had been listening to them, obliged them to make up; he could not have rendered them a more agreeable service.

Meanwhile, Linda, who was dying of the desire to have a bouquet of orange blossom, got up early in the morning; she went down into her flower garden in order to pick some. As she reached out her hand, however, she felt herself stung so violently by the jealous bee that her courage failed her. She went back to her room in a very bad mood. "I don't understand what it is with the tree we found," she said, "but as soon as I try to take the smallest bud, the insects guarding it penetrate me with their stings."

One of her maids, who had wit and was very cheerful, said to her, laughing, "My advice Madame, is that you arm yourself like an amazon, and, following the example of Jason when he went to conquer the Golden Fleece, you go courageously to pick the most beautiful flowers from the pretty tree."

Linda found something amusing in that idea, and immediately equipped herself with a hat covered with feathers, a light breastplate, and gauntlets; to the sound of trumpets, drums, fifes and oboes she went into her garden, followed by all her ladies, who were armored likewise, and who called that fête the war of the insects and the amazons. Linda drew her sword with a very good grace; then, striking the most beautiful branch of the orange tree, she cried: "Appear, terrible bees; I've come to challenge you; are you valiant enough to defend the one you love?"

But what became of Linda, and all those accompanying her, when they heard emerging from the trunk of the orange tree a pitiful: "Alas!" followed by a profound sigh, and they saw blood flowing from the cut branch.

"Heavens!" she cried. "What have I done? What a prodigy!"

She took the bloody branch and attempted, in vain, to reconnect it. She felt herself gripped by terrible fear and anxiety.

The poor little bee, in despair at her dear orange tree's disastrous adventure, thought of appearing in order to seek death in the point of the fatal sword, wanting to avenge her dear prince, but she preferred to live for him; and, thinking of the remedy that he needed, she implored him to allow her to fly to Araby for balm.

In fact, after he had consented to that and they had said a tender and touching adieu, she flew to that part of the world, guided solely by instinct—although, to be more accurate, it was Amour who led her there, and as he flies more rapidly than the most diligent insects, he furnished her with the means of making that great voyage promptly.

She brought back the marvelous balm on her wings and on the tips of her little feet, with which she cured her prince. It is true that that was due less to the excellence of the balm than the pleasure he had in seeing the bee princess take so much care over his misfortune. She put that balm on him every day, and he had great need of it, for the cut branch was one of his fingers, with the consequence that if he had been further mal-treated in the way that Linda had done, he might have re-mained devoid of arms and legs.

How sharply the bee felt the suffering of the orange tree! She reproached herself for having been the cause of it by vir-tue of the urgency she had had to defend his flowers.

Linda, frightened by what she had seen, no longer slept or ate. In the end she decided to end someone in search of fays, in order to try to clarify a matter that seemed to her to be so extraordinary. She dispatched ambassadors, and charged them with great presents, in order to invite them to her court.

Among those who arrived at her court. Queen Trufio was one of the first. There had never been anyone more knowl-edgeable in the art of faerie. She examined the branch and the orange tree; she smelled its flowers and detected a human odor that surprised her. She did not neglect any conjurations, and made such forceful ones that suddenly, the orange tree disap-peared, and a prince was seen, more handsome and better made than any other.

At that sight, Linda remained immobile; she was struck with admiration, and something so particular, for him, that she had already lost her initial indifference when the young prince, occupied with his lovable bee, threw himself at Trufio's feet.

"Great Queen," he said, "I owe you an infinite debt; you have rendered me the usage of life by returning me to my original form; but if you want me to owe you my repose, my joy, and, in sum, more than the daylight to which you have recalled me, render me my princess."

As he finished speaking, he took the little bee, on which he still had his eyes.

"You shall be content," replied the generous Trufio. She recommenced her ceremonies, and Princess Aimée appeared, with all her charms, and there was not one of the ladies who was not moved to envy.

Linda hesitated in her heart as to whether she ought to feel joy or chagrin at such an extraordinary adventure, and particularly the metamorphosis of the bee. In the end, reason prevailed over a passion that was still only nascent. She gave Aimée a thousand caresses, and Trufio begged her to relate her adventures. She had too much obligation to the fay to defer what she wanted of her. The grace and fine manner with which she spoke interested the entire assembly, and when she told Trufio that she had performed so many marvels by means of the virtue of her name and her wand, a cry of joy went up in the room, and every begged the fay to complete that great work.

For her part, Trufio felt an extreme pleasure in everything she heard; she hugged the princess tightly in her arms "Since I have been useful to you without knowing it," she said to her, "Judge, charming Aimée, now that I know you, what I can do for your service. I am a friend of the king, your father, and the queen, your mother. Let us go promptly, in my flying chariot, to the Fortunate Isle, where you will be received as you both merit.

Linda begged them to stay for one day with her while she made them rich presents, and Princess Aimée quit her tiger skin in order to put on clothes of an incomparable beauty.

Understand, now, the joy of our tender lovers; yes, understand it, if possible; but it is necessary for that to have suffered similar misfortunes, to have been among ogres and to have been metamorphosed so many times.

Finally, they departed. Trufio conducted them through the air to the Fortunate Isle. They were received by the king and the queen as the persons they least expected to see again in all the world, and whom they saw again with great satisfaction. The beauty and goodness of Aimée, combined with her intelligence, won her the admiration of her century. Her dear mother loved her recklessly. The great qualities of Prince Aimé charmed no less than his good looks.

Their marriage took place. Nothing has ever been so pompous; the Graces came in their festival costumes; the Amours were there without even having been invited; and by an express order on their part, the eldest son of the prince and princess was named Faithful Amour.

Many other titles were added to that one subsequently, and under all those different titles it is difficult to recover the one born of that charming marriage. Fortunate is the person who encounters it without being misled.

With a tender lover, alone in the middle of woods,
Aimée had at all times an extreme sagacity;
She always listened to the voice of reason,
And conserved the tenderness of her lover.
Beauties, do not believe that to capture hearts,
Pleasures are necessary;
Amour is often extinguished in the midst of favors.
Be proud, be severe,
And you will inspire eternal ardors.

THE GOOD LITTLE MOUSE

There was once a king and a queen who loved one another so much that they made one another's felicity. Their hearts and their sentiments were always in intelligence. They went hunting every day in order to kill hares and red deer; they went fishing in order to catch sole and carp; they went to balls, in order to dance the bourrée and the pavane; they went to great feasts in order to eat roast meats and sugared almonds; and they went to comedies and operas. They laughed, they sang, they did a thousand things to amuse themselves. In sum, it was the happiest of all times. Their subjects followed the example of the king and the queen; they amused themselves in competition with one another. For all those reasons, the country was known as the Land of Joy.

It happened that a neighboring king of King Joyeux lived very differently. He was a declared enemy of pleasures; he only asked for wounds and humps. He had a sullen face, a great beard and sunken eyes; he was thin and stiff, always dressed in black, and his hair was bristling, greasy and dirty. To please him it was necessary to attack and kill passers-by. He hanged criminals personally; he rejoiced in doing them harm. When a good mother loved her little girl or her little boy very much he sent for her and broke their arm or wrung their neck in front of her. His kingdom was known as the Land of Tears.

The evil king heard mention of the satisfaction of King Joyeux. He envied him greatly, and resolved to raise a large army and go and beat him, personally, until he was dead or very ill. He send envoys in all directions to amass men and arms; he had cannons made. Everyone trembled. They said: "Whatever the evil king throws himself into, he'll give no quarter."

When everything was ready he advanced toward the realm of King Joyeux. At that bad news he promptly put himself on the defensive; the queen was dying of fear, and said to him, weeping: "Sire, it's necessary for us to flee; let's try to raise lots of money, and we'll go as far as the earth can take us."

The king replied: "Fie. Madame; I have too much courage; it's better to die than to be a poltroon." He gathered all his men-at-arms, bid the queen a tender adieu, mounted a beautiful horse and departed.

When he was lost to sight she started weeping dolorously and, putting her hands together, she said: "I'm pregnant, alas; if the king is killed in this war I'll be a widow and a prisoner; the evil king will cause me ten thousand woes. That thought prevented her from eating and sleeping.

The king wrote to her every day, but one morning, she saw a courier coming who was riding with all his might. She called to him: "Ho, courier, what news?"

"The king is dead," he shouted. The battle is lost; the evil king will arrive imminently."

The poor queen fell in a faint; she was carried to her bed, and all the ladies around her were weeping, one for her father, another for her son; they were tearing their hair; it was the most pitiful thing in the world."

Suddenly, they heard: "Murder! Thieves!" It was the evil king who was arriving with all his evil subjects; they were killing, for any or no reason, everyone they encountered. He entered into the king's house fully armed and went up to the queen's chamber. When she saw him come in she was so greatly afraid that she plunged into her bed and pulled the covers over her head. He called her two or three times, but she did not say a word. He became annoyed—very annoyed—and said: "I believe you're mocking me; do you know that I can cut your throat right now?"

He uncovered her and tore off her head-dress; her beautiful hair fell over her shoulders. He wound it around his hand two or three times and loaded her on to his back like a sack of wheat; he carried her away like that and mounted his huge horse, which was all black. She begged him to have pity on her; he mocked her, and said: "Cry, lament; that makes me laugh and amuses me."

He took her to his homeland and swore throughout the journey that he had resolved to hang her, but he was told that that would be a pity, and that she was pregnant.

When he knew that, it came into his mind that if she gave birth to a girl he could marry her to his son, and in order to know whether she would, he sent for a fay who lived in the vicinity of his realm. When she came he regaled her better than was his custom; then he took her to a tower, at the top of which the poor queen had a very small and poorly-furnished room. She was lying on the floor, on a mattress that was not worth two sols, where she wept day and night.

One seeing her, the fay was moved; she curtseyed to her and whispered as she embraced her: "Have courage Madame, your misfortunes will end; I hope to contribute to that."

Slightly consoled by those words, the queen caressed her and begged her to have pity on a poor princess who had enjoyed great fortune and who was now very far from it.

They were talking to one another when the evil king said: "Come on, not so many compliments; I brought you here to tell me whether this slave is pregnant with a boy or a girl."

The fay replied: "She is pregnant with a girl, who will be the most beautiful and best-formed princess that has ever been seen; she will wish thereafter for infinite wealth and honors."

"If she isn't beautiful and well-formed," said the evil king, "I'll hang her from her mother's neck and the mother from a tree, without anything being able to prevent me."

After that he went out with the fay, and did not look at the good queen, who was weeping bitterly, for she was saying to herself: *Alas, what can I do? If I have a beautiful little girl he'll give her to his ape of a son, and if she's ugly, he'll hang the pair of us. To what extremity am I reduced? Could I not hide her somewhere, in order that he never sees her?*

The time when the little princess was due to come into the world drew nearer, and the queen's anxieties augmented. She had no one with whom to lament and to console her. The jailer who guarded her only gave her three peas boiled in water for the whole day, with a small piece of black bread. She became thinner than a herring; she was no more than skin and bone.

One evening, when she was spinning—for the evil king was very miserly and made her work day and night—she saw a little mouse, which as very pretty, come in through a hole. She said to herself: "Alas, my little one, what have you come to search for here? I only have three peas for my whole day; if you don't want to fast, go away."

The little mouse ran here and there, and danced and capered like a little monkey, and the queen had such a great pleasure in watching it that she gave it the single pea that remained for her supper.

"Here, little one," she said, "eat; I don't have any more, and I give it to you with a good heart.

As soon as she had done that she saw an excellent grouse on the table, cooked marvelously, and two pots of jam.

"In truth," she said, "a benefit is never lost." She ate a little, but her appetite was gone, after so much fasting. She threw a bonbon to the mouse, which nibbled it, and then began leaping better than before the supper.

Early the following morning the jailer brought the three peas for the queen, which he had put on a large plate in order to mock her; the little mouse came quietly and ate all three, and the bread too. When the queen wanted to eat, she no longer found anything, and became very annoyed with the mouse.

"It's a nasty little beast," she said. "If it carries on, I'll die of hunger."

As she tried to cover up the big plate, which was empty, she found all sorts of good things to eat inside; she was very glad, and ate, but as she ate it came to her mind that the evil king would perhaps kill her child in two or three days, and she left the table in order to weep. Then, raising her eyes to Heaven, she said: "What! Is there no means of salvation?"

As she spoke, she saw the little mouse playing with long pieces of straw; she took them and commenced work. *If I have enough straw,* she thought, *I'll make a covered basket in which to put my little girl, and I'll give her through the window to the first charitable person who wants to take care of her.*

She started to work with good courage, therefore. There was no lack of straw; the mouse always dragged it into the chamber, where it continued to leap, and at meal times, the queen gave it her three peas and found in exchange all kinds of cooked food. She was quite astonished by that, and wondered incessantly who could be sending her such excellent things.

The queen looked out of the window one day to see how long she needed to make the cord to which she would have to attach the basket in order to lower it. Down below she saw a little old woman who was leaning on a stick and who said to her: "I know your trouble, Madame. If you wish, I'll serve you."

"Alas, my dear friend," the queen said to her, "You'd give me great pleasure. Come to the base of the tower every evening; I'll lower my poor child down to you. You can nurse her, and I'll try, if I'm ever rich, to repay you."

"I'm not self-interested," replied the old woman, "But I'm greedy. There's nothing I like as much as a nice plump mouse. If you find any in your attic, kill them and throw them down to me. I won't be ingrate; your baby will be well-off."

Hearing that, the queen started weeping, without making any response, and the old woman, after waiting a while, asked her why she was weeping.

"It's because there's only one mouse in my chamber," she said, "which is so pretty, and so amusing, that I can't resolve to kill it."

"What!" sad the old woman, angrily. "You like a hussy of a little mouse, which nibbles everything, better than a child you're going to have? Well, Madame, you don't have to lament; stay with such good company, I'll have plenty of mice without you. I don't care." She went away, muttering and grumbling.

Although the queen had a good meal and the mouse came to dance for her, she never raised her eyes from the floor, to which she had attached her gaze, and tears ran down her cheeks.

That same night she gave birth to a princess, who was a miracle of beauty; instead of crying like other babies she laughed at her good Maman and held out her little hands, as if she were very reasonable. The queen caressed her and kissed her with all her heart, thinking, sadly: *Poor darling! Dear child! If you fall into the hands of the evil king, that's it for your life.* She enclosed her in the basket with a note attached to her swaddling cloth, on which was written: *This unfortunate little girl is named Joliette.*

When she had left her for a moment without looking at her she opened the basket again, and found her embellished. Then she kissed her and wept more forcefully, not knowing what to do.

But now the little mouse came, and got into the basket with Joliette. "Oh, little beastie," said the queen, "how dearly you cost me to save your life. Perhaps I shall lose my dear Joliette; someone other than me would have killed you and given you to the old glutton; I couldn't consent to that."

The mouse commenced speaking: "Don't repent of it, Madame; I'm not as unworthy of your amity as you believe."

The queen was mortally afraid on hearing the mouse speak, but her fear augmented when she perceived its little muzzle take one the form of a face and its little paws become hands and feet, and it suddenly grew. Finally, the queen, almost not daring to look, recognized her as the fay who had come to see her with the evil king and had made her so many caresses.

She said to her: "I wanted to test your heart; I've recognized that it's good, and that you're capable of amity. We fays, who possess treasures and immense riches, seek the pleasure of life in amity, and we rarely find it."

"Is it possible, beautiful lady," said the queen, embracing her, "that you have difficulty finding friends, being so rich and powerful?"

"Yes," she replied, "for people only love us out of interest, and that scarcely touches us; but when you loved me as a little mouse, it was not for an interested motive. I wanted to test you more rigorously; I took the form of an old woman; it was me who spoke to you from the bottom of the tower, and you were still faithful to me."

With those words she embraced the queen; then she kissed the little princess three times and said: "I endow you, my daughter, with being the consolation of your mother, and richer than your father; with living for a hundred years, always beautiful, devoid of malady, wrinkles and decrepitude."

The delighted queen thanked her and begged her to take Joliette away and take care of her, adding that she gave her to her to be her daughter.

The fay accepted that, and thanked her; she put the baby in the basket and lowered it to the ground, but, having paused for a moment to resume the form of a mouse, when she went down the cord herself she no longer found the child, and came back up, very frightened.

"All is lost," she said to the queen. "My enemy Cancaline has just abducted the princess. It is necessary for you to know that she is a cruel fay who hates me, and, unfortunately, being older than me, she has more power than me. I have no means of extracting Joliette from her vile claws."

When the queen heard such sad news she nearly died of dolor; she wept abundantly, and begged her good friend to try to get the child back, no matter what the cost.

When the jailer came into the queen's room he saw that she was no longer pregnant; he went to tell the king, who came running to demand the child from her, but she said that a fay whose name she did not know have come to take her by force. The evil king stamped his feet and bit his fingernails to the quick.

"I promised to hang you," he said. "I shall keep my word right away."

He dragged the queen to a wood, climbed a tree, and was about to hang her when the fay, who had rendered herself invisible, shoved him rudely. She caused him to fall from the top of the tree; he broke four teeth. While someone tried to refit them, the fay took the queen away in her flying chariot and took her to a beautiful castle. She took great care of her, and if the queen had had Princess Joliette she would have been content, but they could not discover where Cancaline had put her, even though the little mouse did everything she could.

In the end, time passed and the queen's great affliction diminished. Fifteen years had already passed when they heard it said that the son of the evil king was to marry the girl who looked after his turkeys, and that the young woman did not want to do it. It was very surprising that a turkey-girl was refusing to be a queen, but the wedding dress was made and there was a fine wedding to which people came from a hundred leagues around. The little mouse transported herself there; she wanted to see the turkey-girl at her ease.

She went into the poultry-yard and found her there dressed in coarse cloth, barefoot, with a greasy rag on her head. There were garments of gold and silver there, diamonds, pearls ribbons and lace, trailing in the dirt; the turkeys were wandering over them, shitting on them and spoiling them. The turkey-girl was sitting on a large stone.

The king's son, who had a twisted spine, was one-eyed, and lame, said to her rudely: "If you refuse me your heart, I'll kill you."

She replied, proudly: "I won't marry you, you're too ugly and you resemble your cruel father. Leave me in peace with my turkey chicks; I love them more than all your braveries."

The little mouse looked at her in admiration, for she was as beautiful as the sun. As soon as the son of the evil king had gone out, the fay adopted the form of an old shepherdess and said to her: "Good day, my little one; your turkeys are in a good state."

The young turkey-minder looked at the old woman with eyes full of kindness and said to her: "They want me to quit them for an evil crown. What would you advise me to do?"

"A crown is very beautiful, my girl," said the fay. "You won't know the price or the weight of it."

"But yes, I know it," the turkey-girl retorted, immediately, "since I refuse to submit to it. I don't know who I am, though, neither where my father is nor where my mother is. I find myself without relatives and without friends."

"You have beauty and virtue, my child," said the sage fay, "which are worth more than ten kingdoms. Tell me, I beg you, who put you here, since you have no mother or father, relatives or friends?"

"A fay named Cancaline is the reason why I came here. She hated me; she beat me without cause or reason. I fled her one day without knowing where I was going and stopped in a wood. The son of the evil king was walking there, and he asked me whether I wanted to serve in his poultry-yard. I accepted, and I took care of his turkeys. He came to see them all the time, and saw me too. Alas, without my having any desire for it, he came to love me so much that it importunes me greatly."

At that story, the fay began to believe that the turkey-girl was Princess Joliette. She said to her: "My daughter, will you tell me your name?"

"My name is Joliette, if you please."

At that word the fay no longer doubted the truth, and, throwing her arms around her, she nearly devoured her with caresses; then she said to her: "Joliette, I knew you a long time ago; I'm very glad that you are so sage and so well-formed, but I want you to be much cleaner, for you resemble a little ragamuffin. Pick up those beautiful clothes and put them on.

Joliette, who was very obedient, immediately took of the dirty rag she had on her head and shook her hair, which was as blonde as a basin and as loose as gold thread, so that it covered her, falling in curls all the way to the ground. Then, taking in her delicate hands the water of a spring that flowed next to the poultry yard, she wiped the mud off her face, which became as bright as an oriental peal. It seemed that roses were blooming on her cheeks and mouth; her sweet beneath was scented with wild thyme; her body was straighter than a rush; in winter, one might have mistaken her skin for snow, in summer for lilies.

When she was ornamented by diamonds and beautiful garments, the fay considered her like a marvel. She said: "Who do you believe yourself to be, my dear Joliette, for you're very brave?"

She replied: "In truth, it seems to me that I'm the daughter of some great king."

"And would you be glad if you were," said the fay.

"Yes, my good mother," replied Joliette, making a curtsey. "I'd be very glad if I were."

"Well," said the fay, "be content, then. I'll tell you more tomorrow."

She returned diligently to her beautiful castle, where the queen was occupied in spinning silk.

The little mouse cried to her: "Would you like to bet your distaff and spindle, Madame, that I'm bringing you the best news that you've ever heard?"

"Alas," replied the queen, "since the death of King Joyeux and the loss of my Joliette, I'd give all the news in the world for a pin."

"There, there, don't get upset," said the fay. "The princess in marvelously well; I've just seen her. She's so beautiful, so beautiful that she only lacks being a queen."

She told her the whole story, from beginning to end, and the queen wept with joy to know that her daughter was so beautiful, and with sadness to know that she was a turkey-girl. "When we were great monarchs in our realm," she said, "and we had such a good time, the poor deceased king and me, we wouldn't have believed that we'd see our daughter become a turkey-girl."

"It's the cruel Cancaline," added the fay, "who, knowing that I love you, in order to spite me, has put her in that estate, but she'll get out of it or I'll burn my books."

"I don't want her to marry the son of the evil king," said the queen. "Let's go find her tomorrow, and bring her here."

Now, it happened that the son of the evil king, being utterly vexed against Joliette, was sitting under a tree, where he was weeping so forcefully, so forcefully that he was howling. His father heard him; he went to the window and shouted: "What do you have to weep about? How stupid you are!"

He replied: "It's because our turkey-girl doesn't want to love me."

"What!" said the evil king. "She doesn't want to love you? I'll make her love you, or she'll die." He called his men-at-arms and said to them: "Go and fetch her. I'll do her so much harm that she'll repent of being stubborn."

They went to the poultry-yard and found Joliette, who was wearing a beautiful robe of white satin with gold embroidery, red diamonds, and more than a thousand aunes of ribbons everywhere. Never, never ever, had such a beautiful young woman been seen. They dared not speak to her, taking her for a princess.

She said to them, very civilly: "Tell me, pray, whom you are seeking here."

"Madame," they said, "We're looking for a little wretch called Joliette."

"Alas, that's me," she said. "What do you want with me?"

They seized her immediately and bound her hands and feet with thick cords for fear that she might flee. They took her in that fashion to the evil king, who was with his son.

When he saw her so beautiful he could not help being a little moved; doubtless she would have made him feel pity if he had not been the most evil and cruel person in the world. He said to her: "Ha ha, little hussy, little toad, so you don't want to love my son? He's a hundred times more beautiful than you; a single one of his glances is worth more than your entire person. Let's go, love him right way, or I'll have you flayed."

The princess, trembling like a little pigeon, knelt down before him and said: "Sire, I beg you not to flay me; give me a day or two to think about what I ought to do, and then you'll be the master."

His son, in despair, did not want her to be flayed. They agreed together to lock her in a tower where she would not even see the sun.

With that, the fay arrived in her flying chariot with the queen; they learned all that news. Immediately, the queen started weeping bitterly, saying that she was always unfortunate, and that she would rather her daughter were dead than marry the son of the evil king. The fay said: "Have courage; I'll fatigue them so much that you'll be content, and avenged."

As the wicked king was going to bed that fay became a little mouse and burrowed under the bed-head. As soon as he tried to go to sleep she bit his ear; he became very annoyed. He turned on his other side, and she bit his other ear. He cried murder and called for someone to come; they came and found the two bitten ears, which were bleeding so copiously that they could not stem the blood. While they were searching everywhere for the mouse she did the same to the evil king's son. He summoned his servants and showed them his ears, which were entirely skinned; they put plasters on them.

The little mouse returned to the bedroom of the evil king, who was a little drowsy. She bit his nose and started gnawing it. He put his hands to it and she bit and scratched them. He cried: "Mercy!" and "I'm doomed!" She slipped into his mouth and nibbled his tongue, his lips and his cheeks. People came in and saw him in a frightful state, almost unable to speak, because his tongue hurt so much. He made a sign that it was a mouse; they searched the mattress, the bed-head and the little corners, but she was already no longer there.

She ran to do worse to the son, and ate his good eye, for he was already one-eyed. He got up like a furious madman and drew his sword. He was blind. He ran to his father's bedroom; he also had his sword in his hand, storming and swearing that he would kill everyone if they did not catch the mouse.

When the king saw his son so desperate, he scolded him, but the latter, who had his ears in plaster, did not recognize his father's voice; he threw himself upon him. The evil king, very angry, struck him a great blow with his sword, and received another. They both fell to the floor, bleeding like oxen.

All their subjects, who hated them mortally and only served them out of fear, no longer fearing them, tied ropes to their feet and dragged them to the river, saying that they would be very glad to be rid of them.

So there was the evil king dead, and his son with him. The good fay, who knew that, went in quest of the queen; they went to the black tower, where Joliette was locked up under more than forty keys. The fay tapped the thick door three times with a little hazel wand, which opened, and the others did likewise. They found the poor princess very sad, who did not say a single word.

The queen threw her arms round her neck. "My dear darling," she said to her, I'm your Mama, Queen Joyeux." She told her the story of her life.

O good God! When Joliette heard such good news, it would not have taken much for her to die of pleasure. She threw herself at the queen's feet, embraced her knees, moistened her hands with her tears and kissed her a thousand times. She caressed the fay tenderly, who had brought her baskets full of priceless jewels, gold and diamonds, which she set before her. "Let's not amuse ourselves," said the fay. "We need a *coup-d'état*; let's go into the great hall of the castle to harangue the people."

She took the lead, with a grave and serious visage, clad in a robe with a train more than ten aunes long, and the queen another, of blue velvet embroidered with gold, with an even longer train. They had bought their beautiful clothes with them. They all had crowns on their heads, which shone like suns. Princess Joliette followed them, with her beauty and her modesty, which were nothing short of marvelous. They bowed to all those they encountered on the way, to the petty as well as the great. Everyone followed them, eager to know who the beautiful ladies were.

When the hall was full, the good fay told the subjects of the evil king that she wanted to give them for a queen the daughter of King Joyeux, whom they saw; that they would live content under her empire; that if they accepted her, she would find her a husband as perfect as she was, who would always be laughing and who would chase away the melancholy in all hearts,

At those words, everyone cried: "Yes, yes, we want that very much; we've been sad and miserable for too long." At the same time, a hundred sorts of instruments played on all sides; everyone joined hands and danced around the queen, her daughter and the good fay, singing: "Yes, yes, we want that very much."

That was how they were received. No joy has ever equaled it. People sat down at table, they ate, they drank, and then they went to bed to sleep well.

When the young princess woke up, the fay presented to her the most handsome prince who had ever seen the light of day. She had gone in quest of him in the flying chariot, all the way to the end of the earth; he was as lovable as Joliette. As soon as she saw him, she loved him. For his part, he was charmed. As for the queen, she was transported by joy. An admirable meal and marvelous clothes were prepared. The marriage was held with infinite rejoicing.

> *That unfortunate princess,*
> *Whose misfortunes you have just seen,*
> *Abandoned in her prison,*
> *Had experience the rigors of a cruel destiny;*
> *She had mourned since her birth.*
> *Joliette was exposed to death,*
> *If her just recognition*
> *Had not interested in her fate*

That prudent and sage fay,
Who, by a generous effort,
When the queen was menaced by the great peril,
Was able to guide her to port.
All this is nothing but a fable,
Made to amuse whoever reads it;
Nevertheless one will find there
A veritable moral.
To whomsoever does you a favor
Show a grateful soul;
It is the most powerful virtue
To touch and win the heart.

TALES OF THE FAYS

After having experienced all that a long winter has of the most rigorous, the return of the fine season invited several persons of intelligence and good taste to go to Saint-Cloud.[16] Everything there was admired, everything there was praised. Madame D***, who had wearied more rapidly than the rest of the company, went to sit down on the edge of a spring.

"Leave me here," she said. "Perhaps some sylvan or dryad will not disdain to converse with me." Everyone made war on her indolence, but the impatience to see the thousand beautiful things that were offered to their eyes prevailed over the desire they had to stay with her.

"As the conversation you are meditating with the guests of these woods," Monsieur de Saint-P*** said to her, "I will give you *Tales of the Fays*, which will occupy you agreeably."

"It's necessary that I don't have them written," Madame D*** replied, "to allow me at least to anticipate the graces of novelty; but leave me here without scruple; I shall not be idle."

She continued her entreaties in that regard in such a pressing manner that the charming troop drew away.

After having wandered everywhere, they returned to the somber pathway where Madame D*** was waiting for them.

"Ha! You've missed out," exclaimed the Comtesse de F***, approaching her, "What we've just seen is marvelous."

"What has just happened to me," she said, "is no less so. Know that as I was casting my eyes in all directions to distinguish a thousand different objects that I admired, I suddenly

---

[16] The Château de Saint-Cloud, which had been the Hôtel d'Aunay until it was expended in the sixteenth century, was owned in 1697 by Louis XIV's brother Philippe, Duc d'Orléans, the father of the similarly-named future regent.

saw a young nymph nearby, whose soft and shining eyes, cheerful and witty air and gracious and polite manners caused me so much satisfaction as surprise. The light robe that covered her allowed the proportion of her figure to be seen; a knotted ribbon arrested the tresses of her hair at her waist; the regularity of her features had nothing that was not pleasurable.

"I was about to speak to her when she interrupted me with these lines:

When an august prince inhabits this abode,
This superb palace and these tranquil gardens,
Often, from his tranquil court,
Are agreeable refuges,
In everything that is offered to your eyes,
Is there anything that should surprise?
Ought one not to expect
To see so many treasures enrich this beautiful place?
Rhea's fortunate days are made to reign here,
Chagrins fear to enter it,
They are forever banished.
Innocence, games, pleasures and laughter
Reign everywhere in their stead;
These charming arbors and florid beds
Do not fear the effort of the icy season.
See how serene the sky is;
No importunate cloud ever
Covers the face of the sun here,
Countless colors of Flora embellish its bosom;
See what a vivid verdure
Heightens the color so many lovely flowers.
Listen to the birds in these enchanted woods
See in these fertile plains
Those peaceful flocks wandering,
And the springs snaking through flowery meadows;
See these waters bounding to the skies,
Those noisy cascades in the depths of valley,
These tenebrous promenades

With which all the woods are embellished.
The shepherds are more polite here,
The shepherdesses more gracious.
One ceases to boast on seeing these beautiful places,
Of the delectable retreats
That the gods once inhabited,
In the bosom of a durable peace.
Here reigns majesty;
Here, from an agreeable bounty,
Grandeur is inseparable.
But nothing entirely admirable
Comes here to strike my eyes,
Except the incomparable princess
For whom this place is embellished.

"The nymph of Saint-Cloud was as little weary of speaking as I was of listening," Madame D*** continued, "when she seemed to me to be troubled by the noise you were making as you approached. 'Adieu,' she said to me. 'I thought you were alone, but since you are in company, I will see you another time.' As she said that, she disappeared. I confess that I was not overly sorry to see you approaching, for I was beginning to be frightened by such an adventure."

"You are very fortunate," exclaimed the Marquise de ****, "to be in such agreeable commerce, sometimes with the Muses, sometimes with the fays; you cannot be bored, and if I knew as many tales as you, I would think myself a very great lady."

"They are treasures," replied Madame D***, "with which one ordinarily lacks many necessary things; all my good friends the fays have been scarcely prodigal with their favors thus far; I also assure you that I have resolved to neglect them, as they neglect me."

"Ha, Madame," said the Comtesse de F***, interrupting her. "I ask you for mercy for them; you still owe us some of their adventures; this is a place entirely appropriate to tell us about them, and people have never listened to you with more attention than they will today.

"It seems," said Madame D***, that I have divined a part of what you want. Here is a notebook all ready to read to you, and to render it more agreeable I have combined a Spanish novella with it, which is quite true, and of which I know the original."

DON GABRIEL PONCE DE LEON

Don Félix Sarmiento was a man of quality and merit in the kingdom of Galicia. He had married Doña Henrica de Palacios, whose house was no less noble than his own. He had of that marriage a well-made and very honest son named Don Luis, and two daughters so perfect that, for intelligence and beauty, nothing to equal them had been seen in the province.

The virtue and merit of their mother had rendered her commendable to everyone; she was surprised in one of her lands by a malady so prompt and so violent that she scarcely had time to send someone in quest of her sister-in-law in order to put her daughters in her hands.

"There has never been a deposit as dear as the one I am confiding to you," she said to her, "but, my dear sister, promise me that my daughters will rediscover with you all that they are losing in losing me. Love Isidore and Melanie for love of me and for love of them; they have an excellent nature; cultivate it. I promised myself to neglect nothing for their education, but alas, it is necessary for us to separate."

She was interrupted at that point by the tears and sobs of those lovable individuals. Each of them on her knees beside her bed, holding her hands and dissolving in tears, they kissed her with so much respect and love that it seemed they could do no more in being separated from her.

"What, my dear daughters," she said to them, "you're seeking to soften my heart? It seems that you want to make me regret a life that I'm on the point of leaving on the orders of

Providence. Far from enfeebling me, encourage me." Addressing Doña Juana, she went on: "My sister, I beg you not to put them on stage too soon in the theater of society; there are so many things to be feared there, so may charms, it is so dangerous that it requires a great deal of intelligence and reason to know it and to defend oneself from it."

Doña Juana was an old spinster, more severe than all the duennas in Spain put together; she was delighted to hear the last will of her sister-in-law, and without responding to everything tender she had said, she exclaimed: "I swear to you that your daughters will not even have the liberty to see the sun; I shall protect them so well that no one will know that they are in the world; since you are putting them in my charge, I shall be a thousand times more severe with them than you would have been."

A great weakness by which the invalid as overtaken prevented her from replying and moderating such harsh resolutions; her daughters were too occupied with their grief to hear what their aunt said, and nearly died with their mother.

After having rendered her the last duties, Doña Juana took them to a country house near Compostela, which belonged to their father. At that time he was commanding a Spanish contingent in Flanders. He learned of his wife's death and the disposition she had made of his daughters; he was much afflicted by the former and scarcely content with the latter, for he knew his sister's character; her harsh, inflexible and suspicious mind caused him to foresee that his daughters would find a great difference between their mother's conduct and their aunt's. As he was far away, however, and his daughters were young and beautiful, after having examined whether it might not be better to put them in a convent, he decided to leave them with Doña Juana.

Their brother was in Cadiz when he received the news of his mother's death; he took the mail-coach and came to mingle his tears with those of his sisters. I have already said that he was a very honest and well-made young man; his presence soothed the bitterness of their grief in some measure, for there was a narrow union between them.

As soon as they were able to talk in private, they told him that Doña Juana was very ill-humored, that everything displeased her, that she never went out, that she never wanted to see anyone, that she was always grumbling, and that they had strong reasons for regretting the loss they had suffered.

"It's true," said Don Luis, "that Doña Juana has merit and virtue, but it's not a sociable virtue, nor an easy merit. As she is neither beautiful nor young, and has never inspired tender sentiments, she can't suffer anyone taking the most innocent liberty before her. I fear that in the end, she'll become jealous of the daylight that illuminates you, since she has already told me that she will only allow you to go out very rarely, and that, when she is unable to dispense with it, it will be under so many precautions that it will be impossible to see you."

"I assure you, my brother," said Isidore, "that she can follow all her caprices in that regard without my opposing them; I have nothing in my heart that engages me in the commerce of society that she fears so much, and providing that she treats me more gently, I shall be content."

"As for me," added Melanie, "I leave the field free for her; I have not yet seen anyone sufficiently amiable for me to regret seeing anyone."

Don Luis consoled them as best he could: he sent for agreeable books to occupy them, and after staying with them for a month he quit them in order to return to Cadiz, to which his affairs and pleasures recalled him.

He had several friends there who had already perceived his absence, and everyone was wising for his return, but Gabriel Ponce de Leon and Count d'Aguilar, his cousin, testified more eagerness than the others. They sent someone to his house every day, and he had not been back an hour before they came to see him.

The first moments of their conversation were sad, because Don Luis told them about the death of his mother. Moving on then to his sisters he told them about the severity with which Doña Juana was protecting them, that they were beginning to find it tedious, and that it was a pity that his aunt was treating them in that fashion, because they were very amiable. He spoke about their merit with the sincerity of an honest man rather than the modesty of a brother, and the portrait he made of them could not have been more advantageous.

Ponce de Leon refrained from indicating to Don Luis the attention that he paid to his discourse, and suddenly changed the subject. "I'm surprised," he said, "that you have not yet asked me for news of the beautiful Lucile."

"You can believe," replied Don Luis, "that it is not out of indifference. My sentiments for her are too vivid and too affirmed to change, but I thought that I ought to commence by taking to you about my family, since you asked about that."

"Lucile has lost her brother by virtue of a catastrophic accident," said Count d'Aguilar. "She has gone to Seville to collect her succession, and I don't know whether she'll return to Cadiz soon."

"Since she isn't here," Don Luis continued, "I won't stay long; I need to leave tomorrow."

"That's an extraordinary urgency," replied Ponce de Leon, "but remember that you owe us something, and even if it's much less than you owe her, there's an injustice in giving everything to the one and nothing to the others."

"Your rights are inscribed in my heart," replied Don Luis, smiling. "You know that what one feels for one's mistress is so different from what one feels for one's friends that those various sentiments cannot destroy one another."

"Yes," said Count d'Aguilar, laughing in his turn. "You love us very much, but you're quitting us tomorrow to go in search of Lucile. In truth, the rights you leave us in your heart are too limited, and hers too extensive. Could you not, without offending the beauty, wait for her to return here?"

"No, Sire," replied Don Luis, "I could not, without causing her chagrin, and I would die if I caused her chagrin. But as amity is more reasonable than amour, it leaves us a greater liberty; I can quit you without displeasing you, I'm certain, and I'll always find you the same for me."

"Ha!" cried Ponce de Leon. "How glad I am to enjoy all my liberty, and to be able with regard to beauties to do as butterflies fluttering in a flower-bed do, approaching them all and not attaching myself to any."

Don Luis sighed at those words, either because he regretted not being as tranquil as his friend, or because he would already have liked to be at the feet of the person who troubled his tranquility.

They separated with a thousand protestations of amity. Don Luis departed for Seville, as he had resolved to do, and Ponce de Leon remained in Cadiz with Count d'Aguilar, for they lodged together and had nothing hidden from one another.

Ponce de Leon became so pensive, spoke so little and responded so distractedly, that his cousin no longer recognized his humor. He tried to ask him the reason for it several times, but, judging that he had perhaps made some engagement of which he wanted to make a mystery, and that he might cause him pain by pressing the point, he retained all the measures that discretion demands. As he sought nevertheless to discover the truth, he told one of his servants, who was very discreet, to follow Gabriel de Leon everywhere he went, and to take account, as much as he could, of his conduct.

Aguilar, having taken that measure, felt sure that he would soon have news of his cousin; he pretended deliberately to have business, and went out without him, in order to leave him entirely at liberty, but his valet had nothing to tell him in the evening except that he had gone for a walk in a very solitary garden that overlooked the sea, or that he had stayed enclosed in his cabinet all day, and had certainly not talked to anyone.

That conduct surprised the count, and after waiting three weeks, hoping that he would weary of maintaining the silence, he finally broke it himself, and told him that for some time, he had noticed in his behavior things so different from his ordinary procedure that he could no longer resist the anxiety that he felt; that if a melancholy without cause had put him in that state there was reason to fear a serious malady and to prevent it; that if some change in his fortune had occurred, he offered to share his own with him as with another self; and finally, that if he had some other trouble, he ought not to hide it from him, since he was aware of his loyalty and his discretion.

Ponce de Leon only replied with a profound sigh, and the count, who was examining him and looking at him with the utmost attention, continued speaking. "What can be the matter with you?" he said. "You're the most accomplished man in the world; your birth is so illustrious that it is sufficient to mention your name to inspire respect; your father has great wealth, and has already given you a considerable part of it in order to satisfy you. In sum, are you in love? Are you maltreated?"

"Oh, my dear cousin," replied Don Gabriel, "how persistent you are. Can you not love me without putting me to the question?" After a few moments of silence, however, he continued: "But I'm abusing your good will; nothing is more engaging than what you've just said to me, and I sense it keenly. If I've resisted telling you my secret, it's solely for the reason of wanting to conserve your esteem. Alas, will you be able to have any for me when I have made you the confession of my extravagance? Yes, I'm in love, I admit it, and that passion is all the more dangerous because I don't know whether the person who is causing my disquiet merits everything that I am suffering for her. It's Isidore that I love, the sister of Don Luis, whom I've never seen and perhaps never will see, since her aunt is jealous of the sun that shines on her and is keeping her in the country without leaving her any liberty."

Count d'Aguilar listened to his cousin with the utmost astonishment. "If you had seen Isidore," he said, "given what is said about her, I would not be surprised if you loved her; but it's singular, after the long sojourn that you have made in Madrid, and after your voyages to Italy, France and Flanders, where you have seen marvelous women without having the slightest attachment to them, that you have suddenly run aground and delivered yourself without knowing anything of her beauty, her mind or her humor, to the person you have taken it into your head to love."

"That is what causes my shame and my displeasure," said Ponce de Leon. "That is why I didn't dare reveal my secret to you. In the excess of that misfortune, I don't know of any remedy with which to combat my passion."

"Oh, my dear cousin," said the count, "don't be so proud; I can see that our hour has come; you're a rebel who believed yourself to be insensible; Amour wanted to punish you and has given you tenderness for someone you haven't yet seen."

"Don't mock me, please," replied Ponce de Leon. "I've never had less desire to laugh, and if you don't want to treat this matter seriously, I'd rather we stopped talking about it."

Count d'Aguilar told him that what amused him was that Isidore was neither the Infanta of Spain nor the sovereign, and that according to all appearances, if he wanted to ask for her, he would not be refused.

"I believe that, as you do," said Don Gabriel, "but I have another chimera in mind, as difficult to combat as my passion, which is if that my services don't please her, if she doesn't love me before knowing me, her possession might be unable to render me happy; I would always have to tell myself that I owed it to her obedience to her relatives, to my quality and to my wealth. No; I want to owe it to her tenderness, or I would never be content."

"Everything that occupies your mind and your heart," said Count d'Aguilar, "appears to me to be very singular; I feel sorry for you; I lament for myself, in seeing your pains without being able to diminish them. What I will say all my life is that I'm absolutely yours; that if you can imagine some means of arriving at what you desire, and I can be useful to you, you can count on me."

At those words, Don Gabriel could not help embracing his cousin narrowly. "Remember," he said to him, "the word you have given me this evening, for before very long, I shall put you to the proof."

It was so late that they separated. Ponce de Leon esteemed himself less unfortunate, since he had found a confidant, and the count was delighted to know what was preoccupying his cousin, in order to be able to serve or combat his passion, cording to the penchant that he saw in him.

After that first confession, Don Gabriel had no more difficulty in talking about his sentiments to his friend; he sought him out continually as a relief for his woes, and was delighted not to find a spirit of contradiction that would have desolated him, for nothing is more despairing, when one's heart is veritably touched, than to find continual remonstrations in one's path.

Ponce de Leon had wanted to wait for a while to see whether reason might remedy the disorders of his heart, but, seeing that it was weakened by the combats it had already sustained, and that the idea he had formed of Isidore, far from leaving him some repose, continued to persecute him, he resolved to go in search of her and see her. It was scarcely daylight when he went into Count d'Aguilar's bedroom and said to him: "It's necessary to depart, my dear cousin, it's necessary to go to Galicia."

"I understand," the count replied. "It's a question of Isidore, but what have you imagined in order to succeed in what you desire?"

"I imagine," said Don Gabriel, "that having arrived secretly at her home, we set fire to the house and we go into her bedroom by courtesy of the disorder that accidents of that sort always entail, that we recue her, and that I carry her away in my arms. Good God," he continued, "can you understand the excess of pleasure that I shall experience at that moment! Ha! How it will repay me with interest for the sad ones I have experienced thus far!"

"In truth, Don Gabriel," said the count, "you're unwise to want to commence with a conflagration so prejudicial to the best of your friends, Consider that by burning Don Luis's house, which is one of the most beautiful of his properties, you might be doing him a very bad turn. Consider that your dear

Isidore might perhaps by choked by the smoke and flames before you could reach her bedroom to save her, or that something might happen that would cause the two of you to perish, and that this might be the most disastrous expedient you could ever find in your life."

"I've thought," Don Gabriel went on, "that by requesting that land as a part of Isidore's dowry, I wouldn't be doing any harm to Don Luis; but in sum, you appear to me to be so contrary to the proposition that I'll abandon it, provided that you can find a better expedient and that nothing delays our journey."

"This is my sentiment," said the count. "We'll take the mail-coach as far as the stop nearest the castle; we'll take with us pilgrims' habits, we'll dress in such a manner as not to be recognized by anyone. No one will be surprised that on the road to Compostela there are people who pause at a considerable house and remain there for a few hours, at least."

"A few hours!" cried Don Gabriel, "A few hours! How do you expect me to succeed in making her love me in such a short time?"

"I've had an admirable idea," said the count, laughing, "which is that it's necessary to have you buried there. If you're believed to be dead, no one will press you to depart."

Ponce de Leon did not like to hear as much mockery as he was accustomed to give out. "I know full well," he replied, with a chagrined expression, "that you're turning me to ridicule, but to avoid that misfortune, I shall shut up."

The count sensed, but too late, that it is sometimes inappropriate to abandon oneself to the temptation of making a joke; making the reflection that it is always better to sacrifice a good quip to one's friend than one's friend to a good quip, he begged his cousin to forgive that sally. "To return to what occupies you," he continued, "it seems to me to be necessary to pretend that one of us has been wounded; perhaps the old aunt, more charitable to pilgrims than to other people, will keep us in her house."

Don Gabriel approved strongly of that idea. He did not waste a moment before giving the necessary orders for the costumes, and two days later, he departed with his cousin.

Count d'Aguilar did not cede anything, in good looks or stature, to Ponce de Leon; they both had a grand and noble air, an admirable head, and all the mental vivacity and politesse that is natural to Spaniards. Don Gabriel sang so well that the finest masters shut up in his presence; the count played the harp and the guitar as perfectly as anyone in the world. They had learned to ride a horse and dance in France; they knew several languages as well as their own. In sum, one would have searched in vain for cavaliers more accomplished.

Such as I have represented them, they went to the vicinity of Doña Juana's house, each with his hair hidden under a large hat covered by shells, a pilgrim's staff, the calabash, the cape and all the equipage necessary to their pilgrimage. They left a valet at Ciudad Rodrigo, a nearby town, and as they wanted to arrive in the evening, in order to be received more easily, they went to a wood, the avenues of which had been adapted to serve the castle as promenades; it was cut through by streams, the freshness of which kept the grass in the locale always green. The trees, as old as the centuries, offered a thousand refuges to birds, and their interlaced braches provided protection from the glare of the most ardent sun.

"What an abode," cried Ponce de Leon, speaking to the count. "What an abode, my cousin! I would be happy, as the song from *Clélie* says:[17]

> *To live with my Iris in a profound peace*
> *And pay no heed to the rest of the world.*

---

[17] *Clélie* (1654-59) is a ten volume romance by Mademoiselle de Scudéry.

"But that annoying thought would take me a long way if I didn't remember that, thus far, I have nothing to expect of my passion, and perhaps it will be worse in future."

"It's necessary not to despair of your good fortune," replied the count. "Without the kind of caprice you have of making yourself loved before making yourself known, it's certain that your name would smooth out the greatest difficulties and it wouldn't be long before you were happy."

"What do you expect?" said Ponce de Leon. "I'm not the master of doing otherwise. It would be an object of doubt that would torment me for the rest of my life. It's necessary that I make some progress with Isidore before she knows who I am."

Count d'Aguilar was dying of the desire to laugh, but he did not want to do so, and, continuing to walk, they arrived opposite a small pavilion that seemed detached from the castle and terminated the park on the side of the wood. It was ornamented by a large gilded balcony, over which Doña Juana had fitted blinds because her nieces often went there. The bars were so closely packed that they hid a great deal from view,

Silence already reigned everywhere. Our pilgrims approached without making any noise. They placed themselves under windows that were open and heard several people talking inside, but it was impossible to make out what they were saying. When they had finished their discourse, one of the ladies said, quite loudly: "We would have many fine things to say about that if my aunt were not alone, but she likes romances[18] too much to rob her of the pleasure of talking about them anywhere else than with her."

---

[18] Unusually, the author uses the word *romances* here, which is commonly used in France only to refer to ballads; she appears to be attempting a deliberate shift in meaning, attempting to find a better term than *contes* for the particular stories that she and her associates had recently taken to writing—and which, if the views of the storyteller featured in the frame story can be taken seriously, she was already beginning to tire (although that might be a bluff). No one else adopted her in-

Immediately, they got up and left, while Ponce de Leon, who had a great desire to retain the ladies and engage them in conversation, said to Count d'Aguilar: "I'm going to sing a few amorous ballads; perhaps my voice will enable us to make acquaintance."

"You've forgotten," replied the comte, "that one of us must pretend to be injured, and that manner of lamenting and requesting help would be novel."

"That's true," said Don Gabriel, "but it would still be easier for me to attract curiosity by means of a fine song than groans. Nevertheless," he continued, "I ought to follow our original plan, for if my designs were successful, it would seem to me that I was the cause of it."

"To obtain the maximum advantage," said the count, "it's necessary that I'm the one who is injured, and you can play Orpheus. Start singing; perhaps our affairs will go better than we dare hope."

Ponce de Leon sought the most touching and tender words he knew; then, as he gradually raised his beautiful voice, it seemed that the echoes hesitated to respond, for fear of interrupting; everything was in a marvelous silence; the nightingales were listening and the zephyrs held their breath. Count d'Aguilar almost did not recognize his cousin's voice, so embellished did it seem.

After having sung the beautiful aria, he sang another, for which he had made these words:

To set a soul on fire
Amour only needs a moment;
But one suffers a long torment
When the flame must expire.

"I understand well enough for whom you wrote those lines," said the count, interrupting him, and I'm convinced that

---

novative employment of *romance*, and she abandoned it herself, perhaps reluctantly.

you have rendered more than one combat against the violence of such an eccentric passion."

"My reason, as you know," he replied, "has been a very useful auxiliary until now."

"Perhaps," added the count, "in seeing the person you love, it will be easier to cure yourself."

"Ha! I don't flatter myself with that," said Don Gabriel. "And how do I even know that I shall see her? I hoped that my songs might produce some good effect, but nothing has appeared, nothing is being said."

"It's necessary to recommence," said the count, "without tiring."

"What!" exclaimed Ponce de Leon. "You think I'm going to sing all night?"

"You're no less amorous than the nightingales," the count replied, "so you ought not to sing any less than they do."

Ponce de Leon immediately sang a verse:

Amour does not exempt this place
From the troubles and cares one find under his empire;
The proudest heart sighs here,
And knows the troubles that beautiful eyes cause.

Isidore, Melanie and a young woman of condition that they had with them, named Rose, had come downstairs, and were advancing slowly toward the castle, but as soon as they heard that voice, it appeared so marvelous to them that they ran as fast as they could to the pavilion and went back upstairs to the bedroom. They approached the windows with so much precipitation that Ponce de Leon and the count had no doubt that they had come to listen to them.

It is easy to believe that our lover did not neglect anything to charm those ladies, but he said to his cousin from time to time: "I confess to you that I'll greatly regret the trouble I'm taking if Isidore isn't there."

As he was speaking in a whisper, they were agreeably surprised by a little concert that suddenly commenced. It was

Isidore who was playing the harp, Melanie the guitar and Rose the viola. The room seemed brightly illuminated.

Don Gabriel thought he would expire from joy, and flattered himself that he had a part in the symphony and the illumination. But it was not sufficient for him to hear; it was necessary to find some way of seeing. His lightness was useful to him in that occasion; he climbed a tree, and remarked without difficulty the ladies who were holding the instruments. In truth, he was too far away, and the blinds were too thick, for him to have the pleasure of discerning their faces clearly.

They did not play for long, preferring to hear the beautiful voice that had charmed them than to hear themselves. They listened, while Count d'Aguilar began to lament loudly. "How I'm suffering, my brother," he said. "The pain of my injury is augmenting, and if it's necessary for us to spend the night here, I'll be dead tomorrow."

"Alas, what can we do" replied Don Gabriel, "except go to this castle to ask for help?"

They were speaking loudly, in order to be heard.

"They're doubtless travelers," said Isidore. "As the militias are marching toward Tuy, some soldiers might have attacked them."

"Oh, my sister," exclaimed Melanie, "it isn't possible that we should lack charity for people who might be murdered tonight under our windows. It's necessary to talk to them, in order to tell them what they ought to do."

Immediately raising her voice, Isidore said: "You ought to think of coming out of that wood, for it's often dangerous."

Pone de Leon hastened to respond: "We're coming back from Santiago, Madame; thieves attacked us, and my brother received a sword-thrust in the side. In spite of that, he walked on for some time, but his strength has finally abandoned him. I laid him down under these trees, not knowing what would become of us during a night so dark."

"You make us feel a great deal of pity," continued Isidore, "but it doesn't depend on us to receive you here and give your brother the time to heal."

"May Heaven be your recompense, Madame," relied the count. "Will you tell us to whom to address ourselves?"

"Go to the castle," said Melanie. "Ask for the almoner; he has orders to furnish lodgings to pilgrims, and we'll see what help we can bring. Above all, refrain from saying that we've spoken to you, and if you know any romances, don't forget them, for they're well liked here."

As she finished speaking they closed their windows, the candles were snuffed out, and they ran to Doña Juana's room to discover how the affair of the pilgrims was going to pass.

They had not been there long when the almoner came to tell her that young men, one of whom had received a sword-thrust from thieves on the way back from Santiago were asking for shelter, adding that he had never seen such handsome physiognomies, and that to judge their condition by their persons, they must have birth."

"Are they Spaniards?"

"No, Madame, they're Flemings."

"Ah!" she cried. "That's lucky. Perhaps they've seen my brother, and they can give me news of him. I'm very worried about him. If they know romances as well, they'll lack nothing to please me."

"They claim to know admirable ones," said the almoner."

She commanded that they come promptly.

"But Madame" aid the almoner, "the one who is wounded can't wait long to be put to bed."

"Well," she said, "It's necessary to do a work of charity; let them be given a room in the castle; we'll serve them at table."

That was, in fact, one of Juana's principal devotions.

The almoner, who was already prejudiced with an affection for pilgrims, returned to where they were waiting and conducted them to a very pretty apartment, which was the one Don Luis used when he went to that estate. He ordered a good supper for them, and told them that Doña Juana's nieces felt so much pity for them that they wanted to serve them.

After he had quit them, Count d'Aguilar said to his cousin: "Well, my dear brother—for that's what it's necessary to call one another now—here we are in the inaccessible castle, which you almost despaired of ever being able to enter. Don't commencements so fortunate augur well for our designs?"

"Alas, my dear count," replied Ponce de Leon, "I dare not abandon myself yet to presages so flattering; I know from experience that amour isn't without dread and troubles."

"It's seeking gaiety of the heart by tormenting oneself," added the count. "See whether there can be anything prettier than having those beautiful persons at our supper, one cutting up our morsels and the other pouring our drinks. Doesn't it seem to you that we're Amadis, or at least Don Quixotes, that we've arrives in an enchanted palace, that we're expelling the fays that have been guarding it for two or three hundred years, and that princesses are coming thereafter to kiss our hands and disarm us?"

"How cheerful you are," said Don Gabriel, sighing. "It appears that you don't love anything."

"I love you," said the count, "And that's sufficient for me. By the way, I'm not satisfied to have said that it's me who is wounded; it's necessary for me to put on a sad air, and above all, not to eat much, although I'm dying of hunger. Wouldn't it have been a thousand times better for you to play that part, for I'm certain that the presence of Isidore will take the place of everything for you."

"If there were a means," replied Don Gabriel, smiling, "to say that we were mistaken, and that it's me who has the wound, I'd gladly consent to get you out of the embarrassment you're in, but the fault is committed; don't augment it by neglecting anything that depends on you, in order to persuade them that you're very ill."

"As for very ill," exclaimed the count, "I ask for quarter. Find it good that the sword-thrust was light, and that I won't have to stay in bed for long."

As he finished speaking, he threw himself down on the one that had been prepared, and a moment later they heard enough noise to believe that it was the ladies. In fact, they were not mistaken. Doña Juana came in, holding a napkin; Isidore had a gilded silver bowl on a plate, with a broth, and Melanie was carrying two fresh eggs on another.

"This is for the wounded pilgrim," said Doña Juana, approaching the bed on which the count was lying. "He may choose the broth or the eggs."

"Madame," he said, "After having thanked you very humbly for the charity that you are showing to a poor foreigner, who is unknown to you, I will take, if you please, the broth and the eggs with bread, and I might even eat a little meat, for I have lost a lot of blood; if I don't recover my strength, I might never leave here."

"God forbid," said Doña Juana, "that, having received such a great sword-thrust, I allow you to take what you wish; the consequent fever would soon have killed you. Swallow the yolk of an egg, leave the white, and drink a glass of tisane."

At that prescription, the count shivered from top to toe, and Ponce de Leon, who had retired respectfully to a corner, could not help laughing wholeheartedly, albeit quietly enough not to be heard.

Doña Juana had been so surprised by the good looks of Count d'Aguilar and his manner of speaking that she did not think of asking of news of her brother. She was delighted to sense feelings so tender; she attributed them solely to the compassion of seeing a wounded man, far from his homeland and unfortunate, with the consequence that, instead of stifling them, she applauded herself for them in secret and said to herself: *How good I am, how charitable I am! Who else would do as much as me?*

She took his arm in order to feel his pulse. She had a candle brought in order to see the poor moribund, and found a fire in his eyes that dazzled her and a marvelous tint in his complexion. She sustained that one could not have eyes so brilliant without a fever, and commenced to be terribly anxious about the state in which she found her invalid.

"I'm in despair," she said to him, "that you've swallowed an egg; it was necessary to take nothing at all. I want to govern you in my fashion; no one in the world understands it as I do. Listen," she said to her nieces and the servants who had followed them. "I declare to you that if anyone gives him something to eat without my order, there will be dire consequences. Wounds demand a complete fast."

"Oh, Madame," replied the count, sadly, "I'll go mad; I'm not accustomed to the manners of persons of quality; my temperament is opposed to theirs, and what would render them healthy would kill me."

"At least," she said, "I shall make the experiment, and it will instruct me for the future."

After that conversation, she sat down next to the count, still holding his arm in order to feel for the accidents of the pretended fever; turning her gaze away she perceived Ponce de Leon in the corner where he was retrenched. "Approach," she said, "have no fear of ladies who are exercising the right of hospitality with a great deal of joy.

Don Gabriel came to make a profound reverence to her, with a grace so particular that she and her nieces were surprised by it. "Are you brothers?" she asked him.

"Yes, Madame," he said.

"What are your names?"

"My brother, he said, is named Don Estève,[19] and I am Don Gabriel."

"You're from Flanders?"

"We're from Brussels," he replied, "sons of a music master and maker of tales, romances and songs."

---

[19] D'Aguilar's forename is presumably Esteban, but as he is claiming to be a Fleming he would naturally have Frenchified it.

"Romances!" she cried.

"Yes, Madame," he replied. "Tales of fays, ancient and modern."

"Ha!" she added. "It's necessary to tell me one this evening, or I won't sleep. But by the way, have you not seen in the home of the governor of the Low Countries Don Félix Sarmiento?"

"I have had that honor, Madame," said Don Gabriel. "He commands a Spanish contingent; he is a very gallant man, who lives as a great lord. If my father had consented to distance us from his house, he told us that he would have asked him to send us to Andalusia, to the home of his sister and his daughters."

"Why is that?" said Doña Juana, excitedly.

"He said, Madame," Don Gabriel continued, "that his wife had died a little while ago and that his daughters were living in I know not what country, where we could teach them to sing, to play instruments and to dance.."

"It's marvelous," she said, looking at her nieces, "how things come together. Do you know that I am his sister, and these are his daughters? You're only mistaken in the country, for we're in Galicia and you said Andalusia."

"Madame," said Don Gabriel, "those sorts of mistakes are pardonable on the part of foreigners. We are too fortunate to find ourselves in a country of acquaintance."

"By what hazard," she added, "have you come to Santiago?"

"By virtue of a sentiment of devotion," he said, "and a desire to travel at little expense."

"But how did your father," Juana added, "who had refused you to my brother, allow you to depart?"

"Oh, Madame," said Don Gabriel, embarrassed by so many questions, "he is a very good man, too scrupulous to hinder such good work."

Throughout this discourse, the count, whom I shall call Don Estève henceforth, did not say a word, for Doña Juana had forbidden him to speak, and as soon as he opened his mouth she put her hand over it with so much force that he was in great fear of that means of shutting him up. He was in despair at not having left his cousin the care of counterfeiting the invalid.

Ponce de Leon's supper was brought; he wanted, out of respect, to go and eat it in the antechamber, but Doña Juana ordered him to remain, and her nieces to make him eat, while she continued to examine Don Estève's pulse, which seemed to her to be intermittent.

If she had been holding Don Gabriel's, she would not have found it in a better state. He had formed a charming idea of Isidore, but he found her as far above that idea as the sun is above the stars. Whatever care he took to study her, and not to abandon himself to the pleasure that he felt in seeing her, he nevertheless attached his eyes to her sometimes with an expression so passionate that Doña Juana, having remarked it, said to him: "You are looking at my niece a great deal; I would like to know the reason."

"Madame," he said, without embarrassment. "I am something of a physiognomist; I have always had a dominant passion for astronomy, and I dare say that if I have succeeded in anything, it is in horoscopes."

"My God," Isidore said to him, "How much satisfaction I would have in hearing you; I've always wanted to find someone to inform me of my fortune."

"Oh. Madame!" cried Don Gabriel, no longer master of himself, "When one is made like you, what can one not promise oneself?"

"What?" said Doña Juana. "You see a fortunate establishment in her features, then?"

"I see the most beautiful things in the world there," he replied. "I have never seen their equal; I am struck by a surprise that goes as far as rapture."

"That is a science," said Juana, "whose terms have nothing grim or barbaric; it is necessary that I speak to you too, for I want to be knowledgeable regarding my good fortune."

In the meantime the count found himself ill with hunger and ennui, for the old woman had prevented him from eating, as I have already said, and had covered his mouth as if to choke him; he could no longer suffer her near him without the utmost chagrin. In order to get rid of her he begged her to permit that he get up for a while.

"I consent to that," she said, "provided that your brother assures me that he will not give you any of his supper."

Don Gabriel willingly promised what she wished, and although he saw Isidore depart with a great deal of chagrin, and the count had scarcely less with regard to Melanie, they were so glad to be rid of the importunate aunt that they pressed her to go as much as the characters they were playing and the respect that they owed her would permit.

They remained alone with the almoner, and made him understand that for good reasons, it was necessary that he eat or die. The manners of the pilgrims pleased him greatly, he was a man of intelligence, and not having supped himself, he made a third with them. The count recompensed himself at table for everything that he had suffered in the bed, and Don Gabriel, who had not eaten a single morsel with a good appetite in the presence of Isidore imitated his cousin so well that nothing remained.

When they were entirely at liberty to talk, Don Gabriel asked the count whether he had ever seen anything to equal Isidore

"She is a perfect beauty," he said, "but Melanie, in my eyes, has treasures of grace and inexhaustible charms. The finesse of her figure, the vivacity of her complexion, the luster of her black hair, and that air of intelligence and joy spread throughout her person appear to me to be as touching as the mild languor of Isidore."

"I'm very glad," said Ponce to Leon, "that you have paid no attention to her incomparable beauty."

"I don't say that," replied the count. "I agree that she is utterly perfect, but I'm delighted to be sensible to the merit of her sister. Would you have wanted me to become your rival?"

"God forbid!" cried Don Gabriel. "I believe that I would like dying as much."

"By the way," said the count, "You're on the footing here of a skillful astrologer. When you make your predictions, serve my cause with Melanie."

"How can I serve you?" said Ponce de Leon, laughing. "Do you want to love her?"

"I don't have that desire," replied the count, "but at all hazard, serve me."

"If you can keep your liberty," said Don Gabriel, "keep it."

"Eh? What do you want me to do with it here?" said the count, in a jesting tone of anger. "I'll have nothing to compensate me for all that's necessary for me to suffer with Doña Juana. For make no mistake," he added, "she's preparing to exercise my patience, and the interest she's taking in my health already instructs me of that all too well."

It was so late that they ended their conversation. Their bedrooms were only separated by a large hall. They did not sleep much and woke up early in the morning, as people who are beginning to fall in love ordinarily do.

Isidore and Melanie followed their aunt as far as her bedroom; then they went on to their own, and went to bed together. They had done so in the design of talking for a part of the night, but they did not say anything, turning over and over like people more anxious than drowsy.

"Why aren't you asleep, my dear sister; are you ill?" Isidore asked.

"What about you?" replied Melanie. "What's preventing you from sleeping?"

"Having uttered a profound sigh, Isidore replied, briefly: "I don't know."

Their silence recommenced.

After a while, however, Melanie heard her sister sigh again. "Oh, what's this, Isidore?" she said, kissing her. "You have some sadness, and you're hiding it from me? Do you lack confidence in me?"

"It would be the first time in my life," she said, "that that had happened to me," but there are tears so unworthy that one doesn't shed them without shame."

"You're frightening me," said Melanie, tenderly, "although I don't understand what you mean. I'm convinced that you aren't suffering chagrin without a reason. If you love me, confide in me, and don't leave me any longer in the anxiety that you've caused me."

"I swear to you. my sister," Isidore replied, "that I wasn't deceiving you when I replied to you that I don't know what's wrong with me, but since you want something more specific, I confess that after having been in the travelers' room for a time, I found myself so anxious for the one that is wounded, and he appeared to me to be so amiable beneath his poor clothing, that I said to myself, involuntarily: 'What if that young man were of quality and if he were magnificently dressed, since he has such an elevated and noble, being of such mediocre condition?' I was flattering myself that perhaps he had more birth than he wanted to appear, when, to my misfortune, his brother explained to my aunt everything concerning them. They're musicians, my dear Melanie; isn't that and a dagger-thrust the same thing? Me, I said to myself, me, finding myself with an inclination for a man who is so inferior to me, me, who has never felt the slightest weakness for anyone!"

"Oh, my sister," exclaimed Melanie, "the moment of which you're complaining had no less fatality for me then for you. Don Gabriel had already pleased me by virtue of the beauty of his voice; what became of me when I remarked, through that ridiculous pilgrim's habit, an advantageous stature, regular features and such a fine air, that persons more distinguished than him scarcely have."

"However amiable they are," said Isidore, "may heaven preserve us from ever looking at them other than as musicians. I even believe that we ought to hasten their departure."

"Do you want that poor wounded man to die, then?" said Melanie.

"No," she said, "I want him to be cured and to go away, convinced that the best thing for us is to keep away from persons who might cause us difficulty."

"Alas, I consent to that," replied Melanie, "and I'll gladly second you in that design."

They were talking thus when they saw daylight appear, and tried to obtain a few moments of repose.

Doña Juana passed rather bad hours, solely by virtue of the apprehension she had that the pilgrim might be in a worse state than when she had left him; it was so late when he arrived, and there was no means of sending for a surgeon to bandage him, but she had asked for two of the most skillful from Ciudad Real, and as soon as they arrived she took them to the count's room.

He had stayed in bed, very chagrined by the constraint; Ponce de Leon was keeping him company when Juana came in, followed by two men. He did not know at first whether they were domestics, but she told the count that it was necessary to prepare himself for any eventuality; that it might perhaps be necessary to cut his flesh or make incisions, but that he should have no apprehension, because she was putting him in the hands of the most skillful men in Europe.

While she was speaking, one of the surgeons hastened to make lint, and the other arranged his lancets razors, scissors and scalpels on the table, with five or six bottles full of unguents.

It is impossible to comprehend without laughing the embarrassment and anger of the count; he looked at Don Gabriel with furious eyes and let him understand that everything was discovered. Don Gabriel was at least as embarrassed as he was, when he took it into his head to say to Doña Juana: "We never travel, Madame, without bringing a small provision of sympathy powder, the effects of which are always marvelous.

I put some on my brother's wound yesterday evening; I have reason to believe that he will soon be cured."[20]

The surgeons heard that and, seeing that they were surplus to requirements, protested against such a pernicious secret; they even said that a little witchcraft entered into it, and that the Holy Inquisition would not suffer that it cured. Doña Juana was on the point of taking flight at the redoubtable name of the Inquisition, but the count reassured her; he told her that the powder was composed with simples, that he had made it himself, and that if she wished, he would give her the secret.

"At the very least," she replied, "permit the surgeons to see your wound. If it's in a good state, they won't make it worse."

"I shall do nothing of the sort," he said, quietly and with an air of confidence that gave him pleasure, "for you know, Madame, the character of these sorts of people."

She agreed with him, and paid them so liberally for their trouble that they went away very satisfied.

As she had no desire to quit Count d'Aguilar, she searched for a pretext that might keep him with her, and addressed Ponce de Leon. "Since you know romances," she said to him, "you would give me a singular pleasure by recounting one for me, because I'm very fond of them."

"I will obey you, Madame," he said, in a respectful manner, and he commenced immediately.

THE SHEEP

---

[20] Sympathy power was a kind of quasi-magical medicine commonplace in the seventeenth century. It was sometimes applied to the weapon that had caused a wound rather than the wound itself, but the version promoted in England by Sir Kenelm Digby, whose main ingredient was iron sulfate, was claimed to be effective in curing wounds inflicted by blades by means of direct application.

In the fortunate times when the fays lived, a king reigned who had three daughters; they were beautiful and young; they had merit, but the youngest was the most amiable and the best loved; her name was Merveilleuse. The king, their father, gave her more robes and ribbons in a month than he gave the others in a year, but she had such a good little heart that she shared everything with her sisters, with the consequence that the union between them was great.

The king had bad neighbors, who, weary of leaving him in peace, made war against him so forcefully that he feared being beaten if he did not defend himself. He assembled a large army and went on campaign. The three princesses remained with their governor in a castle where they received good news of the king every day, sometimes that he had taken a town, or won a battle; in the end, he did so much that he vanquished his enemies and expelled them from his estates. Then he came back quickly to his castle, in order to see little Merveilleuse again, whom he loved so much.

The three princesses had made three satin dresses, one green, one blue and the last white; their gems matched the dresses; the green had emeralds, the blue turquoises and the white diamonds, and thus adorned they went to meet the king, singing verses that they had composed about his victories:

> *After so many illustrious conquests,*
> *What joy to see one's father and king again!*
> *Inventors of pleasure, let us celebrate a thousand fêtes,*
> *Let everyone here submit to his laws,*
> *And let us try to prove our tenderness,*
> *By means of eager cares and songs of delight.*

When he saw them so beautiful and so cheerful he embraced them tenderly, and gave Merveilleuse more caresses than the others.

A magnificent meal was served; the king and his three daughters sat down at table, and as he drew consequences from everything, he said to the eldest: "Tell me, why have you put on a green dress?"

"Milord," she said, "having known your exploits, I thought that green would signify my joy and the hope of your return."

"That's very well said," said the king. And you, my daughter," he continued, "why have you put on a blue dress?"

"Milord," said the princess, "to mark that it is necessary incessantly to implore the gods in your favor, and that on seeing you, I believe I can see the sky and the most beautiful stars."

"Why," said the king, "you speak like an oracle. And you, Merveilleuse, what reason have you for your white costume?"

"Milord," she said, "because it suits me better than the other colors."

"What, little coquette," said the king, very annoyed. "You only had that intention?"

"I had that of pleasing you," said the princess. "It didn't seem to me that I ought to have any other."

The king, who loved her, found the affair so well accommodated that he said that that little turn of wit pleased him, and that there was even artistry in not having declared her thought all at once.

"Well," he said, "I've supped well; I don't want to go to bed so soon; tell me the dreams you had on the night preceding my return."

The eldest said that she had dreamed that he brought her a dress in which gold and precious stones shone more brilliantly than the sun. The second said that she had dreamed that he brought her a dress and a golden distaff in order to spin chemises. The youngest said that she had dreamed that he had married her second sister, and that on the wedding day, he had held up a golden ewer, and had said to her: "Come here, Merveilleuse, so that I can wash you."

The king, indignant at that dream, frowned and made the ugliest grimace in the world; everyone knew that he was annoyed. He went into his bedroom and went to bad abruptly; his daughter's dream kept coming back into his head.

That insolent child, he thought, *would like to reduce me to becoming her domestic. I'm not astonished that she put on the white satin dress without thinking about me; she thinks me unworthy of her reflections, but I can forestall her evil design before it happens.*

He got up in a fury, and although it was not yet daylight he sent for the captain of is guards and said to him: "You've heard the dream that Merveilleuse has had; it signifies strange things against me. I want you to take possession of her right away, take her into the forest, and cut her throat. Then bring me her heart and tongue, for I don't intend to be deceived; or I'll put you to death cruelly."

The captain of the guards was very astonished to hear such a barbaric order. He did not want to oppose the king, for fear of embittering him further and that he might give the commission to someone else. He told him that he would take away the princess, that he would cut her throat and bring him back her heart and tongue.

He went immediately to her chamber, where he had great difficulty getting anyone to open up for him, but it was very early. He told Merveilleuse that the king was asking for her. She got up promptly. A little Mooress named Patypata took the train of her dress; her little monkey and her little dog ran after her. Her monkey was named Grabugeon and the dog Tintin.

The captain of the guards obliged Merveilleuse to go downstairs, and told her that the king was in the garden taking the fresh air. She went in. He made a semblance of searching for him, and not having found him, he said; "Doubtless the king has gone all the way to the forest." He opened a little door and took her into the forest.

Daylight was already beginning to appear. The princess looked at her conductor; he had tears in his eyes, and he was so sad that he could not speak.

"What's the matter with you?" she said with a charming air of kindness. "You seem very afflicted to me."

"Oh, Madame," he exclaimed, "who wouldn't be, at the deadliest order that has ever been given? The king wants me to murder you here and take him your heart and tongue; if I fail, he'll put me to death."

The poor princess, frightened, went pale and began to weep very softly; she resembled a little lamb about to be immolated. She attached her beautiful eyes to the captain of the guards and looked at him without anger. "Will you have the courage," she said, "to kill me—me, who has never done you any harm? If I had merited my father's hatred I would suffer its effects without a murmur, but alas, I have shown him so much respect and attachment that he cannot complain without injustice."

"Have no fear, beautiful princess," said the captain of the guards, "that I am capable of lending my hand to such a barbaric action, and I would rather resolve myself to the death with which he threatens me; but if I stabbed myself, you would be in so greater security. It's necessary to find a means for me to return to the king and convince him that you are dead."

"What means can we find?" said Merveilleuse. "For he wants you to take him my tongue and my heart; without that, he won't believe you."

Patypata, who had listened to everything, and whom neither the princess not the captain of the guards had even perceived, sad as they were, advanced courageously and came to throw herself at Merveilleuse's feet. "Madame," she said, "I've come to offer you my life. It's necessary to kill me; I will be only to content to die for such a good mistress."

"I shall not take it, my dear Patypata," said the princess, kissing her. "After such a tender expression of your amity, your life is no less precious to me that my own."

Grabugeon advanced and said: "You're right, my princess, to love a slave as faithful as Patypata; she can be more useful to you than me. I offer you my tongue and my heart with joy, wanting to immortalize myself in the empire of the apes."

"Of, my little Grabugeon," replied Merveilleuse, "I cannot bear the thought of taking your life."

"It would be insupportable for me," cried Tintin, "being the good dog that I am, for another to give their life from my mistress; I must die or no one must die."

With that, a great dispute rose up between Patypata, Grabugeon and Tintin; they all started shouting. In the end, Grabugeon, more excited than the others, went to the top of a tree, let herself fall head first and killed herself. Whatever regret the princess had, she consented, since she was dead, to the captain of the guards taking her tongue; but it was so small— for in total it was no larger than a fist—that they judged with great dolor that the king would not be deceived by it.

"Alas, my dear little monkey," said the princess, "now you are dead, without your death making my life safe."

"It's for me that that honor is reserved," said the Mooress. At the same time, she took the knife that had been used on Grabugeon and plunged it into her throat.

The captain of the guards wanted to take away her tongue, but it was so black that he dared not flatter himself that he could deceive the king with it."

"Am I not very unfortunate?" said the princess, weeping. "I am losing everything that I love, and my fortune is not changing."

"If you had wanted to accept my proposition," said Tintin, "you would only have had me to regret, and I would have had the advantage of being regretted alone."

Merveilleuse kissed her little dog, weeping so abundantly that she could do no more; she drew away promptly, with the result that when she came back she no longer saw her conductor; she found herself in the company of her Mooress, her monkey and her dog. She could not go away until she had put them in a ditch that she found by chance at the foot of a tree. Then she wrote these words on the tree:

Here lie three mortals
All equally faithful,
Who to conserve my days
Cut their own short.

Then she thought about her safety. As there was none for her in the forest, which was so close to her father's castle that the first passers-by might see her and recognize her, or lions or wolves might eat her like a pullet, she started walking as fast as she could. But the forest was so large and the sun was so ardent that she was dying of heat, fear and lassitude. She looked in all directions without seeing any end to the forest. Everything frightened her; she still believed that the king would run after her to kill her; it is impossible to describe her sad plaints.

She walked without following any certain route; the bushes tore her beautiful dress and wounded her white skin. Finally, she heard sheep bleating. *Undoubtedly*, she said to herself, *there are shepherds here with their flocks; they could guide me to some hamlet where I could hide in the costume of a peasant. Alas*, she continued, *it is not sovereigns and princes who are always the most fortunate. Who would have believed in all the realm that I am a fugitive, that my father, without any reason, desires my death, and that it is necessary to disguise myself in order to avoid it?*

As she made those reflections she advanced toward the place where she had heard bleating, but what was her surprise, on arriving in a rather spacious area surrounded by trees, to see a large sheep whiter than snow, with gilded horns, a garland of flowers around its neck, its legs surrounded by strings of pearls of a prodigious size, and several chains of diamonds, lying on orange blossom. An awning of golden cloth suspended in the air prevented the sun from inconveniencing it. A hundred ornamented sheep were around it, which were not grazing, but some were taking coffee, sorbets, ice cream or lemonade and others strawberries, cream and jam. Some were playing bassette, others lansquenet; several had golden collars enriched with gallant mottoes, pierced ears, ribbons and flowers in a thousand places.

Merveilleuse was so astonished that she was almost paralyzed. She was searching with her eyes for the shepherd of such an extraordinary flock when the most beautiful sheep came toward her, bounding and leaping. "Approach, divine princess," it said to her, "have no fear of animals as gentle and peaceful as us."

"What a prodigy! Sheep who can talk!"

"Oh, Madame," it said, "your monkey and your dog talked so nicely; have you any reason to be astonished?"

"A fay," Merveilleuse replied, "had given them the gift of speech. That is what rendered the prodigy more familiar."

"Perhaps we have had a similar adventure," said the sheep, smiling sheepishly. "but my princess, what has guided your steps here?"

"A thousand misfortunes, Sire Sheep,"[21] she said. "I am the most unfortunate person in the world. I'm searching for a refuge against the fury of my father."

"Come, Madame," replied the sheep. "Come with me; I offer you one that will only be known to you, and you will be the absolute mistress of it."

"It's impossible for me to follow you," said Merveilleuse. "I'm so weary that I'm dying of it."

The sheep with the gilded horns ordered that someone go in quest of its chariot. A moment later, six goats arrived harnessed to a pumpkin of prodigious size, in which two people could sit quite comfortably. The pumpkin was dry, and there were good feather and velvet cushions everywhere inside. The princess placed herself in it, admiring such a novel equipage.

---

[21] The word *mouton* [sheep] is a masculine noun in French, so the masculine pronoun would naturally be attributed to this one even if the individual in question were not obviously male; he is never identified within the story as a *bélier* [ram], so I have retained the straightforward translation.

The master sheep entered the pumpkin with her, and the goats ran as fast as they could to a cavern, the entrance of which was sealed by a large stone. The gilded sheep touched it with its foot; immediately, it fell. It told the princess to enter without fear. She thought that the cavern was utterly frightful, and if she had been less alarmed nothing could have obliged her to descend into it, but such was the force of her apprehension that she would have jumped into a well. She did not hesitate, therefore, to follow the sheep, which walked ahead of her.

It made her descend so far, so far down that she thought she was going at least to the antipodes, and she was sometimes afraid that it was conducting her to the realm of the dead. Eventually, she suddenly discovered a vast plain dotted with a thousand different flowers, the pleasant odor of which surpassed all those she had ever scented. A wide river of orange-flower water was flowing around it; springs of Spanish wine, rosolis, hypocras and a thousand other kind of liquors formed cascades and charming little streams. The plan was covered with singular trees; there were entire avenues in which grouse, better skewered and better cooked than at La Guerbois,[22] were hanging on the branches; there were other avenues of quail and young rabbits, turkeys, pullets, pheasants and ortolans. In certain areas where the air seemed more obscure, it was raining lobster bisque, tonic soups, *foie gras*, shredded *ris de veau*, white sausages, tortes, pâtés, dry and liquid jam, louis d'or, écus, pearls and diamonds. The rarity of that rain, and the entire assembly of utility, would have attracted good company if the big sheep had had a better humor and more familiarity, but all the chronicles that mention him affirm that he maintained more gravity than a Roman senator.

As it was the most beautiful season of the year when Merveilleuse arrived in that beautiful place, she did not see any other palaces than a long series of orange trees, jasmines,

---

[22] Madame Guerbois' famous cabaret was opened on the Butte Saint-Roch in the early seventeenth century.

honeysuckle and little musk-roses, the interlaced branches of which formed cabinets, halls and bedrooms, all furnished with gold and silver, with large mirrors, chandeliers and admirable pictures.

The Master Sheep told the princes that he was the sovereign of the realm, and that for some years he had had sensible reasons to be afflicted and to shed tears, but that it was only up to her to enable him to forget his misfortunes.

"The manners you have, charming sheep," she told him, "are so generous, and everything that I see here appears so extraordinary to me, that I don't know what to think about it."

She had difficulty finishing these words because she saw a troop of nymphs of admirable beauty appear before her. They presented her with fruits in amber baskets, but when she tried to approach them their bodies gradually drew away; she reached out her arm in order to touch them, but felt nothing, and she realized that they were phantoms.

"Oh, what's this?" she cried. "In what company am I?"

She started to weep, and King Mouton—for that was his name—who had left her for a few moments, having returned to her and seen her tears flowing, was so bewildered by it that he nearly died at her feet.

"What's the matter, beautiful princess?" he said. "Has someone in this place lacked the respect that is due to you?"

"No," she said, "I'm not complaining; but I have to confess that I'm not accustomed to living with the dead and sheep who can talk. Everything here frightens me, and whatever obligation I have to you for having brought me here, I'd have even more if you were to take me back to the world."

"Don't be frightened," replied the sheep. "Deign to listen to me tranquilly, and you'll know my deplorable adventure.

"I was born on the throne. A long sequence of kings that I had for ancestors had assured me of the possession of the most beautiful realm in the world; my subjects loved me and I was feared and envied by my neighbors. I was esteemed, with some justice; it was said that no king had ever been more worthy of being. My person was not indifferent to those who saw me.

"I was very fond of hunting, and, allowing myself to be carried away one day by the pleasure of following a red deer, which drew me away from those who were accompanying me. I suddenly saw it plunge into a pond. I pushed my horse into it with as much imprudence as temerity, but on advancing a little, instead of the freshness of water I felt an extraordinary heat. The pond dried up, and through an opening from which terrible fires emerged, I fell into the depths of a precipice, in which nothing could be seen but flames.

"I believed myself doomed, when I heard a voice that said to me: 'It needs nothing less than fire, ingrate, to warm your heart.'

"'Oh!' I cried. 'Who is complaining here of my coldness?'

"'An unfortunate person,' replied the voice, 'who adores you hopelessly.'

"At the same time he fires were extinguished; I saw a fay whom I had known since my most tender youth, whose age and ugliness had always frightened me. She was leaning on a young slave of incomparable beauty; she had golden chains that marked her condition sufficiently.

"'What prodigy is passing here, Ragotte?' I said to her— that was the fay's name. 'Is it by your orders?'

"'Who else?' she replied. 'Have you not known my sentiments until now? Must I have the shame of explaining myself? Have my eyes, once sure of their effects, lost all their power? Consider how I am lowering myself; it is me who is making you the confession of my weakness, for although you are a great king, you are less than an ant before a fay like me.'

"'I am whatever you please,' I said to her, with an impatient attitude and tone, 'but in sum, what are you demanding of me? Is it my crown, my cities, my treasures?'

"'Ha, wretch!' she replied, disdainfully, 'My scullions, if I wished, would be more powerful than you. I'm demanding your heart; my eyes have requested it a thousand times over;

you have not understood them—or, to put it better, you have not wanted to understand them. If you were engaged to another,' she continued, 'I would leave you to progress in your amour; but I had too much interest in enlightening you not to have discovered the indifference that reigns in your heart. Well, love me,' she added, tightening her mouth to make it more agreeable, and rolling her eyes. 'I'll be your little Ragotte; I'll add twenty kingdoms to the one you possess, a hundred towers full of gold, five hundred full of silver; in a word, anything you wish.'

"'Madame Ragotte,' I said to her, 'it's not in the depths of a hole where I thought I'd be roasted that I want to make a declaration to a person of your merit; I beg you, by all the charms that render you amiable, to put me at liberty, and then we'll see together what I can do for your satisfaction.'

"'Ha! Traitor!' she cried. 'If you loved me, you wouldn't seek the road to your kingdom; you'd be content in a grotto, in a foxhole, in the woods in the deserts. Don't believe that I'm a novice; you're thinking of escaping, but I warn you that its necessary for you to remain here, and the first thing you will do is to look after my sheep; they are intelligent, and talk at least as well as you.'

"At the same time, she advanced into the plain where we are and showed me her flock. I hardly looked at them; the beautiful slave who was with her had seemed marvelous to me; my eyes betrayed me. The cruel Ragotte took account of it, threw herself upon her and plunged a stiletto so far into her eye that the admirable individual lost her life instantly.

"At that disastrous sight I threw myself upon Ragotte and I would have immolated her to such dear manes if she had not rendered me immobile by means of her power. My efforts were futile; I fell to the ground, and I was searching for a means to kill myself in order to deliver myself from the state that I was in when she said to me with an ironic smile: 'I want you to know my power; you're a lion at present; you'll become a sheep.'

"Immediately, she touched me with her wand and I found myself metamorphosed as you see. I did not lose the usage of speech, nor the sentiments of dolor that I owed to my estate. 'You shall be a sheep for five years,' she said, 'and absolute master of this beautiful place, while, away from you and no longer seeing your agreeable face, I shall only think of you with the hatred that I owe you.'

"She disappeared; and if anything had been able to soften my disgrace, it would have been her absence. The talking sheep who are here recognized me as their king; they told me that they were unfortunates who had displeased the vindictive fay for various different reasons, that she had composed a flock of them, and that their penitence was not as long for some as for others. In fact," he added, "from time to time they become once again what they were before, and quit the flock.

"As for the others, they are rivals or enemies of Ragotte, whom she has killed for a century or less, and who then return to the world. The young slave I mentioned is of that number; I have seen her several times subsequently, with pleasure, although she does not speak to me, and in wanting to approach her, it was annoying to know that she was only a shade. Having remarked one of my sheep close to that little phantom, however, I understood that he was her lover, and that Ragotte, susceptible to tender impressions, had wanted to take him away from her.

"That reason distanced me from the slave shade, and for three years I have not felt any penchant for anything except my liberty. That is what engages me to go to the forest occasionally. I saw you there, beautiful princess," he continued, "Sometimes on a chariot that you guided yourself with more skill than the sun has on guiding his own, sometimes hunting on a horse that seemed indomitable by anyone but you. Then, running lightly in the plain with the princesses of your court, you won the prize like another Atalanta. Oh, princess, if in all those times when my heart rendered you secret prayers, I had dared to speak to you, what would I not have said to you? But how would you have received the declaration of an unfortunate sheep like me?"

Merveilleuse was so troubled by all that she had heard thus far that she was almost unable to respond. She made him honest replies, however, that left him some hope, and said that she was less fearful of the shades since they would live again one day. "Alas," she continued," if only my poor Patypata, my dear Grabugeon and the pretty Tintin, who died to save me, could have a similar fate, I would not find it so tedious here."

In spite of King Mouton's disgrace, he had a few admirable privileges. "Go," he said to his grand squire—a very good looking sheep—"in quest of the Mooress, the monkey and the dog; their shades will divert our princess."

A moment later, Merveilleuse saw them, and although she could not approach them closely enough to touch them, their presence was an infinite consolation to her.

King Mouton had all the intelligence and delicacy that could form agreeable conversations. He loved Merveilleuse so passionately that she also came to consider him, and subsequently to love him. A pretty sheep, very mild and affectionate, cannot fail to please, especially when one knows that he is a king and that his metamorphosis will end. So the princess spent her fine days pleasantly, awaiting a more fortunate fate. The gallant sheep was only occupied with her; he arranged fêtes, concerts and hunts; his flock seconded him, and even shades played their parts therein.

One evening, couriers arrived, for he sent for news carefully, and always knew the best. Someone came to tell him that Merveilleuse's elder sister was about to marry a great prince, and that nothing was more magnificent than all the preparations that were being made for the wedding.

"Oh, how unfortunate I am not to see so many beautiful things," cried the young princess. "Here I am underground with shades and sheep, while my sister is going to appear adorned like a queen; everyone will pay court to her, and I shall be the only one not to share in her joy."

"Of what are you complaining, Madame?" the king of the sheep said to her. "Have I refused to let you go to the wedding? Depart when you please, but give me your word to come back; if you don't consent to that, you'll see me expire at your feet, for the attachment I have for you is too violent for me to be able to lose you without dying."

The tender Merveilleuse promised the sheep that nothing in the world could prevent her return. He gave her an equipage proportionate to her birth; she dressed superbly, and did not neglect anything that might augment her beauty. She mounted a chariot of mother-of-pearl drawn by light bay hippogriffs newly arrived from the antipodes. He had her accompanied by an infinite number of officers richly clad and admirably well made; he had sent far and wide for them in order to make up her cortege.

She went to the palace of the king, her father, at the moment when the wedding was being celebrated. As soon as she entered, she surprised everyone who saw her by the splendor of her beauty and that of her gems; she heard nothing around her but acclamations and praise. The king looked at her with an attention and pleasure that made her dread being recognized, but he was so convinced of her death that he did not have the slightest idea of it.

Even so, the apprehension of being arrested prevented her from remaining until the end of the ceremony; she left abruptly, and left behind a little coral casket garnished with emeralds; inscribed on it in diamonds was: *gems for the bride.* It was opened immediately, and what was not found therein? The king, who had hoped to catch up with her and was burning to know who she was, was in despair at no longer seeing her. He gave an absolute order that if she ever came back, all the doors were to be closed on her and that she should be retained.

Short as Merveilleuse's absence had been, it had seemed to the sheep to last a century. He waited for her on the bank of a spring in the densest part of the forest; he had laid out immense riches there to offer her in recognition of her return. As soon as he saw her he ran toward her, leaping and bounding like a real sheep; he made her a thousand tender caresses, he lay down at her feet, he kissed her hands, he recounted his anxieties and his impatience. His passion gave him an eloquence by which the princess was charmed.

After a time, the king married his second daughter. Merveilleuse heard about it and begged the sheep to permit her, as he had done before, to go and see a fête in which she was so strongly interested. At that proposition he felt a dolor of which he was not the master; a secret presentiment announced his misfortune to him, but as it is not always in us to avoid it, and his complaisance for the princess prevailed over all other interests, he did not have the strength to refuse.

"You want to quit me, Madame," he said to her. "That effect of my misfortune comes from my evil destiny rather than from you. I consent to what you wish, and I can never make you a sacrifice more complete."

She assured him that she would delay as little as the first time; that she felt keenly all that being distance from him could produce; and she implored him not to worry. She made use of the same equipage that had conducted her before and she arrived as the ceremony commenced. In spite of the attention that people were paying to it, her presence caused a cry of joy and admiration to rise up, which attracted the eyes of all the princes to her; they could not weary of gazing at her, and found her a beauty so uncommon that they were ready to believe that she was not a mortal woman.

The king was so charmed to see her again that he only took his eyes off her to order that all the doors be firmly closed in order to retain her.

When the ceremony was on the point of conclusion, the princess got up promptly, wanting to slip away through the crowd, but she was extremely surprised and afflicted to find the doors closed.

The king approached her with great respect and a submission that reassured her. He begged her not to deprive them so soon of the pleasure of seeing her and of being at the celebratory feast that he was giving the princes and princesses. He took her into a magnificent hall where the entire court was. He picked up a golden basin and a vase full of water himself, in order to wash her beautiful hands.

At that moment she was no longer mistress of her transport. She threw himself at his feet and embraced his knees. "Here is my dream accomplished," she said. "You have come to wash me on the day of my sister's wedding, without anything unfortunate happening to you."

The king recognized her with much less difficulty because he had already thought more than once that she resembled Merveilleuse perfectly. "Oh, my dear daughter," he said, embracing her and shedding tears, "can you forget my cruelty? I wanted your death because I thought that your dream signified the loss of my crown. It also signified," he continued, "now your sisters are married, and they each have one, that mine would be for you." At the same time he stood up and placed it on the head of the princess; then he cried: "Long live Queen Merveilleuse!"

All the court cried likewise; the two sisters of the young queen came to throw their arms around her neck and made her a thousand caresses. Merveilleuse lost herself, she was so glad; she was weeping and laughing at the same time; she embraced one, she spoke to the other, she thanked the king, and among all those different things she remembered the captain of the guards to whom she had so much obligation, and asked for him insistently; but she was told that he was dead, and she felt that loss keenly.

When she was at table the king begged her to recount what had happened o her since the day that he had given such fatal orders against her. Immediately, she began speaking with an admirable grace, and everyone listened attentively.

While she forgot herself in company with the king and her sisters, however, the amorous sheep saw the hour of the princess's return pass, and his anxiety became so extreme that he as no longer the master of it.

"She no longer wants to come back!" he cried. "My unfortunate form of a sheep displeases her. Oh, too unfortunate lover, what will I do without Merveilleuse? Ragotte, barbaric fay, what vengeance are you not taking for the indifference I have for you?"

He lamented for a long time, and, seeing that night was approaching without the princess appearing, he ran to the city. When he reached the king's palace he asked for Merveilleuse, but as everyone already knew about her adventure and no one wanted her to return with the sheep, they refused harshly to let him see her. He uttered plaints and regrets capable of moving anyone except the soldiers who were guarding the door of the palace. Finally, penetrated by dolor, he threw himself to the ground and rendered his life there.

The king and Merveilleuse were unaware of the tragedy that had just occurred. He proposed to his daughter to mount a chariot and allow themselves to be seen throughout the city, by the light of thousands of torches, which were at the windows and in the large squares; but what a spectacle it was for her, on emerging from the palace, to find her dear sheep lying on the paving stones, no longer breathing!

She leapt out of the chariot and ran to him; she wept; she groaned; she knew that her lack of exactitude had caused the death of the royal sheep. In her despair, she thought she would die herself.

Everyone can agree, then, that the most elevated persons are subject, like the others, to the blows of fortune, and that they often experience the greatest misfortunes at the moment when they believe that all their wishes have been granted.

Often, the most beautiful gifts of the heavens
Only serve for our ruination
The striking merit that one requests of the gods,
Is sometimes the sad origin of our woes.
The royal sheep would have suffered less
If he had not ignited the fatal flame
That Ragotte avenged on him, on her rival;

It was his merit that doomed him.
He should have had a more propitious destiny.
Ragotte and her presents could do nothing for him;
He hated without pretence, loved without artifice,
And did not resemble the men of today.
Even his death will seem rare to us,
And only appropriate to King Mouton.
One does not see anyone nowadays
Dying when their ewes go astray.

Doña Juana, who was a connoisseur of romances, gave great applause to that one; she lamented the fate of the unfortunate sheep, and criticized the indolence of Merveilleuse. She had never been in a better mood.

Finally, she withdrew; it was time to devote herself to her toilette; she consulted all the mirrors in her apartment with an attention that she had perhaps never had before. She dressed diligently, and, going to the bedroom of her nieces, who were out of bed, she said: "How indolent you are. I've already seen the pilgrims. I've heard the prettiest romance in the world and made fifty tours of the house. If you were charitable you'd have imitated me and you wouldn't have eyes so swollen with sleep. See how awake mine are."

Isidore and Melanie had a great deal of difficulty refraining from laughing, for Doña Juana had eyes so small and sunken that if they had been less red it would be no exaggeration to say that one would have had difficulty seeing them.

They told her that they had headaches, and did not know whether they ought to return to the foreigners' room.

"You're already weary of them," said Juana, "because they're not great lords; personally, I like them because of their poverty. Can anything be more touching than fining oneself far from one's homeland, attacked by thieves and wounded? I confess that it penetrates me, and in order to enable them to regain the money that was taken from them, I've resolved to retain them here for a time, in order to show you everything that my brother desired that they come to teach you."

"What, Madame!" cried Isidore. "You want to keep people you don't know, who might perhaps by ignorant in their professions, who will more easily make us forget what we already know than inform us of what we do not?"

"You oppose yourselves to everything I want, my nieces," said Doña Juana, angrily. "I don't intend to give you masters against your will, but at least you'll permit me to take one for myself; I'd be very glad to sing with a little method and to take up playing the guitar again. Fifty years ago I played it quite well, and with a little study I'll recover what I knew; you'll be very glad to hear me then."

As she was rather thrifty, Isidore thought there was a sure means of having the pilgrims sent away in telling her that there was nothing more ridiculous than finding them in her apartment, singing or playing instruments, with a leather cap, shells, a frightful hat and calabashes, and that it would be necessary to dress them.

"You'd be very glad if they stayed like that," she said, in order to mock them, "but your brother has left very neat clothes here, and I intend to give them to them."

"Perhaps my brother isn't as charitable as you, Madame," Melanie added.

"So much the worse for him," retorted the old woman, brusquely. "It's my duty to help him go to paradise, if I can, and the surest means is to distribute charities at his expense."

She went out immediately, and her two nieces remained alone.

"Oh, my dear sister," said Melanie, "our aunt is losing her mind; at her age, she wants singing and dancing masters; can anything be more bizarre? It's certain that she's in love with one of the foreigners: that's a prodigy at which one can't be sufficiently astonished."

"What do you expect?" said Isidore, sadly. "It's our misfortune that's the cause of it; if we had an interest in the affair she'd turn around completely; in the end, it's necessary to find in our courage all the strength we need."

While they were getting dressed, Doña Juana engaged in a battle against the count, who wanted to get up and to eat something more solid than the thin chicken soup and refreshing purgative herbs that she brought him. At the word "purgative" he thought he would lose his mind, and looked askance at his cousin. "Yes," he said, "if the sympathy powder doesn't cure me today, I'll go mad."

Doña Juana, seeing him so annoyed, became annoyed in her turn and told him that he would have difficulty recovering his health; that she predicted a malign fever; that the vivacity of his eyes was a sure indication of it; that apparently he had it in mind to die; that she had done everything she could to acquit her conscience and that he could purge himself or not, as he pleased.

He could see by her somber expression that she was not content; he replied that, far from wanting to die, he had never loved life so much since she had deigned to interest herself in his; that he wished for its conservation in order to offer her his very humble services and to publish her generosity everywhere. She was easily appeased, and to make him see that she did not want to give him anything that she would not take herself, she swallowed the soup that had caused their dispute in front of him; she thought she might die of it, so effective was it, and she began to perceive that it would be necessary to quit the company imminently in order to return to her room.

"Well," exclaimed the count, as soon as he no longer saw her, "is there a similar fury and a misfortune equal to mine in being exposed to all her caprices? If they go on, and you don't become the object of them in your turn, I'll be in despair."

"My dear cousin," said Don Gabriel, laughing, "you sometimes give me the impression of being more interested in yourself than my project; but fundamentally, would you have been so very ill if you had taken the chicken soup mixed with a few purgative drugs?"

"Yes," said the count, angrily, "mingled with Hell and all its demons. I protest to you that if I had not seen Melanie and did not have a great desire to see her again, whatever you said and did, I'd abandon you in your enterprise. Alas," he continued, "I spoke only too truly when I sad that this castle was inhabited by a fay; but I added that we'd expelled her, and for my sins, we've retained her."

"You make strange lamentations," said Don Gabriel. "Stay and rest. I promise you that my powder will have cured you by this evening, and that the wound will be so completely closed that we won't even be able to see the scar."

"I wish to heaven that you were as skillful for wounds of the heart," cried the count, "for I repeat to you that I feel that the one that was inflicted on my yesterday is deep and will last a long time."

"How I love you," exclaimed Ponce de Leon, "for admitting your defeat so frankly. You know from experience that I have sometimes merited your pity, in a time when you had a great desire to refuse it to me."

When the time for the midday meal arrived Doña Juana did not find herself in a state to go to the pilgrims' room, but as the apprehension that her invalid might eat too much was tormenting her even more than the medicine she had taken she summoned her nieces in order to command them to make sure of it.

"Don't leave his room," she said, "until his brother is away from the table."

"But Madame," said Isidore, "it seems to me that your almoner is far more appropriate than we are to take care of such matters. We'll instruct him to do it, if you please."

"What!" cried Doña Juana, "always opposed to my will, devoid of charity for the poor, devoid of good will for foreigners, devoid of obedience for your aunt!" She was no angry that her nieces did not wait for everything she wanted to say to them; they left promptly.

They stopped in a gallery that it was necessary to traverse in order to reach the count's bedroom, and looked at one another sadly. "Can there be an eccentricity similar to our aunt's?" Isidore said to her sister. "She is obstinate in making us see the people who are the most dangerous in the world to us. If they had birth, wealth and attachment for us she'd want to hide us at the bottom of a well."

"But my sister," Melanie interjected, "What she's doing isn't with a view to exposing our hearts; I'm sure that she'd be in despair at encountering us in her path, She thinks that we are only made for serving her inclinations; she loves Don Estève; fire has never taken hold of a combustible material more rapidly than it has in her heart; she even wants to learn to sing and play the guitar. Would we be able to help dying of laughter if we didn't have a thousand subjects of chagrin?"

"What you say is true," said Isidore, "but how can we help rendering justice to the foreigners?"

"It's necessary always to keep in mind," Melanie continued, "that they're so far beneath us that it's impossible for our hearts to be made for either of them, and that it would be better to die than to have something for which to reproach ourselves."

At that moment they found themselves so fortified against their own penchant that they entered the pilgrims' room boldly.

The count was in bed, bearing less resemblance to a poor voyager than a man of quality; his underwear was perfectly beautiful; they had a good provision of it in a little valise. As musicians are almost always with persons of quality, they are usually very neat, so he did not hide his lace and allowed the flame-colored ribbon at his neck and his wrists to be seen. Don Gabriel had also taken off his pilgrim's cape and given a couple of strokes of the comb to his hair, with the consequence that he attracted no less attention than his cousin.

Although Isidore and her sister were followed by their maidservants, and they had commanded the almoner to come, they nevertheless found themselves embarrassed in the bedroom of two men who were not their near relatives; that was something so extraordinary in Spain that it require nothing less than their aunt's stubbornness to smooth out all the difficulties.

Melanie told the comte, smiling, that Doña Juana was so interested in his cure that she had ordered her to make him die of hunger and that she had come expressly to prevent him eating.

"Doña Juana," he said, gazing at her with as much tenderness as respect, "will easily prevent me eating if she sends you to forbid me, Madame, but I doubt that, in seeing you, my cure will be very assured."

"As for me," said Don Gabriel to Isidore, "I find that there is so much compassion for the sick here that I no longer fear falling ill."

"Do you feel some disposition of that kind?" asked Melanie, hastily.

"Yes," he replied. "I have an anxiety and a continuous heart-ache."

"That's unfortunate," added Isidore, "for we were hoping that you would sing us one of those beautiful arias that delighted us yesterday evening."

"Oh, Madame," he said, "I will always find the strength to obey you; it is sufficient for you to command something."

"But," she continued, "may we not soon hear Don Estève according his harp with your voice?"

"That will be this very evening, Madame," he said, "for my wound is healing so well that I shall be able to get up without difficulty."

"This is the time," Melanie continued, "when we are going to give you a meal. As soon as you have eaten, we shall withdraw."

"What, Madame!" said the count, interrupting. "We're going to spend all day without seeing you? I declare that it will be impossible for me to be as well this evening as I promised you."

"Unless Doña Juana has a whim to send us back here, replied Isidore, "I doubt that we shall come back."

A meal was brought to Don Gabriel, but he was so occupied with the pleasure of gazing at and listening to the woman he loved that he had no appetite. Doña Melanie pressed him to eat, and Isidore continued to talk to the count. Finally, they came to believe that they were preventing Don Gabriel from eating and the count from getting up. As they were less partisan in the matter of fasting than their aunt and they believed that the invalid might have need of some nourishment, they withdrew.

Meanwhile, Doña Juana, who thought of everything, sent them her nephew's clothes. He had had them made for the country—which is to say, in the French style. They had no difficulty in putting them on, laughing wholeheartedly.

"Don Luis," they said, "would be a clever man if he could divine that we were wearing his clothes at the present moment and were in his house."

They joked about that for some time, but Don Gabriel suddenly changed the subject. "Did you notice," he said, "the indifference with which the beautiful Isidore treated me? She scarcely deigned to respond to me, and two or three times I surprised her eyes attached to you in a very obliging manner; I would have deemed myself very happy if she had looked at me in the same way."

"That's a pure vision," replied the count, "but what is not one is that Melanie was doing in your regard what you think Isidore was doing in mine. She praised your voice to the point of exaggeration and she admired everything you said. Oh, my cousin, how apprehensive I am that you might make two conquests here rather than one."

"I have more faith than you," replied Don Gabriel, "for I confess to you that she seemed to have rather gracious manners for me, but Isidore recompensed you with interest."

"I conclude from all that," said the count, that we are not agreeable to either one of them. I should be neither surprised nor alarmed by that," he continued, immediately. "One does not make so much progress in so little time."

"I have a cruel anxiety," added Ponce de Leon, "that if you are still obstinate in being cured this evening, it might be necessary to depart tomorrow, for what pretext would we have for remaining?"

"I assure you," the count replied, "that I have no intention of exposing myself further to the importunate charity of Doña Juana. If she had wanted to make you die of hunger, render you mute and deliver you to torturers in the form of surgeons, and, to complete your disgrace, give you chicken water to drink, I'm convinced that you would have found as little humor in it as me."

"And you say that you are touched by Melanie's charms?" said Ponce de Leon, looking at him intently. "Good God, your passion is weak."

"That lovely person would please me infinitely," said the count, "if I could flatter myself that I please her, but I confess to you that, however shameful it might be, I cannot remain in bed any longer. Put yourself there in your turn, utter loud cries, complain of a pain in your side; I'll say that it's a pleurisy, and Doña Juana will have you bled charitably, until it kills you."

Vexed as Don Gabriel was, he could not help laughing at such an imagination. "I need all my strength," he said, "to sustain the coldness of Isidore."

"In order not to lose mine," replied the count, "I'm going to eat."

Ponce de Leon kept him company, and ate more like a famished traveler than a man very much in love.

The two sisters went of Doña Juana's room to pay their court to her and inform her of the good health of the pilgrims. Her own was beginning to improve slightly, for she had suffered strangely all morning. She told them that if it were true that the sympathy powder put a wounded man in a state to get up so rapidly then she would never use anything else in her maladies; that she wanted to learn the secret of it and make some for herself and all her friends.

"But," she continued, "do you believe that that poor wounded man can come into my room this evening?

"I have no doubt of it," Melanie told her. "He has the best face in the world, and I'm much mistaken if they don't put on a little concert to divert you."

"How glad I am," she exclaimed, "that hazard turned their steps toward the castle. It's necessary that they receive such good treatment here that they have reason to praise it everywhere."

Her nieces went to their apartment, and having eaten, they shut themselves in together.

"Tell me your news," said Melanie to Isidore. "What is your situation? Are you stronger or weaker?"

"I'm the most unfortunate person in the world," she replied. "I have no less chagrin than shame, not to be able to hate a man who has come to trouble my repose. You've remarked," she continued, "that I didn't say much and dreamed a great deal. I've examined my sentiments, and...no, I don't want to talk about it anymore." She fell silent.

"Melanie looked at her for a long time without saying anything.

"You feel pity for me, don't you?" Isidore continued

"Whatever pity I have for you," said Melanie, "it can't equal what I have for myself, for I sense the magnitude of my trouble more, and I believe you to be more courageous."

"Oh, my sister, what use is courage," cried Isidore, "when it is combated by our inclination?"

"But do you not think," added Melanie, "that these foreigners would be delighted to remain here?"

"Their fortune is so limited," said Isidore, "that it wouldn't surprise me at all."

"I don't know whether they're rich or poor," added Melanie. "What is constant is that to judge each of them by his person and his intelligence, one would take them for princes rather than ordinary men."

"A truce on visions, my poor Melanie," said Isidore, interrupting her. "They're only musicians; they told us that without wanting to leave us in an agreeable uncertainty, and I admire the sincerity they had."

"I protest to you," said Melanie, "that I can't believe them. Would it be the first time that someone has disguised his birth?"

"No," said her sister, "but one ordinarily represents oneself as more illustrious than one really is; one doesn't see people pretending to be peasants when they're gentlemen."

Juana, feeling much better, sent someone to enquire as to whether the pilgrims wanted to come to her room, because she would be very glad to see them, provided than Don Estève was not suffering.

At that compliment they both became anxious.

"What I fear," said Don Gabriel, "is that it's a matter of dismissing us, and I have a good mind to go to bed."

"Oh, you've waited too long," relied the count, laughing. "You must come, but let it be without dread; there's no appearance that after having found my pulse intermittent yesterday she'll want to throw is out today, and either I don't know my *virtuoso* or that one doesn't hate us."

Thus, Don Gabriel, reassured, followed the man who had been sent in quest of them. The count only went slowly—for fear, he said, of reopening his wound.

As soon as Doña Juana perceived them, she assumed and expression of gaiety by which all her maidservants were astonished; she had them sit down next to her, whatever good reasons they alleged for not taking that liberty. She begged them to give her the pleasure of singing.

The count acquitted himself no less well that Ponce de Leon; having perceived a harp in the corner of the room he asked Doña Juana if she would permit him to play it. She said that she would be delighted. Someone was sent on her order to inform the nieces; as soon as they had arrived, the count commenced singing words that he had composed expressly in order to touch the pitiable Juana in their favor.

O Heaven, banish our alarms
Stem the flow of our tears;
Along with our woes

Put an end to our pains.
In our danger, what power
Will undertake our defense?
Who will save us from furious thieves
Who are desolating this place?
O Heaven, banish our alarms
Stem the flow of our tears;
Along with our woes
Put an end to our pains.

Doña Juana, transported with admiration on hearing the young musician sing so perfectly, and finding at the same time that he was a poet, interrupted at that point.

"By Santiago, protector of Spain," she cried, "You need have no more fear of thieves; you are in a good house, you will not depart so soon, and when that happens, you shall have a good escort, so that there will be no more reason for you to be afraid."

At those words the two pilgrims made reverences and gave thanks without measure and without number. She begged them to continue their concert, and they did their best to do so.

It is easy to believe that the ladies were so favorably prejudiced in favor of the pilgrims that they heard them with an extreme pleasure, but they were nevertheless all discontented, for their eyes and sighs had no intelligence. Ponce de Leon only had eyes for Isidore, who turned hers toward the comte; the latter saw Melanie with an extreme pleasure but Melanie was only thinking of Don Gabriel.

As for Doña Juana, she praised the count and persecuted him fruitlessly; he said nothing obliging to her. She flattered herself more than the others, believing that it was an effect of his respect and that he dared not listen to the movements of his heart, but our lovers were not deceived, and were greatly afflicted. As soon as they had ceased singing, she asked them whether they wanted to attempt to show her music and how to play instruments—"And perhaps," she added, "I shall even learn to dance, as soon as I am cured of a sciatic gout that has been tormenting me for thirty years; and don't think I'll be put off; I'll keep you for twenty years if necessary."

They told her that she did them too much honor; that they would accept with pleasure to spend their life in her service, but that before engaging themselves to do so, they begged her to permit them to write to their father in order to know his will. Far from opposing it, she praised them for it extremely.

Immediately, she picked up a guitar, and played a few chords with her thin, stiff hands; her fingers trembled when she wanted to draw out the sound of a chord. It was necessary to have strong reasons not to burst out laughing, but the count, who had not lacked choice for his master, repressed all his gaiety when he thought about young Melanie's indifference. The two pilgrims, having finished the concert, retired because it was already very late, and the ladies went to their apartment.

Seeing her sister in a profound sadness, Isidore said to her: "I shall not ask you, my dear Melanie, what is wrong; I can judge the state of your heart by that of my own. We are in love, and as if that misfortune were not great enough, we find no recognition in the sentiments of those foreigners."

"It's necessary not to believe that they're insensible to us," said Melanie, "But by an unequaled fatality, their hearts or ours are mistaken; we do not love the one who loves us, we love the one who does not love us."

"Oh, my sister, my sister," Isidore interrupted, "You've said it; our hearts are mistaken; to what, great God, are they descending? But ought we to be annoyed about the snag we have encountered? It might be a means of cure? If their attachment had responded to our esteem, we would have more combats to render, instead of which, we can say to one another, let us cease, let us cease to show good will to ingrates."

"Why call them ingrates?" cried Melanie. "They're more to be pitied than blamed; perhaps it's even by politics that they are behaving thus."

"Prudence in this regard seems to me to be out of place," said Isidore. "They would have done much better not to mark any passion; but as soon as they wanted to express it, for what motives would they betray their thoughts? No, no, my dear, it's an error. Don Estève loves you, and Don Gabriel doesn't hate me; as for my aunt, she's a rival, I haven't seen her, at any other time, turn her eyes as she turned them this evening. I sometimes feared that it might go as far as convulsions."

"Well," cried Melanie, after having though for a while, "may chagrin do what pride was unable to do; since the foreigners are unable to love us as they ought, let's avoid them, without seeking with gaiety of heart to make ourselves suffer."

Isidore agreed with her.

Alas, they both wanted it, but there was no question of them having the strength to do it.

Ponce de Leon and the count lamented as much as them the fatality of their destiny. They deemed themselves fortunate to have attracted the attention of Isidore and Melanie, but they did not want to become rivals, nor change the initial object that had charmed them.

"Haven't I been repaid well?" said Don Gabriel, "for the passion that I conceived for Isidore? When I look at her, she attaches her eyes to you, and it seems that she is demanding the reason for the liberty I'm taking."

"Melanie follows the same conduct," replied the count. "I haven't been able to attract any honesty on her part; to hear her, there's as much difference between us as there is between a phoenix and a crow. You've seen the manner in which Doña Juana has conceived an affection for me."

"She's certainly your partisan," said Ponce de Leon, "but it's not up to her to console you."

"It's an augmentation of the chagrin I have to support alone," said the comte, "for I'll be obliged to have a complaisance for her, which isn't a cheerful prospect especially when one has a head full of anxiety."

Several days passed without Ponce de Leon or the count daring to declare to Isidore or to Melanie the sentiments they had for them.

"I would have spoken already," Don Gabriel said, "If I had known what I ought to expect from my confession. I can see only too clearly than I'm not loved by the person I love."

"I dare not say anything either," replied the count. "Even without Melanie's indifference, what I could I promise the character I'm playing? Is a musician born for a young woman of quality and merit? Why do you want to remain unknown any longer? Let's commence by informing them of our birth; perhaps they'll treat us more favorably?"

"What!" interrupted Ponce de Leon. "You want to add to our displeasures that of being rejected in our own name?"

"You hold your name in higher esteem than your heart, then," said the count, brusquely, "since you're protecting one more than the other. But after all, you'll be satisfied; I promised to be guided by your enlightenment; it's necessary for you to get us out of this affair with honor."

"I fear everything and have very little hope," replied Don Gabriel, "And however useful you were to me, I'd give half my life for you not to have come here."

"I wish to Heaven I hadn't!" cried the count. "I was tranquil, I was content, I could certainly have done without being amorous."

As he concluded those words, rather loudly, he heard a sound, and he was afraid that someone might have been near enough to the room to her them. In order to clarify the matter he got op, and, looking toward the door, he was surprised to see Doña Juana. She put a finger over her mouth and made a sign to him to follow her; she went to the gallery.

It was easy to understand by the expression on her face that something was happening in her mind that was agitating her. The count sensed very clearly then how dear Melanie was to him; he feared that Doña Juana knew his secret, and that she would oblige him to leave. He was so troubled that he thought twenty times over of accusing himself and making himself known, but in the end he waited for her to speak.

"You are in love, Don Estève" she said to him, "and I am not surprised that your heart has not consulted your reason, and that the inequality you find between the beloved person and yourself has not been able to deter you. You are of an age when ambition is not ill-befitting, but why do you make a confidence to your brother of something you ought to hide from everyone?"

The manner in which Doña Juana was speaking appeared so obliging and so distant from the one she ought to have had if she had known that her niece was the object of that passion that he began to doubt that she had heard everything. Not wanting to aid in his condemnation, he uttered a profound sigh without replying.

"I understand that sigh all too well," she continued, softening. "It ought to annoy me, if I were capable of anger against you. But in the end, what views could you have? A person of my birth cannot marry a man who is inferior to her."

The count's seriousness nearly failed when he realized what she meant. "The sentiments of the heart, Madame," he said, "do not always depend on us; I know well enough to what my misfortune condemns me. I shall die; that is the only remedy I can envisage."

"You cannot envisage any other?" she said, peering at him with her little red yes. "In truth, you make me feel a great pity; I am too interested in what concerns you to..."

She was about to explain herself in his favor when Melanie came in. As soon as she perceived the count with her aunt she wanted to go away, but Juana called out to her.

"Come, my niece," she said to her, "and listen to the romance that I promised to tell the other day. I'll commence...I learned it from an old Arab slave; she knew a thousand fables of that old Locman,[23] celebrated throughout the Orient, who is thought to have been none other than Aesop. The character, so naïve and infantile, that romances have doesn't please everyone equally; many fine minds regard them as works better

---

[23] Locman or Luqman is a mythical fabulist who supposedly lived in the eleventh century B.C., after whom the first thirty sura of the Quran are named.

suited to nurses and governesses than delicate people. I'm nevertheless convinced that there is an art in that sort of simplicity, and I have known persons of very good taste who sometimes made them their favorite amusement."

"I'm not surprised by that, Madame," replied the count. "The mind takes pleasure in variety. Whoever does not want to read tales or hear them told, renders himself ridiculous; whoever proposes them as very grave things lacks judgment; and whoever wants to write them in an overblown and pompous style takes away too much of the character that is appropriate to them; but I'm convinced that, after a serious occupation, one can play with them."

"It seems to me," added Melanie, who had not yet spoken, "that it is necessary to render them nether feathery nor rampant, that they ought to hold to a milieu that that is more light-hearted than serious, and above all to propose them as bagatelles to with the listener alone has the right to put a price."

It is a romance of the simplest sort that I'm going to tell you," said Juana. "You can put on it whatever price you please, but I can't help saying that those who compose them are capable of more important things when they want to take the trouble."

FINETTE CENDRON[24]

There was once a king and a queen who had handled their affairs badly. They had been expelled from their kingdom. They sold their crowns in order to live, then their

---

[24] The fact that this story blatantly combines motifs that are prominent in both of the *contes de fées* published by Mademoiselle de L'Héritier in 1696, combined with L'Héritier's efforts of promoting the genre, suggests strongly that those stories preceded this one, although it also seems probably that this one preceded Perrault's highly derivative "Cendrillon"—a nickname also used herein.

clothes, their underwear, their lace and all their furniture, piece by piece. The second-hand dealers were weary of buying, because they sold something new every day,

When the king and queen were very poor, the king said to his wife: "Here we are, outside our kingdom; we no longer have anything; it's necessary to earn our living and that of our poor children; think of what we can do, for until now I've only known the métier of king, which is very easy."

The queen had a great deal of intelligence. She asked for a week to think about it. At the end of that time she said to him: "Sire, it's necessary for us not to be afflicted; you have only to make nets, in which you'll catch birds by hunting and fish by fishing. While the cords are being worn away, I'll spin to make others. With regard to our three daughters, they're frank idlers who think they're still great ladies; they want to be damsels. It's necessary to take them away, so far way that they'll never come back; for it will be impossible for us to furnish them with enough clothes for their taste."

The king commenced weeping when he saw that it was necessary to separate from his children. He was a good father, but the queen was the mistress. He went along, therefore, with everything she wanted. He said to her: "Get up early tomorrow morning and take our three daughters wherever you think appropriate."

While they were completing that arrangement, Princess Finette, who was the youngest of the daughters, was listening through the keyhole. When she had discovered the design that her Papa and Mama had she went as quickly as she could to a large grotto a long way from their home, where the fay Merluche lived, who was her godmother.

Finette had taken two pounds of fresh butter, eggs milk and flour in order to make an excellent cake for her godmother. She commenced her journey cheerfully, but the further she went, the wearier she became. Her shores were worn away completely in the soles and her dainty little feet were grazed so much that she was in a pitiful state. She could do no more, and she sat down in the grass, weeping.

A beautiful Spanish horse passed that way, fully saddled and bridled; it had more diamonds in its horse-blanket that it required to but three cities, and when it saw the princess it started to graze placidly beside her, bending its hocks; it seemed to be making her a reverence.

"Nice horsey," she said, "Would you be so kind as to carry me to my godmother, the fay? You'd give me great pleasure, or I'm so tired I could die; but if you serve me on this occasion, I'll give you good oats and good hay; you'll have fresh straw to lie down in." The horse lowered itself almost to the ground in front of her, and young Finette jumped on to it. It started running so lightly that it seemed to be flying like a bird. It stopped at the entrance to the grotto, as if it had known the way, and it knew it very well, for it was Merluche, who, having divined that her goddaughter wanted to come and see her, had sent her the fine horse.

When she had gone in she bowed deeply three times to her godmother and picked up the hem of her dress, which she kissed. Then she said: "Good day, godmother; how are you? Here's butter, milk, flour and eggs that I've brought you for you to make a good cake in the local manner."

"Be welcome, Finette," said the fay. "Come here so I can kiss you." She kissed her twice, for which Finette was very grateful, for Madame Merluche was not a common-or-garden fay. She said: "Now, my goddaughter, I want you to be my little chambermaid; undo my hair and comb it."

The princess did her hair and combed it very adroitly.

"I know," said Merluche, "why you've come here. You've listened to the king and queen, who want to take you away and lose you, and you want to avoid that misfortune. Here, you have only to take this ball of thread; the thread will never break. Attach the end to the door of your house and hold it in your hand. When the queen has left you, it will be easy to come back by following the thread."

The princess thanked her godmother, who filled a sack with beautiful clothes, all gold and silver. She kissed her, and made her mount the pretty horse again, and in two or three moments it returned her to the door of Their Majesties' little house.

Finette said to the horse: "My little friend, you're very handsome and very good; you go more rapidly than the sun; I thank you for your trouble; return whence you came."

She went into the house very quietly and hid her sack under her bed-head. She went to bed without making any semblance of anything.

As soon as daylight appeared, the king woke his wife. "Let's go, let's go, Madame," he said to her, "get ready for your journey. Immediately she got up, put on her big shoes, a short skirt and a white camisole and picked up a staff. She summoned the eldest of her children, who was called Fleur-d'Amour, the second, Belle-de-Nuit, and the third, Fine-Oreille—that was why she was usually called Finette.

"I dreamed last night," said the queen, "that it's necessary for us to go and see my sister; shell treat us well, we'll eat and laugh as much as we like."

Fleur-d'Amour, who was in despair at being in a desert, said to her mother: "Let's go. Madame, wherever you please, provided I get outside, it doesn't matter to me." The other two said as much.

They took their leave of the king, and all four of them set forth. They went so far, so far that Fine-Oreille had a great fear of not having enough thread, for it was nearly a thousand leagues. She always walked behind her sisters, passing the thread adroitly through the bushes.

When the queen thought that her daughters could no longer find their way back she went into a large wood and said to them: "Sleep, my little ewes. I shall be like the shepherdess who watches over her flock for fear that the wolf might eat them."

They lay down on the grass and went to sleep. The queen quit them, thinking that she would never see them again. Finette closed her eyes but did not sleep.

If I were a bad girl, she said to herself, *I'd go right away and let my sisters die here, for they beat me and scratch me until I bleed. In spite of all their malice, though, I don't want to abandon them.*

She woke them up and told them the whole story. They began to weep and begged her to take them with them, promising that they would give her their beautiful dolls, their little silver house, their other toys and their bonbons.

"I know full well that you won't do anything," said Finette, "but I'll be a good sister anyway." She got to her feet and followed the thread, and the princesses too, with the result that they arrived almost immediately after the queen.

As they stopped at the door, they heard the king say: "It grips my heart seeing you come back alone."

"Good," said the queen. "We were too embarrassed with our daughters."

"Still," said the king, "if you'd brought back my Finette I'd have consoled myself for the others, for they didn't love anything."

They knocked, *tap, tap.*

The king said: "Who's there?"

They replied: "It's your three daughters, Fleur-d'Amour, Belle-de-Nuit and Fine-Oreille."

The queen started to tremble. "Don't open it," she said. "They must be spirits, for it's impossible that they've come back."

The king was as cowardly as his wife, and he said: "You're deceiving me; you're not my daughters."

But Fine-Oreille, who was clever, said to him: "I'll bend down Papa, look at me through the cat-hole, and if I'm not Finette I consent to have the whip."

The king looked, as she had told him to do, and as soon as he had recognized her he opened the door. The queen made a semblance of being very glad to see them; she told them that she had forgotten something, and that she had come to find it, but she would surely have come to find them. They pretended to believe her, and went up into the little grain-loft where they slept.

"Well, my sister," said Finette, "you promised me a doll, give it to me,"

"Truly, you had only to wait there, you little rogue," they said, "You're the cause of the king not regretting us." Then they took their distaffs and beat her like plaster.

When they had between her well she went to bed; and as she was covered in cuts and bruises she was unable to sleep, and she heard the queen say to the king: "I'll take them in another direction, much further, and I'm certain that they'll never come back."

When Finette heard that plot she got up very quietly in order to go to see her godmother again. She went into the henhouse, took two pullets and a master cock, and wrung their necks, and then two little rabbits that the queen nourished on cabbages in order to have an occasional feast. She put them all in a basket and left. She had not walked for a league, dying of fear, when the Spanish horse arrived at a gallop, snorting and whinnying. She thought she was done for, that some men-at-arms were about to catch her. When she saw the pretty horse all alone she mounted up, delighted to be so comfortable; she arrived promptly at her godmother's home.

After the ordinary ceremonies, she presented her with the pullets, the cock and the rabbits, and begged her for the aid of her good advice, because the queen had sworn that she would take them to the end of the world.

Merluche told her goddaughter not to be afflicted; she gave her a sack full of ashes. Carry the sack in front of you," she said, "shake it and walk over the ashes, and when you want to come back you only have to look at the impressions of your footsteps; but don't bring your sisters back; they're too malicious, and if you bring them back I don't want to see you again."

Finette took her leave of her, taking away, on her order, thirty or forty millions in diamonds in a little box, which she put in her pocket. The horse was all ready, and took her back, as usual.

At daybreak, the queen called the princesses; they came, and she said to them: "The king isn't very well; I dreamed last night that it's necessary to pick flowers and herbs in a certain country where they're very excellent; they'll rejuvenate him; that's why we're going right away."

Fleur-d'Amour and Belle-de-Nuit, who did not believe that their mother still had a desire to lose them, were afflicted by the news. It was necessary to go, however, and they went so far that they had never made such a long journey. Finette, who did not say a word, kept behind the others, and shook her sack marvelously, without the wind or the rain spoiling anything.

The queen, who was convinced that they could never find the way back, remarked one evening that her three daughters were fast asleep; she chose that time to quit them, and returned home.

When it was daylight and Finette knew that her mother was no longer there, she awoke her sisters. "We're alone here," she said. "The queen has gone."

Fleur-d'Amour and Belle-de-Nuit started to cry; they tore their hair and bruised their faces with their fists. They cried: "Alas, what are we going to do,"

Finette was the best girl in the world; she took pity on her sisters again.

"See what I'm risking," she said, "for when my godmother gave me the means to return, she forbade me to show you the way, and said that if I disobeyed her, she didn't want to see me anymore."

Belle-de-Nuit threw her arms around Finette's neck, and so did Fleur-d'Amour; they caressed her so tenderly that it needed no more for all three of them to return together to the king and the queen.

Their Majesties were very surprised to see the princesses again; they talked about it all night, and the youngest, who was not called Fine-Oreille for nothing, heard them make a new plot, and that the next day, the queen would set out on campaign again.

She ran to wake her sisters. "Alas," she told them, "we're doomed. The queen wants absolutely to take us into some desert and leave us there. Because of you I've annoyed my godmother, I daren't go to find her as I always did before."

They remained in great difficulty, and said to one another: "What are we going to do?"

Finally, Belle-de-Nuit said to the other two: "It's necessary not to be embarrassed. Old Merluche hasn't so much intelligence that there isn't a little left for others. We only have to load ourselves with peas; we'll drop them along the road and we'll come back. Fleur-d'Amour thought the expedient admirable; they filled their pockets. As for Fine-Oreille, instead of taking peas, she took the bag of beautiful clothes and he box of diamonds, and as soon as the queen called them they were all ready.

She said to them: "I dreamed last night that in a country, which it isn't necessary to name, there are three handsome princes who are waiting for you in order to marry you, and I'm going to take you there to see whether my dream is true."

The queen led the way and her daughters followed, dropping peas without worrying about anything, for they were certain of returning to the house. This time, the queen went even further than she had been before, but during a dark night she quit them and came back to find the king. She arrived very weary, and very glad no longer to have such a large household on her hands.

The three princesses, having slept until eleven o'clock in the morning, woke up., Finette was the first to perceive the absence of the queen. Although she was prepared for it, she wept nevertheless, trusting more for her return on her godmother the fay than the cleverness of her sisters. Very frightened, she went to tell them that the queen had gone and that it was necessary to follow her as quickly as possible.

"Shut up, little baboon," replied Fleur-d'Amour. "We'll find our way when we want, you're playing the inappropriately hasty old woman now."

Finette dared not reply; but when they tried to find the way back, there was no longer any trace of the path; the pigeons, of which there were a large number in that region, had come to eat all the peas. They started to weep until they screamed.

After having gone for two days without eating, Fleur-d'Amour said to Belle-de-Nuit: "Have you anything to eat, my sister?"

"No," she said.

She said the same thing to Finette.

"I haven't got anything either," she said, "but I've just found an acorn."

"Ha!" said the one. "Give it to me!"

"Give it to me!" said the other.

Each of them wanted to have it.

"The three of us won't sate our hunger with one acorn," said Finette. "Let's plant it. Something might come from it that might serve us."

They consented to that, although there was scarcely any appearance that a tree would grow in a land where there were none. Nothing could be seen but cabbages and lettuces, which the princesses ate. If they had been delicate they would have died a hundred times over. They almost always slept under the stars; every morning and every evening all three of them went in turn to water the acorn, and they said: "Grow, grow, lovely acorn."

It began to grow visibly. When it reached a certain size, Fleur-d'Amour wanted to climb it, but it was not strong enough to bear her weight; she felt it buckling beneath her and came down immediately. Belle-de-Nuit had the same adventure. Finette, being much lighter, remained there for longer, and her sisters asked her: "Can't you see anything, my sister?"

She replied: "No, I can't see anything."

"Oh, the oak tree isn't high enough," said Fleur-d'Amour—so they continued to water the acorn and say to it: "Grow, grow, lovely acorn." Finette never failed to climb it twice a day.

One morning, when she was there, Belle-de-Nuit said to Fleur-d'Amour: "I've found a sack that our sister has hidden from us; what can there be inside?

"She told me that it was old lace that she was repairing," Fleur-d'Amour replied.

"Personally, I think it's bonbons," added Belle-de-Nuit. She was greedy, and wanted to see. She did, indeed, find all the king and queen's lace, but they served to hide Finette's fine clothes and the box of diamonds. "Well! Could there be a greater little rogue!" she cried. "It's necessary to take it all for ourselves and put stones in its place." They did that promptly.

Finette came back without perceiving the malice of her sisters, for she did not think of ornamenting herself in a desert; she only thought about the oak tree, which had become the most beautiful of all oaks.

Once, when she climbed up it and her sisters, according to their custom, asked her whether she had discovered anything she shouted: "I've discovered a large house, so beautiful, so beautiful that I can't say it enough; the walls are made of emeralds and rubies, and the roof of diamonds. It's all covered in little golden bells; the weathervanes go back and forth with the wind."

"You're lying," they said. "It's not as beautiful as you say."

"Believe me," Finette replied, "I'm not a liar. Come here and see for yourselves; my eyes are completely dazzled."

Fleur-d'Amour climbed the tree; when she had seen the castle she could not shut up about it. Belle-de-Nuit, who was very curious, did not fail to climb up in her turn; she was as rapturous as her sisters.

"Certainly," they said, it's necessary to go to that palace. "Perhaps we'll find handsome princes there who will be only too glad to marry us."

All evening long, they talked about nothing but their plan. They lay down on the grass; but when Finette appeared to them to be fast asleep, Fleur-d'Amour said to Belle-de-

Nuit: "Do you know what we ought to do, my sister? Let's get up and put on the rich clothes that Finette has brought."

"You're right," said Belle-de-Nuit."

They got up, therefore, curled their hair, powdered their faces and then put on beauty-spots and the beautiful gold and silver dresses all covered with diamonds. There had never been anything so magnificent.

Finette was unaware of the theft that her wicked sisters had committed. She took her sack with the design of getting dressed, but only found pebbles; at the same time she perceived her sisters, who were dressed up like suns. She wept, and complained to the treason they had committed. They laughed at her and mocked her.

"Is it possible," she said, "that you have the courage to take me to the castle without adorning me and making me beautiful?"

"We only have enough for ourselves," replied Fleur-d'Amour. "You'll only get blows if you importune us."

"But those clothes that you're wearing are mine," she continued. "My godmother gave them to me; they're nothing to do with you."

"If you say any more," thy sad, "We're going to kill you, and we'll bury you without anyone knowing."

Poor Finette was careful not to irritate them; she followed them meekly, and walked a little way behind them, only able to pass for their servant,

The closer they came to the house, the more marvelous it seemed to them.

"Ha!" said Fleur d'Amour and Belle-de-Nuit. "How well we're going to amuse ourselves! What god cheer we'll have! We'll eat at the king's table, but poor Finette will wash the dishes in the kitchen, because she's dressed like a scullion, and if anyone asks who she is, let's refrain carefully from calling her our sister; it's necessary to say that she's a little village milkmaid."

Finette, who was full of intelligence and beauty, was in despair at being so maltreated.

When they reached the door of the castle, they knocked. Immediately, a frightful old woman came to open it. She only had one eye in the middle of the forehead, but it was larger than five or six others, a flat nose, a dark complexion and a mouth so horrible that it was scary. She was five feet tall and thirty around.

"What brings you here, unfortunate young women?" she said to them. "Don't you know that this is the ogre's castle, and that you'll scarcely be sufficient for his breakfast? But I'm better than my husband. Come in, I won't eat you all at once, and you'll have the consolation of living for two or three days more."

When they heard the ogress speak thus, they fled, thinking that they could get away, but a single one of her strides was worthy fifty of theirs; she ran after them and caught them, one by the hair and the others by the skin of the neck, putting them under her arm. She threw all three of them into a cellar that was full of toads and snakes, and they were treading on the bones of the people the ogres had eaten.

As she wanted to eat Finette immediately, she went in search of vinegar, oil and salt in order to eat her in a salad, but she heard the ogre coming and, thinking that the princesses had white and delicate skin, she resolved to eat them all by herself, and promptly put them in a large tub, where they could only see out through a hole.

The ogre was six times as tall as his wife; he spoke, the house shook, and when her coughed it resembled bursts of thunder. He only had one huge horrible eye; his hair was all bristly; he was leaning on a log that he used as a walking-stick. He had a covered basket in his hand; he took out fifteen little children that he had stolen on the roads, and which he swallowed like fifteen fresh eggs.

When the three princesses saw that, they trembled in the tub. They did not dare weep loudly for hear that he might hear them, but they said to one another in whispers: "He's going to eat us all alive; how are we going to save ourselves?"

The ogre said to his wife: "Do you know, I can smell fresh flesh? I want you to give it to me."

"Good," said the ogress. "You always think you can smell fresh flesh, and it's your sheep that have passed through."

"Oh, I'm not mistaken," said the ogre. "I smell fresh flesh, for sure. I'm going to search everywhere."

"Search," she said. "You won't find anything."

"If I find that you're hiding it from me," the ogre replied, "I'll cut off your head to make a bowling-ball."

She was frightened by that threat and said: "Don't get annoyed, my little ogrelet; I'll tell you the truth. Three young girls came today, whom I captured, but it would be a pity to eat them, because they can all do sorts of things. As I'm old, it's necessary that I repose; you can see that our beautiful house is very untidy, that our bread isn't baked, that the soup no longer seems as good to you, and that I don't seem so beautiful to you anymore, because I'm killing myself with hard work. They can be my servants. I beg you, don't eat them right away; if you want to do it someday, you'll still be the master of that."

The ogre had a great deal of difficulty promising her not to eat them right away. "Let me do it," he said. "I'll only eat two of them."

"No, you shan't eat them."

"Well hen, I'll only eat the smallest one."

"No," she said, "You won't eat any of them."

Finally, after much contestation, he promised not to eat them. She thought secretly: *When he goes hunting, I'll eat them, and I'll tell him that they've run away.*

The ogre came out of the cellar; he told her to bring them to him. The poor young women were almost dead of fear, but the ogress reassured them. When he saw them, he asked them what they could do. They replied that they could sweep, that they could sew and spin marvelously, that they made such good stews that people ate them all the way to the dish, and that as for bread, cakes and pastries, people came to their house in search of them from a thousand leagues around.

The ogre was greedy. He said: "All right, let's put these good workers to work. But," he said to Finette, "when you've lit the fire in the oven, how can you tell whether it's hot enough?"

"Milord," she replied, "I throw butter into it, and then I taste it with my tongue."

"Well then," he said, "light the oven."

That oven was as large as a stable, for the ogre and the ogress ate more bread than four armies. The princess made a frightful fire there; it was ablaze like a furnace, and the ogre, who was present, waiting for the soft bread, ate a hundred lambs and a hundred suckling pigs. Fleur-d'Amour and Belle-de-Nuit kneaded the dough.

"Well," said the master ogre, "is the fire hot enough?"

"Milord," said Finette, "You'll see." She threw a hundred pounds of butter into the depths of the oven in front of it, and then said: "It's necessary to feel it with the tongue, but I'm too small."

"I'm tall," said the ogre, and, bending down, he plunged so far forward that he could not get out again, with the result that he burned all the way to the bones.

When the ogress came to the oven she was very astonished to find a mountain of the ash of her husband's bones.

Fleur-d'Amour and Belle-de-Nuit, who saw that she was very afflicted, did their best to console her, but they feared that her dolor might calm down too soon and that, having an appetite, she might put them in a salad, as she had already thought of doing.

"Have courage, Madame," they said to her, "You'll find some king or marquis who'll be happy to marry you."

She smiled a little, showing teeth longer than a finger.

When they saw that she was in a good mood, Finette said to her: "If you want to take off those horrible bearskins in you're wearing and dress more fashionably, we can do your hair marvelously; you'll be like a star."

"Let's see what you can do," she said, "but be sure that if there are any ladies prettier than me, I'll chop you up like mincemeat."

With that, the three princesses took off her bonnet, and started combing and curling her hair; while they were amusing her with their chatter, Finette took an ax and dealt her such a great blow from behind that it separated her body from her head.

There had never been such delight; they went up on to the roof of the house to divert themselves by ringing the golden bells. They went into all the rooms, which were lined with pearls and diamonds, and had furniture so rich that they were dying of pleasure. They laughed and sang; they did not lack anything; there was wheat, jam, fruits and dolls in abundance.

Fleur-d'Amour and Belle-de-Nuit lay down in brocade and velvet beds and said to one another: "Now we're richer than our father was when he had his kingdom, but we still lack being married, and no one will come here; this house surely passes for a cut-throats' den, for no one knows that the ogre and ogress are dead. It's necessary that we go to the nearest city to be seen with our beautiful clothes, and it won't take us long to find good financiers who'll be very glad to marry princesses."

As soon as they were dressed they old Finette that they were going for a walk that that she was to stay in the house and do the cleaning and the washing, and that everything had to be neat and tidy when they got back; if not, they would beat her.

Poor Finette, whose heart was constricted by dolor, remained alone in the lodgings, sweeping, cleaning and washing without repose, and always weeping.

How unfortunate I am, she said to herself. *Because I disobeyed my godmother, all sorts of disgraces have overtaken me; my sisters have stolen my rich clothes; they make use of them to adorn themselves. But for me, the ogre and his wife would still be alive and well; what advantage have I obtained from killing them? Wouldn't it have been better for them to eat me than to live like this?*

When she had said that, she wept until she choked. Then her sisters arrived laden with Portuguese oranges, jam and sugar, and they said to her: "Oh, what a beautiful ball we've been to! How many people there were! The king's son danced there; everyone made us a thousand honors. Come on, take our shoes off and clean us up, that's your job."

Finette obeyed, and if by chance she uttered a word of complaint they threw themselves upon her and beat her enough to leave her for dead.

The following day they went to the city again and came back to relate marvels.

One evening, when Finette was sitting rather close to the fire on a heap of ashes, not knowing what to do, she searched the cracks in the fireplace, and found a little key that was so old and dirty that she had all the difficulty in the world cleaning it up. When it was bright, she realized that it was gold, and thought that a golden key ought to open a nice little casket. She immediately started running all over the house, trying the key in locks, and finally found a casket that was a masterpiece.

She opened it; inside there were clothes, diamonds, lace, underwear and ribbons worth immense sums. She did not say a word about her good fortune, but waited impatiently for her sisters to go out the next day. As soon as she no longer saw them, she adorned herself, with the result that she was more beautiful than the sun and the moon.

Thus attired she was at the same ball where her sisters were dancing, and although it was not a masked ball, she had changed so much for the better that they did not recognize her. As soon as she appeared in the assembly, a murmur of voices rose up, some of admiration and others of jealousy. She was asked to dance, and she surpassed all the ladies in dancing as she surpassed them in beauty. The mistress of the house came to her, and having made her a profound reverence, begged her to tell her what she was called, in order never so forget the name of such a marvelous person. She replied, politely, that she was known as Cendron.

There was no lover who would not have been unfaithful to his mistress for Cendron, and no poet who was not seeking rhymes for Cendron; no nickname had ever made so much noise in such a short time; he echoes only repeated praise for Cendron; no one had enough eyes to gaze at her or enough mouth to laud her.

Fleur-d'Amour and Belle-de-Nuit, who had initially caused a great stir in the places where they had appeared, seeing the welcome that was given to the newcomer, were dying of chagrin, but Finette cleaved a path through all of it with the best grace in the world; it seemed, from her manner, that she had been born to command.

Fleur-d'Amour and Belle-de-Nuit, who only saw their sister with the soot of the hearth on her face, smeared with more dirt than a little dog, had lost the idea of her beauty so completely that they did not recognize her at all; they paid their court to Cendron like the others.

As soon as she saw that the ball was about to end she left quickly, returned to the house, undressed diligently, and resumed her rags. When her sisters came home, they said to her, "Oh, Finette, we've just seen a young princess who is utterly charming; she's not a she-monkey like you; she's as white as snow, redder than roses; her teeth are pearls, her lips coral; she has a dress that weighs more than a hundred pounds, it's nothing but gold and diamonds. How beautiful she is! How lovable she is!"

Finette muttered between her teeth: "So I was, so I was."

"What are you buzzing?" they said.

"So I was," Finette replied, even more quietly.

That little game went on for a long time; hardly a day went by without Finette changing clothes, for the casket was enchanted, and the more one took out of it, the more it filled up again, and she was so fashionable that the ladies only dressed on her model.

One evening, when Finette had danced more than usual and had been rather late in leaving, wanting to make up the time lost and arrive home before her sisters, walking as fast as she could, she dropped one of her slippers, which was red velvet embroidered with pearls. She did everything possible to find it on the road but the night was so black that it was wasted effort. She returned to the house with one foot shod and the other bare.

The next day, Prince Cheri, the elder son of the king, while going hunting, found Finette's slipper; he picked it up, looked at it, admired its smallness and elegance, turned it over and over, kissed it, cherished it and took it away with him. From that day on he no longer ate; he became thin and changed, as yellow as a quince, sad and depressed. The king and the queen, who loved him recklessly, sent in all directions for good game and jam; it was less than nothing for him; he looked at all that without responding to the queen when she spoke to him.

They sent in quest of physicians everywhere, as far afield as Paris and Montpellier. When they arrived, they were taken to see the prince, and after having considered them for three days and three nights without losing sight of him, they concluded that he was in love and that he would die if no remedy was found.

The queen, who loved him madly wept as if to dissolve at being unable to discover who it was with whom he was in love, in order that he could marry her. She brought all the most beautiful ladies into his bedroom, but he did not deign to look at them. Finally, she said to him: "My dear son, you're going to make us choke with grief, for you're in love and you're hiding your sentiments from us. Tell us who you want and we'll give her to you, even if she's only a simple shepherdess."

The prince, emboldened by the queen's promises, took the slipper out from beneath his bed-head and showed it to her. "Here, Madame," he said. "This is the cause of my trouble; I found this pretty little dainty doll-like slipper while going hunting, and I shall only ever marry the person who can put it on."

"Well, my son," said the queen, "don't be afflicted; we'll find her."

She went to give that news to the king. He was very surprised, but he commanded that men be sent with drums and trumpets to announce that all the married and unmarried women come to put the slipper on, and that whichever one it fitted would marry the prince.

Everyone, having heard what was at stake, cleaned their feet with all sorts of liquids, creams and lotions. There were ladies who had them peeled, in order to have more beautiful skin; others fasted or had them flayed in order to have smaller ones. They came in a host to try on the slipper; not one of them could put it on, and the more that came unsuccessfully, the more afflicted the prince became.

Fleur-d'Amour and Belle-de-Nuit made themselves up one day so boldly that it was astonishing. "Where are you going?" Finette asked them.

"We're going to the capital city, where the king and queen live," they said, "to try on the slipper that the king's son has found, for if it fits one of us, he'll marry her and we'll be queens."

What about me?" said Finette. "Aren't I going?"

"Truly," they said, "you're a fine stuffed goose. Go water our cabbages; you're good for nothing."

Finette immediately thought that she should put on her most beautiful clothes and go to attempt the adventure like the others, for she had a slight suspicion that she would succeed in it; what caused her difficulty was that she did not know the way; the ball at which she went to dance was not in the capital city.

She dressed magnificently; her dress was blue satin, covered with stars and diamonds; she had a sun on her head and a full moon on her back; all that shone so brightly that one could not look at her without blinking.

When she opened the door to go out, she was very astonished to find the beautiful Spanish horse that had taken her to her godmother's house. She caressed him and said to him: "Be welcome, my little horsey; I'm obliged to my stepmother Merluche." He bent down; she sat on him like a nymph. He was covered in little golden bells and ribbons; his blanket and bridle were priceless, and Finette was thirty times as beautiful as Helen of Troy.

The Spanish horse went lightly, its little bells going *ding, ding, ding*. Fleur-d'Amour and Belle-de-Nuit, having heard them, turned round and saw her coming, but how surprised they were at that moment! They recognized her as Finette Cendron. They were very dirty; their beautiful clothes were covered in mud.

"My sister," cried Fleur-d'Amour, speaking to Belle-de-Nuit, "I protest to you that that's Finette Cendron."

The other cried likewise, and as Finette went past them her horse splashed them and made them masks of filth.

She started to laugh and said to them: "Highnesses, Cendrillon scorns you as much as you merit." Then, passing by like an arrow, she was gone.

Belle-de-Nuit and Fleur-d'Amour looked at one another. "Are we dreaming?" they said. "Who can have given Finette those clothes and a horse? What a marvel! Fortune will favor her; she's going to put on the slipper, and we'll only have the pain of a wasted journey."

While they were despairing, Finette arrived at the palace; as soon as people saw her, everyone believed that she was a queen; the guards presented arms, the drums were beaten, the trumpets were sounded, all the doors were opened and those who had seen her at the ball went ahead of her, saying: "Make way, make way, it's the beautiful Cendron, the marvel of the universe."

She entered with that apparel into the bedroom of the dying prince; he cast his eyes upon her and was charmed, wanting her to have a foot small enough to put on the slipper. She put it on immediately, and showed its counterpart, which she had brought with her expressly.

At the same time, people cried: "Long live Princess Cherie, long live the princess who will be our queen."

The prince got out of bed and came to kiss her hands; she found him handsome and full of intelligence; he made her a thousand amities. The king and queen were informed, and came running. The queen took Finette in her arms, called her daughter, her darling, her little queen, gave her admirable presents, which the liberal king outbid. Cannons were fired; all the violins and bagpipes were played; people talked about nothing but dancing and rejoicing.

The king, the queen and the prince begged Cendron to consent to be married.

"No," she said, "It's necessary before then that I tell you my story"—which she did, in a few words.

When they knew that she had been born a princess there was quite another joy; it would not have taken much for them to have died of it; but when she told them the names of the king, her father, and the queen, her mother, they realized that they were the ones who had conquered their kingdom. They announced that to her, and she swore that she would never consent to her mirage unless her father's estates were returned to him. They promised her that, for they had more than a hundred kingdoms, and one fewer was of no significance.

Meanwhile, Belle-de-Nuit and Fleur-d'Amour arrived. The first news they heard was that Cendron had put on the slipper. They did not know what to do or say; they wanted to go home without seeing her, but when she discovered that they were there she had them come in, and instead of looking at them unkindly and punishing them s they merited, she got up, went to them and embraced them tenderly. Then she presented them to the queen, saying to her: "Madame, these are my sisters, who are very amiable; I beg you to love them."

They were so confused by Finette's kindness that they could not say a word. She promised them that they would return to their kingdom, and that the prince wanted to return it to their family. At those words they threw themselves on their knees before her, weeping with joy.

The wedding was the most beautiful that has ever been seen. Finette wrote to her godmother and put the letter, with great presents, on the pretty Spanish horse, begging her to find the king and queen, tell them about her good fortune, and that they had nothing more to do than return to their kingdom.

The fay Merluche acquitted that commission very well. Finette's mother and father returned to their estates and her sisters were queens as well as her.

> *To extract from an ingrate a noble vengeance,*
> *Imitate the prudence of young Finette,*
> *Do not cease, like her, to pour forth benefits;*
> *All your presents and services,*
> *Will be as many secret vengeances.*
> *Those who prepared tortures in a troubled heart,*
> *Belle-de-Nuit and Fleur-d'Amour,*
> *Were more cruelly punished*
> *When Finette showed them infinite mercy,*
> *Than if the cruel ogre had taken their lives;*
> *Follow at all times her maxim,*
> *And think in your resentment,*
> *Than a magnanimous heart can never*
> *Be avenged more generously.*

It is easy to imagine how, by virtue of complaisance, the count and Melanie proclaimed of the romance that none had ever been so gallant, and above all, so well told.

Juana was delighted. "You see," she added, "That it's as pretty as Don Gabriel's."

"Oh, Madame," said the count, "nothing equals yours." He would have extended himself further in the praise that she enjoyed so much, if she had not been informed that the Archbishop of Compostela had just arrived, and that he was already in his apartment.

She hastened to go and receive him. Melanie wanted to go with her, but the count could not help retaining her.

"You're going to find me very bold, Madame," he said to her, "but I have only stopped you in order to talk to you about my respectful passion. Yes, Madame, I love you." He paused at that point, and then resumed speaking. "You're blushing at such a bold confession, but don't judge the heart that I offer you by my scant fortune; I am certain that it can work miracles in my favor, if you have some generosity for me."

"A truce on visions, Don Estève," she said, looking at him with an expression full of scorn. "The best thing that your temerity can bring you is that I keep silent and regard you in the future as an insensate."

The comte was thunderstruck; he was on the point of replying that if Don Gabriel had spoken in the same terms she would not have responded with so much bitterness, but he overcame his chagrin, and dared not hinder her from leaving the gallery

He was pacing back and forth, thinking about his adventure when Don Gabriel, anxious as to what Doña Juana wanted of him, came to find him, and the chagrin that appeared on his face alarmed him more than a little.

"Tell me our destiny," he said.

"I know nothing of yours," the count replied, in a chagrined manner. "As for mine, I surely have no reason to be satisfied. Melanie has just treated me as a wretch; she is retrenching herself on the obscurity of my birth, but it's you who are putting me in a bad light with her."

"Well, my cousin," replied Ponce de Lon. "Am I any better placed in my affairs? Isidore looks at me with an insupportable scorn; however, I cannot neglect declaring my passion to her, even if she adds further displeasures to those she has already given me."

"You have less reason to complain than me," the count continued. "Isidore is the sole object of your concern, but in my regard, it's necessary that I have a ridiculous complaisance for old Juana, and that I give her moments that I could employ better. Just now, for example, she made me hear that she doesn't hate me and that she is convinced that I adore her. Can one fall into such extravagance? I don't believe that if Melanie continues to mistreat me, I can suffer the aunt's good treatment patiently."

He continued talking, but Ponce de Leon made no reply.

"What's the matter with you, then?" said the count. "You're very pensive."

"I'm composing the couplets of a song," he replied, "for the tune that Isidore likes so much. When it's finished, you can tell me what you think."

"I advise you not to rely on my advice," said the count. "I have no liberty of mind at the moment."

As they were about to emerge from the gallery they heard their names called by Juana's principal duenna; she had come in search of them in order to sing for the Archbishop of Compostela, but they knew him too well to risk appearing before him; they excused themselves with a cold in the head and a violent headache. In the dread that they would be pressed to go, they went into the park and climbed up to a room that overlooked the wood.

It recalled a thousand things to the memory of our pilgrims, one complaining of having come in search of troubles and worries, and the other afflicted by having found so little return in a heart that could make the felicity of his life. They gazed at the wood, and agreed that they would have done better to stay there than to have a star so fatal in their amours.

"For is there a similar bizarrerie?" Don Gabriel continued. "Isidore looks at you favorably, Melanie would receive my prayers; it isn't to her that I address them, and you only have indifference for the one who loves you."

"If only we could change places," said the count, "our felicity would depend on us again."

"Ha! What a proposition!" cried Don Gabriel. "Would you be capable of wishing what you're saying?"

"Yes, certainly," said the count. "I'd wish it with all my heart, but my heart understands its interests so poorly that it doesn't want it."

They stayed in that place until they had heard the archbishop go by, returning to Compostela. Immediately, they went down into the park, and, traversing one of the pathways, they perceived Isidore with Melanie. They had been in Juana's room for such a long time that they were very glad to come out for a walk.

"Let's go into the arbor," said Ponce de Leon to his cousin. "I'll sing the aria that Isidore loves; perhaps she'll come."

He was not mistaken in that conjecture; but as Melanie was angered against the count she begged her sister to stop near the arbor, and told her why. They slipped between the trees, but not so quietly that Ponce de Leon did not hear them nearby. He did not delay in singing these words;

Do not resist Amour,
Isidore, lay down your arms;
All hearts must, in their turn
Sense the power of his charms.

Sooner or later the god prevails,
And our resistance is vain;
It is better to give one's heart
Than to wait for it to be taken.

What would you do if Amour,
To punish your resistance,
Came in your declining days
To make you sense his power?

Unable o stifle the amour
By which your heart was attained,
You would be heard, every day,
Uttering this futile plaint:

Alas, potent master of the gods
In whom my hope is founded
Render some charms to my eyes,
Or blind the whole world.

Don Gabriel was about to continue when Doña Juana entered like a fury; she had been so anxious about the headache of her dear pilgrim that as soon as the archbishop had gone she had run into the pathways of her park, where she knew that he had gone, The voice of Don Gabriel had attracted her. She had hidden in a little wood, and had been surprised to hear her niece named in the first couplet, but when he sang those about an old woman she had no doubt that they were about her.

Hurling herself into the arbor, as I have already said, she said: "So, Don Gabriel, it's with satirical songs that you repay the good welcome you've received from me! You give pretty advice to my niece, and you treat me in a jesting manner!"

It would be difficult to express the surprise of our two lovers; the consequences of such a sharp anger had never been so apprehensively anticipated. It was then that they sensed everything that they might lose if she obliged them to leave. The count was beginning to excuse Don Gabriel when Isidore and Melanie, urged by a dread that they could not overcome, came to join the conversation.

"What, Madame," they said to their aunt, "Do you no longer remember that my sister and I made that song in your room, that it was to divert you, and that you wanted me to make a few more couplets? I taught them to Don Gabriel, and if it causes you chagrin now, it is us that it is necessary to forbid to sing it."

It is true that the two beautiful young women had made up songs, but not true that they had made up that one; however, the manner in which they asserted it convinced Doña Juana. She had an extreme joy at not being turned to ridicule, and suddenly calmed down.

"I am sorry," she said to Ponce de Leon, "to have appeared to you to be embittered, but put yourself in my place; if those couplets were about me, nothing would be more disobliging."

Don Gabriel said the most honest things in the world to her, and, turning to Isidore, he said: "What do I not owe you, Madame? You have justified me. I would die of dolor if Doña Juana had suspected me of ingratitude." Afterwards speaking quietly enough only to be heard by her, he continued: "Yes, Madame, I would have died of dolor if it had been necessary to distance myself from you."

She only replied with a gaze that had nothing terrible about it.

When he had retired with his cousin, they embraced, and the count spoke. "Admit the truth," he said. "Our old lady gave us a great scare."

"I haven't yet recovered from it," replied Don Gabriel, "And if I make any more songs in my life in which she has a part, I want..."

"But also," said the count, interrupting, "of what futile verbiage have you gone in search? Instead of declaring your passion to Isidore, you recount the follies of her aunt!"

"Oh," said Don Gabriel, "the declaration was coming in its turn; I didn't have time to sing it."

"Believe me," said the count, laughing, "do it in prose."

"You think, then," said Don Gabriel, "that I ought to regret having made those couplets; I assure you, however, that Isidore might have more indulgence for poets than other people, for she looked at me with an expression of good will that I haven't experienced before."

"If Melanie proves to be of a similar humor," said the count. "I'll write verses day and night."

In fact, the following day, as he sang very tender lines, she gave him her notebook and asked him to write them down. He thought for a moment and, profiting from the opportunity, instead of doing as she asked, he wrote:

Can the most rebellious heart
Resist for very long
The assiduous and constant cares,
That a faithful lover renders?

She read those lines and, taking her handkerchief with a disdainful expression, she erased them. The count felt extremely piqued, but let nothing show. "You've punished me well, Madame," he said, "for that little trick. If you're agreeable to handing me your notebook again, I'll put what you wish therein."

She gave it to him, and he wrote these words to the tune of a minuet that he had taught her:

You scorn a faithful heart,
I feel the rigors of the most terrible fate;
My dolor is more than mortal,
But I cannot find death.

Melanie appeared even more offended by the latest lines than the previous ones. Addressing Don Gabriel, she said: "Your brother is using with me a manner so familiar that it seems that we are equals."

"I know only too well who I am and who you are," said the count, "but Madame, everything renders me criminal in your eyes; you make me feel harshly the misfortune I have in being without merit."

Isidore, who was listening, had a malign joy in his pain. "My sister is proud and a little grim," she said to him, laughing.

"Alas, Madame," added Ponce de Leon, "Are you any less so than her?"

At that question she remained embarrassed; the person who asked it was not sufficiently agreeable to her for her to want to reply to it in an agreeable manner.

It was thus that those four individuals, who could have made one another's felicity, tormented one another by virtue of the bizarrerie of their star.

Meanwhile, Doña Juana was only occupied with her obsession with the count. She summoned him to her cabinet, and after a preamble whose conclusion he awaited with dread, she continued: "Don Estève, I find you such a gallant man that although I have resolved never to submit to the harsh laws of marriage, I believe that I can take other measures without risking anything. My father having been governor of Lima, he acquired great wealth, and has left me more in Mexico than in Spain. If you would like to come there with me, I will share my fortune with you, for I could not decently stay in this country after having married you, whereas in that one, no one would know who you are and we would be happy there. Examine that proposition; if it suits you, it is necessary to embark soon, for the galleons are on the point of departure."

The count was surprised by a proposition so extravagant; he thought that a refusal would be too piquant, and that it was necessary only to elude the affair. "I cannot mark you all my gratitude, Madame," he said, "for your generosity; I sense that I would never be ingrate for it, and to commence rendering myself worthy of it, I will make you a confession of my fortune.

"A very rich young widow, having acquired a great deal of amity for me, received me frequently in her home, and proposed marriage to me; I accepted that offer with joy; my father was delighted by it; the contract and the engagement followed shortly thereafter. In sum, on the day appointed for our marriage, I went to find her with my family and I married her in a country house near Antwerp. But we had not been together for a week when her first husband arrived; he was believed to have perished ten years before. My wife—or, to put it better, his—pretended not to recognize him. The scandal of the affair was considerable, and my displeasure so violent, that I left the care of it to my father and departed with my brother for Santiago. I beg you, Madame," he continued, "to permit me to discover what has been regulated before departing for Mexico."

"That is very just," replied Doña Juana, anxiously, "and I confess that if I had thought you were married, I would have stifled immediately the obliging sentiments that I had for you; for, in sum, you love that woman and you will always be chagrined by having lost her."

"Oh, Madame, how easily I would have consoled myself with you," he said, kissing her hand, "but you can see that it is necessary for my marriage to be broken."

The good lady agreed, although her tenderness was strong enough to enable her to pass over all the scruples of polygamy.

Don Gabriel was waiting for his cousin with the utmost anxiety; he still feared that some unfortunate contretemps might make him known, and that Doña Juana would oblige them to leave, but he was reassured when he heard the count returning, singing these words that he had made for Juana, and which he was pronouncing indistinctly because of consequences:

> *Iris passes in spite of years*
> *For the younger sister of spring;*
> *Without seeking other reasons*
> *In metamorphoses,*
> *Iris is replete with buds,*
> *And the springtime of roses.*

"I was alarmed," said Ponce de Leon, "But you appear to me to be to cheerful for my fears to be well founded."

"Indeed," the count replied, "I have good reason, and you'll agree when I tell you that I've come to invite you to my wedding."

"Your wedding!" Ponce de Leon interrupted. "What, to Isidore?"

"No," said the comte, smiling, "I haven't had the bad taste to choose a young and beautiful woman; I'll tell you that the marriage will be in Mexico, in the great city of Lima, with the very amiable and very charming Doña Juana."

"How long have you been raving mad?" Don Gabriel responded.

"A truce on madness," said the count. "The matter is very serious, but there's a slight difficulty in our marriage; it's that my wife who is in Brussels, might well not intend to be mocked."

Ponce de Leon burst out laughing; the count could not help doing likewise. He told him afterwards more seriously, what had happened, and Don Gabriel told him that he was very apprehensive of the outcome of all this intrigue.

It was already late enough for Ponce de Leon that Count d'Aguilar not to want to separate; they went to bed together.

The count was not yet asleep when he heard his door open quietly. He was all the more surprised because he usually took away the key, but he was even more so on seeing a man and a woman come in. He nudged his cousin, and without saying anything to him for fear of being heard, he obliged him to look.

The moon illuminated the room brightly enough for them to see everything that was happening.

They thought at first that it was Doña Juana who had come to take liberties with the count, but why bring a man and stand in a corner? Don Gabriel remembered that Isidore had looked at him with rather obliging eyes and flattered himself than she might have repented of her indifference and wanted to talk to him, but the hour seemed very suspect for such a sage person, and it was not in the count's room that she would have come to look for him. He therefore feared that if it were really her, she might be there for his cousin, since she had always testified more good will toward him.

That was what was passing through their minds when the lady, speaking in a low voice, said: "How I fear the humor of your aunt, Don Luis! With what eye will she see me after that I have dared to do for you?"

"Have no fear, beautiful Lucile," he said. "Doña Juana will be supportive; my sisters will not neglect anything to please you; you are at home here, but it's too late to wake them; that's what obliges me to leave you in my bedroom, so that you can spend the rest of the night here, and I take measures to ensure that no one knows where we are."

"In fact," she said, "the fury of my relatives will be extreme; this succession, which enriches me, renders me more considerable in their eyes than my own person. Alas, Don Luis, what will you do to appease them?"

"I will love you more than anything in the world, my dear Lucile," he continued, "and I hope to make them know that it is by virtue of the movements of a violent passion that I resolved to abduct you; for, after all, I have enough wealth and birth to..."

He did not finish, for the count had been seized by such a violent desire to cough, which he had been holding back for a quarter of an hour, that he finally had to cough in spite of his efforts.

At that sound, the startled Lucile would have run away if Don Luis, on entering the room, had not taken the precaution of locking the door.

He took a few steps toward the bed, very surprised to find on the chairs clothes that he had left in his wardrobe; he did not understand by what spirit of familiarity someone had taken it into his head to take them and wear them, for he knew well enough that whoever had coughed was the same person who put on his clothes.

He was about to open the curtain when he suddenly stopped; then, returning to Lucile, he said: "I don't know what to resolve. Perhaps the man who has just coughed is asleep, and has not heard us; perhaps he is even deaf; that is not impossible."

"But even if he is deaf and asleep," said Lucile, "will he not necessarily see us in this room, unless God grants us the mercy that he is also blind?"

At those words, Ponce de Leon and his cousin burst out laughing, and drew the curtain.

"My dear Don Luis," they said, "approach your best friends, and know that we have no less need of your discretion that you have of ours."

Don Luis recognized the voice of his friends with all the more astonishment because he had mourned their deaths.

Since their departure from Cadiz, accompanied only by a valet de chambre, no one in the world had had any news of them, and as a troop of thieves was running the country, so cruel that they gave no quarter, it was believed that they had fallen into their hands and had been murdered. It was easier for Don Luis to imagine that their spirits had returned from the other world than to imagine them full of life in the house of Doña Juana, the most severe of all spinsters, who captivated even more the persons over whom she could extend her domination.

Lucile trembled, and Don Luis thought about an event so singular, without making any response.

"Approach, my dear friend," said the count, "We have infinite measures to take with you."

Don Luis, very emotional, ran to them with open arms. "How can I explain my joy and my surprise to you?" he said. "Your absence from Cadiz threw me into the utmost anxiety; I'm delighted that the rumors that are running around are false. But to find you in my room when I thought I was alone here with Doña Lucile! To find you in the home of my torturer of an aunt! What does this mean? Do my sisters have some part in it? Don't disguise anything from me."

"Yes, Don Luis," exclaimed Don Gabriel, "Your sisters have some part in it; I felt myself so touched by the elder of whom you spoke, and of whom you gave me a very advantageous description that I was only occupied which the means of seeing her. I would have concerted them with you if you have not already left for Seville; I even regarded the execution of my design as an impossibility, by reason of the severe guard that Doña Juana maintained over them, and I believe that I would not have dared to attempt the adventure if my cousin, sensitive to my pain, had not imagined a disguise, in favor of which we were received here."

The count then told him everything that had happened, about his passion for Melanie, and even the proposition that Juana had made that he go with her to Mexico.

Don Luis listened to them with a great deal of pleasure. His sisters could not hope, without a particular good fortune, to find such good matches. He knew their personal merit, their great birth and their fortune. He embraced them with all this heart, and testified the veritable joy he felt in having found them.

"However," he said, "I foresee a few difficulties that time will have to aid us to overcome. You tell me that the hearts of those young persons are not disposed as you would wish; my aunt's will be animated by wrath when she sees as a nephew a man whom she intends to make her husband. Don Gabriel has a father who might perhaps destine him for some other alliance, and I have such a great affair on my hands because of Lucile, whose relatives will pursue me, that it might be necessary for me to go to Portugal with her."

"You're overwhelming us," replied Ponce de Leon. "Your foresight is making us envisage obstacles that our amour had hidden from us; but in spite of all that you have just said to us, we are resolved to persevere, and to die rather than fail in our passion."

Lucile had not wanted to approach the count or Ponce de Leon, although she knew them. It did not seem decorous for her to see them in bed; she had always remained in the place where she had first sat down, and as Don Gabriel remarked that Don Luis was anxious about seeing her pass a bad night, he advised him to take her into his room; it was only separated from the one where they were by a great hall.

Don Luis proposed that to the amiable person; she was very glad of it, and threw herself on to the bed fully dressed. Having closed the door on her, Don Luis returned to find his friends, for he had a key to that room, which is how he had entered it so easily.

They agreed together that he would tell his sisters the secret of the pilgrims' disguises and he would engage them to do some violence to their penchants in order to accord their inclinations with those of Don Gabriel and the count; that as soon as they consented to that, they would write to their fathers on either part, in order to have their agreement, and that they would refrain carefully from letting Doña Juana know the trick they had played on her until things were in a state to be concluded.

The conversation of the three friends took them until eight o'clock in the morning. Don Luis, occupied with Lucile, entered quietly into her room; he saw that she was asleep; he dared not wake her, and in the same fashion he went into Doña Juana's apartment.

All the women were surprised to see him; he was not expected. His aunt was the most astonished. He asked to speak to her, and told her that for two years he had been received in Lucile's home with the agreement of her entire family; that in those days she had had little wealth, that he only loved her because of her virtue and her good qualities; that she was not unaware that her marriage with him had been resolved, but that the brother of the beautiful young woman had been murdered and she had become one of the richest heiresses in Andalusia; that her grandfather, no longer wanting to give her, had made her go from Cadiz to Seville; that he had held her in his house with the intention of marrying her with the son of one of his friends; that he had not been able to suffer an affront that dishonored him, in causing him to lose his mistress; and that, in intelligence with her, he had abducted her; that he begged her to receive her well and to testify to him, in a matter so pressing, the good will that she had always had for him.

Doña Juana was very uncertain as to what she ought to do; she dreaded scandal, and she had no doubt that Lucile's relatives would cause her trouble for having received her. In truth, the castle where she lived was not hers, but it seemed to her that she was nevertheless responsible for what happened therein. But as, in addition, she could not keep the musicians without Don Luis finding something to criticize in her conduct, and might perhaps suspect the design that she had to go abroad with the one she loved, an idea occurred to her that she judged very good.

"My nephew," she said, "if you had taken my advice before the execution of your project, I would not have neglected anything to deflect you from it. Whatever advantages you imagine in the alliance you desire, the consequences seem to me so perilous, as long as you are at odds with Lucile's family, that I fear everything. This, then, is the temperament that it is necessary to adopt. I have a house near Seville. I will go there with your sisters, and I will soothe the irritated spirits while you stay here. It is necessary that you marry Lucile as soon as we have departed. You see that, in that way, no one will have any reason to pursue us and we shall still be in a state to serve you."

Don Luis could not help approving his aunt's design. He understood that it was the best way of engaging Lucile not to delay his happiness, for if she were not his wife, how would she be able to remain alone with such an amiable man? Whereas, if she remained with Doña Juana, she would have to await the final decision of her relatives. He testified to his aunt that he liked the expedient very much. Thereafter, he went to his sisters' room, whom he found already up and dying to see him.

After having given marks of a reciprocal amity, Don Luis told them about the progress of his passion for Doña Lucile and her abduction. They interrupted him at that point to express the anxiety that that affair caused them, with regard to all the consequences that it might have. He told them that he could not even hope that death would deliver him of the cruelest of his enemies, because he was not old, even though he was the grandfather of his mistress.

"As soon as we're dressed," they told him, "we'll go to find her and you ought to be persuaded of the care that we shall take to please her."

"You won't be together long," said Don Luis. "Doña Juana wants to leave immediately for Andalusia. She fears that there might be a scandal, and she claims that she will be in a better position to serve me there than elsewhere."

They agreed with that in their turn.

Continuing the conversation, Don Luis said: "Doña Juana spoke to me about two pilgrims who, returning from Santiago, were wounded near the house, whom she received, and that they know music well enough to show you, if they were not so young and well-made. I approve strongly of their sojourn in your company, but in truth, if it is necessary for you to learn to sing and play instruments, it's necessary to find women who can perfect you, without retaining foreigners who are not accustomed to Spanish manners, who would become too familiar, and whom one would despair of having kept."

While he was speaking he studied the faces of his sisters; he saw them change color, and easily divined the cause.

"Have you said that to Doña Juana?" Isidore asked.

"I have not failed," replied Don Luis, "and I found some reluctance to send them away, but I told her firmly that it was necessary, and that I would take care of it, but being afraid that I might maltreat them, she told me that she wanted to do it herself."

"They'll soon be leaving, then?" Melanie interrupted, sadly.

"Today, I hope," Don Luis continued.

"And what do you find dangerous in leaving them?" asked Isidore. "You must have a very low opinion of us, to believe that persons of such an obscure birth might make some disadvantageous impression in our minds."

"I'm not anxious on your account, my sister," he added. "I only fear the public, whose judgments, often false and wrong, are nevertheless decisive and without appeal. I'm convinced that you'll approve of my conduct."

Isidore and Melanie, penetrated by dolor, strove to hide the cause from their brother. "I've never seen you so melancholy, my dear sisters," he said. "Have you some sort of regret for these foreigners?"

"We're afflicted," said Isidore, "By your insulting suspicions."

"Say rather," he said, "that you're afflicted by the inequality you find between yourselves and them, and that otherwise, they appear to you to be amiable enough not to displease you."

"In truth," cried Melanie, "you're trying to push us to the limit!"

Their anger amused Don Luis greatly. "Let's make peace," he said, embracing them tenderly. "It's necessary to unravel this mystery for you. It's for you that they became pilgrims. Don Gabriel Ponce de Leon belongs to one of the most illustrious houses that we have in Europe. Don Manuel Ponce de Leon, Duke of Arcos,[25] from whom the kings of Xerica descend, was his ancestor, and he had for relatives the kings of Leon; it was that Don Manuel who sustained the oppressed innocence of the Queen of Granada, whose husband, King Chico, wanted to put to death. Alonso d'Aguilar also fought for her; he was not inferior either in birth or merit to any of the great lords of Andalusia; it is from him that Esteban, Count d'Aguilar is descended, who passes here for a musician; their wealth is so considerable that they can sustain their rank with splendor; I have no friends in the world dearer to me than them or who merit my attachment more. They love

---

[25] The reference is unlikely to be to Manuel Ponce de Leon, sixth Duke of Arcos (1633-1693), because he was not contemporary with the Moorish King of Granada known and "el rey chico" [the little king], who reigned a century earlier, when Rodrigo Ponce de Leon was the first duke and Luis Cristobal Ponce de Leon was the second. As Gabriel is fictitious, however, it would be unwise to expect too much historical accuracy in his ancestry.

you; they want to marry you. Judge my joy, my sisters, to be able to hope for such a fine alliance, and that they might render you as happy as I have always wanted you to be."

He shut up at that point. But instead of responding to him, they looked at one another, and then stared at him, as if trying to penetrate whether he had told them the truth.

"You doubt my sincerity," he continued, "and the malice that I've just exercised against you gives you reason. However, be certain that I have never spoken more seriously in my life. We spent the night together; they told me about their passion for you, your manners toward them, and Doña Juana's extravagances."

"Oh, my brother," cried Isidore, "I know now that this isn't a game! How difficult it would be, too, that men so perfect, so well-born, with so much intelligence and so many good qualities, could be what they said they were. It came to me twenty times over that there was something hidden in this pilgrimage, which I could not unravel."

"But my dear brother," Melanie interrupted, "Since you have so much part in the amity of Don Gabriel, he has doubtless told you for which of us he has more inclination?"

"Yes, my sister," replied Don Luis. "He has made me that confidence, He declares himself for Isidore, and Count d'Aguilar for you."

At those words, the two beautiful young women went pale. Their hearts had already made a choice, and each of them believed that it could not change. Don Luis examined them for some time; it would not have been difficult for him to divine what he knew already, but he did not want to let anything show, for fear that they might complain of the indiscretion of their lovers.

"It appears to me," he said, "that you have some repugnance for them. Please, my dear sisters, make the decision that reason dictates to you. Fortune is favorable to you; don't neglect it, love who loves you. I'm not only advising you as your brother, I'm advising you as your friend, and I beg you to want to explain yourselves with them favorably, in order that they can take just measures and enable their relatives to agree to what they desire most in the world, and which will render you the most fortunate.

"The manner in which you are speaking to us is so obliging, my brother," said Isidore, "that there is no means of hiding our secret from you. We are in love, but we love those who do not love us. Don Gabriel pleases Melanie, the count appears lovable to me. Can we adopt other sentiments? Oh, if we were the mistresses of them, we would only have had indifference."

"I want to believe," Don Luis interrupted, "that your prejudice is not so strong that you cannot change it, when that change would be so advantageous to you. Adieu; I'll quit you. Make your reflections. I'm going to find Lucile, and I'll wait for you in her room."

Din Luis had hardly gone out when they began to weep. "Can there be a fate more bizarre?" cried Isidore. "What ought to cause me joy afflicts me to excess. I learn that this pretended musician is a man of the highest quality; that fortunate change would fill me with joy if I did not learn at the same time that he does not love me, and that he only thinks of you."

"I lament my destiny as much," said Melanie; "however appropriate to make me blush my sentiments for Don Gabriel might have been, I could hope that the recognition, and even the vanity, of having engaged a heart like mine might be able to attach him, and that he might only seek to please me; now I know him, for what can I hope? He is worthy of you, he loves you, you will love him, my sister, you will love him."

Without making any response Isidore held her head inclined over one of her hands, and with the other she wiped away a few tears that she could not retain. In the end, she raised her head, and looked at her sister. "Would you like," she said to her, "that in order to put you in possession of the property that you envy me, and which is indifferent to me, that I give you the strongest mark to tenderness that one can promise a god sister? I shall make myself a nun. It will be necessary then that Don Gabriel renders homage to your merit and that he will forget me forever."

"God forbid," cried Melanie, "that I accept such a proof of your amity, my dear sister; I would soon follow you into a retreat that you would only have chosen in my consideration; and, supposing that I were ingrate enough to consent to it, would Don Gabriel pardon me for it?"

"He would not know the reasons for my retreat," said Isidore

"And even if he did not know them, would it be a consequence that I would possess his heart? No, my dear Isidore, I am convinced that the heart wants to be surprised; he is already accustomed to seeing me; my face, my conversation, the turn of my mind, are not new to him; I would lose you and I would not gain anything."

"But if it is true that the first moments of acquaintance," said Isidore, "decide, according to you, the consequence of a passion, we will never love those who love us, and we will continue to love those who do not love us."

"I hope otherwise," Melanie interrupted. "The metamorphosis that has just taken place in favor of the musicians might perhaps dispose our hearts to what they desire, and as we have always taken care to hide our sentiments from them, I cannot help thinking that in belonging to them they might be touched by them."

"Alas," Isidore continued, "You're in great error in thinking that they have not penetrated our secret; our eyes have spoken in spite of us, and the language of the eyes is often the most intelligible."

Melanie was about to reply when someone came to tell them to dress promptly. Doña Juana wanted them to come with her to Lucile's room in order to offer her everything that might depend on them for her satisfaction.

They did not want to add anything to their natural charms; they braided their hair negligently and mingled it with jonquils and jasmines; they were as brilliant as the dawn; their clothing was a light white fabric; that is the most usual mourning for young women of quality in Spain, and the beauty of their figure was not hidden by the large cloak that they wore when they went out; they were so majestic and so noble that they could not be more perfect; but the tears they had shed took away from their eyes something of the vivacity that rendered their gaze so difficult to sustain.

They went to find their aunt; she went immediately to Lucile's room. She was on her bed, overwhelmed by the fatigue of the journey and the scant repose that she had taken since her departure from Seville. Anxiety was not the least of the causes that changed her air of joy into an air of melancholy that added to her charms; she was young, well made and she had the intelligence and all the manners of a young person of quality.

Doña Juana showed her a great deal of amity; she told her that if she entered into her family she would be dearly loved, that she would have no reason to regret the steps that she had taken for Don Luis. Isidore and Melanie gave her the same assurances in a manner so tender and engaging that they made her well aware of the amity that they had or their brother. Lucile, for her part, did not miss any opportunity to testify the joy she had in finding herself with them and being so well received.

Juana interrupted the conversation, however. "Among all the good qualities that render you lovable," she told her, "my nephew has told me about one that is very much to my liking."

"Oh, I understand you, Madame," Lucile replied, with a gracious smile. "He has doubtless told you that I am a great teller of romances."

"It is true," Juana continued, "that I have the folly of loving them, as if I were only four years old, and I beg you right away to be kind enough to tell me one, if you are not too tired."

Lucile replied, with a great deal of politeness, that in truth, she was rather tired, but that she did not want to defer the pleasure of giving marks of her complaisance. She pondered for a moment, and then commenced.

FORTUNÉE

There was once a poor laborer who, seeing that he was on the point of dying, did not want to leave in his succession any points of dispute for his son and daughter, whom he loved tenderly.

"Your mother brought me for a dowry," he told them, "two stools and a mattress. There they are, with my chicken, a pot of carnations and a plain silver ring that a great lady who stayed in my poor cottage gave me. She said as she left: 'My good man, here is a gift that I'm making you; be careful to water the carnations well and hold on to the ring carefully. Furthermore, your daughter will be an incomparable beauty; name her Fortunée, give her the ring and the carnations, to console her for her poverty.' So, my dear Fortunée," added the worthy man, "you shall have both of them; the rest will be for your brother."

The laborer's two children seemed content; he died. They wept, and there was no dispute regarding their shares. Fortunée thought that her brother loved her, but when she wanted to sit down on one of the stools he said, with a grim expression: "Keep your carnations and your ring; as for my stools, don't disturb them, I like order in my house."

Fortunée, who was very meek, started weeping quietly; she remained standing, while Bedou—that was the brother's name—was better seated than a doctor. When supper time came, Bedou had an excellent fresh egg from his unique chicken, and he threw the shell to his sister. "Here," he said; "I've nothing else to give you; if you don't like it, go and hunt frogs. There are some in the nearby marsh."

Fortunée made no reply. What would she have replied? She raised her eyes to the heavens again, wept again, and then went into her bedroom.

She found it richly perfumed, and, not doubting that it was her carnations. She approached them sadly and said to them: "Beautiful carnations, whose variety gives me an extreme pleasure to see, who fortify my afflicted heart with the sweet perfume you spread, have no fear that I'll let you lack water and detach you from your stems with cruel hand; I'll take care of you, since you're my only wealth."

As she finished speaking she looked to see whether they needed watering; they were very dry. She took her pitcher and went by moonlight to the spring, which was some distance away.

As she had walked quickly she sat down on the bank to rest. But she had scarcely done so than she saw a lady coming whose majestic bearing responded well to the numerous retinue that accompanied her; six maids of honor sustained the train of her mantle; she was leaning on two others; her guards were marching before her, richly clad in amaranth velvet embroidered with pearls; one carried an armchair of golden cloth, on which she sat down, and a campaign awning that was tautly stretched.

At the same time, a table was set up, covered with golden vessels and crystal vases. She was served an excellent supper on the bank of the spring, the soft murmur of which seemed to harmonize with several voices, which sang these words:

> *Our woods are agitated by the softest zephyrs,*
> *Flora shines on these banks;*
> *Under this somber foliage*
> *Enchanted birds express their desires.*
> *Occupy yourself with hearing them;*
> *And if your heart wants to love,*
> *There are pleasant objects that can charm you:*
> *One will glory in going there.*

Fortunée sat in a little corner, not daring to stir, so surprised was she by all the things that were happening. After a moment, the great queen said to one of her squires: "It seems to me that I perceive a shepherdess near that bush; have her approach."

Immediately, Fortunée advanced, and, although she was naturally timid she nevertheless made a profound reverence to the queen, with so much grace that those who saw it were astonished. She took the hem of her robe, which she kissed, and then stood before her, lowering her eyes modestly; her cheeks were covered with a blush that heightened the whiteness of her complexion, and it was easy to remark in her manners the air of simplicity and mildness that is charming in young persons.

"What are you doing here, beautiful girl?" the queen said to her. "Don't you fear thieves?"

"Alas, Madame," said Fortunée, "I only have a coarse dress; what would they gain from a poor shepherdess like me?"

"You're not rich, then?" said the queen, smiling.

"I'm so poor," said Fortunée, "that all I inherited from my father was a pot of carnations and a silver ring."

"But you have a heart," added the queen. "If someone wanted to take it from you, would you want to give it to him?"

"I don't know what it is to give my heart, Madame," she replied. "I've always heard it said that without one's heart, one can't live, that when it's wounded it's necessary to die, and in spite of my poverty, I'm not sorry to be alive."

"You'll always be right, beautiful girl, to defend your heart. But tell me," continued the queen, "have you supped well?"

"No, Madame," said Fortunée. "My brother has eaten everything."

The queen commanded that a place be set for her, invited her to sit at the table, and served her the best of what she had.

The young shepherdess was so surprised with admiration, and so charmed by the queen's generosity, that she could scarcely eat a morsel.

"I'd like to know," said the queen, "what you came to the spring to do so late."

"Madame," she said, "here's my pitcher. I came in quest of water to water my carnations."

As she spoke she bent down in order to pick up her pitcher, which was beside her, but when she showed it to the queen she was astonished to find that it was gold, covered with large diamonds and filled with water that seemed admirably good. She dared not take it away, fearing that it was not hers.

"I give it to you, Fortunée," said the queen. "Go and water the flowers of which you take care, and remember that the Queen of the Woods wants to be your friend"

At those words, the shepherdess threw herself at her feet. "After having rendered you very humble thanks, Madame," she said, "for the honor you are doing me, I dare to take the liberty to ask you to wait here for a moment. I will go fetch you half my wealth, which is my pot of carnations, which can never be in better hands than yours."

"Go, Fortunée," the queen said to her, touching her cheeks lightly. "I consent to stay here until you return."

Fortunée took her golden pitcher and ran to her little bedroom; but while she had been absent, her brother Bedou had gone in there; he had taken the pot of carnations and left a large cabbage in its place. When Fortunée perceived the wretched cabbage, she fell into the utmost affliction, and remained very irresolute as to whether she should return to the spring.

Finally, she determined to do it, and put herself on her knees before the queen. "Madame," she said to her, "Bedou has stolen my pot of carnations; all that remains to me is my ring; I beg you to receive it as a proof of my gratitude."

"If I take your ring, beautiful shepherdess," said the queen, "you will be ruined."

"Oh, Madame," she said, with a spiritual expression, "if I possess your good graces, I cannot be ruined."

The queen took Fortunée's ring and put it on her finger; immediately, she mounted a coral chariot enriched with emeralds, drawn by six white horses, more beautiful than the sun's team. Fortunée followed it with her eyes for as long as she could; finally, the different routes of the forest hid it from view. She returned to Bedou's cottage, full of that adventure.

The first thing she did on going into her bedroom was to throw the cabbage out of the window, but she was astonished to hear a voice that cried: "Oh, I'm dead!"

She did not understand that plaint, for ordinarily, cabbages do not speak.

As soon as it was daylight, Fortunée, anxious about her pot of carnations, went downstairs to search for it, and the first thing she saw was the wretched cabbage. She gave it a kick, saying: "What are you doing here, after being in my bedroom instead of my carnations?"

"If I hadn't been carried there," replied the cabbage, "it wouldn't have entered my head to go there."

She shivered, for she was very afraid, but the cabbage said then: "If you care to take me back to my comrades, I'll tell you in two words that your carnations are in Bedou's mattress."

Fortunée, in despair, did not know how to get them back. She had the generosity to plant the cabbage, and then took her brother's favorite chicken and said to it: "Nasty, beast, I'll pay you back for all the chagrin that Bedou has given me."

"Oh, Shepherdess," said the chicken, "let me live, and as my humor is loquacious, I'll tell you surprising things. Don't believe that you're the daughter of the laborer in whose home you were nourished. No, beautiful Fortunée, he wasn't your father, but the queen who gave you the light of day already had six daughters, and as if she were the mistress of having a son, her husband and father-in law told her that they would stab her to death unless she gave them an heir. The poor afflicted queen became pregnant; she was imprisoned in a castle and guards stationed with her—or, to put it better, executioners—who had orders to kill her if she had another daughter.

"The princess, alarmed by the misfortune that threatened her, no longer ate or slept. She had a sister who was a fay; she wrote to her about her just fears. The fay was pregnant and knew that she would have a son. When she gave birth, she charged the zephyrs with a basket, in which she placed her son, very neatly, and she gave them the order to take the little prince into the queen's bedroom, in order to exchange it with the daughter she would have, That foresight served no purpose, because the queen, not receiving any news from her sister, took advantage of the good will of one of her guards, who took pity on her and enabled her to escape with a rope ladder. As soon as you came into the world, the afflicted queen, seeking a hiding-place, arrived in this little house, half-dead of lassitude and dolor.

"I was laborious," said the chicken, "and a good nurse. She charged me with you and recounted her misfortunes to me, which she found so overwhelming that she died without having time to instruct us as to what to do with you.

"As I've liked to chat all my life, I couldn't help talking about that adventure, with the consequence that a beautiful lady came here one day, to whom I told everything I knew about it. Immediately, she tapped me with her wand and I became a chicken, without being able to talk any more. My affliction was extreme and my husband, who was absent at the time of that metamorphosis, never knew anything about it. When he returned he searched for me everywhere; finally, he thought that I had drowned, or that the animals of the forest had devoured me. The same lady who had done me so much harm passed through here a second time; she ordered him to call you Fortunée and made him a present of a silver ring and a pot of carnations; but while she was here, twenty-five of your father's guards arrived, who were searching for you with evil intentions. She said a few words and turned them into green cabbages, whose number includes the one you threw out of your window yesterday evening. I hadn't heard him talk before, and I couldn't talk myself; I don't know how we got our voices back."

The princess was very surprised by the marvels that the chicken had just recounted to her; she was still full of generosity, and said to her: "You make me feel great pity, my poor nurse, in having become a chicken; I'd very much like to return your original form if I could, but let's not despair of any-thing. It seems to me that all the things you've just told me can't remain in the same situation. I'll go look for my carnations, for I love them uniquely."

Bedou had gone to the wood, unable to imagine that Fortunée would take it into her head to search his mattress; she was delighted by his absence, and flattered herself that she would not find any resistance, when she suddenly saw a large quantity of prodigious rats, armed for war. They were arranged in battalions, with the famous mattress behind them and the stools to the sides. Several large mice formed the reserve corps, resolved to fight like amazons. Fortunée was very surprised; she dared not go any closer, for the rats threw themselves upon her, bit her and drew blood.

"What!" she cried. "My carnations, my dear carnations, will you remain in such bad company?"

Suddenly, she had an idea: perhaps the perfumed water that she had in a golden vase might have a particular virtue. She ran in quest of it; she threw a few drops of it over the furry population; as she did so the rodents ran away into their holes, and the princess promptly took her beautiful carnations, which were on the point of dying, so much need did they have of being watered.

She poured all the water in the golden vase over them, and was smelling them with a great deal of pleasure when she heard a very soft voice emerging from between the branches, which said to her: "Incomparable Fortunée, this is the happy and so much desired day to declare my sentiments for you; know that the power of your beauty is such that it can even render flowers sensible."

The princess trembled with surprise at having heard a cabbage, a chicken and a carnation speak, and having seen an army of rats. She went pale and fainted.

Bedou arrived then. Labor and the sun had warmed his head; when he saw that Fortunée had come in search of her carnations and that she had found them, he dragged her as far as the door and put her outside.

She had scarcely felt the fresh air than she opened her beautiful eyes. She perceived the Queen of the Woods next to her, still charming and magnificent.

"You have a nasty brother," she said to Fortunée. "I saw the inhumanity with which he threw you out here. Would you like me to avenge you?"

"No, Madame," she said. "I'm not capable of being annoyed, and his bad nature won't change mine."

"But I have a presentiment," added the queen, "that that vulgar laborer is not your brother. What do you think?"

"All appearances persuade me that he is, Madame," replied the shepherdess, modestly, "and I ought to believe them."

"What!" the queen continued. "Have you not heard it said that you were born a princess?"

"I was told that a little while ago," she replied, "but I dare not boast of something of which I have no proof."

"Oh, my dear child," added the queen, "How I love you in that humor! I know now that the obscure education you have received has not stifled the nobility of your blood. Yes, you are a princess, and it has not depended on me to protect you from the disgraces that you have experienced until the present hour."

She was interrupted at that point by the arrival of a young adolescent more beautiful than the day. He was dressed in a long jacket of gold and green silk, fastened by large emerald, ruby and diamond buttons. He had a crown of carnations and his hair covered his shoulders. As soon as he saw the queen he put one knee on the ground and saluted her respectfully.

"Ah, my son, my lovable Carnation," she said to him. "The fatal time of your enchantment has now ended, thanks to the aid of the beautiful Fortunée. What a joy it is to see you!" She hugged him tightly in her arms.

Turning toward the shepherdess then, she said: "Charming princess, I know everything that the chicken told you, but what you do not know is that the zephyrs that I had charged with putting my son in your place put him into a flower-bed while they went to search for your mother, who was my sister. A fay to whom none of the most secret things were unknown, with whom I had quarreled a long time ago, had watched very carefully for the moment of my son's birth, which she had foreseen. She immediately changed him into a carnation, and in spite of my science, I could not prevent that misfortunate.

"In the chagrin to which I was reduced I employed all my art to search for some remedy, and I found none more assured than brining Prince Carnation into the place where you were nursed, divining that when you had watered the flowers with the delicious water that I had in a golden vase, he would speak, he would love you and in future, nothing would trouble your repose. I also had the silver ring, which it was necessary that I receive from your hand, not unaware that it was the mark by which I would know you when the time came that the charm lost its force, in spite of the rats and mice that our enemy would put on campaign to prevent you from touching the carnations.

"Thus, my dear Fortunée, if my son marries you with this ring, your felicity will be permanent. See now whether the prince appears lovable enough for you to receive him as a husband."

"Madame," she replied, blushing, "you are heaping me with graces. I know that you are my aunt, that by means of your knowledge, the guards sent to kill me were changed into cabbages and my nurse into a chicken, and that in proposing the alliance of Prince Carnation to me you are doing me the greatest honor to which I can aspire. But may I tell you my uncertainty? I do not know his heart, and I am beginning to sense for the first time in my life that I could not be content if he did not love me."

"Have no uncertainty about that, beautiful princess," the prince said to her. "A long time ago you made the impression in me that you want to make at present, and if the usage of a voice had been permitted to me, what would you not have heard every day about the progress of a passion that was consuming me? But I am an unfortunate prince, for whom you only feel indifference."

Then he recited these lines:

While I retained the form of a carnation,
You gave me your tender cares;
You came sometimes to admire without witnesses
The eccentric colors of my brilliant flowers.
For you I spread my sweetest perfumes.
I affected in your eyes a new beauty;
And when I was far from you
A mortal dryness
Proved all too well that, secretly consumed,
I always languished in cruel anticipation
Of the object that had charmed me.
You were favorable to my dolors,
And your beautiful hand,
Watered my bosom with pure water,
And sometimes our adorable mouth,
Gave me kisses, alas, full of sweetness.
In order better to enjoy my good fortune,
And prove to you my fires and my gratitude,
I would have liked, at such a sweet moment,
Some magical power
To extract me from a sad enchantment.
My wishes were granted, I see you, I love you;
I can tell you about my torment;
But unhappily for me, you are no longer the same.
What prayers have I formed? Just gods, what have I done?

The princess appeared very content with the gallantry of the prince; she praised that improvisation lavishly, and although she was not accustomed to hearing poetry, she talked about it like a person of good taste.

The queen, who was only suffering that she was clad as a shepherdess with impatience, touched her, wishing her the richest garment that had ever been seen. At the same time, her white cloth was change into silver brocade embroidered with carbuncles; from her raised hair, a long veil of golden-tinted gauze fell and her black tresses were ornamented with a thousand diamonds; her complexion, the whiteness of which was dazzling, took on colors so vivid that the prince could scarcely sustain the glare.

"Oh, Fortunée, how beautiful and charming you are!" he cried, sighing. "Will you be inexorable to my pains?"

"No, my son, said the queen. "Your cousin will not resist your prayers."

While they were talking thus, Bedou, who was returning to his labor, passed by. Seeing Fortunée like a goddess, he thought he was dreaming. She called to him with a great deal of kindness, and begged the queen to have pity on him.

"What, after having treated you so badly!" she said.

"Oh, Madame," replied the princess, "I'm incapable of avenging myself."

The queen embraced her, and praised the generosity of her sentiments. "To content you," she added, "I shall enrich the ingrate Bedou."

His cottage became a furnished palace full of silver. His stools did not change form, nor his mattress, in order to enable him to remember his original estate, but the Queen of the Woods polished his mind; she gave him politeness and changed his face. Bedou then found himself capable of gratitude. What did he not say to the queen and the princess to testify his own on that occasion!

Then, at a stroke of the wand, the cabbages became men and the chicken a woman. Only Prince Carnation was discontented; he was sighing after the princess. He implored her to make a resolution in his favor. Finally, she consented: she had seen nothing that was not lovable, and everything else that was lovable was less so than the young prince.

The Queen of the Woods, delighted by such a happy marriage, did not neglect anything in order for it to be sump-

tuous. The fête lasted for several years, and the happiness of
the tender spouses lasted as long as their lives.

> *Without the help of any fay.*
> *One could tell from what parents*
> *The amiable Fortunée emerged.*
> *The brilliant virtue by which she was adorned*
> *Were as many sure guarantees*
> *That she was born of a fine blood.*
> *Merit and virtue alone*
> *Are the veritable nobility.*
> *O you whom honor invests*
> *Do not show pride and weakness;*
> *Learn from me this lesson:*
> *In vain of an ancient family*
> *You will boast the illustrious name.*
> *Whoever has virtue, in spite of a humble estate,*
> *Passes for noble, or worthy of being;*
> *But your honors and your splendor*
> *Will not make you recognized as noble.*

When Lucile had finished her romance Juana and her
nieces thanked her for the pleasure she had given them.

"The delicacy of your intelligence appears in all things,"
they said to her, "even a little tale, which is quite sterile in
itself, you have made infinitely valuable."

"It is true," added Don Luis, "That there is a brilliant genius that draw everything out of obscurity and give value to
the slightest bagatelles."

Lucile defended herself with as much politeness as modesty from the praise that was given to her. At that moment
someone came to tell Doña Juana that the meal was served;
she begged her nephew to eat with the pilgrims and to give
them a favorable welcome.

As soon as the ladies had left the table, Don Luis and the
pilgrims came to find them, but Juana took Lucile by the hand
and took her into her cabinet. After having paid her further

compliments she told her that she was in accord with her nephew to go to one of his estates near Seville; that she was leaving her with a sensible regret, but after the step she had made in favor of Don Luis she could not forbid her to complete her happiness by means of her marriage; that, by that means, her glory would not suffer, and, in remaining with a spouse that one loves one scarcely perceives the ennuis of solitude.

Lucile could not help blushing on hearing talk of such a prompt marriage; she replied to Doña Juana very honestly that she wanted in future to regulate her conduct by her orders; that she felt keenly the departure that she was meditating, but, believing it to be necessary to her repose, she dare not try to deflect her from it.

Isidore and Melanie came in at that point, and made her a great many compliments; they were already so prejudiced in one another's favor that seeing one another and loving one another was the same thing; they testified that they had a sensible regret in quitting her.

"I'm very unfortunate," Lucile said to them, "to be bringing so much trouble among you; it's me who is driving you away from your house; I imagined a thousand pleasures in your company. I could not have resolved to leave Seville if I had not been filled with that flattering idea; but you're quitting me."

Words so tender reawakened the idea in the hearts of the two sisters the cruel separation from Ponce de Leon and the count; they thought of the pain they would have in no longer seeing them; they sighed; a few tears flowed from their eyes. Deceived by such obliging marks of amity, Lucile threw her arms around them and embraced them tightly, mingling her sighs and tears with theirs.

While they were weeping and afflicted, Don Luis was consoling Ponce de Leon and Count d'Aguilar; he rendered them an account of the situation of their affairs; they finally knew that Isidore loved the one who did not love her and that Melanie was in the same situation. They were able to hope that time, perseverance and reason might change their hearts, but they foresaw an imminent separation. Oh, what a torment it is to be drawing away from a person one loves, without being loved!

As Don Luis understood all the cruelty of their condition, he tried to soothe them by saying: "Don't be afflicted, my dear friends; I hope that my sisters will understand their veritable interests, and I hope that today will give you the means of talking to them, for there is every appearance that Doña Juana will be leaving here very promptly."

"We hope for everything of your cares," they replied, "and measure our gratitude by the grandeur of the obligation; for, in sum, we regard being loved by those amiable persons as the sovereign happiness."

Doña Juana was thinking less about her journey than of finding a means of taking away her dear musician; she feared that a few bad jokes might be made about it and was waiting with an extreme impatience for the pretended marriage with which the count had amused her to be broken in order to conclude her own. After having made a thousand reflections, her tenderness prevailed over all the regard that she owed herself; she sent someone to find the count and went into her cabinet with him.

Finding herself able to speak to him freely, she said: "Don Estève, I am quitting this house in order to go to Andalusia; would you like to come with me?"

"I will follow you anywhere, Madame," he exclaimed, "only too happy if you will permit me to do so." In fact, he was delighted by the prospect of making that journey with Melanie.

Doña Juana said to him everything that she could imagine of the most obliging, and as the hope of accompanying his mistress put him in a very good mood in his turn, he said a thousand things as agreeable as they were charming.

Everything was in that state when, that evening, Doña Juana was in the pavilion on the park. On the side of the drawing room that overlooked the park there was a small cabinet, of which she kept the key. It was filled with books and papers; she wanted to find some there to take with her. As she hardly ever went there, Don Luis and his sisters had no reason to believe that she was there when they went there in order to converse with Ponce de Leon and Count d'Aguilar.

Don Luis quit them at the bottom of the staircase. "I'll go and invite my friends to come," he said. "If you love me, and if you love yourselves, be careful of their hearts; don't neglect such a good establishment."

Doña Juana, hearing the sound of voices, removed the key of the cabinet and shut herself inside.

Scarcely had her nieces come in than, casting her eyes in the direction of the wood, Isidore said: "There, my dear sister, is the place fatal to our repose, the place where we head those amiable pilgrims for the first time; could we have believed that it was in order to see us that they were playing such a role?"

"Oh, my sister," Melanie interrupted, "how content I would be if their hearts, or if ours, had not erred in their choice; but what are we going to say to them? Are we going to confess our sentiments?"

"How can we resolve to do that, my dear Melanie?" exclaimed Isidore. "Is it not already too much to listen to theirs? Are we not wounding our duty in consenting to this kind of rendezvous? And is not my brother, who is leading us into an adventure so new to us, too new himself to the rules of decency?"

"Before coming here," interrupted Melanie, "it would have been very appropriate to make the reflections that you are making now, but do you know, my sister, that what I fear above all else is that Doña Juana might discover my sentiments."

"She would certainly be annoyed," replied Isidore, "as she nourishes such tender ones for the count and is making herself a green costume embroidered with gold, with which she wants to surprise us as soon as it's finished."

"That isn't possible," said Melanie. "You're attributing too much extravagance to her for me to believe it."

"I protest to you that it's the truth," she added, "and if you take note, the majority of women don't want to regulate their garments to their age; they think they can deceive the public with a pink ribbon, but in my view, they only deceive themselves."

"What!" said Melanie, bursting into laughter. "I shall see my old aunt as green as a cicada?"

"Yes, my sister," said Isidore. "You'll see her as a cicada, to please her dear musician."

Melanie was about to respond when he came in with Ponce de Leon; all of them made profound reverences, in such an embarrassed fashion that it appeared that each of them was thinking a great deal without daring to declare their sentiments.

Finally, Isidore spoke. "If we have not rendered you everything that is owed to your birth and your merit," she said to them, "that fault must be imputed to you, since the mystery you made of it was the cause."

"Oh, Madame," said Ponce de Leon, "we are not asking for compliments. You are aware of our passion and our designs; deign to approve them, and we will be only too glad. You cannot doubt," he continued, "that your merit has produced its full effect us, since we left Cadiz expressly to see you, and, knowing the excessively severe conduct of Doña Juana, appeared in such a singular disguise. It required nothing less than a violent passion for us to resolve to take such steps, but if we were capable of making them before seeing you, of what have we been rendered capable after seeing you?"

"Yes, Madame," the count interjected, wanting to speak in his turn. "Yes, beautiful Melanie, that passion would make me attempt anything, provided that you approve it, and that, of the many prayers and sighs I have consecrated to you, some are agreeable to you. When my complaisance for Don Gabriel obliged me to accompany him, I regarded amour as a terrible reef to be avoided at all costs; the state in which I saw it inspired me with such a distance from light gallantry that I would have sworn that I would never engage my days. Oh God, how briefly my resolution lasted when I saw you; my excessively charmed heart surrendered without the slightest combat; it seemed that there was nothing that it would not do for love of you."

"The just dread that you had of loving, Sire," Melanie replied to the count, "ought to be a lesson to forbid me any engagement."

"Yes, Madame," he replied. "I confess that Don Gabriel's chagrins were so violent that I have been close to renouncing his amity a hundred times. Alas, you have taken all too much care to justify them in my mind; I have learned, in knowing you, that there is a fatal moment in which it is finally necessary to surrender—but what am I thinking, in naming that moment fatal? If you wished, Madame, it would be the most fortunate of my life."

Melanie's silence and embarrassment threw the count into a confusion of thought so terrible that he dared not speak to her again. She saw his condition in his eyes.

"Sire," she said to him, "the admission for which you are asking does not depend sufficiently on me; you are not unaware of what I owe to my family, and what I owe to myself."

A conversation so tender could not be general for long. Ponce de Leon wanted to speak to Isidore in private; he advanced with her toward a platform garnished with several piles of cushions. For her part, Melanie sat down against the door of the cabinet in which the god Juana was locked; the count set himself at her feet, and no matter how quietly they were speaking, she could hear them clearly.

Good God, what a quarter of an hour for that poor individual! She discovered at the same moment that the musician, Don Estève, her lover, was none of that; that he had a noble birth and a great amour for her niece; that he wanted to marry her; that he was not neglecting anything to touch her heart; that he was employing oaths, sighs and promises; that Melanie did not appear insensible to them; and that she was the dupe of that entire adventure; that the count had made a fool of her with the chimerical design of her marriage. Finally, to drive her patience to the limit, he sang these words to Melanie, which he had fitted to a passacaglia that she loved:

Often, in some secret place,
Thinking she can talk without dread,
In a languid and discreet tone,
Juana makes this plaint to Heaven.
That the white hair and sad aspect,
And the wrinkles of old age
Can inspire respect,
But produce no tenderness.

In sum, nothing was lacking in that conversation to convince Doña Juana of her misfortune. It is difficult to understand how she could sustain it; she said subsequently that she had fallen into weakness and did not have strength enough to open the door and appear in a place to which she would have brought a great deal of disturbance.

Isidore and Melanie heard with pleasure the protestations that were made to them of loving them until death; they were even penetrated by the conviction that they ought not to hope that their lovers might change that resolution, the one to give it to Isidore and the other to attach it to Melanie; that they would remain fixed in their initial design; and, considering their merit and all the advantages that they would find in their alliance, they thought very seriously that they ought not to reject them and that it was necessary to render justice to the sentiments they had for them.

Never had two lovers been more satisfied; they commenced to have hopes with which they had not dared to flatter themselves until then. They had always been apprehensive that Isidore, prejudiced for the count, and Melanie for Don Gabriel, would refuse to adopt other impressions. They quit them with an extreme difficulty; they had not yet savored such sweet moments, and the novelty augmented the pleasure of them.

Those two beautiful young women, penetrated to the depths of their souls, applauded themselves for having made such glorious conquests; but the first impressions they had taken were still to strong too change at the whim of their desires; they believed that a little time was necessary for them to be sure of their own sentiments.

Ponce de Leon and his cousin went to join Don Luis in Lucile's room while Isidore and her sister returned to their apartment.

Then Doña Juana, having recovered somewhat from her astonishment and her dolor, returned to the castle and shut herself in her cabinet in order to write this letter to Count d'Aguilar:

The nobility of your birth does not shelter you from the just reproaches that I owe you. You have feigned a wound, you have assumed a name. I have not only received you in my home, I have received you in my heart. Alas! I exercised hospitality in your regard while you were meditating my doom. I have two nieces as young as they are innocent; you and your relative used the liberty of seeing them to engage their hearts, in order to treat them subsequently as you have treated me. Do not believe that I am cowardly enough to forget your ingratitude; I shall carry the memory and the resentment to the tomb; for, in sum, what did I not want to do for you, at a time when my ignorance made you appear far below me? The generosity of my heart merited all the gratitude of yours, but far from feeling any, you take me as the subject of your satirical songs. I would be in despair at experiencing such unworthy treatment if fortune did not furnish me with a prompt vengeance. Yes, Sire, my vengeance will be my consolation; I shall take away from you those you love; an austere convent will answer to me for the future of their conduct, and if they make an alliance with you I will disinherit them.

As soon as that letter was finished and she had employed a few more hours in tranquilizing her dolor, she summoned her majordomo and told him that she wanted to depart at midnight; that he should sent her equipage to the gate of the park; that she would take as few people as possible and that he was to keep the matter secret.

Then she spoke to her nephew. "Believe me," she said, "Don't waste a moment before marrying Lucile, her it is to be feared that her relatives will come to abduct her from you in their turn, and since you love her, and find so many advantages therein, to avoid them being belied, it's necessary for you to go to Compostela tonight in quest of permission to marry her here."

That advice accorded to well with Don Luis's passion for him to raise any difficulties: he told Juana that he would go to talk to Lucile and mount his horse immediately thereafter.

Thus the adroit Juana distanced her nephew, having almost as much chagrin against him as against the pilgrims, of whom she knew that he was a friend. Wanting to testify an entire liberty of mind, in order that they did not acquire any suspicion of her departure, however, she appeared cheerful and content, and even had them sing Spanish words that evening that she had just fitted to a very agreeable saraband. As they discovered the state of her soul well enough, here is the translation:

> *Glory, pride, severe honor,*
> *Return, if possible, return to my heart;*
> *Alas, dared you not forbid me?*
> *I cherished an ingrate who scorned my prayers,*
> *He refused to hear*
> *The fiery sighs of my amorous heart.*
> *I know too well his rigorous scorn.*
> *He prefers another lover;*
> *But far from stifling my unfortunate amour,*
> *My tenderness, alas, is augmented.*

The agreeable company, knowing nothing of the subject that had given rise to those words, gave their all in singing them in order to pay court to Doña Juana, and Count d'Aguilar, who found a great interest in treating her kindly, approached her and said to her, tenderly: "Of what are you thinking, Madame, to write lines so sad? Have you ever found a rival in your path who dared to dispute the possession of some heart with you?"

"No," she replied, with a forced smile. "What I have just enabled you to hear does not regard me; it was by pure caprice that I made those words."

Isidore, Melanie and Ponce de Leon did not understand the mystery of it, but they said to one another in whispers: "Does it not seem to you that the good aunt has guessed? Could there be anything more appropriate to what has happened today?" Then they adopted pretexts and burst out laughing.

She was more informed than they believed of their intrigues, with the consequence that she penetrated their gazes and gestures, and it is difficult to comprehend the violence that she exerted on herself not to speak.

In the end, she said at nine o'clock that it was late; immediately, everyone said good night, and retired.

At midnight exactly she went into her nieces' room and made them get up; she did not quit them thereafter. They looked at one another without saying anything, equally surprised by such a prompt and secret departure. They did not see either their brother or their lovers appear; they went through the park without even saying adieu to Lucile. All that surprised them greatly and threw them into great consternation. They climbed into a carriage and departed for Andalusia.

Everything was in a silence that did not presage anything disastrous to the two pilgrims when, at about ten o'clock in the morning, the almoner came into the count's room and gave him Doña Juana's letter. He was surprised by that, but he was much more so what it contained. He gave it to Don Gabriel and asked the almoner whether they had all departed. He said yes, and after having replied to a few other questions, he withdrew.

"We've been betrayed!" cried the count. "But by whom? And how? We haven't confided our secret to anyone capable of revealing it; Don Luis has too much honor, Lucile is too discreet. Is it possible that Isidore or Melanie has done us such a bad turn?"

"It isn't easy to believe," Don Gabriel interjected. "Doña Juana seems irritated against them; you can see that she is threatening them with a convent and disinheritance. If they had given her an account of our passion and consented to go away, she wouldn't be so discontented with them."

"It's necessary that we've been overheard," replied the count, "for she knows who we are, including the unfortunate couplet of the song that I only made two days ago."

Don Gabriel was thinking profoundly while he spoke; he started thinking in his turn, and resumed speaking to exclaim: "There's no doubt about it; someone was listening in the drawing room in the park. I remember that when Melanie sat down near the cabinet I heard noises several times, and even thought I heard someone sighing, without it ever crossing my mind that someone might be in there. Oh, good God," he continued, "if that was Juana, as I can no longer doubt, why didn't she come out to strangle me?"

"What she's just done to us," replied Don Gabriel, sadly, "is more cruel than death. Believe me, she's sufficiently avenged; she's taken away what is dearer to us than the light. I shall never see Isidore again; you will never see Melanie. Alas, the charming liberty of seeing them, of speaking to them, of walking with them, has been suddenly stolen from us. We're going to find Doña Juana, irritated, oppose to all our designs. She'll prejudice her brother against us; it's to be feared that his nieces, unsure in their sentiments, might change them, by virtue of constraint, or complaisance for her. How many misfortunes and difficulties I foresee!" he continued. "I'm dying of dolor and rage, without knowing what to decide."

A profound silence followed those sad reflections; one might have taken them for statues rather than living men; but that lethargy did not last long. The almoner came in, with a fearful expression.

"The castle," he told them, "is invested by armed men who are demanding entry. All that I have been able to do is to close the doors, but they're threatening to break them down with axes. If they decide to do it, we're not in a state to prevent them."

Don Gabriel and the count were as surprised by that as they were irresolute as to what they ought to do about it.

"Let's conserve Lucile for Don Luis," cried the count. "It's the most essential service that we can render him."

"But how?" said Don Gabriel. "Do you intend to hold a siege against that small army?"

"No," he replied. "I intend that we mount horses and take Lucile away. We'll go out through the park; it's unlikely that anyone is on that side. We'll go to Tuy, we'll pass over the river at Ministrio and when we reach Valencia we'll have nothing more to fear, because it belongs to the king of Portugal."

"What embarrasses me," said the almoner, "is that the horses that are still here aren't worth much, and the matter is so urgent that we can't look elsewhere."

"There's no other course to take," cried Don Gabriel. "Let's go right away."

They were about to go to Lucile's room to tell her what was happening when she came into theirs. "Oh, Sire," she said to the count, who advanced first, "I'm doomed if you can't find a means to save me; my father is here with the man he destines for me as a husband; I recognized them both from the tower, which I climbed. They're accompanied by a considerable number of my relatives and their friends. Alas, wretch that I am," she continued, weeping, "is it necessary that I cause so much disorder in my family and so much displeasure to Don Luis? For after all, imagine his dolor if, for the recompense for his trouble, he sees me on his return in the hands of a rival."

"Beautiful Lucile," the comte said to her, "Be persuaded that we shall serve you with no less ardor than if Don Luis would if he were here. We've resolved to take you away immediately; it's necessary not to delay for a moment."

As he finished speaking they obliged her to go downstairs; she was covered in her mantle. Don Gabriel mounted a horse and took her behind him; the count had a mule of which the almoner usually made use. They emerged from the park without any obstacle and drew away as quickly as they could, but their equipage was very poor, and in the situation they were in it was impossible to send to Ciudad Rodrigo in quest of their valet and the horses that had been waiting them there since Doña Juana had received them in her home.

Don Fernand de la Vega, who wanted to marry Lucile, piqued with honor and amour, did not neglect anything to irritate her father and his relatives. As soon as they had arrived he feared that Don Luis and she might escape by some back door; he had engaged peasants to watch for them; the latter knew about the park gate; they pretended to be laboring in a nearby field, but as soon as they had seen Lucile and the two riders accompanying her they gave that information to Don Fernand. He was a reckless young man, devoid of bravery, brutal and capable of an evil action. He was convinced that if he attacked Don Luis without an advantage he would not achieve his objective. He took one of his cousins and two valets, all equally well-mounted.

They knew the road that Lucile had taken, and without any reflection they went by another route into a dense wood, where they had time to hide and take all the measures necessary not to miss their coup.

Thus covered by the bushes, they were cowardly enough to fire without quarter on Don Gabriel and the count. Don Gabriel was wounded in the knee and the count's right arm was broken. His mule, frightened by the noise and the fire, took flight with such fury that the count, no longer having the strength to retain it, tried to throw himself to the ground, but his foot remained caught in the stirrup. He fell without being able to disengage it, and his head took the whole weight of his body. He had never been in such a deplorable state; the umbrageous mule ran in all directions; eventually, the girth-strap of the saddle broke, and he remained by the side of the road, drowned in his own blood.

Don Luis was returning diligently from Compostela with the permission that he had requested from the archbishop; his tender heart promised him an imminent felicity; he already believed himself to be the most fortunate of all men.

Oh, how little reason one has to count on the benefits if life; they so often escape us when we think we are most certain of them! That was what happened on this occasion.

Don Luis perceived a man half-dead; the blood that covered the face prevented him from recognizing him, but whatever haste he was in to arrive home he did not want to leave to a gentleman and a valet who were accompanying him the care of helping him. He approached. Oh God, could a more veritable friend than him be encountered? He leapt from his horse to the body of the count; he embraced him; he could not hold back his tears, and while his valet brought water from a spring that chanced to be not far away, he and his gentleman looked at the wounds by which the count was covered.

Finally, he began to breathe; then he opened his eyes and recognized Don Luis. "What are you doing here?" he said, in a voice so faint that it was hardly audible. "Run after Lucile; she has been abducted in the nearby wood, where Don Gabriel has been wounded."

At news so disastrous, Don Luis nearly expired. What could he do in such an extremity? Two friends dead or alive, a mistress so dear in the power of his most terrible enemies! Very rapidly, however, he made the decision to follow her. He left his gentleman with the count, commanded his valet to search for help, and addressed his friend: "I'm going to help

Lucile and Don Gabriel. I'll try to avenge you. You'll see me again soon.'"

He mounted his horse, his heart so constricted that he was suffering as much as one can suffer, and although the count's weakness had prevented him from giving him any details, he could imagine well enough who the thief of his property was.

He rode toward the wood at top speed; he could hear loud shouting within it; he even seemed to recognize the voice of his dear Lucile. It was indeed her, who was putting up as much resistance as she could to Don Fernand and one of his valets, who were trying to put her on a horse.

Don Gabriel had already taken the lives of two of the assassins, and the others would have met a similar fate if they had dared to fight him, but they remained hidden behind the trees and had fired a shot from there that brought him down. Lucile, no longer having a defender, had tried to flee, but Don Fernand de la Vega had retained her and had done her enough violence for her to allow herself to be led away.

At that sight, Don Luis, more furious than a young lion from whom a hunter is snatching his prey, threw himself at the two cowardly adversaries, sword in hand; to defeat them cost him very little although it bought him glory. What carnage! Four men dead on one side, Don Gabriel lying on the other with no sentiment of life.

Don Luis and Lucile ran to him; that scene was no less sad than the one that had passed with Count d'Aguilar. Don Luis found himself in a strange embarrassment, for if he abandoned his friend, it would be the utmost cowardice, but if he retained Lucile in that place he risked losing her a second time. As he was thinking profoundly he heard a noise; it was his gentleman. He commanded him to go promptly in quest of people to carry Don Gabriel to the home of one of his friends, whose house was nearby. In the meantime, he obliged Lucile to hide in the densest part of the wood.

What did he not fear after the extreme misfortune of his two friends? He dreaded that the fatality of his star might extend as far as his mistress, that some snake or some other venomous animal might sting her in the place where he had left her alone. Oh, how his soul was penetrated by dolor! What anxiety he felt! Amour, cruel amour, it is you who causes the greatest woes of life!

Although Don Gabriel seemed to be dead, Don Luis could not lose the hope of seeing him recover from that pitiful state. He followed him to his friend's house with Lucile. By means of remedies he was brought round from his unconsciousness, and it was judged that his wounds were not dangerous. Don Luis, having thus deposited him in the hands of a very honest man, and knowing that the count was in a house whose master he knew well, he left his gentleman to take care of both of them, in association with his friend's two sons, who were very brave young men. He said adieu to his dear Ponce de Leon, assuring him that Isidore would not belong to anyone but him.

He could not talk to him for long and thanked him for the generous manner in which he had helped Lucile, without inconveniencing him. He departed with her at nightfall and went to Portugal, where he married her.

The grandfather of the beautiful young woman, having entered with his friends into the castle of Felix Sarmiente, remained there tranquilly, waiting for Don Fernand de la Vega to bring Lucile back. The night was already far advanced without them having received news of him. Anxiety took possession of their minds; they sent people to search for him, and someone came to inform them of their misfortune.

Nothing equaled the affliction by which Lucile's father and de la Vega's were seized, but as those two old men were unaccustomed to vigorous actions, as soon as they were no longer animated by the young people who had accompanied them, they only thought of returning to Seville in order to continue the procedures they had commenced against Don Luis.

The irritated Doña Juana took on departure the road to Malaga without saying anything to her nieces. She took them straight to the convent of the Hieronymite nuns where they had been brought up.[26] After having talked to the abbess in private she shut herself in with Isidore and Melanie.

"I did not want to speak to you sooner," she told them, "about the subjects of complaint that I have against you, but know that I am not unaware of any of them; that I am dying of dolor that you have been capable of suffering disguised young lords in your presence, who will doom you in society; and that to expiate such frightful conduct I am leaving you here, from which you will only emerge on the order of your father."

"Madame," replied Isidore, with a pride that did not distance her at all from the respect that she owed her, "we have nothing for which to reproach ourselves, and if it is true that you know the things that have happened, you know that we only learned the names of those lords on the day when we departed with you by night; you can still remember that, when you resolved to let them stay, we neglected nothing to make them leave. Were we in intelligence with you, Madame, since we had difficulty in seeing them in our house? It is true that they spoke to us about their sentiments without offending us; we found them very advantageous, and if we had the honor of being in your good graces you would not lose an opportunity so favorable to establish us."

Doña Juana, lacking good arguments to respond to her nieces, had no lack of insults; she heaped them with them, for her infatuation for the count, far from being diminished by absence, acquired new force, and the scant hope that remained of engaging him completed rendering her furious.

Isidore and Melanie entered the convent; they believed that they would find there all the honest liberty that their good conduct merited, but scarcely had the doors closed on them than they were told that they could not see anyone, that they could not write, and that they would not be let out of sight.

---

[26] The Hieronymites were nuns of the Order of Saint Jerome, strongly favored by the kings of Spain from their foundation in the fourteenth century.

Doña Juana had made the abbess believe that men of a condition far below theirs wanted to abduct them, that they had given them their hands, and that they could not be watched too closely.

That precaution was the cause of the old lady's designs not succeeding. The abbess chose among the nuns those who had the most birth in order to place them with the beautiful prisoners; among them, Iphigenie d'Aguilar was the first appointed, because she only had commerce with her relatives, and because the wretches of the sort Doña Juana had depicted as the lovers of her nieces were far from such a character.

Doña Iphigenie had a great deal of intelligence and mildness; she found so much merit in the new inmates that, seeing them in an extreme melancholy, she neglected nothing to extract them from it, but it was not long before she needed herself the consolation that she tried to give them; she received a letter that her brother, Count d'Aguilar, had written to her; he informed her of the state he was in, without telling her the reason for his combat, content to recommend himself to her prayers because he was dangerously wounded, and telling her that Don Gabriel Ponce de Leon was as bad as him.

Isidore, having remarked an extraordinary pallor on Iphigenie's face, asked her the cause. Iphigenie told her that she was very afflicted, and gave her the letter. On reading it, Isidore uttered a loud scream and let herself fall into an armchair; Melanie came running. Unable to speak, Isidore handed her the count's letter. Melanie testified no less affliction than her sister.

Until that moment, Iphigenie had not told them her family name; her modesty prevented her from boasting of those sorts of advantages, which were scarcely appropriate to a nun. Thus, they had never had occasion to talk to her about the count and Don Gabriel; but the sensibility that they testified on that occasion passed far beyond what one ordinarily has for a new friend; she saw them weeping more bitterly than her, and their acquaintance was so recent that she dared not attribute it to a dolor of that nature.

She looked at them without speaking; finally, Isidore, understanding a part of what was passing through her mind, said to her: "Cease to be surprised, Madame, by the state in which you see us. We are beloved, and we have to confess to you that we are not indifferent to Count d'Aguilar and Don Gabriel Ponce de Leon; it is because of them that we are here; however many difficulties they have caused us, gods, how mild they would be in comparison with the cruel news that we have learned."

"What! My dear brother and my dear cousin love you?" said Doña Iphigenie, "embracing Isidore and Melanie. You wish them well, you're suffering for them, and I did not know sooner that I am doing them harm! Alas, can you forgive me for all my actions of espionage?" After a few moments of silence she continued: "Yes, of course you will forgive me, by virtue of the care I shall take in future to please you; my heart has not waited for me to know you by your own names to attach itself to you."

"Madame," replied Melanie, "a secret presentiment inspired in it the tenderness we owe you, in relation to Count d'Aguilar and Don Gabriel, but what can we do to relieve them?"

"It's necessary to write to them," said Iphigenie. "I shall send an express bearer of your letters. It was futile for your aunt to order that you be captive here; I assure you that she will be poorly obeyed."

Isidore and Melanie thanked her for the pleasure that she gave them, and they wrote without delay. Isidore's letter to Don Gabriel was in these terms:

You will be as surprised to learn that I am with the Hieronymites of Malaga as I have been to learn of your wound. What can have happened to you, sire, since our separation, and is that separation not painful enough without it being followed by further disgraces? If you love me, do not neglect a health in which I am as interested as you wish. Come here as promptly as you can, and be persuaded, sire, that your memory will keep me faithful company.

Melanie wrote to Count d'Aguilar:

You are far away, and you are in peril: so many woes at once, sire! If it were sufficient to share them to soothe you, alas, how I would be useful to you! My dolor and my anxiety are frightful; I shall have little repose until I see you.

They also wrote to their brother. Iphigenie, having made a package of all those letters, charged a man of confidence with them.

It is easy to judge the joy that the count received, by means of news so dear and so unexpected; it contributed more to his recovery than all the remedies he was given. Don Gabriel was with him in the same room; as soon as he could suffer a litter, he had been carried there. The testimony of good will that he received from Isidore filled him with satisfaction. They begged Don Luis's gentleman to write all that had happened since Juana's departure in order to inform the ladies.

As the count was very ill he was only able to write these few lines to Melanie:

You will see me soon at your feet, the most respectful of all lovers.

Ponce de Leon wrote to Isidore:

We believed that we would follow you, when a thousand accidents succeeded one another to stop us, but Madame, can there be a more agreeable surprise than that of receiving a note from your hand? With what transport I saw those testimonies of your good will! I am unable to make you understand them better than by talking to you about my passion; it is such that, on the point of losing my life, I only regretted you. In fact, you take the place of everything for me; I am fortunate, Madame if I hold some place for you.

The messenger made all the necessary diligence in order not to leave Iphigenie and the two amiable sisters for long in the anxiety they had regarding the health of the cavaliers. The character of their letters appeared to them to be so tender and so touching that thy resolved to render an entire justice to their sentiments, to love the ones who loved them, and to second the steps that they wanted to take for their marriage.

They wrote in that spirit to Don Luis, and as he was only waiting for their consent to send Don Felix Sarmiente the request that Don Gabriel and the count were making for his sisters, it was no longer a question of anything but knowing the final resolution of the two lovers. When he wrote to them, they outbid that urgency and declared that even if Doña Juana disinherited them, that would not be an obstacle, since they loved them enough not to regard, in marrying them, anything but their persons.

Don Gabriel wrote to inform his father, who was in Madrid, of the sentiments he had for Isidore, and as the latter only wanted for his son an amiable and virtuous young woman, he willingly gave his support to what they desired, and he charged his brother, the Comte de Leon, who was in Cadiz, to take all the cares necessary for the affair.

Don Felix Sarmiente felt so honored by the alliance that his son proposed for his sisters that he judged it necessary to go to Malaga in order to smooth out all the difficulties, for Don Luis's lawsuit did not permit him to come to Andalusia.

The lovers and their mistresses received that good news with a satisfaction difficult to express. Don Gabriel and the count were soon in a state to go to Malaga; they arrived at the same time as their uncle and Don Felix, who, having communicated with one another regarding the marriage, also went there

Meanwhile, Doña Juana, sad and desolate, was nurturing her own poison in a country house, where her brother went to find her in order to beg her to come to her nieces' weddings. A thunderbolt would not have been more terrible; she said everything that her rage could make her imagine in order to break the affair, but Don Felix was already forewarned and her fury had no more effect than her remonstrations and her threats.

When she saw that the thing was without remedy, she went to Seville and gave all her wealth to Lucile's grandfather and Don Fernand's father, on condition that they maintain an eternal lawsuit against her family. They were, however, parties too scantly redoubtable to make trouble for very long against persons as distinguished by their merit and their quality. An accommodation was proposed to them, which they accepted with joy.

Thus, the marriages of Don Gabriel and Isidore, and Count d'Aguilar and Melanie, were completed in a matter of days with all possible magnificence and all the satisfaction that ought to be imagined between persons so accomplished, who loved one another so dearly.

As for Juana, she would have been ruined by the foolish donation she had just made if Don Felix had not fortunately found the means to appease Lucile's father. After having forgiven Don Luis for her abduction, he gave his daughter Juana's wealth as well as his own, and as that wealth returned to the Sarmiente family, they had the generosity of allowing Juana to enjoy it. She retired for the rest of her life to the Carmelites of Seville.

As soon as Madame D*** had finished, the company was informed that a large collation was served in the cabinet of verdure near the spring.

"Let's go there," said Comtesse de F***. "I consent to that, provided that I'm promised that when we leave the table, we finish the reading of this notebook, for I'm convinced by what we have heard so far and what remains to be read that we would lose many pleasant things."

Everyone applauded what the comtesse desired.

"Since you wish it," said Madame D***, we'll recommence with the tale of Babiole; there are still a few others, with another Spanish novella, which will perhaps not displease you.

BABIOLE

There was once a queen who could not wish for anything, in order to be happy, except to have children; she talked about nothing else, and said incessantly that the fay Fanferluche, having come to her birth, and not having been satisfied by the queen, her mother, had flown into a fury and had wished her nothing but chagrins.

One day, when she was afflicted all alone by her fireside, she saw a little old lady descend through the chimney, as tall as a handspan; she was sitting astride three strands of rush and was wearing a hawthorn branch on her head; her costume was made of insect wings; two nutshells served her as boots. She walked in the air, and having made three tours of the room she stopped before the queen. "For a long time," she said, "you have been murmuring against me, accusing me of your displeasures and holding me responsible for everything that happens to you. You believe, Madame, that I'm the cause of your having no children; I've come to announce a child to you, but my apprehension is that she will cost you many tears."

"Oh, noble Fanferluche," cried the queen, "Don't refuse me your pity and your aid; I promise to render you all the services that are in my power, provided that the princess you are promising me will be my consolation and not my penalty."

"Destiny is more powerful than me," replied the fay. "All that I can do to mark my affection for you is to give you this sprig of hawthorn. Attach it to your daughter's head as soon as she is born; it will protect her from several perils."

She gave her the hawthorn and disappeared in a flash.

The queen remained sad and thoughtful. *For what have I wished?* she said to herself. *A daughter who will cost my many tears and many sighs. Would I not have been happier not having any?*

The presence of the king, whom she loved dearly, dissipated a part of her displeasure. She became pregnant, and her only concern, during her pregnancy, was recommending to her closest confidantes that as soon as the princess was born, the thorn-flower—which she kept in a golden box covered in diamonds, as the thing in the world she held in highest esteem—should be attached to her head.

Eventually, the queen gave birth to the most beautiful creature that has ever been seen; the hawthorn flower was attached to her head diligently, and at the same instant—O marvel!—she became a little she-monkey, leaping, running and capering around the room, without anything lacking.

At that metamorphosis, all the ladies uttered frightful screams, and the queen, more alarmed than anyone, nearly died of despair. She shouted to them to take away the bouquet she had over her ear; they had a thousand difficulties catching the monkey, and they took away the fatal flowers, but in vain; she was already a monkey, a confirmed monkey. Not wanting to suckle, nor to play the infant, she only required walnuts and chestnuts.

"Barbaric Fanferluche!" cried the queen, dolorously, "What have I done to you, to treat me so cruelly? What will become of me? What shame for me; all my subjects will believe that I've made a monster; what will the king's horror be for such a child? She wept, and begged her ladies to advise her as to what to do in such a pressing occasion.

"Madame," said the oldest one, "It's necessary to persuade the king that the princess is dead, and to shut this she-monkey in a box in order to throw it to the bottom of the sea, for it would be a frightful thing if you kept any longer a little beast of that nature."

The queen had some difficulty in resolving to do that, but when she was told that the king was coming to her room, she was so confused and so troubled that without further deliberation, she told her maid of honor to do anything she wanted with the monkey.

It was taken into another apartment; it was shut in a box, and one of the queen's valets de chambre was ordered to throw it in the sea; he departed immediately.

The princess was, therefore, in extreme peril, but the man, having found the box beautiful, was reluctant to destroy it. He sat down on the shore and took the monkey out of the box, firmly resolved to kill it, for he did not know that it was his sovereign, but as he was holding it, a loud noise that surprised him obliged him to turn his head; he saw an uncovered chariot drawn by six unicorns, glittering with gold and precious stones; several instruments of war preceded it. A queen, in a royal mantle, was sitting on cushions of golden cloth and holding her son, aged four years, in front of her.

The valet de chambre recognized the queen who was the sister of his mistress; she had come to see her in order to rejoice with her, but as soon as she was told that the little princess was dead she had departed, very sad, to return to her realm. She was in a profound reverie when her son cried: "I want the monkey! I want to have it!"

Having looked, the queen perceived the prettiest monkey there had ever been. The valet de chambre looked for a means to flee, but was prevented from so doing. The queen gave him a large sum of money, and, finding the monkey gentle and pretty, named her Babiole. Thus, in spite of the rigor of her fate, she fell into the hands of the queen, her aunt.

When she had arrived in her estates, the little prince begged her to give him Babiole, in order to play with her. He wanted her to be dressed like a princess; new dresses were made for her every day, and she was taught only to walk on her hind feet.

It was impossible to find a more beautiful she-monkey with better manners. Her little face was as black as jet, with a white beard and red patches at the ears; her hands were no larger than a butterfly's wings, and the vivacity of her eyes marked so much intelligence that no one had reason to be astonished by all the things she did. The prince, who loved her dearly, caressed her incessantly; she refrained carefully from biting him, and when he wept, she wept too.

She had been with the queen for four years when she began one day to stammer like a child who wants to say something; everyone was astonished by that, but there was a much greater astonishment when she began to talk in a soft and clear little voice, so distinct that not a word was lost.

What a marvel! Babiole was talking, Babiole was reasoning! The queen wanted to see her again, in order to be amused; she was taken to her apartment, to the great regret of the prince; it cost him a few tears, and to console him he was given dogs and cats, birds and squirrels, and even a little horse called Criquetin, who danced the saraband—but all that was not worth as much as a single word from Babiole.

For her part, she was more constrained in the queen's apartment than the prince's; it was necessary for her to respond like a Sibyl to a hundred clever and savant questions, which she was sometimes unable to disentangle. As soon as an ambassador or a foreigner arrived, she was made to appear in a velvet or brocade robe, a jacket and collar; if the court was in mourning she dragged a long mantle and crepes, which fatigued her greatly. She was no longer given the liberty of eating what she liked; the physician prescribed for her, and that scarcely pleased her, for she was as willful as a she-monkey born a princess.

The queen gave her masters who exercised the vivacity of her mind fully; she excellent at playing the harpsichord, a marvelous one was made for her in an oyster shell. Painters came from the four corners of the world, especially Italy, to paint her; her renown flew from one pole to the other, for a monkey that talked had not yet been seen.

The prince, who was as handsome as Amour is represented, gracious and intelligent, was a prodigy no less extraordinary. He came to see Babiole; he sometimes amused himself with her; their conversations, from playful and joyful, sometimes became serious and moral. Babiole had a heart, and that heart had not been metamorphosed like the rest of her little person; she therefore acquired a tenderness for the prince, and it became so strong that it became excessive.

The unfortunate Babiole did not know what to do; she spent nights on the top of a widow-shutter, or the corner of a mantelpiece, without wanting to go into her neat and clean padded and feathered basket. Her governess—for she had one—often heard her sighing, and sometimes lamenting; her melancholy increased along with her reason, and she never saw herself in a mirror without wanting to break it, with the result that it was ordinarily said that the monkey was still a monkey, that Babiole was unable to rid herself of the natural malice of her family.

The prince having grown up, he loved hunting, balls, the theater, arms and books, and of the monkey there was almost no mention any longer. Things went very differently on her side; she loved him more at twelve years of age than she had at six; she sometimes reproached him for his neglect; he thought she was quite justified, as he gave her for all reckoning a lady-apple or a glazed chestnut.

Finally, Babiole's reputation caused rumor in the realm of Monkeys; King Magot had a great desire to marry her, and with that design he decided to send a celebrated ambassador to obtain her from the queen; he had no difficulty in making his intentions clear to his prime minister, but would have had infinite difficulty expressing them without the aid of parrots and magpies, commonly known as margots; the latter chattered a abundantly, the jays that were following the equipage would have been hard pressed to jabber less than them.

A large monkey named Mirlifiche was the leader of the embassy; he had a cardboard carriage made on which were painted the amours of King Magot with Monette Guenuche, famous in the Magotic Empire; she had died pitilessly under the claws of a wild cat, unaccustomed to her teasing. The pleasures that Magot and Monette had enjoyed during their marriage were therefore represented, and the good nature with which the king had mourned her demise. Six white rabbits from an excellent warren drew the carriage, called by virtue of honor the corps carriage. Then came a chariot of straw painted in several colors, in which were the she-monkeys destined for Babiole; it was necessary to see how they were adorned; they genuinely looked as if they were going to a wedding.

The rest of the cortege was made up of little spaniels, greyhound pups, Spanish cats, Muscovite rats, a few hedge-hogs, subtle weasels and greedy foxes, some pulling carts and others carrying the baggage. Mirlifiche, above all, graver than a Roman dictator and wiser than Cato, rode a young grey-hound, which could amble better than any English guildsman.

The queen did not know anything about this magnificent embassy when it appeared outside her palace. The burst of laughter of the people and her guards having obliged her to put her head out of the window, she saw the most extraordinary cavalcade that she had ever seen in her life.

Immediately, Mirlifiche, followed by a considerable number of monkeys, advanced toward the chariot of she-monkeys and, giving his paw to the stoutest one, called Gigogna, he helped her down; then, releasing the little parrot that was to serve as an interpreter, he waited for the beautiful bird to be introduced to the queen and to request an audience on his behalf.

The parrot rose slowly into the air, came to the window from which the queen was looking out and said to her, in the prettiest voice in the world: "Madame, Count Mirlifiche, the ambassador of the celebrated Magot, king of monkeys, re-quests an audience with Your Majesty in order to discuss a very important mater."

"Handsome parrot," said the queen, caressing it, "com-mence by having a bite to eat and a drink. After that, I consent that you go to tell Count Mirlifiche that he and those accom-panying him are very welcome in my estates. If the voyage he has made from Magotia has not fatigued him too much, per-haps he would like to enter the audience hall shortly, where I shall await him with all my court.

At those words, the parrot lowered its paw twice, flapped its wings, sang a little song as a sign of joy and resumed its flight; it perched on Mirlifiche's shoulder and reported the favorable response it had just received into his ear. Mirlifiche was not insensible to it; he asked one of the queen's officers via Margot, the magpie, which had been promoted to deputy interpreter, if he would be kind enough to give him a room in which to relax for a few moments. A drawing room was immediately opened, paved with marble, gilded and decorated, which was one of the cleanest in the palace.

He went in with a part of his retinue, but as the monkeys were great rummagers by profession they discovered a certain corner in which many pots of jam were arranged; also being very gluttonous, one held a crystal cup full of apricots another a bottle of syrup, this one pies, another marzipan.

The avian folk that formed the cortege were annoyed to be a feast at which there was no hempseed or millet, and one jay, a great chatterbox by profession, flew into the audience hall and approached the queen respectfully. "Madame," it said, "I am too much You Majesty's servant to be the benevolent accomplice of the damage that it being done to your sweet jams; Count Mirlifiche had already eaten three jars himself; he was scoffing the fourth without any respect for royal majesty when, my heart penetrated, I came to give you the information."

"Thank you, little jay, my friend," said the queen, smiling, "but I dispense you of having so much zeal for my pots of jam; I abandon them in favor of Babiole, whom I love with all my heart."

The jay, a little ashamed of the tattling it had just done, withdrew without saying a word.

A few moments later the ambassador entered with his retinue; his costume was not entirely fashionable, for, since the return of the famous Fagotin,[27] who had shone so much in

---

[27] As previously noted, Fagotin was famous as a companion of the puppeteer Brioché, allegedly killed by Cyrano de Berge-

society, no good model had come forward: his hat was pointed, with a bouquet of glass plumes, a baldric of blue paper covered with golden dimples, large knee-breeches and a cane. The parrot, who was reputed to be a good poet, having composed a very serious speech, advanced as far as the foot of the throne, where the queen was seated; he addressed Babiole, and spoke thus:

> *Madame, know the power of your eyes*
> *For amour of which Magot feels the violence.*
> *These monkeys and cats, this pompous cortege,*
> *These birds, everything here speaks of his fires.*
> *When a savage cat attesting fury,*
> *Monette—who was a cherished she-monkey*
> *Madame, I can only compare her with you—*
> *Was stolen from Magot her husband,*
> *The king swore a hundred times to his manes,*
> *That he would conserve an eternal love for her.*
> *Madame, your charms have expelled from his heart*
> *The tender memory of his first ardor.*
> *He only thinks of you; if you knew, Madame,*
> *To what excess he has carried his flame,*
> *Doubtless your heart, sensible to pity,*
> *To soothe his woes would take the half!*
> *He who was once seen big, fat, well and light,*
> *Is now unquiet, all undone and thin,*
> *An eternal worry seems to be consuming him,*
> *Madame, how keenly he feels what it is to love!*
> *The olives and walnuts for which he was avid,*
> *No longer appear to him more than insipid,*
> *He is dying; it is to you he has recourse!*
> *You alone can conserve his days.*
> *I will not tell you the charming advantages*

---

rac, who was deceived by his costume into mistaking him for a man, and reacted accordingly when he thought he was being attacked by the playful animal.

That you will find on our happy shores.
Figs and grapes are there to harvest
The most beautiful fruits are ever in season.

The parrot had hardly finished his discourse when the queen cast her eyes upon Babiole, who found herself so nonplussed that no one has ever been more so. The queen wanted to know her sentiment before replying. She told the parrot to let the ambassador understand that she favored the pretentions of his king in everything that depended on her.

The audience over, she withdrew, and Babiole followed her into her cabinet.

"My little she-monkey," she said. "I confess to you that I would greatly regret your going away, but there is no means of refusing Magot, who is asking for you in marriage, for I have not forgotten that his father put two hundred thousand monkeys on campaign in order to sustain a great war against mine; they would eat so many of our subjects that we would be obliged to make a rather shameful peace."

"That signifies, Madame," relied Babiole, impatiently, "that you are resolved to sacrifice me to this vile monster in order to avoid his anger, but I beg Your Majesty at least to grant me a few days to make my final resolution."

"That is just," said the queen. "Nevertheless, if you believe me, make up your mind promptly; consider the honors that are in preparation for you, the magnificence of the ambassador and what maids of honor you have been sent. I am sure that Magot never did as much for Monette as he is doing for you."

"I don't know what he did for Monette," replied little Babiole, disdainfully, "but I know full well that I am untouched by the sentiments with which he is distinguishing me."

She got up immediately, curtseyed with good grace and went to find the prince in order to tell him her dolors.

As soon as he saw her he cried: "Well, my Babiole, well shall we be dancing at your wedding?"

"I don't know, Sire," she said, sadly, "but the state in which you find me is so deplorable that I am no longer the mistress of keeping my secret from you, and although it costs my modesty, it is necessary that I confess that you are the only one whom I could desire for a husband."

"For a husband!" said the prince, bursting out laughing. "For a husband, my she-monkey! I'm charmed by what you tell me, but I hope that you will excuse me if I don't accept the proposal, for, in sum, our stature, our appearance and our manners are scarcely suitable."

"I am in accord with that," she said, "and above all, our hearts do not resemble one another. You are an ingrate; I perceived that a long time ago, and I have been very extravagant to love a prince who merits it so little."

"But Babiole," he said, "think of the difficulty I would have in seeing you perched on the tip of a sycamore, holding on to a branch by the end of your tail; believe me, let us turn that affair into a joke for your honor and mine. Marry King Magot in favor of the good amity he has for us; send me the first Magotin of your fashion."

"You are fortunate, Sire," added Babiole, "that I do not have the mind of a she-monkey entirely; another than me would already have put out your eyes, bitten your nose and torn off your ears; but I abandon you to the reflections that you will make one day regarding your unworthy procedure."

She could not say any more; her governess came to fetch her. Ambassador Mirlifiche had rendered to her apartment with magnificent presents.

There was a dressing-table made of spider-webs embroidered with little glow-worms; an egg-shell contained combs, a bigarreau cherry serving as a pin-cushion, and all the linen was garnished with paper lace. There was also a basket containing several shells, neatly sorted, some to serve as pendant ear-rings, others as hairpins, all of that shone like diamond. What was even better were a dozen jars full of jam with a little glass box in which a walnut and an olive were enclosed, but the key was lost—about which Babiole did not care.

The ambassador made her understand by grunting, which is the language that is used in Magotia, that his monarch was more touched by her charms than he had been in his life by any she-monkey; that he had built her a palace at the top of a fir tree; that he send her those presents, including good jam, to mark his attachment to her; that the king his master could not testify his amity better.

"But," he added, "the strongest proof of his tenderness, and to which you will be most sensible, Madame, is the care that he has taken to have himself painted in order to advance for you the pleasure of seeing him."

Immediately, he deployed a portrait of the king of the monkeys sitting on a large block of wood holding an apple, which he was eating.

Babiole turned her eyes away, in order not to gaze any longer at a face so disagreeable, and, grunting three or four times, she made Mirlifiche understand that she was obliged to his master for his esteem, but that she had not yet determined whether she wanted to marry him

However, the queen had resolved not to attract the anger of the monkeys, and, not believing that many ceremonies were required in order to send Babiole where she wanted her to go, she had everything prepared for her departure. At that news, despair took entre possession of her heart. The scorn of the prince on the one hand, and the indifference of the queen on the other, and more than all that, the idea of such a husband, caused her to make the resolution to flee, That was not such a difficult thing to do; since she had talked, she was no longer attached; she came, went and returned to her room by the window as often as the door.

She hastened to depart, therefore, leaping from tree to tree and from branch to branch all the way to the bank of a river. The excess of her despair prevented her from understanding the peril into which she was about to put herself by trying to swim across, and without examining the question she threw herself in; immediately, she sank to the bottom. As she had not lost her judgment, however, she perceived a magnificent grotto ornamented with shells. She hastened to enter it; she was received there by a venerable old man, whose white beard descended all the way to his waist; he was lying on reeds and gladioli, wearing a crown of wild poppies. He was leaning against a rock from which several springs ran that swelled the river.

"Hey, what brings you here, little Babiole?" he said, holding out his hand.

"Sire," she replied, "I am an unfortunate she-monkey. I'm fleeing a frightful monkey that they want to give me as a husband."

"I know more about your news than you think," added the sage old man. "It's true that you abhor Magot, but it's no less true that you love a young prince, who only has indifference for you."

"Oh, sire," cried Babiole, sighing, "let's not talk about that; the memory augments all my dolors."

"He won't always be rebellious to amour," the host of the fish continued. "I know that he's reserved for the most beautiful princess in the world."

"Unfortunate that I am," continued Babiole, "He will never be for me, then!"

The fellow smiled, and said: "Don't be afflicted, good Babiole; time is a grandmaster; only be careful not to lose the little glass box the Magot sent you, and which you happen to have in your pocket. I can't tell you anymore. Here's a tortoise that travels at a good pace; sit on it, and it will take you where you need to go."

"After the obligations I owe to you," she said to him, "I can't neglect knowing your name."

"My name is Biroquoi," he said, "father of Biroquie, a rather large and rather famous river, as you can see."

Babiole climbed on to the tortoise with a good deal of confidence; they traveled for a long time in the water, but, after what seemed like a long detour, the tortoise reached the bank. It would be difficult to find anything more elegant than its English saddle and the rest of its harness; it even had little saddle-pistols, for which two crayfish shells served as holsters.

Babiole was traveling with an entire confidence in the promises of the sage Biroquoi when she suddenly heard a loud noise. Alas, alas, it was the ambassador Mirlifiche, with all his mirlifichons, who were returning to Magotia, sad and desolate at Babiole's flight. One monkey of the troop had climbed a walnut tree while foraging in order to knock down nuts and nourish the magotins, but he was scarcely at the top of the tree than, looking in all directions, he perceived Babiole on the poor tortoise, which was making its way slowly across open country. At that sight he started crying so loudly that the monkeys assembled and asked him in their language what the matter was. He told them. Immediately, the parrots, magpies and jay were unleashed, which flew to where she was, and on their report, the ambassador, the she-monkeys and the rest of the equipage ran and arrested her.

What a displeasure for Babiole! It would be difficult to have a greater and more sensible one; she was constrained to climb into the corps carriage; it was immediately surrounded by the most vigilant she-monkeys, a few foxes and a cock, which perched on the imperial, standing sentinel day and night. A monkey took the tortoise in hand, as a rare animal, and the cavalcade continued its journey, to the displeasure of Babiole, who had no company except for Madame Gigogna, a peevish and disobliging she-monkey.

After three days, which had passed without any adventure, the guides having gone astray, they all arrived in a large and famous city that was completely unfamiliar, but having perceived a magnificent garden, the gate of which was open, they stopped there and occupied it, like a conquered country. One cracked nuts, another guzzled cherries, another stripped a plum-tree; in the end, there was not a single little monkey who did not go foraging and did not make a store.

It is necessary to know that the city in question was the capital of the realm where Babiole had been born; that the queen, her mother, was still there; and that since the misfortune she had experienced of seeing her daughter metamorphosed into a monkey by a sprig of hawthorn, she had never wanted to suffer in her estates any monkey of any species, or anything that might remind her of the fatality of her deplorable adventure.

A monkey was regarded there as a disturber of public repose. With what astonishment, therefore were the people struck, on seeing a cardboard carriage, a chariot of painted straw and the rest of the most surprising equipage that had ever been seen since tales have been tales and fays have been fays.

The news flew to the palace; the queen was panic-stricken; she thought that the simian population wanted to attack her authority. She promptly assembled her council, had them all condemned as criminals of lèse-majesté, and, not wanting to waste the opportunity to make an example famous enough to be remembered in future, she sent her guards into the garden with orders to capture all the monkeys.

They threw large nets over the trees; the hunt was soon complete, and, in spite of the respect due to him in the quality of ambassador, that individual found himself utterly scorned in the person of Mirlifiche, who was thrown pitilessly into the depths of a cellar under a large empty building, where he and his comrades were imprisoned, along with the lady she-monkeys and damsels accompanying Babiole.

For her part, she experienced a secret joy at this new disorder. When disgraces reach a certain point, one no longer hears anything, and even death can be envisaged as a benefit; that was the situation in which she found herself, her heart occupied with the prince who had scorned her and her mind filled by the frightful idea of King Magot, whose wife she was on the point of becoming.

Furthermore, it is necessary not to forget to say that her costume was so pretty and her manners so uncommon that those who had captured her paused to consider her as something marvelous, and when she had spoken to them, there was further astonishment. They had already heard mention of the admirable Babiole. The queen who had found her, and who did not know about her niece's metamorphosis, had often written to her sister that she possessed a marvelous she-monkey and begged her to come and see her, but the afflicted queen had passed over that article without wanting to read it.

Finally, the guards, rapturous with admiration, took Babiole into a large gallery and made her a little throne there; they placed her on it, more like a sovereign than a prisoner, and the queen, happening to pass by, was so surprised by her pretty figure and the gracious compliment that she paid her that, involuntarily, nature spoke in favor of the infanta.

The queen took her in her arms. The little creature, animated for her part by emotions that she had not felt before, threw her arms around her and said things so tender and engaging that she evoked the admiration of all those who heard her.

"No, Madame," she cried, "it is not the fear of an imminent death, with which I her that you are threatening the fortunate race of monkeys, that frightens me and engages me to seek means of pleasing you and soothing you; the end of my life is not the greatest misfortune that can happen to me, and I have sentiments so far above what I am that I would regret the slightest step for my conservation; it is, therefore, in relation to you alone, Madame, that I love you; your crown touches me far less than your merit."

In your opinion, how could one reply to a Babiole so complimentary and so reverential? The queen, as mute as a carp, opened two wide eyes, thought she was dreaming, and felt that her heart was very emotional.

She took the she-monkey into her cabinet. When they were alone, she said to her: "Don't defer for a moment telling me your adventures, for I sense that of all the small animals that populate the menageries and that I keep in the palace, you will be the one I like best. I even assure you that in your favor I will grant mercy to the monkeys accompanying you."

"Oh, Madame," she cried, "I don't request any for them. My misfortune has caused me to be born a monkey, and that same misfortune has given me a discernment that will make me suffer until death; for, in sum, what can I feel when I see myself in my mirror, small, ugly and black, with paws covered in fur, a tail, and teeth ever ready to bite, while, in addition, I do not lack intelligence, I have taste, delicacy and sentiments?"

"Are you capable," the queen asked, "of having that of tenderness?"

Babiole sighed, without making any reply.

"Oh," the queen continued, "it's necessary to tell me whether you love a monkey, a rabbit or a squirrel, for if you are not too engaged, I have a dwarf that might suit you very well."

At that proposition Babiole assumed a disdainful expression, which made the queen burst out laughing. "Don't get annoyed," she said, "and tell me by what hazard you can talk."

All that I know about my adventures," replied Babiole, "is that the queen, your sister, had scarcely quit you after the death of the princess, your daughter, than she saw while passing along the sea shore one of your valets de chambre who wanted to drown me. I was snatched from his hands by her order, and by virtue of a prodigy by which everyone was equally surprised, speech and reason came to me. I was given masters who taught me several languages and to play instruments. Eventually, Madame, I became sensible of my disgraces, and…but what's wrong, Madame?" she exclaimed, on seeing the queen's face pale and covered in cold sweat. "I remark an extraordinary change in your person."

"I'm dying!" aid the queen, in a feeble and poorly articulated voice. "I'm dying, my dear and too unfortunate daughter. It's today, then, that I find you again!"

With those words, she fainted. Babiole, frightened, ran to call for help. The queen's ladies hastened to give her water, to unlace her and to put her to bed, Babiole burrowed into it with her; no one even noticed her, she was so small.

When the queen came round from the long faint into which the discourse of the princes had thrown her, she wanted to remain alone with the ladies who knew the secret of the fatal birth of her daughter. She told them what had happened, by which they remained so bewildered that they did not know what advice to give her, but she commanded them to tell her what they thought it appropriate to do in such a circumstance. Some said that it was necessary to strangle the she-monkey, others that she should be imprisoned in a hole, and yet others wanted to throw her in the sea again.

The queen wept and sobbed. "She has so much intelligence," she said. "What a pity to see her reduced by an enchanted bouquet to this wretched estate! But fundamentally," she continued, "she's my daughter, she's my blood, and it's me who attracted the evil Fanferluche to her; is it just that she should suffer the hatred that the fay has for me?"

"Yes, Madame," cried the old maid of honor, "it's necessary to save your glory; what would people think in society if you declared that a monkey is your infanta? It isn't natural to have such children, when one is as beautiful as you."

The queen lost patience on hearing her argue thus. She and the others sustained with no less vivacity that it was necessary to examine the little monster, and by way of conclusion she decided to imprison Babiole in a castle, where she would be well nourished and well treated for the rest of her life.

When she heard that the queen wanted to put her in prison, Babiole slipped very gently along the gap behind the bed and, throwing herself from the window into a tree in the garden she ran away, all the way to that great forest, and left everyone in confusion, unable to find her.

She spent the night in the hollow of an oak tree, where she had time to moralize on the cruelty of destiny, but what gave her more pain was the necessity in which she had been put of quitting the queen. However, she preferred to exile herself voluntarily and remain mistress of her liberty rather than lose it forever.

As soon as it was daylight she continued her journey, without knowing where she wanted to go, thinking and re-thinking a thousand times over about the bizarrerie of such an extraordinary adventure. "What a difference here is," she cried, "between what I am and what I ought to be!" Tears ran abundantly from poor Babiole's little eyes.

She set forth again as soon as day dawned; she feared that the queen would have her followed, or that one of the monkeys escaped from the cave might take her to King Magot in spite of herself. She went so far, so very far, without following any road or path, that she arrived in a great desert where there was no house or tree, no fruits, grass or any spring. She set out into it without reflection, and when she began to get hungry she realized, too late, that it had been very imprudent to travel in such a country.

Two days and two nights went by without her being able to catch a grub or a gnat. The fear of death gripped her; she was so weak that she fainted. She lay down on the ground, and eventually remembering the olive and the walnut that were inside the little glass box, she judged that she might make a light meal of them. Joyful at that ray of hope, she took a stone, smashed the box and bit into the olive.

She had hardly touched it with her teeth, however, than a great abundance of perfumed oil emerged from it, which fell on to her paws; they became the most beautiful hands in the world. Her surprise was extreme. She took the oil and rubbed herself all over with it. A marvel! She became so beautiful, instantly, that nothing in the world could equal her.

She felt her large eyes, her small mouth, and her shapely nose. She was dying of the desire to have a mirror. Finally, she decided to make one of the largest shard of glass from her box. When she saw herself, what joy! What an agreeable surprise! Her garments had grown with her; she was well coiffed, her hair had a thousand curls, her complexion had the freshness of spring flowers.

One the first moments of surprise had passed, hunger made itself felt more urgently, and her regrets were strangely augmented.

"What!" she said. "So beautiful and so young, born a princess as I am, it's necessary for me to perish in this sad place! Oh, barbaric fortune that led me here, what fate have you ordered for me? Is it to afflict me further that you have made such a fortunate and unexpected change in me? And you, venerable river Biroquoi, who saved my life so generously, will you let me perish in this frightful solitude?

The infanta asked for help in vain; everything was deaf to her voice. The necessity of eating tormented her to such a point that she took the walnut and broke it; but when she threw away the shell she was very surprised to see architects, painters, masons, upholsterers, sculptors and a thousand other sorts of workmen emerged from it.

Some designed a palace, others built it and others furnished it. Some painted the apartments, some cultivated the gardens; everything shone with gold and azure; a magnificent meal was served to her; sixty princesses better dressed than queens, led by squires and followed by their pages, came to pay her great compliments and invited her to the feast that was awaiting her. Immediately, without having to be begged, advanced promptly toward the hall, and there, in a regal manner, she ate like a starveling.

Scarcely had she left the table than her treasurers brought before her fifteen thousand coffers as large as hogsheads, filled with gold and diamonds. They asked her whether she was agreeable that they pay the workers who had built her palace. She said that it was just, on condition that they also built a city, that they get married and stay with her. All of them consented to that; the city was finished in three quarters of an hour, although it was five times as large as Rome. That was a great many prodigies to emerge from a single little nut.

The princess meditated sending a famous embassy to her mother, the queen, and to make a few reproaches to the young prince, her cousin. While waiting to take the necessary measures for that, she amused herself watching tourneys, for which she always gave the prizes, playing games, seeing plays, hunting and fishing—for a river had been conducted there. The rumor of her beauty spread throughout the world; kings came to her court from the four corners of the earth, along with giants taller than mountains and pygmies smaller than rats.

One day, when there was a great celebration, in which several knights were breaking lances, it happened that they became irritated with one another; they fought and wounded one another. Angrily, the princess descended from her balcony in order to recognize the guilty parties, but when they were disarmed, what became of her when she saw the prince, her cousin!

Although he was not dead, he was so nearly dead that she thought she would die herself of surprise and dolor. She had him carried to the finest apartment in the palace, where nothing was lacking of everything necessary to his cure: physicians from Chowdhury, surgeons, ointments, broths and syrups. The infanta made bandages and slings personally; her eyes were bathed by tears, and those tears must have served as a balm for the invalid. He was, in fact, ill in more ways than one, for, without counting half a dozen sword-thrusts and as many lance-thrusts that had pierced him through, he had been in the court incognito for a long time and had experienced the power of Babiole's beautiful eyes in a manner that would not be cured as long as he lived. It is easy to judge at present, therefore, a part of what he felt when he was able to read on the face of the lovable princess that she was in the utmost dolor at the state to which he was reduced.

I shall not pause to repeat all the things with which his heart furnished him in order to thank her for the generosity that she was showing to him; those who heard him were surprised that a man who was so ill could manifest so much passion and gratitude. The infanta, who blushed more than once, begged him to shut up, but the emotion and ardor of his discourse took him so far that she saw him suddenly fall into a frightful agony.

She had armed herself until then with constancy; finally, she lost control of herself to such an extent that she tore out her hair, uttered loud screams and gave everyone reason to believe that her heart was facile of access, since she had acquired so much tenderness for a stranger in such a short time, for no one knew in Babiola—that was the name she had given to her realm—that the prince was her cousin and that she had loved him since her earliest childhood.

It was while traveling that he had stopped in the court, and as he did not know anyone to introduce him to the infanta, he thought that nothing would be better than to perform in front of her five or six heroic gallantries—which is to say, to cut off the arms and legs of knights in tourneys—but he could not find any sufficiently complaisant to suffer it. There was, in consequence, a rude melee; the strongest battled the weakest, and the weakest, as I have already said, was the prince.

Babiole, in despair, wandered the high roads without a carriage and without guards. She entered thus into a wood and fell in a faint at the foot of a tree, from which the fay Fanferluche, who never slept and was always seeking opportunities to do harm, came to take her away in a cloud blacker than ink, which traveled faster than the wind.

The princess remained unconscious for some time; finally, she came round. No surprise was ever equal to hers on finding herself so far from the ground and so close to the Pole. The floor of the cloud was not solid, with the result that in running back and forth she seemed to be walking on feathers. The cloud split, and she had a great deal of difficulty preventing herself from falling. She did not find anyone to whom to complain, for the wicked Fanferluche had rendered herself invisible. She had time to think about her dear prince and the state in which she had left him, and she abandoned herself to the most dolorous sentiments that can occupy a soul.

"What!" she cried. "I'm still capable of surviving the man I love, and the apprehension of an imminent death can find some place in my heart! Oh, if the sun wanted to roast me, what a good office it would be rendering me; or if I could drown myself in a rainbow how content I would be! But alas, the entire zodiac is deaf to my voice; Sagittarius has no arrows, Taurus any horns or Leo any teeth. Perhaps the earth will be more obliging, and will offer me the tip of a rock on which I can kill myself. Oh, Prince, my dear cousin, why are you not here to see me make the most tragic somersault that a desperate lover can ever turn."

As she finished speaking, she ran to the end of the cloud and hurled herself like a violently-unleashed arrow.

All those who saw her believed that it was the moon that was falling, and as it was then waning, several people who worshiped it and did not see it again for some time, put on full mourning and were convinced that the sun had done it that bad turn out of jealousy,

Whatever desire the infanta had to die, she did not succeed; she fell into the glass bottle into which the fays ordinarily put their ratafia out in the sun—but what a bottle! There is no other in the world that is as large. Fortunately, it was empty, for she would otherwise have drowned like a fly.

Six giants were guarding it; they recognized the infanta immediately; they were the same ones that had resided in her court and who loved her. The malign Fanferluche, who left nothing to chance, had transported them there, each on a flying dragon, and the dragons in question guarded the bottle while the giants slept. While she was there, there were many days when she regretted her monkey pelt; she lived like a chameleon on air and dew.

The infanta's prison was unknown to anyone; the young prince did not know it. He was not dead, and asked for Babiole incessantly. He perceived well enough, by the dolor of those who served him, that there was a subject of general dolor in the court; his natural discretion prevented him from trying to penetrate it, but when he was convalescent he became so insistent that he was given the news of the loss of the princess, which no one had had the courage to give him.

Those who had seen her enter the wood sustained that she had been eaten by lions; others believed that she had killed herself in despair, yet others that she had lost her mind and that she was wandering through the world.

As that last opinion was the least terrible, and it sustained the prince's hope somewhat, he settled upon it, and departed on Criquetin, which I have mentioned previously but without saying that he was the eldest son of Bucephalus and one of the best horses that had been seen in that century. He put the bridle on his neck and let him wander at will; he called to the infanta, but the echoes alone replied to him.

Finally, he arrived on the bank of a great river, Criquetin was thirsty; he went into it in order to drink, and the prince, in accordance with his custom, started to shout with all his might: "Babiole, beautiful Babiole, where are you?"

He heard a voice, the softness of which seemed to rejoice the waters; the voice said to him: "Advance, and you shall know where she is."

At those words, the prince, as reckless as he was amorous, gave two thrusts of the spurs to Criquetin; he swam, and found a gulf into which the rapid water precipitated him. He fell to the bottom, convinced that he was going to drown.

Fortunately, he arrived in the abode of the worthy Biroquoi, who was celebrating the marriage of his daughter with one of the richest and most serious rivers in the country; all the fishy deities were in his grotto; tritons and sirens were making an agreeable music there, and the river Biroquie, lightly dressed, was dancing olivettes with the Seine, the Thames, the Euphrates and the Ganges, who had certainly come a long way to amuse themselves together.

Criquetin, who knew how to behave, stopped very respectfully at the entrance to the grotto, and the prince, who knew how to behave even better than his horse, made a profound reverence and asked whether it was permitted for a mortal to appear in the midst of such a fine company.

Biroquoi took it upon himself to speak, and replied in an affable manner that it would be an honor and a pleasure for them. "I've been waiting for you for several days, Sire," he continued. "I am in your interests, and those of the infanta are dear to me. It's necessary that you get her out of the fatal place in which the vindictive Fanferluche has put her in a prison, which is a bottle."

"Oh, what are you telling me?" cried the prince. "The infanta is in a bottle?"

"Yes," said the sage old man. "She is suffering a great deal, but I warn you, sire, that it will not be easy to vanquish the giants and the dragons that are guarding her, unless you follow my advice. It's necessary to leave your beautiful horse here and mount a winged dolphin that I bred for you a long time ago."

He summoned the dolphin, saddle and bridled, which made voltes and curvets so well that Criquetin was jealous.

Biroquoi and his companions immediately hastened to arm the prince. They equipped him with a brilliant armor of golden carp scales and coiffed him with the shell of a huge snail, shaded by the tail of a large cod raised in the form of a plume. A naiad girded him with an eel, from which a redoubt-able sword made of a long fishbone was suspended. Finally, he was given a large turtle-shell, of which he made a shield. In that equipage, he did not know whether small fry might mistake him for the god of Soles, for it is necessary to tell the truth: that young prince had a certain air about him that is rarely encountered among mortals.

The hope of soon recovering the charming princess he loved inspired a joy in him of which he had not been capable since her loss, and the chronicle of this faithful tale relates that he ate with a good appetite in Biroquoi's abode, and that he thanked the entire company in uncommon terms. He bid adieu to his Criquetin, and then mounted the flying fish, which departed immediately.

At the end of the day the prince found himself so high that, in order to rest for a while, they entered the realm of the

Moon. The rarities that he discovered there would have been capable of making him pause if he had had a desire less pressing than that of extracting his infanta from the bottle in which she had been living for several months.

The dawn had scarcely appeared when he found her, surrounded by the giants and dragons that the fay, by the virtue of her little wand, had retained beside her. The fay had so little belief that anyone might have enough power to deliver her that she relied on the vigilance of those terrible guards to make her suffer.

The beautiful princess was gazing pitiably at the sky, and addressing her sad plaints to it, when she saw the flying dolphin and the knight who had come to liberate her. She would not have thought that adventure possible, although she knew from her own experience that he most extraordinary things were rendered familiar for certain persons.

Might it be by the malice of some fay, she wondered, *that that knight is being transported through the air? Alas, how I pity him, if it is necessary for a bottle or a carafe to serve him as a prison like mine.*

While she was reasoning thus, the giants, who perceived the prince above their heads, thought he was a kite and shouted to one another: "Catch it, catch the string; it will amuse us." But when they bent down to pick it up he fell upon them, and with cut and thrust he hacked them into pieces, like a deck of cards sliced through the middle and cast to the wind.

At the noise of that great combat the princess turned her head, and she recognized her young prince. What joy to be certain of his life! But what alarm to see him in such evident peril, in the midst of those terrible colossi and the dragons that were hurling themselves upon him! She uttered frightful screams, and the danger he was in nearly caused her to die.

However, the enchanted fishbone with which Biroquoi had armed the prince's hand did not deal any futile blows, and the nimble dolphin, which rose and dived so appropriately, also gave him marvelous aid, with the result that in very little time, the ground was covered by the monsters.

The impatient prince, who could see his infanta through the glass, would have smashed it to smithereens if he had not feared wounding her with them. He made the decision to descend through the neck of the bottle. When he reached the bottom, he threw himself at Babiole's feet and kissed her hand respectfully.

"Sire," she said to him, "It is only just that in order to protect your self-esteem, I tell you the reasons that I had for interesting myself so tenderly in your conservation. Know that we are close relatives, that I am the daughter of the queen, your aunt, and the same Babiole that you found in the form of a she-monkey on the shore of the sea, and who had the weakness thereafter to testify to you an attachment that you scorned."

"Oh, Madame," cried the prince, "ought I to believe an event so prodigious? You have been a monkey, you have loved me, I have known you, and my heart has been capable of refusing the greatest of all goods!"

"I would have a very poor opinion at present of your taste," replied the infanta, smiling, "if you had been able to conceive some attachment for me then; but Sire, let us depart; I'm weary of being a prisoner and I fear my enemy. Let us go to the abode of the queen, my mother, to render her an account of so many extraordinary things that ought to interest her."

"Let's go, Madame, let's go," said the amorous prince, mounting the winged dolphin and taking her in his arms. "Let's go, and return to her in you the most lovable princess that there is in the world."

The dolphin rose up slowly, and flew away toward the capital where the queen spent her sad life. The flight of Babiole did not leave her a moment's repose; she could not help thinking about her, remembering the pretty things she had said to her, and she would have give half her realm to see her again, monkey as she was.

When the prince arrived, he disguised himself as an old man and asked for a private audience.

"Madame," he said, "I have studied since my earliest youth the art of necromancy; you ought to judge therefore that I am not unaware of the hatred that Fanferluche has for you and the terrible effects that have ensued therefrom; but wipe away your tears, Madame, the Babiole that you saw so ugly is now the most beautiful princess in the world; you will soon have her with you if you are willing to pardon the queen, your sister, for the cruel war she has made on you and conclude the peace by means of the marriage of your infanta with the prince, your nephew."

"I cannot flatter myself with what you are saying to me, sage old man," replied the queen, weeping. "You are trying to soothe my distress, but I have lost my daughter; I no longer have a husband; my sister claims that my realm belongs to her; and her son is as unjust as she is; they are persecuting me, and I can never make an alliance with them."

"Destiny has ordered otherwise," he continued. "I have been chosen to tell you that."

"Oh, what good would it do me to consent to that marriage?" added the queen. "The evil Fanferluche has too much power and malice; she will always oppose it."

"Have no fear, Madame," replied the old man. "Only promise me that you will not oppose the desired marriage."

"I will promise anything," cried the queen, "provided that I see my dear daughter again."

The prince left and ran to the place where the infanta was waiting. She was surprised to see him disguised, and that obliged him to tell her that for some time, the two queens had had great interests to disentangle, and that there was a great deal of bitterness between them, but that, in sum, he had just made his aunt consent to what he wanted.

The princess was delighted; she went to the palace; all those who saw her pass by found such a perfect resemblance between her and her mother that they hastened to follow her, in order to discover who she was.

As soon as the queen perceived her, her heart was so strongly agitated that she needed no further evidence of the verity of the adventure. The princess threw herself at her feet; the queen received her in her arms; and after having remained for a long time without speaking, wiping their tears away by means of a thousand tender kisses, they said to one another everything that can be imagined in such an occasion. Then the queen, casting her eyes upon her nephew, gave him a very favorable welcome, and reiterated to him what she had promised the necromancer.

She would have spoken for longer, but the noise that was being made in the courtyard of the palace obliged her to put her head out of the window. She had the agreeable surprise of seeing her sister arriving, recognizing with her the veritable Biroquoi, and the good Criquetin was also in the company.

Each party uttered loud cries of joy for the other; everyone ran to see one another with inexpressible transports. The celebrated marriage of the prince and the infanta was concluded right away, in spite of the fay Fanferluche, whose knowledge and malice were equally confounded.

One ought to fear the presents of an enemy,
Who appears to your eyes to want to engage you,
And protests to you that they love you,
When in secret they are seeking revenge.
The infanta whose adventure I trace here,
Would, in a lovable form,
Have seen fortunate days go by,
If from the unjust Fanferluche
She had not received poisoned gifts
That changed her into a monkey,
Such a catastrophic change
Could not protect her soul
From the arrows of an amorous flame.
She dared to choose a prince for a lover.
I know many in the present century,
Whom a she-monkey would find ugly
But of whom the great men aspire
To captivate the heart;

DON FERNAND DE TOLEDO

The Count de Fuentes had spent almost all his life in Madrid. His wife was the most tedious and most insupportable person in the world; while her husband was young she persecuted him with a frightful jealousy; when he was old, she persecuted her children.

She had two daughters and a nephew; the elder daughter was called Leonore; she was pale, blonde and piquante; her figure had something easy and noble; all her features were regular and the character of her mind seemed so mild and judicious that she attracted the esteem and amity equally of those who knew her. Doña Matilde was the younger; she had lustrous black hair, a vivid and uniform complexion, bright eyes, admirable teeth, an air of gaiety, and manners so charming that she pleased no less than her sister. Don Francisco, their cousin, attracted the esteem and distinction of all persons of merit so strongly that he was seen with pleasure everywhere.

They had for neighbors two young noblemen who were relatives and friends; one was named Don Jaime de Casarreal and the other Don Fernand de Toledo; they lived together, so close to the house of Count de Fuentes, that they linked a narrow amity with Don Francisco. As they were often in his house, they saw his cousins; to see them and to love them were the same thing.

The sisters would not have been insensible to their merits if the vigilance of their mother had not come to trouble those dispositions, by means of furious threats that if they ever spoke to Don Jaime and Don Fernand she would put them in religion for the rest of their life. She added to those threats two watchers more terrible than Argus, but those further obstacles only served to augment the passion of the cavaliers that the countess wanted to repel.

She discovered that they were making new gallantries to her daughters every day; she flew into a terrible wrath, and, knowing that her nephew, less severe than her, was furnishing his friends with a thousand innocent opportunities to see his cousins, either on their balconies, through shutters or in the garden, where they sometimes went to take the air, she wore herself out scolding incessantly and gaining nothing over the perseverance of the young lovers.

In order to disconcert their measures absolutely, one day when her husband had gone to the Escorial to pay his court, she departed with her daughters in a carriage as closed as a coffin, and even sadder for them than if it had really been one. She went with them to considerable lands that the Count de Fuentes had near Cadiz.

She left a letter for him in which she begged him to come and find her and to bring his nephew, but the Count de Fuentes, who had been weary for a long time of his wife's eccentricities, was in no hurry to go and join her. He thanked Heaven for a separation that he had desired for a long time, and pitied his two daughters for being incessantly exposed to their mother's ill humor.

When Don Jaime and Don Fernand learned from Don Francisco of the departure of their mistresses, they thought they might die of chagrin and racked their brains for all imaginable means of recalling them to Madrid; but Don Francisco said that if they put any of them to usage, it would be a means of preventing them from returning. When they saw that the matter was without remedy in that direction, they resolved to go to Cadiz and to find some favorable moment to talk to them.

They begged Don Francisco to join them so insistently that he could not refuse. Apart from the fact that the Count de Fuentes, who did not want to quit the court, was quite willing for his nephew to go any keep the countess company, she was very glad to see him. Some time passed before she discovered that Don Fernand and Don Jaime had arrived; they saw her daughters in the evening through a barred window that overlooked a small street along with no one passed. In that place they lamented their destiny; they swore an eternal fidelity to one another, and consoled themselves with hopes that flattered their sentiments.

Although they had a thousand things to desire more agreeable than the ones that they enjoyed, they were nevertheless glad to be able to deceive the countess; but the duennas that had been placed with them understood their duty too well to be duped by young lovers. They were surprised at the grille; whatever promises and pleas they could make, it did not prevent the old women from going to tell the countess what they knew.

At that news, the furious mother got up, and although it was not yet daylight, she climbed into a carriage with her daughters, with whom she quarreled a great deal, and went to shut herself away with them in and almost inaccessible mansion a day's ride from Cadiz.

It is easy to imagine the further disorder that such an abrupt departure brought to our lovers; there were sighs and laments on both sides, and when Don Francisco went to Las Peñas—that was the name of the countess's country house— he was charged with letters and a thousand small presents for his cousins. He obliged them to receive them, because he knew his friends' veritable sentiments and was assured that they wanted to marry them.

Scarcely had he returned from Las Peñas than Don Fernand and Don Jaime pestered him to return, and they implored him to find a way of taking them with him, in order that they could see their de mistresses again; but the matter was so delicate that Don Francisco hesitated to attempt it, and contented himself with procuring them the means to write.

After he had spent a few days with his aunt and his cousins, as he was on the point of quitting them, the countess told Don Francisco that she knew that an ambassador from the

King of Morocco had recently arrived in Cadiz, and that if anything pressed her to return there, it was the desire to see him before he left. He thought immediately that that opportunity, well managed, might become useful to his friends to procure them the pleasure of speaking to his cousins. With that in mind, he replied to the countess that he was already acquainted with the ambassador's two sons, that they had intelligence and politesse, and that if she wanted to promise him to receive them with all the ceremonies that persons of their nation required, it would be easy to bring them to her house, because they gave particular consideration to women of quality, and he had no sooner mentioned hers than they were burning with impatience to pay their court to her.

That was one of the great weaknesses of that good lady; her cabinet was full of her old titles and her arms had even been put on her parrot's cage. Don Francisco, who knew her perfectly on that article, immediately added: "You'll admit, Madame, that if the children of the Moroccan ambassador have come so far in search of you, the nobility of your birth must be known even in their country, and consequently, this visit might be joined to the ornaments that you put in your genealogical tree."

The countess, who did not lack curiosity or vanity, thought that, in fact, it might cause considerable rumor in her province, with the consequence that she seemed delighted by her nephew's proposition. "You think of everything," she said, "and I give you a veritable credit for that attention. Don't neglect anything, then, to procure me the pleasure of receiving in my house those excellent Mohammedans."

Don Jaime and his cousin came to meet Don Francisco in order to advance by a few moments the satisfaction they promised themselves of learning news of their mistresses. After having read their letters and thanked him for the good offices he was rendering them in that regard, Don Francisco told them that his aunt had an extreme passion to see the children of the Moroccan ambassador; that the good part of the idea was that his cousins knew nothing about the deception that he had premeditated for them, and that they would be able to surprise them in a manner that always pleases. Then he told them what had passed between the countess and himself.

"I advise you to disguise yourselves and to study the new characters that it is necessary to put on stage; for my part, I promise to play mine well."

The two lovers were charmed by Don Francisco's imagination; they could not praise his intelligence and skill sufficiently. They did not waste a moment in dressing themselves up; they ordered rich coats of gold cloth garnished with gemstones; scimitars whose hand-guards were garnished with diamonds; turbans, and all the equipage necessary for a masquerade of that sort. Fortunately, they found a painter who made them an oil composed to render their complexion as dark as it was necessary to be.

When everything was ready for that little voyage Don Francisco sent one of his servants to the countess to notify her of the day when he would bring the ambassador's sons. She became very active, and took extreme care to receive the illustrious Moors well. She ordered her daughters not to neglect anything to appear amiable in their eyes, and her severity, which extended over all the nations of the world, abandoned her with regard to that of Morocco, because, being very devout, she regarded them as barbarians and enemies of the faith. On that basis, it was, in her thinking, quite impossible for a Spanish woman ever to love a man who was not baptized; and by the effect of that prejudice, she judged that there was no risk in letting her daughters see the gallant Africans.

As they were to arrive in the evening, the entire mansion was illuminated by an infinite number of candles. She received them on the staircase, and they made her such extraordinary reverences in saluting her, raising and lowering their hands so many times and making such sudden and frequent exclamations of *hi, ha* and *ho* that Don Francisco, who was constraining himself not to laugh, was on the point of choking.

For her part, the countess made them a thousand compliments, but she could not prevent herself making a little sign of the cross every time they said "Allah." It was not without an extreme gratitude that she received from their hands pieces of brocade fabrics, fans, Chinese boxes, stones engraved with a marvelous workmanship and other considerable rarities, which they had bought for her and her daughters. They told them that they were common items in their country, and were careful to speak Spanish badly enough that they could hardly be understood.

The good countess was transported by all those honors, but while they were talking to her with all the distractions that amour causes when one sees that one is loved, and whatever violence they exerted upon themselves not to look at their mistresses they always attached their eyes to them, Doña Leonore felt a secret anxiety that nevertheless flattered her heart; she could not discern the cause of it, and although she knew Don Fernand's eyes and remarked some of the features of Don Jaime in the face of one of the Moors, what means was there of discovering them under complexions so dark and such extraordinary garments?

The countess led them to a large gallery ornamented by paintings; she directed their attention to one that she had bought recently, of Amours playing games, the smallest of which was covering his face with a mask in order to frighten the others. Don Fernand praised the imagination of the painter and the excellence of his work, in terms that showed well enough his intelligence and the justice of his taste; he stopped there, without letting any affectation appear. While the countess was talking to her nephew, the amorous Moor took a pencil and wrote at the feet of the little masked amour: *I am hiding from everyone, in order to see your beautiful eyes.*

Scarcely had Lenore looked at those characters than she sensed a great disturbance mingled with joy. Don Fernand knew that she had penetrated the mystery and that she was not sorry to see him; he seemed even more cheerful and witty. In conversation he said a thousand pretty things in which Leonore had reason to be interested, but whatever pleasure she had in hearing them, she could not help separating herself from the company and taking her sister aside.

"Oh, my dear Matilde," she said to her, "are you not afraid, like me, that Don Fernand and Don Jaime will be recognized?"

"I don't understand you," replied Matilde. "What are you talking about?"

"Alas, poor girl," Leonore continued, smiling, "how poorly your heart serves you. What! You haven't yet noticed that that Moor who doesn't quit you is Don Jaime, and that the other, who has talked to me, is Don Fernand?"

"Is that possible?" exclaimed Matilde. "Are you telling me the truth, my sister? But the attention he has in looking at me," she continued, "and my presentiments, don't allow me to doubt it."

As they approached them again they heard the countess propose that they go into the garden, where she had arranged an illumination that was perceptible in the depths of a rather distant wood, which produced a charming effect.

The entire company went along a long pathway, which was enclosed by a double row of channels; jasmines interlaced with orange trees and honeysuckle formed a large enclosure at the end, open in several places. A fountain rose up in the middle, and fell back on itself with a soft murmur; it animated the nightingales to make more noise than it did. Everyone exclaimed that the enclosure was the true abode of the pleasures; they placed themselves on grass seats; iced drinks were served, chocolate and jam, while awaiting supper time.

As the countess was seeking to divert the Moors, and romances were very much in fashion, she asked Doña Leonore to recite one that she had learned not long ago. The beautiful young woman dared not demur; her mother had raised her on the basis of not eluding the least of her orders; she commenced immediately in these terms.

THE YELLOW DWARF

There was once a queen, to whom there remained, of the several children she had had, only one daughter, who was worth more than a thousand; but, her mother being a widow and having nothing in the world as dear as that young princess, she had such a terrible apprehension of losing her that she did not correct any of her faults. The result was that the marvelous person in question, whose beauty seemed more celestial than mortal, and destined to wear a crown, became so proud and so carried away by her nascent charms, that she was scornful of everyone.

The queen, her mother, aided her by means of her caresses and her complaisance, to persuade herself that there was nothing that was worthy of her. She was almost always seen dressed as Pallas Athena or Diana, followed by the first ladies of the court, dressed as nymphs. Finally, to add the final touch to her vanity, the queen named her Toute-Belle, and, having had her painted by the most skillful painters, she sent her portrait to several kings with whom she maintained a narrow amity. When they saw that portrait there was none who could defend himself from the inevitable power of her charms; some fell ill, others lost their minds, and the most fortunate arrived in good health in her proximity—but as soon as they saw her, those poor princes became her slaves.

There has never been a court more gallant and more polite. Twenty kings tried, in competition, to please her; and after having spent three or four hundred millions merely in giving her a fête, if they had extracted a "That's pretty" from her, they thought themselves well recompensed.

The adoration that they had for her delighted the queen; there was no daybreak when seven or eight thousand sonnets did not arrive at her court, as many elegies, madrigals and songs, sent by all the poets in the universe. Toute-Belle was the unique object of the prose and the poetry of the authors of her time; fires of joy were never made except with those verses, which sparkled and burned better than any kind of wood.

The princess was already fifteen years old; no one dared aspire to the honor of being her husband, although there was no one who did not desire that status. But how could a heart of that character be touched? One could have oneself hanged five or six times a day to please her, and she would have treated it as a bagatelle. Her lovers murmured against her cruelty; and the queen, who wanted her to marry, did not know what to do to resolve her to it.

"Wouldn't you like," she said to her sometimes, "to reduce a little the insupportable pride that makes you regard with scorn all the kings who come to your court? I want to give you to one of them; don't you have any complaisance for me?"

"I'm so happy," Toute-Belle replied. "Permit, Madame, that I remain in tranquil indifference; if I had ever lost it, you might have been sorry."

"Yes," replied the queen, "I would have been sorry if you loved someone beneath you, but look at those who are asking for you, and know that there is no one elsewhere who is worth as much as them."

That was true, but the princess, prejudiced with regard to her merit, believed that she was worth even more, and gradually, by virtue of her stubbornness in remaining unwed, she began to cause her mother so much chagrin that the queen repented, but too late, of having had so much complaisance for her.

Uncertain as to what she ought to do, she went on her own to seek a celebrated fay, who was known as the Fay of the Desert; but it was not easy to see her, because she was guarded by lions. The queen would have been prevented from doing so if she had not known for a long time that it was necessary to throw them a cake made from millet flour, candied sugar and crocodile eggs. She kneaded the cake herself and put it in a small basket under her arm.

As she was wearied by having walked for such a long time, not being accustomed to it, she lay down at the foot of a tree in order to take a little rest. Gradually, she became drowsy, and when she woke up, she only found her basket; the cake was no longer there. To complete her misfortune she heard the lions coming, which were making a great deal of noise, for they had scented her.

"Alas, what will become of me?" she cried, dolorously. "I shall be devoured."

She wept, and, not having the strength to take a step to run away, she stood against the tree where she had fallen asleep. At the same time, she heard: *chet, chet, hem, hem*. She looked in all directions, and on raising her eyes she perceived in the tree a little man who was only a cubit tall.

He was eating oranges, and he said to her: "Oh, Queen, I know you well, and I know the fear you have that the lions will devour you; it's not without reason that you're afraid, for they've devoured many others; and to complete the disgrace, you have no cake."

"It's necessary to resolve myself to death," said the queen, with a sigh. "Alas, I'd have less pain if my dear daughter were married."

"What! You have a daughter?" cried the Yellow Dwarf—he was so-called because of the color of his complexion and the orange tree in which he lived. "Truly, I rejoice, for I've been searching for a wife on land and sea; if you want to promise her to me, I'll protect you from lions, tigers and bears."

The queen looked at him, and was scarcely less frightened by his horrible little face than she already was by the lions. She was pensive, and made no reply.

"What! You're hesitating, Madame?" he cried. "It's necessary that you don't love life."

At the same time, the queen perceived the lions at the top of a hill; they were running toward her. Each of them had two heads, eight feet and four rows of teeth, and their skin was as hard as tortoiseshell and as red as morocco leather. At that sight, the poor queen, more tremulous than a dove when it perceives a hawk, cried with all her might: "Milord Dwarf, Toute-Belle is yours."

"Oh," he said, disdainfully, "Toute-Belle is too beautiful, I don't want her. Keep her."

"Oh, milord," continued the afflicted queen, "don't refuse her; she's the most charming princess in the world."

"Well," he replied, "I'll accept her out of charity, but remember the gift that you've made me of her."

Immediately, the orange tree in which he was perched opened up, and the queen threw herself into it recklessly. It closed again, and the lions did not catch anything.

The queen was so troubled that she could not see a door fitted into the tree. Finally, she perceived it, and opened it. It opened into a field of nettles and thistles, surrounded by a muddy ditch; a little further away there was a small house, very low, with a thatched roof. The Yellow Dwarf came out of it with a cheerful expression. He was wearing sabots and a jacket of coarse yellow cloth; he had no hair, huge ears, and every appearance of a little scoundrel.

"I'm delighted, Madame my mother-in-law," he said to the queen, "that you can see the little country house where your Toute-Belle will live with me. She can nourish a donkey on nettles and thistles, which will carry her on excursions; she can shelter under the rustic roof from the insults of the seasons; she can drink this water and eat a few frogs that grow fat therein. Finally, she will have me beside her night and day, handsome, healthy and vigorous, as you see me; for I'll be very sorry if her shadow keeps her closer company than me."

The unfortunate queen, suddenly considering the deplorable life that the dwarf was promising her dear daughter, and unable to sustain an idea so terrible, fell to the ground unconscious, without having had the strength to utter a single word in response.

While she was in that state she was transported to her bed, very properly, with the most beautiful nightcap and a fontange of the finest quality that she had ever put on.

The queen woke up, and remembered what had happened to her; she did not believe any of it, for, finding herself in her palace in the middle of her ladies, with her daughter beside her, there was scarcely any appearance that she had been in the desert, that she had run such great perils and that the dwarf had got her out of it on conditions so harsh as to give him Toute-Belle. However, the nightcap of rare lace and the ribbon astonished her as much as the dream she thought she had had, and in the excess of her anxiety she fell into a melancholy so extraordinary that she could hardly speak, eat or sleep.

The princess, who loved her with all her heart, was very anxious; she begged her several times to tell her what was wrong, but the queen, seeking pretexts, sometimes replied that it was an effect of her poor health, and sometimes that one of her neighbors was threatening her with a great war.

Toute-Belle could see clearly that her responses were plausible, but that fundamentally, there was something else, which the queen was determined to hide from her. No longer being the mistress of her anxiety, she made the resolution to go and find the famous Fay of the Desert, whose knowledge created abundant rumor everywhere. She also desired to ask her advice as to whether to remain a maiden or to marry, for everyone was pressing her so strongly to choose a husband.

She took care to knead herself the cake that was to appease the fury of the lions, and, making a semblance of going to bed early, she went out via a little hidden stairway, her face covered by a large white veil that fell all the way to her feet. Thus clad, she walked on her own toward the grotto where the clever fay lived.

On arriving at the fatal orange tree that we have already mentioned, however, she saw it so covered with fruits that the desire took her to pick some. She put her basket down on the ground and took some oranges, which she ate. When it was a question of finding her basket and her cake again, however, there was no longer anything there. She became anxious, and afflicted, and suddenly saw beside her the frightful little dwarf that I have already described.

"What's the matter, beautiful girl?" he said. "What have you to bemoan?"

"Alas, who wouldn't weep?" she said. "I've lost my basket and my cake, which were so necessary to me in order to reach the Fay of the Desert safely."

"Well, what did you want with her, beautiful girl?" said the little ape. "I'm her relative and her friend, and at least as skillful as her."

"The queen, my mother, has fallen into a frightful sadness recently, which makes me fear for her life, and I have it in mind that I might be the cause of it, because she wants me to marry. I confess to you that I haven't found anyone worthy of me; all those reasons engaged me to want to speak to the fay."

"Don't go to the trouble, princess," the dwarf said to her. "I'm better able than she is to enlighten you on those matters. The queen, your mother, is chagrined because she has promised you in marriage..."

"The queen has promised me!" she said, interrupting. "Oh, doubtless you're mistaken. She would have told me, and I have too much interest in it for her to engage me without my consent."

"Beautiful princess," said the dwarf, suddenly throwing himself to his knees, "I flatter myself that the choice won't displease you, when I've told you that it's me who is destined for that good fortune."

"My mother wants you for a son-in-law!" cried Toute-Belle, recoiling a few steps. "Is there any folly similar to yours?"

"I care little," said the dwarf, "for that honor. Here come the lions; in three snaps of the teeth they'll have avenged me for your unjust scorn."

At the same time, the princess heard them coming, with long howls.

"What will become of me?" she cried "What! Shall I finish my beautiful days thus?"

The malevolent dwarf looked at her and laughed disdainfully. "You'll at least have the glory," he said to her, "of not misallying your splendid merit with a miserable dwarf like me."

"Please don't be annoyed," said the princess, putting her beautiful hands together. "I'd rather marry all the dwarfs in the world than perish in such a frightful manner."

"Look at me carefully, princess, before giving me your word," he replied, "for I don't intend to surprise you."

"I've looked at you," she told him. "The lions are getting closer; my fear is increasing; save me, save me, or the fear will kill me."

In fact, she had scarcely finished speaking than she fell unconscious—and without knowing how, she found herself in her bed, with the most beautiful linen in the world, the most beautiful ribbons and a little ring made of a single red hair, which was so tight that it seemed to her that it was attached to her skin, and that she would not be able to remove it from her finger."

When the princess saw all those things, and she remembered what had happened during the night, she fell into a melancholy that surprised and worried the entire court. The queen was more alarmed than anyone; she asked her hundreds of times what was wrong, but she was obstinate in concealing her adventure.

Finally, the estates of the realm, impatient to see their princess married, assembled and then came to find the queen to beg her to choose a husband as soon as possible. She replied that she would like nothing better, but that her daughter testified so much reluctance to do so that she advised them to go and find her and harangue her. They did so right away.

Toute-Belle had reduced her pride a good deal since her adventure with the Yellow Dwarf; she could not see any better way of getting out of the affair than to marry some great king, against whom the little ape would not be in a state to dispute such a glorious conquest. She therefore responded more favorably than had been hoped, that although she would have esteemed herself fortunate to remain unmarried all her life, she consented to marry the King of the Gold Mines. He was a very powerful and very well made prince who had loved her with the utmost passion for several years, and who had not had any reason until then to flatter himself with any return.

It is easy to judge the excess of his joy when the charming news was known, and the fury of all his rivals, at losing forever a hope that nourished their passion; but Toute-Belle could not marry twenty men; she had even had difficulty choosing ne, for her vanity was undiminished and she was firmly convinced that no one in the world could be comparable to her.

Everything necessary for the greatest fête in the world was prepared; the King of the Gold Mines sent for such prodigious sums that the sea was entirely covered with the ships that were bringing them. People were sent to the most polite and elegant courts in the world, particularly that of France, to obtain everything there was of the rarest, in order to adorn the princess. She had less need than anyone else of accoutrements to heighten beauty; hers was so perfect that nothing could be added to it, and the King of the Gold Mines, seeing himself on the point of being happy, no longer quit the charming princess.

The interest that she had in knowing him obliged her to study him with care; she discovered in him so much merit, so much intelligence, sentiments so keen and delicate—in sum, such a beautiful soul in such a perfect body—that she commenced to feel for him a part of what he felt for her. What happy moments there were for both of them when they found themselves at liberty, in the most beautiful gardens in the world, to discover all their tenderness. Those pleasures were often seconded by those of music. The king, always gallant and amorous, made verses and songs for the princess; this is one that she found very agreeable:

These woods, on seeing you, are ornamented with foliage,
> *And these meadows make their charming colors shine,*
> *The zephyr makes flowers boom beneath your feet;*

The amorous birds redouble their singing;
In this charming abode;
Everything laughs, recognizing the daughter of Amour.

Everyone was at the pinnacle of joy. The king's rivals, in despair at his good fortune, had quit the court and returned to their realms, overwhelmed by the sharpest dolor, unable to witness Toute-Belle's marriage. They bid her adieu in such a touching manner that she could not help feeling sorry for them.

"Oh, Madame," the King of the Gold Mines said to her, "What larceny are you committing against me today? You accord your pity to lovers who have been paid too well for their troubles by a single one of your glances."

"I would be sorry," said Toute-Belle, "if you were insensible to the compassion that I testified to the princes who are losing me forever; it's a proof of your delicacy, which I hold to your credit; but sire, their state is so different from yours; you ought to be content with me; they have so little reason to laud themselves that you ought not to push your jealousy any further."

The King of the Gold Mines, confused by the obliging manner in which the princess took something that might have caused her chagrin, threw himself at her feet and kissed her hands; he asked her for pardon a thousand times.

Finally, the day so much anticipated and so much desired arrived; everything being ready for Toute-Belle's wedding, the instruments and trumpets announced the great celebration to the entire city. The streets were carpeted, they were strewn with flowers; people flocked in crowds to the main square of the palace.

The delighted queen had scarcely gone to bed; she got up before the dawn to give the necessary orders and to chose the precious stones with which the princess would be adorned; there was nothing but diamonds all the way to her shoes, which were made of them; her silver brocade robe was decorated with a dozen sunbursts that had been bought very dear, but nothing was more brilliant, and there was only the beauty of the princess that could be more splendid. A rich crown ornamented her head; her hair hung down to her feet, and the majesty of her stature distinguished her from all the ladies accompanying her.

The King of the Gold Mines was no less accomplished and no less magnificent; his joy appeared in his face and all his actions; no one approached him who did not return charged with his liberalities, for he had arranged in the tower of the festival all a thousand barrels full of gold, and great sacks of pearl-embroidered velvet full of pistoles, each of which could hold a hundred thousand. They were given out indifferently to those who held out their hands, with the result that the little ceremony in question, which was one of the least useful and least agreeable of the wedding, attracted many people who were insensible to all the other pleasures.

The queen and the princess were advancing in order to go out with the king when they saw two large guinea fowl entered a long gallery drawing a very poorly-made box; behind it came an exceedingly old lady, whose advanced age and decrepitude were no less surprising than her extreme ugliness. She was leaning on a crutch; she had a black taffeta ruff, a red velvet hood and a tattered farthingale. She made three circuits with the guinea fowl without saying a word, then stopped in the middle of the gallery and brandished her crutch in a menacing manner.

"Ho ho, Queen! Ho ho, Princess!" she cried. "You expect, then, to break with impunity the word that you've given to my friend the Yellow Dwarf! I am the Fay of the Desert. Without him, without his orange tree, don't you know that my great lions would have devoured you? Such insults are not suffered in the realm of Faerie. Think promptly of what you ought to do, for I swear by my escutcheon that you'll marry him, or I'll burn my crutch."

"Oh, Princess," said the queen, weeping, "What am I learning? What have you promised?

"Oh, my mother," replied Toute-Belle dolorously, "what have you promised yourself?"

The King of the Gold Mines, indignant at what was happening, and that the malevolent old woman was opposing his felicity, approached her, sword in hand, pointing it at her breast.

"Wretch," he said to her, "leave this place forever, or the loss of your life will avenge me for your malice."

He had scarcely pronounced those words than the top of the box leapt up as far as the ceiling with a frightful noise, and the Yellow Dwarf was seen to emerge, mounted on a huge Spanish cat. He came to place himself between the Fay of the Desert and the King of the Gold Mines.

"Young hothead," he said, "do not think of outraging this illustrious fay; it is with me alone that you have to deal. I am your rival; I am your enemy. The infidel princess who wants to give herself to you has given me her word, and received mine. See whether she does not have a ring of one of my hairs. Try to take it off and you will see by that little trial that your power is less than mine."

"Miserable monster," the king said to him, "Do you really have the temerity to call yourself the adorer of this divine princess and to pretend to such a glorious possession? Think that you are an ape, whose hideous face makes the eyes hurt, and that I would already have taken your life if you were worthy of such a glorious death."

The Yellow Dwarf, offended in the depths of his soul, applied the spur to the belly of his cat, which commenced mewling frightfully and, leaping here and there, it frightened everyone except for the brave king, who was pressing the dwarf closely when he drew a large cutlass with which he was armed, and, challenging the king to combat, he descended to the palace square with a strange noise.

The angry king followed him with long strides. Scarcely were they face to face, and the entire court was on balconies, when the sun suddenly turned as red as if it had been bloodied; it darkened to such a point that people could scarcely see.

Thunder and lightning seemed to want to destroy the world, and the two guinea fowl appeared at the sides of the malevolent dwarf, like two giants taller than mountains, which projected fire from their mouths and eyes, with such abundance that one might have thought it as an ardent furnace.

All those things would not have been capable of frightening the magnanimous heart of the young monarch; he displaced an intrepidity in his gaze and in his actions that reassured all those who were interested in his conservation, and which might perhaps have embarrassed the Yellow Dwarf; but his courage was not proof against the state in which he saw his dear princess when he saw the Fay of the Desert, coiffed like Tisiphone, her head covered with long serpents, mounted on a winged griffin, armed with a lance with which she struck her so rudely that she made her fall into the arms of the queen, bathed in her own blood.

That tender mother, more wounded by the thrust than her daughter had been, uttered screams and made laments that are indescribable. The king lost his courage and his reason then; he abandoned the combat and ran to the princess to help her; but the Yellow Dwarf did not give him time to reach her. He launched himself with his Spanish cat on to the balcony where she was; he snatched her from the queen's hands and those of all her ladies. Then, leaping from the roof of the palace, he disappeared with his prey.

The king, confused and motionless, was gazing with the utmost despair at an adventure so extraordinary and to which he had been unfortunate enough not to be able to bring any remedy, when to complete his disgrace, he sensed his eyes clouding over. They lost the light and someone of extraordinary strength carried him away into the vast spaces of the air.

What disgrace! Amour, cruel Amour, is it thus that you treat those who recognize you as their conqueror?

The evil Fay of the Desert, who had come with the Yellow Dwarf to second him in his abduction of the princess, had scarcely seen the King of the Gold Mines when, her barbaric heart becoming sensitive to the merit of the young prince, she had wanted to make him her prey. She transported him to the depths of a frightful cavern, where she charged him with chains, which she attached to a rock. She hoped that the fear of an imminent death would make him forget Toute-Belle and engage him to do what she wanted.

As soon as she had arrived she returned his sight, without setting him free, and, borrowing from the art of faerie the graces and charms that nature had refused her, she appeared before him as a lovely nymph that hazard had brought into that place.

"What do I see?" she cried. "What, it's you, charming prince! What misfortune overwhelms you and retains you in such a sad abode?"

The king, taken in by such deceptive appearances, replied: "Alas, beautiful nymph, I don't know what the infernal fury who brought me here wants of me. Although she took away the usage of my eyes when she abducted me, and has not appeared since, I nevertheless recognized by the sound of her voice that it was the Fay of the Desert."

"Oh, Sire," cried the false nymph, "if you are in the hands of that woman, you will only get out of them after having married her. She has played this trick on more than one hero, and she is the least tractable person in the world in her obstinacy."

While she was pretending to share abundantly in the king's affliction he perceived the feet of the nymph, which were like those of a griffin; it was by that feature that the fay could always be recognized in her different metamorphoses, for with regard to that griffinage, she did not have the power to change.

The king did not let anything show, and, speaking to her in a confidential tone, he said: "I don't feel any aversion for the Fay of the Desert, but it is insupportable to me that she protects the Yellow Dwarf against me and that she keeps me in chains like a criminal. What have I done to her? I loved a charming princess; but if she set me free, I sense that gratitude would engage me only to love her."

"Are you speaking sincerely?" asked the deceived nymph.

"Don't doubt it," said the king. "I do not have the art of pretence, and I confess that a fay might flatter my vanity more than a simple princess. But even if I have to die of amour for her, I will always testify hatred to her until I am the master of my liberty."

Deceived by those words, the Fay of the Desert made the resolution to transport the king into a place as agreeable as that solitude was frightful, with the result that, obliging him to mount her chariot, to which she had attached swans instead of the bats that normally conducted it, she flew from one pole to the other.

But what became of the king when, while traversing the vast space of the atmosphere thus, he perceived his dear princess in a castle made entirely of steel, the walls of which, struck by the sun's rays, made ardent mirrors that burned all those who attempted to approach it? She was in a boscage, lying on the edge of a stream, with one of her hands under her head, while she seemed to be wiping away tears with the other. As she raised her eyes toward the heavens to ask for some aid she saw the king pass over with the Fay of the Desert, who, having employed the art of faerie, in which she was expert, to appear beautiful in the eyes of the young monarch, also appeared to those of the princess to be the most marvelous young woman in the world.

"What!" she cried. "Am I not unhappy enough, then, in this inaccessible castle to which the Yellow Dwarf has transported me? Is it necessary that, to complete my disgrace, the demon of jealousy should come to persecute me? Is it necessary that I learn, by such an extraordinary adventure, of the infidelity of the King of the Gold Mines? He has believed, in losing sight of me, that he is liberated from all the oaths he made to me. But who is that redoubtable rival, whose fatal beauty surpasses mine?"

While she was speaking thus, the amorous king felt a mortal pain in drawing away with so much velocity from the dear object of his wishes. If he had not known the power of the fay so well he would have attempted everything to get away from her, either by killing himself or by some other means that he amour and his courage would have furnished him, but what could he do against such a powerful person? Only time and cleverness could extract him from her hands.

The fay had perceived Toute-Belle, and sought in the king's eyes to penetrate the effect that the sight produced on his heart. "No one can tell you better than me," he said, "what you want to know. The unexpected encounter with an unfortunate princess for whom I had a attachment before acquiring one for you, moved me somewhat; but you are so far above her in my mind that I would rather die than commit an infidelity to you."

"Oh, Prince," she said, "can I flatter myself that I have inspired you with sentiments so advantageous in my favor?"

"Time will convince you of it, Madame," he told her, "but if you want to convince me that I have some part in your good graces, don't refuse your help to Toute-Belle."

"Do you know what you are asking of me?" said the fay, looking at him askance. "You want me to employ my science against the Yellow Dwarf, who is my best friend, in order that I extract from his hands a proud princess whom I can only regard as my rival."

The king sighed, without responding. What could he have responded to that penetrating individual?

They arrived in a vast meadowland dotted with a thousand different flowers. A profound river surrounded it, and several streams ran gently beneath leafy trees, where one found an eternal freshness. In the distance, a superb palace could be seen rising up, the walls of which were transparent emeralds.

As soon as the swans conducting the fay's chariot had landed under a portico, the pavement of which was diamond and the vaults ruby, a thousand beautiful women appeared on all sides, who came to welcome her with great acclamations of joy. They sang these words:

> *When Amour wants to win the victory over a heart*
> *Efforts to resist him are superfluous;*
> *One only augments his glory;*
> *The most powerful conquerors are the first defeated.*

The Fay of the Desert was delighted to hear her amours sung. She took the king to the most superb apartment that was ever seen in fay memory, and left him there for a few moments, in order for him to think that he was not absolutely captive. He had no doubt that she was not far away, and that in some hidden place she was observing what he was doing. That obliged him to approach a large mirror and address it: "Faithful adviser, permit me to see what I can do to render myself agreeable to the charming Fay of the Desert, for the desire that I have to please her occupies me incessantly."

Immediately, he combed his hair, powdered his face, put on a beauty spot, and, seeing on a table a costume more magnificent than his own, he put it on diligently.

The fay came in, transported by a joy that she was unable to moderate. "I give you credit," she told him, "for the care you are taking to please me; you found the secret even without seeking it; judge then, sire, whether it will be difficult for you when you want to do it."

The king, who had his reasons for saying sweet things to the aged fay, did not spare them, and gradually obtained the liberty to go for walks along the sea shore. By means of her art she had rendered it s terrible and stormy that there was no pilot bold enough to navigate in the vicinity, so she had nothing to fear from the complaisance that she had for her prisoner; she felt some relief from his troubles in being able to dream alone, without being interrupted by his malevolent jailer.

After having walked across the sand for some length of time, he bent down and inscribed these verses with a cane that he was holding in his hand:

*Finally I am at liberty
To soothe my dolors with a flood of tears;
Alas, I no longer see the charms
Of the adorable object that enchanted me.
You who render this shore inaccessible to mortals,
Stormy sea, terrible sea,
Who drive the furious winds,
Sometimes as far as Hell and sometimes as far as Heaven,*

*My heart is even less peaceful
Than you appear to my eyes.
Toute-Belle! Oh, barbaric destiny
I have lost the object of my amour;
Oh Heaven, whose sentence separates us,
Why defer taking my life?
Divinity of the waves,
You have felt the power of amour;
Emerge from your profound grottoes,
Help a lover reduced to despair.*

As he was writing, he heard a voice that attracted all his attention involuntarily, and, seeing the waves swelling, he was looking in all directions when he perceived a woman of extraordinary beauty. Her body was only covered by her long hair, which, gently agitated by zephyrs, was floating on the surface. She was holding a mirror in one hand, and a comb in the other; a long fish-tail with fins terminated her body.

The king was very surprised by such an extraordinary encounter; as soon as she was close enough to be able to speak she said to him: "I know the sad state to which you are reduced by separation from your princess and the bizarre passion that the Fay of the Desert has conceived for you. If you wish, I can take you away from this fatal place where you might perhaps languish for more than thirty years."

The king did not know how to respond to that proposition. It was not for lack of desire to escape from captivity, but he feared that the Fay of the Desert might have borrowed that form in order to deceive him.

As he was hesitating the siren, who divined his thoughts, said: "Don't believe that it's a trap that I'm extending for you. I have too much good faith to want to serve your enemies. The procedure of the Fay of the Desert, and that of the Yellow Dwarf, have embittered me against them. I see your unfortunate princess every day; her beauty and her merit cause me an equal pity, and I repeat to you that if you have confidence in me, I can save you."

"I have such a perfect confidence," cried the king, "that I will do everything you order me to do; but since you have seen my princess, give me news of her."

"We would lose too much time talking," she told him. "Come with me; I will take you to the Steel Castle and leave on this shore a form that resembles you so closely that the fay will be duped by it."

Immediately, she cut marine rushes; he made a large bundle of them and, blowing on them three times, she said to them: "Marine rushes, my friends, I order you to remain lying on the sand without departing until the Fay of the Desert comes to take you away."

The rushes appeared covered in skin, so similar to the King of the Gold Mines that he had never seen anything so surprising; they were dressed in a costume like his; they were pale and distressed, as if he had drowned. At the same time, the good siren had the king sit down on her large fish-tail, and both of them headed out to sea with a equal satisfaction.

"I can tell you now," she said to him, "that when the evil Yellow Dwarf had abducted Toute-Belle, he put her behind him in his terrible Spanish cat, in spite of the wound that the Fay of the Desert had inflicted. She had lost a lot of blood, and was so troubled by that adventure that her strength abandoned her; she remained unconscious throughout the journey, but the Yellow Dwarf did not want to stop to help her until he was secure in his terrible Steel Palace. He was received there by the most beautiful women in the world, whom he had transported there. All of them competed to show him their urgency to aid the princess. She was put into a bed with golden sheets, decorated with pearls larger than walnuts."

"Oh!" cried the King of the Gold Mines, interrupting the siren. "He has married her; I'm swooning; I'm dying."

"No, Sire," she said to him. "Don't worry; Toute-Belle's firmness has preserved her from the violence of the frightful dwarf."

"Finish, then," said the king.

"What more have I to tell you?" the siren continued. "She was in the wood when you passed over; she saw you with the Fay of the Desert, who was disguised so that she seemed to possess a beauty superior to her own. Her despair could not understand; she thought that you loved the fay."

"She thought that I loved her!" cried the king. "Just gods, into what fatal error has she fallen, and what must I do to correct her error?"

"Consult your heart," replied the siren, with a gracious smile. "When one is strongly engaged, one has no need of advice."

As she finished speaking they arrived at the Steel Castle; the side facing the sea was the only place that the Yellow Dwarf had not dressed with the formidable walls that burned everything.

"I know full well," the siren said to the king, "that Toute-Belle is on the bank of the same stream where you saw her as you passed over, but as you will have enemies to battle before arriving there, here is a sword with which you can attempt anything and confront the greatest perils, provided that you do not drop it. Adieu; I shall retire beneath the rock you can see; if you need me in order to conduct you further with your dear princess, I shall not fail, for her mother, the queen, is my best friend, and it is in order to serve her that I came to find you."

As she finished speaking she gave the king a sword made of a single diamond; the sun's rays were not as bright; he understood all its utility, and could not find terms strong enough to express his gratitude. He begged her to be kind enough to substitute for them by imagining what a well made heart is capable of feeling for such great obligations.

It is necessary to say something about the Fay of the Desert. As she did not see her amiable lover return, she hastened to go in search of him. She was on the shore with a hundred young women of her retinue, all laden with magnificent presents for the king. Some were carrying large baskets full of diamonds, others golden vases of marvelous workmanship, several of ambergris, coral and pearls; others had bales of cloth on their heads of an inconceivable richness, a few others fruits, flowers, and even birds.

But what became of the fay who was marching after that gallant and numerous troop, when she perceived the marine rushes so similar in form to the King of the Gold Mines that no difference was recognizable? At that sight, struck by astonishment and the sharpest dolor, she uttered a scream so terrible that it penetrated the heavens, made mountains tremble, and echoed all the way to Hell. Furious Megaera, Alecto and Tisiphone would not have taken on faces more redoubtable than the one she displayed.

She threw herself on the king's body, she wept, she howled, she tore apart fifty of the most beautiful young women who had accompanied her, immolating them to the manes of the dear departed. Finally, she summoned eleven of her sisters, who were fays like her, begging her to aid her to make a superb mausoleum for the young hero. There was not one of them who was not duped by the marine rushes. That is rather surprising, for fays know everything, but the clever siren knew even more than them.

While they were furnishing the porphyry, the jasper, the agate and the marble, the statues, the devices, the gold and the bronze to immortalize the memory of the king they believed to be dead, he was thanking the amiable siren, imploring her to accord him her protection; she promised that with the best grace in the world, and disappeared from his sight. He had nothing more to do than advance toward the Steel Castle.

Thus guided by his amour, he marched with long strides, looking with curious eyes to see whether he could perceive his adorable princess, but he was not without occupation for long. Four terrible sphinxes surrounded him, and, throwing themselves upon him, their terrible claws would have torn him to pieces if the diamond sword had not commenced to be as useful to him as the fay had predicted. He had scarcely made it shine in the eyes of the monsters than they fell inert at his feet.

He struck each one a mortal blow, and then, advancing again, he found six dragons covered with scales more difficult to penetrate than iron. Frightening as that encounter was, he remained intrepid, and, as he made use of his redoubtable sword, there was not one that he did not cut in half.

He was hoping that he had overcome the greatest difficulties when one that was even more embarrassing arrived. Twenty-four nymphs, beautiful and gracious, came to meet him holding long garlands of flowers, with which they blocked the passage.

"Where do you want to go, Sire?" they asked him. "We're committed to guard this place; if we let you pass, infinite misfortunes will overtake you and us; please, don't persist. Would you want to steep your victorious hand in the blood of twenty-four innocent young women, who have never caused you any displeasure?"

At that sight, the king remained nonplussed and in suspense; he did not know what to resolve, having made a profession of respecting the fair sex, of being a knight to all excess; was it necessary on this occasion to exert himself to destroy it? But a voice that he heard suddenly fortified him.

"Strike, strike; don't spare any," the voice said to him, "or you'll lose your princess forever."

At the same time, without saying anything to the nymphs, he threw himself into their midst, broke their garlands, attacked them without quarter and dissipated them in a moment.

That was one of the last obstacles that he was to find; he entered into the little wood where he had seen Toute-Belle.

She was there, on the edge of the spring, pale and languid. He approached her, trembling; he wanted to throw himself at her feet, but she drew away from him with as much haste and indignation as if he had been the Yellow Dwarf.

"Don't condemn me without hearing me, Madame," he said to her. "I am neither infidel nor culpable; I am an unfortunate who has displeased you without wanting to."

"Oh, barbarian," she cried, "I saw you traversing the atmosphere with a person of extraordinary beauty. Was it in spite of yourself that you were making that journey?"

"Yes, Princess," he said to her, "it was in spite of myself; the wicked Fay of the Desert was not content to chain me to a rock; she abducted me in a chariot to one of the ends of the earth, where I would still be languishing without the unexpected aid of a benevolent siren, who brought me here. I have come, Princess, to extract you from the hands that retain you captive. Don't refuse the help of the most faithful of lovers."

He threw himself at her feet and caught hold of her dress. Unfortunately, he dropped his redoubtable sword. The Yellow Dwarf, who was hiding in a lettuce, no sooner saw it out of the king's hand than, knowing its power, he threw himself upon it and seized it.

The princess uttered a terrible scream on seeing the dwarf, but her plaints only served to embitter the little monster. With a few words from his grimoire he made two giants appear, who charged the king with chains and irons.

"Now," said the dwarf, "I am master of my rival's destiny; but I will accord him life and the liberty to leave this place, provided that you consent to marry me without delay."

"Oh, I would rather die a thousand time," cried the amorous king.

"Is there anything so terrible, alas, sire, as that you should die?" said the princess.

"Is there anything so frightful, as that you should become the victim of this monster," replied the king.

"Let us die together, then," she continued.

"Leave me, my princess, the consolation of dying for you."

"I consent instead," she said to the dwarf, "to what you want."

"Before my eyes," said the king, "before my eyes you will make him your husband, cruel princess; life will be odious to me."

"No," said the Yellow Dwarf, "it will not be before your eyes that I become her husband; a beloved rival is too odious to me."

As he finished speaking, in spite of the tears and cries of Toute-Belle, he struck the king straight in the heart and laid him at his feet. The princess, unable to survive her dear lover, let herself fall on to his body, and was not long before uniting her soul with his.

It was thus that those illustrious unfortunates perished, without the siren being able to bring any remedy to it, for the force of the charm was in the diamond sword. The malevolent dwarf preferred to see the princess deprived of life than see her in another's arms.

The Fay of the Desert, having learned of that adventure, destroyed the mausoleum that she had built, conceiving as much hatred for the memory of the King of the Gold Mines as she had conceived passion for his person. The helpful siren, desolate at such a great misfortune could obtain nothing from destiny except to metamorphose them into palm trees.

Those two perfect bodies became two beautiful trees; always conserving a faithful love for one another, they caressed one another with their interlaced branches, and immortalized their fires by their tender union.

One who promises in a shipwreck
A hecatomb to the immortals,
Does not only go to kiss their altars
When he finds himself on the shore.
Everyone makes promises in danger;
But let the danger of Toute-Belle

When Leonore had finished her romance, everyone thanked her urgently for the pleasure she had just given them.

"I am mistaken," said Don Francisco, "if that is not the composition of the lovely Leonore or young Matilde; I remark therein a delicate turn that greatly resembles that of their intelligence."

"If I had imagined it," she replied, modestly, "I would merit little praise. These sorts of works appear to me to be very easy, and simply relating something requires no great genius."

"You have said enough," said Don Jaime, in his jargon, "to persuade us that Don Francisco knows your character; one can judge your modesty by the scorn that you have for such a witty romance."

The entire company got up, testifying that it was necessary to enjoy the liberty that the country gives, and as they separated into several groups, it was not difficult for Don Fernand to find the means of conversing with Leonore. After having walked with the countess, he quit her adroitly and went in search of his mistress; he perceived her traversing the arbor of jasmines; he stopped her respectfully and, finding himself alone with her, he could not help falling at her feet.

"Is there anyone more fortunate than me?" he said to her. "I am at your feet, Madame, and I can tell you that I adore you."

"I do not think," the beautiful young woman replied, in a modest and embarrassed manner, "that the liberty in question is as well-established as you imagine; for in sum, sire, ought I not remove it from you?"

"No, Madame," he replied, "no, you are too amiable and too good to punish me so rudely for an offence that I am not the master of having committed; you have forced me to give you my heart; is it not permissible to talk to you about your conquest? Alas, Madame," he continued, "I can only talk to you about that; if I dared would I not talk to you about the return that I merit?"

"I have never seen so much ground covered in such little time," she said. "I do not know yet whether I ought to accord you permission to talk to me. But alas," she said, interrupting herself, how can I refuse it to your merit, to the sincerity of your intentions, to my penchant, to your entreaties, and to what you have done, sire, to prove your urgency to me, for can anything equal your perseverance?"

"I shall never be capable of lacking it, Madame," replied Don Fernand. "The ill humor of the countess will not deter me, and I am already too well rewarded for my disguise, and the complaisance I have for her, since I find myself at your feet, that you have suffered the confession of my passion, that I can flatter myself that my cares, my respects and my constancy might one day touch you."

"I do not forbid you to hope," Leonore said to him. "Think about rendering your sentiments as agreeable to my father as they might be to me, and..."

She was unable to continue a conversation that was beginning to be so tender; her disturbance completed explaining what she thought; and the rapturous Don Fernand was on the point of dying at her feet when, involuntarily, he took one of her hands. As he tried to kiss it, however, he suddenly felt someone pull his foot so rudely that he fell on his nose.

What became of him when, getting up abruptly with the design of avenging the insult that had just been made to him before Leonore's eyes, he saw the countess, like a phantom? Neither he nor his mistress had perceived that she was behind them, and that she was listening to them.

The suspicious old woman had scarcely perceived that the pretended Moor had quit her adroitly to return to the enclosure than she feared that one of her daughters might be there; and, coming after him as quietly as she could, she had seen by the light of several candles that had been put in crystal chandeliers that the African was at Leonore's feet. Transported by fury as she was, she had the patience to listen to the whole conversation of the tender lovers; but when he took her daughter's hand she did not judge it appropriate to remain a benevolent spectator any longer.

"Aha, Don Fernand," she cried, "so it's you who has taken the trouble to disguise yourself as a Moor, in order to continue your attentions to Leonore, and that imprudent girl is sufficiently deprived of reason to listen to you and permit you to kiss her hand?"

Leonore and Don Fernand were so confused that it is easier to imagine their condition than to describe it. However, as he flattered himself that the countess might not have heard what they had said, he soon recovered his composure and tried to react boldly.

"What!" he replied "Is it a crime in Spain to speak to a young woman, and to kiss her hand? In my country it is a mark of respect."

"And in my country," said the countess angrily, "it's a proof that one has lost it. But Moor or Castilian, know that I am not in a humor to be your dupe any longer."

With that, charging her daughter with the cruelest reproaches, she obliged her to return to the house with Matilde, where she locked them both up under twenty keys.

Don Fernand and Don Jaime were so desperate that, but for Don Francisco, they would have opposed violence to violence. The illumination and the supper that had been prepared disappeared suddenly, as if by enchantment. She said the harshest things in the world to her nephew, and told him that if he did not leave immediately with "those two demons"—that was what she called the cavaliers—she would be driven to extremes against them, of which all of them would have reason to repent.

No fête had ever concluded in such a disastrous manner. The two lovers and their friends were in despair at leaving their mistresses in such terrible hands, but they feared even more that the countess might explode, and when one is veritably in love one is more interested in the repose of the beloved person than one's own satisfaction.

They departed without even having supped, half-dead of hunger and rage. They sustained their masquerade with the rest of the company, so far as it as possible, saying that the ambassador had just sent for them; they threatened the countess with Mohammed and Aly, and to complain to the court of Spain about her excesses, for which they hoped to find a means of avenging themselves as soon as they had returned to Morocco.

That only served to irritate her further; she called them disturbers of the public peace, thieves of hearts, men devoid of faith and law. She became so heated in making them reproaches that they thought it better to leave than see the furious woman any longer. They had a mortal displeasure at having spoken so little to their mistresses and leaving them exposed to the ill humor of that terrible mother.

She sometimes doubted that they were Don Fernand and Don Jaime, for they were perfectly disguised, but in the end, she was convinced that they were two Spaniards who had only come to her house in order to see and speak to her daughters.

As they returned to Cadiz they did not have the strength to talk to one another for a long time; the different reflections to which they abandoned themselves took them so far that it was difficult to come back from them. But whatever chagrin Don Francisco had, as he had not been as piqued by the game as the others, he spoke to them first.

"Although I don't want to insult your misfortune by untimely reproaches," he said, "I can't help asking you, my dear Don Fernand, what imprudence led you to throw yourself at Leonore's feet in a garden where her mother might surprise you?"

"It's true," added Don Jaime, "that without that unfortunate impulse gripping me, everything was going very well, and I was talking to Matilde without anyone perceiving it."

"You cold-blooded individuals," replied Don Fernand, "can talk at your ease about that adventure. Alas, if you loved as much as I do, how much difficulty you would have found in being with Leonore without testifying to her by some transport the state of your soul."

Don Jaime waited impatiently for him to finish in order to say to him, in harsh manner: "You pretend to the glory of loving Leonore more than I love Matilde?"

"Yes, I pretend to that," added Don Fernand, "and I will sustain it to you."

Don Jaime, full of vivacity, opened the door of the carriage and jumped to the ground. "Come and sustain it then," he said, "drawing his sword."

Don Fernand immediately leapt down into the meadow, and Don Francisco ran forward to put himself between them. "What fury is animating you?" he cried. "You want to kill one another for such a reason? Live, live for the women you love; it's to them alone that it's necessary to prove the grandeur of your passion, without undertaking a combat by which they would be offended if it came to their knowledge."

Good as those arguments were, the two lovers had a strong desire to cross swords and avenge upon one another the mortal chagrin they had against the Countess de Fuentes. In the end however, the pleas of their friend appeased them; they climbed back into the carriage, ashamed of a promptitude that offended the sincere amity that they had always sworn to one another.

On the other hand, Don Francisco was anxious about the quarrel that he had created with his aunt in taking the supposed African to her home; he could not imagine any means of appeasing her, and he feared that she might oblige her husband to enter into her resentment.

Having remarked his anxiety, Don Fernand told him that he was in despair at all the contretemps that they had encountered, without flattering himself that the return of his father would succeed in calming the tempest.

As they entered Don Francisco's abode they were told that the Marquis de Toledo had arrived. Don Fernand and Don Jaime appeared to be delighted by that; they repeated all the assurances they had already given their friend with regard to marrying his cousins, if the Count de Fuentes consented to it.

Don Fernand begged him to confide to him the portrait of Lenore that he had had for a short time, in order to convince his father that no one was more lovable than her. Don Francisco, who wanted that marriage as ardently as him, made no difficulty about giving it to him, understanding that his cousin would be one of the most fortunate women in the world to marry a man of such great quality and such great merit. Don Fernand thanked him a thousand times for the pleasure he was giving him, and retired with Don Jaime filled with the sweetest hopes. They resolved together to have Doña Matilde requested at the same time.

They talked to one of their friends immediately about the pleasure they would find in those marriages, and begged him to talk to the Marquis de Toledo and to bring him to want them. Don Fernand added that it was necessary to make his father understand that he could not find a young woman more virtuous or more amiable; that he had even judged it appropriate to show him her portrait in order to convince him by means of his own eyes of a part of what he was told. He gave that of his mistress to his friend, in order that he would not lose any time in showing it to him.

They did not fail, for their part, to go to see the Marquis de Toledo; and Don Fernand, who had reasons for seeking to please him, had never seemed so glad of his return, so complaisant or so assiduous.

Meanwhile, their friend, in order to give them pleasure, went to see the Marquis, whom he made to understand so clearly the advantages that he would encounter in an alliance with the Count de Fuentes, that he promised to work for what his son desired.

"I've brought you the portrait of the charming young woman," continued his friend, "and I'm convinced that, without counting her beauty, which is perfect, you will have a good opinion of her on the basis of her physiognomy alone."

The marquis appeared charmed to such a point that he requested that the charming portrait be left with him for the rest of the day. When he was alone, he looked at it with an extraordinary attention and pleasure. He commenced to envy the good fortune of his son.

What felicity, he thought, *to please such a lovable young woman? But*, he continued, *what am I thinking in wanting to unite her with my son when I'm not yet of an age to renounce marriage? Let's discover a few particularities of her humor; that will determine me absolutely.*

He sent for Don Fernand, and after having applauded his choice, he questioned him about the intelligence and character of his mistress. The amorous Spaniard only spoke of her with the exaggerations of a lover, and not without a natural eloquence, with the result that the marquis wearied as little of interrogating his son as the latter did of responding to him—and, not knowing the pain he was preparing for himself, he remarked with pleasure the attention with which his father was listening to him. He took it as such a good augury that he almost did not put his happiness in doubt, for he knew well enough that the Count de Fuentes would not refuse him. Thus, he continued to proclaim the marvels of his mistress, in order to engage him to advance is marriage. His father promised to favor his amour and to give him news soon.

Don Fernand, transported by joy, gave him thanks proportionate to the good fortune for which he enabled him to hope. As soon as he had retired he wrote to Lenore regarding the state into which he had put his pretentions; she received the letter thanks to the cares of her cousin, in spite of the vigilance of the countess.

While Don Fernand and his beautiful mistress were congratulating themselves on such flattering hopes, the Count de Fuentes, persecuted by continual letters from his wife came to find her at Las Peñas in order to put her in repose regarding the sentiments of jealousy that had reignited in her soul.

As soon as Don Fernand knew that, he informed his father, and as the latter knew the count well he wrote him a note asking if he could talk to him elsewhere than at his home. They arranged a meeting at the house of a common friend.

After the initial civilities, the Marquis de Toledo said to the count: "I've come to ask you for a pledge of my amity and give you one of mine that might surprise you if the subject in question were not appropriate to work miracles. I've me to ask you for the amiable Leonore, whose beauty and youth would rejuvenate me, to the point of not being entirely disagreeable to her. Accord her to me, Sire, and in order that our houses might be more narrowly linked, give the amiable Matilde to my son."

The Count de Fuentes responded to that request with all the civility and testimonies of joy that the marquis could have promised himself; they embraced, and gave one another their word; and, the affair having been settled between them, they resolved to keep it secret.

The Count de Fuentes did not dispense with speaking about it to his wife, in order to obtain her consent, but he begged her at the same time to say nothing to her daughters, thinking that it was sufficient for him to approve of something for her to be content with it.

On returning to Cadiz the Marquis de Toledo told Don Fernand that everything was going well, and that he would soon be happy, without going into further detail, with the result that he could not be enlightened regarding the bad turn his father had done him. As they both had reasons for impatience, they both wanted to hasten the day of the marriage.

Don Jaime, who had no less passion for Matilde than Don Fernand for Leonore, did not fail to press the Marquis de Toledo to make his request, in order that the two sisters could be married at the same time. The old marquis refrained carefully from informing him of what had happened; on the contrary, he promised to serve him usefully. Fearing that he trick he was playing on his son and his friend might be discovered before it had its effect, however, he pressed for the return of Leonore and Matilde to Cadiz. The Count de Fuentes, who was bored with the country, was not sorry to have a pretext to bring his family back to a more agreeable location.

It would have been very difficult for two men as clear-sighted as Don Fernand and Don Jaime not to discover the perfidy that was being plotted against them; they discovered it, therefore, and how did they receive that news?

Everything violent that despair, amour and anger can inspire was assembled in their hearts; the state that Don Fernand's was in when he made the reflection that the object of his fury sand vengeance was his own father is indescribable.

"Alas," he said to Don Francisco, "it isn't him that I ought to punish, but myself; it was me who showed him the portrait of my beautiful mistress; I informed him too carefully of her good qualities; how could I believe that he would be capable of seeing her with indifference? Does not Amour have arrows for all ages and all times? What was I thinking, then, wretch that I am, when I enabled him to see that charming person?"

Then passing from that reflection to others more violent, he said: "Am I capable of excusing the man who has just stolen from me the woman I love? No, no, consideration, respect, I shall no longer listen to you, and it will only be at the end of my life that another will assure himself of the possession of my mistress."

Don Jaime, who was not given pause by such great regards, promised himself a vengeance proportionate to the insult that he had received.

Knowing that Leonore and Matilde were to arrive the following day, they begged Don Francisco to go to meet them in order to inform them of what was happening. He wanted to take that step, in spite of all the chagrin of his aunt, to whom he had written in vain to try to justify himself regarding the adventure of the Moors. He did not fail to give Leonore Don Fernand's letter, which was conceived in these terms:

The excess of my dolor is far above the words I can use to express it to you. It is my father, beautiful Leonore, who wants to extinguish my hopes, to snatch your heart from me and marry you. I am no longer in possession of myself since that frightful news. I no longer know what I am or what I am doing. You alone can prevent all the misfortunes of my life; permit me to take you to a place that will serve as a refuge for our amour. It is the only remedy for evils so pressing; but Madame, if you refuse, I shall no longer seek anything but death.

Don Francisco found the Countess de Fuentes on the point of quitting Las Peñas. He talked to his cousins in favor of the disorder of their departure. O God, what was their dolor at such fatal and unexpected news! A thunderbolt would have surprised them less and desolated them less.

"Why are you so afflicted?" Don Francisco said to them. "Do you not see that if you consent, Don Fernand and Don Jaime will protect you from this cruel marriage? But it's necessary, in order to succeed in that, for you to play your roles well, and that when you go to Cadiz, you seem cheerful and content; under those conditions, I assure you that all will go in accordance with your desires."

"Oh, my dear cousin," said Leonore, "You flatter us too much; after this misfortune we have everything to dread and very little for which to hope; however, I am resolved to follow your advice and I shall hide my dolor to the extent that it depends on me. Return to Cadiz, I implore you; assure Don Fernand that I am ready to do whatever you wish."

"Tell Don Jaime the same thing for me," added Matilde, to whom he had written the most tender letter in the world. "Assure him that neither my hand nor my heart will ever belong to anyone but him."

"That isn't sufficient," Don Francisco interrupted. "It's necessary to write, and for me to carry your orders."

Leonore immediately charge him with a note. of which these were the words:

Don Francisco will tell you in what state I am; and sincerely, I do not believe that I could have resisted the excess of my displeasure without flattering myself that that design you have formed might succeed. I approve, Sire, and I will go with you with pleasure under conditions appropriate to virtue and decency.

Matilde's note for Don Jaime contained these few words:

Do not expect eloquent laments on my part; the blow threatens you kills me, and great dolors are ordinarily mute; but as they sometimes lead to the last extremities, count on me to second your designs, in order to unite our destiny forever.

Don Francisco returned to Cadiz; the lovers of his two cousins were waiting for him impatiently; they were delighted with their generous resolutions. While they were giving the necessary orders, the sisters arrived, and were able to dissimulate the just displeasures by which they were overwhelmed

They were scarcely in Cadiz when the Marquis de Toledo came to see them without Don Fernand. He had declared his intentions to him in a very embarrassed manner, assuring him that if he conformed to them with a good grace there was nothing he could not expect from his amity. Don Fernand had exerted the utmost violence to constrain himself, and replied briefly that he would obey his orders.

The marquis had not neglected anything to conceal some of his years from the eyes of young Leonore; powder, good odors, diamonds and embroidery had all be employed. He said everything to her he could imagine of the most obliging; she responded to him with a great deal of modesty. The visit was short, and as soon as her had returned home he sent Leonore and Matilde the most beautiful gems in the world. They were looking at them sadly when Leonore remarked a little note in a box covered in emeralds. She opened it and found these words:

*We shall enter your garden tonight. Be there, beautiful
Leonore, Doña Matilde; have mantles in order not to be recognized; everything is ready in order to put you in security.*

They slipped away that evening and went at the appointed hour into the garden. Don Francisco, who had been informed of everything, accompanied them, and it was him who
opened a door, of which he had taken the key, to the two lovers. They had hidden their faces with their cloaks, and seeing
their mistresses covered in their mantles they took them away
diligently and secretly.

They found a carriage at the end of the street that they
instructed to take the road to the port, where a lighter was
waiting for them with a few gentlemen; they climbed into it
and were promptly rowed away.

They joined the ship that was waiting for them, which
immediately set sail for Venice. Leonore and Matilde were
taken by the captain to the poop cabin. A fresh wind that got
up was very favorable to the flight of the tender lovers; each
of them, placed next to his mistress, testified his joy and gratitude. But the sisters found themselves slightly astonished by
the step they had just taken; young women who had spent their
entire lives with a mother more rigid than any other, could
well reflect on a step of that nature.

Don Fernand had no difficulty in penetrating their state
of mind; he felt anxious about it, and as he was being very
amusing, in order to distract them from the profound reverie to
which they seemed to have abandoned themselves, he proposed to tell them a tale, since they did not want to go to bed.
They were delighted, and wanted to go up on deck, because
the night was fine, the moon shining, he sea so mild and calm
that it was only agitated by zephyrs. The captain asked for
permission to stay with them.

GREEN WORM[28]

There was once a great queen who, having given birth to twin girls, invited a dozen fays of the neighborhood to come and see them and to endow them, as was the custom in those days—a very convenient custom, for the power of fays almost always repaired what nature had spoiled; but sometimes, it spoiled what nature had done well.

When the fays were all in the banqueting hall a magnificent meal was served to them. Everyone was about to sit down at table when Magotine came in; she was the sister of Carabosse, who was no less malevolent than her. At that sight, the queen shivered, fearing some disaster, for she had not invited her to come to the feast. Hiding her anxiety carefully, however, she went in quest herself of a green velvet armchair embroidered with sapphires. As she was the oldest of the fays, all the others moved aside to make room for her, and each one whispered: "Let's hasten to endow the little princesses, my sister, in order to forestall Magotine."

When she was offered an armchair she said rudely that she did not want one, and that she was big enough to eat standing up; but she was mistaken, for the table being a little high, she could not even see it, she was so small. She had a chagrin in consequence that augmented her ill humor further.

"Madame," the queen said to her "I beg you to take a place at the table."

"If you wanted to have me there," the fay replied, "You should have invited me, like the others; you only want pretty, benevolent and magnificent people like my sisters at your

---

[28] The original title, *Serpentin vert*, could refer to anything green and serpentine; the noun often refers to a paper steamer or the coiled tube of a still, but it rarely refers to a snake (and the author deliberately avoided titling the tale *Le Serpent vert*). The creature in the story, although initially introduced as a snake, is possessed of wings and claws, and is thus clearly a kind of dragon, so I have preferred the translation "worm."

court; as for me, I'm too ugly and too old; but with that, I have no less power than them, and without boasting, perhaps I have more."

All the fays pressed her so much to go the table that she consented to it. First, a golden basket was placed on it with a dozen bouquets of gems inside; the first comers each took theirs, with the result that none remained for Magotine. She started to mutter between her teeth. The queen ran to her cabinet and brought her a casket of perfumed Spanish leather covered with rubies and filled with diamonds; she begged her to receive it, but Magotine shook her head and said: "Keep your jewels, Madame, I have plenty of them; I only came to see whether you had thought about me, but you have neglected me greatly. With that she tapped the table with her wand, and all the meat with which it was laden was changed into fricasseed snakes; the fays were so horrified that they threw away their napkins and quit the feast.

While they were talking about the bad turn that Magotine had just done them, that barbaric little fay approached the cradle where the princesses were enveloped by sheets of golden cloth, and were the prettiest in the world. "I endow you, she promptly said to one, with being perfect in ugliness." She was about to give some malediction to the other when the fays, who were very emotional, came running and stopped her from doing so, with the consequence that the evil Magotine broke a glass panel and, passing through it like a flash of lightning, disappeared from sight.

The queen hardly felt the bounty of a few gifts that the benevolent fays were able to endow the princess; she only felt the dolor of finding herself the mother of the ugliest creature in the world. She took her in her arms and had the chagrin of seeing her become uglier from one moment to the next. She tried in vain to do herself violence in order not to weep in front of the fays, but she could not help it, and the pity they felt for her was immeasurable.

"What can we do, my sister?" they said to one another. "What can we do to console the queen?"

They held a great council, and then told her to listen less to her dolor, because there was a time marked where her daughter would be happy."

"But will she be beautiful?" the queen interrupted. "Will she be beautiful?"

"We can't explain ourselves further," they replied. "Let it suffice for you, Madame that your daughter will be content."

She thanked them very much, and did not fail to charge them with presents, for even though the fays are very rich, they always like to be given something, and that custom has passed since to all the people of the earth, without time having destroyed it.

The queen called her elder daughter Laidronnette the younger one Bellotte; their names suited them perfectly, for Laidronnette became so frightful that whatever intelligence she had, it was impossible to look at her; her sister was embellished, and appeared utterly charming, with the result that Laidronnette, having already reached twelve years of age, came to throw herself at the feet of the king and the queen to beg them to permit her to go and shut herself away in the Castle of Solitude in order to hide her ugliness and not desolate them any longer. They loved her in spite of her deformity, with the consequence that they had some difficulty consenting to it, but they still had Bellotte, and that was enough to console them.

Laidronnette asked the queen only to send her nurse with her and a few officers to serve her. You need have no fear, Madame," she said, "that anyone will abduct me; and I confess that, being made as I am, I would even like to avoid the light of day."

The king and queen accorded her what she wanted; she was taken to the castle she had chosen. It had been built several centuries before; the sea came all the way to beneath its windows, and served it as a moat. A vast nearby forest furnished promenades, and several meadows terminated the view. The princess played instruments and sang divinely well.

She remained in that agreeable solitude or two years, where she even wrote a few book of reflections, but the desire to see the king and queen again obliged her to mount a carriage and go to the court. She arrived as Princess Bellotte was about to be married; everyone was joyful. When they saw Laidronnette they had chagrined expressions; she was not embraced or caressed by any of her relatives, and for her only welcome she was told that she had grown even uglier.

She was advised not to appear at the ball, but that if she wanted to see it they would contrive some hole through which she could look. She replied that she had not come to dance or listen to violins; that she had been in the solitary castle for such a long time that she had been unable to help quitting it in order to render her respects to the king and queen; that she knew with a sharp dolor that they could not suffer her; and that she would therefore return to her desert, where the trees, the flowers and the springs did not reproach her for her ugliness when she approached them.

When the king and queen saw that she was so annoyed they told her that by doing some violence to themselves they could allow her to stay with them for a few days. As she had courage, however, she replied that she would have too much difficulty quitting them if she spent that time in such good company. They wanted her to go away too much to retain her, so they told her coldly that she was right.

Princess Bellotte gave her for a wedding present an old ribbon that she had worn all winter on her sleeve, and the king she was marrying gave her some purple taffeta with which to make a skirt. If she had followed her impulse she would have thrown the ribbon and the taffeta in the faces of the generous people who regaled her so poorly, but she had so much intelligence, sagacity and reason that she did not want to testify any bitterness; she departed, therefore, with her nurse to return to her castle, her heart so full of sadness that she made the entire journey without saying a word.

One day, when she was in one of the darkest paths of the forest, she saw a large green serpent under a tree, which raised its head and said to Laidronnette: "You're not the only unfortunate one; look at my horrible form, and know that I was born more beautiful than you."

The frightened princess only heard half those words; she fled, and did not dare to go out for several days, so fearful was she of a similar encounter. Finally, bored with being always alone in her room, she went downstairs in the evening and went to the sea shore.

She was walking slowly, thinking about her sad destiny, when she saw a small boat coming toward her, gilded and painted with a thousand different devices. The sail was gold brocade, the mast cedar-wood and the oars carambola. It seemed that hazard alone was navigating it, and when it stopped near the shore, the princess, curious to see all those beauties, climbed into it. She found it garnished with crimson velvet with a gold backcloth, and what served as nails were made of diamond.

Suddenly, the boat drew away from the shore. The princess, alarmed by the peril she was running, took the oars in order to try to go back, but her efforts were futile; the wind that was blowing elevated the waves and she lost sight of the land. No longer perceiving anything but the sky and the sea, she abandoned herself to fortune, convinced that it would scarcely be favorable to her, and that Magotine was doing her another bad turn.

It's necessary to die, she said to herself. *What secret movements make me fear death? Until now, alas, have I known any of the pleasures that can make it hated? My ugliness frightens even my nearest relatives; my sister is a great queen and I am relegated to the depths of a desert, where the only company I have found is a talking snake. Isn't it better for me to perish than to drag myself through a life as tedious as mine?*

These reflections dried up the princess's tears. She looked with intrepidity to see from which direction death would come. She seemed to be inviting it not to be late, when she saw something serpentine in the water that was approaching her boat, and which said to her: "If you were in a humor to receive me help from a poor Green Worm like me, I'm in a position to save your life."

"Death scares me less that you," cried the princess. "If you want to give me some pleasure, never show yourself to my eyes."

Poor Green Worm uttered a long hiss—that is the fashion in which snakes sigh—and without making any reply, it sank beneath the waves.

What a horrible monster, the princess said to herself. *It has green wings, its body is a thousand colors, its claws are ivory, its eyes fiery and its head is bristling with long hairs. Oh, I'd rather perish than owe my life to it. Bu*t, she went on, *what attachment does it have to following me, and by what adventure can it speak, as if it were reasonable?*

She was still thinking about it when a voice, responding to her thought, said to her: "Know, Laidronnette, that it is necessary not to scorn Green Worm, and if it were not saying something harsh to you, I would assure you that he is less ugly in his species than you are in yours. Far from wanting to annoy you, though, one would like to soothe your pains, if you would consent to it."

That voice surprised the princess greatly, and what it had said appeared so unbearable that she would not have had enough strength to retain her tears, but she suddenly made a reflection and cried: "What! I don't want to mourn my death because I'm reproached for my ugliness. What good would it do me, alas, to be the most beautiful person in the worlds; I would perish nonetheless; it ought to be a motive of consolation, to prevent me from regretting life."

While she was moralizing thus, the boat, still floating at the whim of the wind, broke up against a rock; no two pieces of wood remained together. The poor princess felt that all her philosophy could not hold out against such an evident peril. She found a few fragments of wood, which she took in her arms, and feeling herself buoyed up, she arrived fortunately at the foot of the huge rock.

Alas, what became of her when she saw that she was tightly embracing Green Worm! As it perceived the terrible fear that she had, it drew away slightly, and shouted at her: "You'd fear me less if you knew me better; but it's the rigor of my destiny to frighten everyone."

Immediately, it threw itself into the water, and Laidronnette remained alone on a rock of prodigious size.

In no matter what direction she cast her eyes, she saw nothing to soften her despair. Night was approaching; she had no provisions to eat, and did not know where to retire.

I thought, she said, sadly, *that I'd end my days in the sea; doubtless their final period will be here. Some marine monster will come to devour me, or lack of nourishment will take my life.*

She went to sit down on top of the rock. As long as there was daylight, she gazed at the sea, and when night had fallen completely she took off her purple taffeta skirt, covered her head and face with it; and then remained this, very anxious about what was going to happen.

Finally, she went to sleep, and it seemed to her that she heard various instruments. She persuaded herself that she was dreaming, but a moment later, she heard these lines being sung, which seemed to be made for her:

Suffer that here Amour wounds you,
That his tender fires are felt here.
That god banishes our sadness;
We please ourselves in this happy abode;
Suffer that here Amour wounds you,
That his tender fires are felt here.

The attention that she paid to those words woke her up completely. *With what good and ill fortune am I menaced?* she wondered. *In the state I am in, do fine days still remain to me?* She opened her eyes with a sort of dread, apprehensive that she might find herself surrounded by monsters; but what was her surprise when, instead of that savage rock she found herself in a chamber paneled with gold; the bed on which she was lying responded perfectly to the magnificence of the most beautiful palace in the world.

She asked herself a hundred questions about that, unable to believe that she was really awake. Finally, she got up, and ran to open a glazed door that opened on to a spacious balcony, from which all that the beauties of nature, seconded by art, can contrive on earth was revealed: gardens full of flowers, fountains, statures and rare trees; forests in the distance; palaces, the walls of which were ornamented with precious stones, and the roofs with pearls, so marvelously made that they were as many masterpieces; a calm and placid sea, covered with a thousand different sorts of boats, whose sails, banners and streamers, agitated by the wind, had the most agreeable effect on the sight.

"Gods!" she cried. "Just gods! What do I see? Where am I? What a surprising metamorphosis! What, then, has become of that frightful rock, which seemed to threaten the stars with its sullen points? Was it me that nearly perished yesterday in a boat and was saved by a Worm?"

She spoke thus; she walked back and forth; she stopped; finally, she heard a noise in her apartment; she went in and saw a hundred pagodas coming, clad in a hundred different fashions; the largest were a cubit high, the smallest no more than four fingers; some were beautiful, gracious and agreeable others hideous, of a frightful ugliness; there were some made of diamonds, emeralds, rubies, pearls, crystal, silver, brass, bronze, iron, wood and clay; some had no arms, others had no feet, mouths extending to the ears, eyes askew and noses crushed; in a word, there was no more difference between the creatures that inhabit the world than there was between those pagodas.[29]

---

[29] The model for these "pagodas" is not the building itself but the humanoid figures often found at the entrance or in association with them; pagodas and their decorations became fashionable in seventeenth-century France; there was a notorious

The ones that presented themselves before the princess were the delegates of the realm; after having made a speech mingled with a few very judicious reflections, they said to her, in order to divert her, that for some time they had been traveling the world, but that in order to obtain permission from their sovereign, they had sworn an oath to her on departure not to speak; that they had been so scrupulous that they did not want to move their heads, nor their feet, nor their hands, but that the majority had not been able to help it, having traveled the world thus, when they returned, entertaining their king with the story of everything most secret that happened in the various courts where they had been received.

"It is, Madame," the delegates added, "a pleasure that we will give you sometimes, for we have orders not to neglect anything to distract you; instead of bringing you presents, we have come to divert you by means of our songs and dances. Immediately, they started to sing these words, while dancing a round dance with Basque tambourines and castanets.

> *Pleasures are charming*
> *When they follow pains*
> *Pleasures are charming*
> *After long torments.*
> *Don't break your chains.*
> *Young lovers.*
> *Pleasures are charming*
> *When they follow pains*
> *Pleasures are charming*
> *After long torments.*
>
> *By dint of suffering inhumane rigors,*
> *You'll find happy moments;*
> *Pleasures are charming*

---

example at Versailles, and the Pagoda of Chanteloup commissioned by the Duc de Choiseul can still be seen, along with its Oriental garden.

When they had finished, the delegate that had served as spokesman said to the princess: "Here, Madame, are a hundred pagodines who are destined for the honor of serving you; everything you could want in the world will be accomplished, provided that you stay among us."

The pagodines appeared in their turn; they were holding baskets proportionate to their stature, filled with a hundred different things, so pretty, so useful, so well made and so rich that Laidronnette could not weary of admiring them, of praising them and exclaiming about the marvels she saw.

The most apparent of the pagodines, which was a little figure of diamond, proposed that she go into the bath grotto because the heat was increasing. The princess walked beside the one that showed her the way, between two rows of bodyguards of a stature and bearing to make ne die of laughter. She found two crystal tubs garnished with gold, full of water of an odor so fine and rare that she was surprised by it. An awning, gold mingled with green, rose above it.

She asked why there were two tubs; she was told that one was for her and the other for the sovereign of the pagodas,

"But where is he?" she exclaimed.

"Madame," one said, "he is presently at war; you will see him when he returns."

The princess asked whether he was married, she was told that he was not, and that he was so lovable that he had not thus far found anyone worthy of him.

She did not take her curiosity any further; she undressed and got into the bath. Immediately, the pagodas and pagodines began to sing and play instruments; some had theorbos made of walnut shells, others had viols made from almond shells, for it as necessary that the instruments be proportionate to their stature, but all of it was so accurate and harmonized so well that nothing as more enjoyable than concerts of that sort.

When the princess got out of the bath, she was presented with a magnificent dressing gown; several pagodines playing flutes and oboes marched ahead of her singing verses praising her. She entered thus into a chamber where her clothes were laid out. Immediately, pagodine wardrobe mistresses and chambermaids came and went, coiffing her, dressing her, praising her and applauding her; there was no longer any question of ugliness, purple skirts it dirty ribbon.

The princess was veritably astonished. *Who*, she wondered, *can have procured me such an extraordinary good fortune? I was on the point of perishing, I was awaiting death, I could not hope for anything else, and yet I suddenly find myself in the most agreeable and magnificent place in the world, where everyone testifies more than joy on seeing me.*

As she had infinite intelligence and good will, she conducted herself so well that all the little creatures that approached her were charmed by her manners.

Every day, when she got up, she had new garments, new lace, new gemstones; it was still a pity that she was so ugly, but because she could not suffer from it she began to find it less disagreeable, by virtue of the great care that was taken to adorn her. There was no time when a few pagodas did not arrive and render a account of the most secret and most curious things that were happening in the world: peace treaties, leagues to make war, treasons and ruptures of lovers, infidelities of mistresses, despairs, reconciliations, disappointed heirs, broken marriages, old widows remarrying inappropriately, treasures discovered, bankruptcies, fortunes made overnight, fallen favorites, sieges of forts, jealous husbands, coquettish women, bad children, destroyed towns—in sum, what did they not tell the princess in order to amuse or occupy her?

Sometimes there were pagodas who had bellies so inflated and cheeks so swollen that it was surprising. When she asked them why they were like that they told her: "As it's not permitted for us to laugh, not to talk, in society and we incessantly see such risible things there, and almost intolerable stupidities, the desire to mock is so powerful that we swell up, it's really a hydropsy of laughter, of which we're cured as soon as we're here."

The princess admired the good minds of the pagodine population, for one could indeed have swelled up with laughter if it were necessary not to laugh at all the impertinences they saw.

There was no evening when one of the best plays of Corneille or Molière was not performed. Balls were very frequent; the smallest figures, in order to take advantage of everything, danced on tightropes in order to be more visible. Furthermore, the meals that were served to the princess could have passed for feasts of solemn festivals. She was brought serious, gallant and historic books.

In sum, the days flowed by like moments, although, in truth, all those witty pagodas appeared to be insupportably tiny, for it often happened that when she went for a walk she put thirty or so in her pockets in order to entertain her; it was funniest thing in the world to hear them chatting with their little voices, as clear as those of marionettes.

Once, it happened that the princess, not sleeping, said: "What will become of me? Will I always be here? My life is passing more agreeably that I would have dared to expect, but my heart lacks something. I don't know what it is, but I'm beginning to feel that this succession of the same pleasures, which isn't varied by any events, seems insipid."

"Oh, Princess," said a voice, "isn't that your fault? If you wanted to love, you'd discover very quickly that one can remain for a long time with the person one loves in a palace, or even in a frightful solitude, without wanting to go out."

"What pagoda is speaking to me?" she asked. "What pernicious advice is it giving me, contrary to all the repose of my life?"

"It's not a pagoda," was the reply, "that is warning you about something you will do sooner or later; it's the unfortunate sovereign of this realm, who adores you, and who only dares tell you so while trembling."

"A king adores me!" replied the princess. "Has that king eyes, or is he blind? Has he seen that I'm the ugliest person in the world?"

"I've seen you, Madame," replied the invisible individual. "I haven't found you such as you represent yourself, and whatever your person, your merit or your disgraces, I repeat to you that I adore you, but my respectful and fearful amour obliges me to hide."

"I am obliged to you for that," said the princess. "What would I do, alas, if I loved something?"

"You would be the felicity of the person who cannot live without you," he said, "but if you do not permit him to appear, he will not dare to do so."

"No," said the princes, "No, I don't want to see anything that engages me too strongly."

The other ceased to respond to her, and she spent the rest of the night very occupied with that adventure.

Whatever resolution she had not to say anything that had the slightest relationship to that adventure, she could not help asking the pagodas whether their king had returned. They said no. That response, which accorded poorly with what she had heard, worried her; she nevertheless asked whether the king was young and well made. She was told that he was young, that he was well made and very lovable. She asked whether they often had news of him; she was told that they received it every day.

"But does he know that I'm in his palace?" she added.

"Yes, Madame," was the reply. "He knows everything that happens in your regard. It interests him, and couriers depart every hour who go to tell him your news."

She fell silent, and commenced to dream much more frequently than she had been accustomed to do.

When she was alone, the voice spoke to her. She was sometimes afraid of it, but it sometimes gave her some pleasure, for there was nothing so gallant as everything that it said to her.

"Whatever resolution I've made never to love," the princess replied, "and whatever reason I have to defend my heart from an engagement that can only be fatal, I confess to you that I would be very glad to know a king whose taste is as bizarre as yours; for if it is true that you love me, you are perhaps the only person in the world who can have such a weakness for a person as ugly as me."

"Think whatever you please about my character, my adorable princess," the voice replied, "I find enough to justify you in your merit; it isn't that alone that obliges me to hide. I have reasons so sad that if you knew them you wouldn't be able to refuse me your pity."

The princess then pressed the voice to explain, but the voice no longer spoke; she only heard it uttering long sighs. All those things worried her. Although he was an unknown and hidden lover, he rendered her a thousand cares. To add to that, the place where she found herself made her wish for a company more appropriate than that of pagodas. That was why she began to suffer ennui everywhere. Only the voice of the invisible individual had the ability to occupy her agreeably.

On one of the darkest nights of her tears, when she was asleep, she perceived, on waking up, that someone was near her bed. She thought that it was the pagodine of pearls, which, having more intelligence than the others, sometimes came to converse with her. The princess reached out to pick her up, but someone took her hand, held it tightly, kissed it, and a few tears fell upon it; the individual was so emotional that he could not speak. She had no doubt that it was the invisible king.

"What do you want with me, then?" she said to him, sighing. "Can I love you without knowing you and without seeing you?"

"Oh, Madame," was the reply, "what conditions do you attach to the sweetness of pleasing you? It's impossible for me to allow myself to be seen. The malevolent Magotine, who did you a bad turn, is the same one who condemned me to a penitence of seven years; five have already gone by; two still remain, all the bitterness of which you would soothe if you would accept me as a husband. You will think that I am very bold, and that what I ask of you is absolutely impossible, but Madame, if you knew how far my passion goes, and how far the excess of my misfortunes goes, you would not refuse the favor that I ask of you."

Laidronnette became annoyed. As I have already said, she found that the invisible king had everything that could please intellectually, and amour took root in her heart under the specious name of a generous pity. She replied that she required a few more days in order to make up her mind. It was a great deal to have got her to the point of only deferring for a few days something with which one ought to flatter oneself.

The fêtes and concerts redoubled; nothing was sung to her any longer but wedding songs; she was brought presents incessantly, the magnificence of which surpassed anything that had ever been seen; the assiduous amorous voice paid court to her as soon as night fell, and the princess went to bed early in order to have more time to converse with it.

Finally, she consented to take the invisible king for her husband, and she promised him not to see him until after his penitence was finished. "It would be all over for you and for me," he said, "if you had that imprudent curiosity; it would be necessary for me to recommence my penitence and for you to share the punishment with me; but if you can prevent yourself from following the bad advice that will be given to you, you will have the satisfaction of finding me in accordance with your heart, and rediscovering at the same time the marvelous beauty that the malevolent Magotine took from you.

Delighted by that new hope, the princess swore a thousand oaths to her husband to have no curiosity contrary to his desires. Thus, the wedding was completed without noise and without splendor, but the heart and the mind settled their account nonetheless.

As all the pagodas sought urgently to divert their new queen, one of them brought her the story of Psyche, which a very fashionable author had just put into beautiful language.[30] She found many things in it that related to her own adventure, and such a violent desire took hold of her to see her father and her mother in her home, with her sister and her brother-in-law, that nothing the king could say was capable to getting rid of that fantasy.

"The book that you are reading," he added, "can tell you into what misfortunes Psyche fell. Please profit from it in order to avoid them."

She promised more than he asked. Finally, a vessel laden with pagodas and presents was dispatched with letters from Queen Laidronnette to the queen, her mother. She implored her to come and see her in her realm, and the pagodas were given permission for that one time only to speak elsewhere than in their own land.

The loss of the princess had not failed to touch the sensibility of her near relatives; she was thought to be dead, with the result that her letters were infinitely agreeable to the court; and the queen, who was dying to see her again, did not resist for a moment departing with her daughter and son-in-law. The pagodas, who alone knew the way to their realm, conducted the entire royal family there, and when Laidronnette saw her parents she nearly died of joy. She read and reread Psyche, in order to be on her guard against all they might say, and above all what she ought to reply, but however hard she tried she went astray in a hundred places. Sometimes the king was with the army, sometimes he was ill and in such a bad humor that he did not want to see anyone, sometimes he was making a pilgrimage, then he was hunting or fishing. In sum, it seemed that she was engaged to say nothing that would hold up, and that the barbaric Magotine had disturbed her mind.

---

[30] The reference is to an elaboration composed in the 1690s of Jean de La Fontaine's poem "Les Amours de Psyche et de Cupidon" (1669); the expanded version, combining verse with prose, proved very popular.

Her mother and father conferred together, and concluded that she was deceiving herself, with the consequence that, by virtue of an ill-judged zeal, they resolved to talk to her. They acquitted that task with so much skill that they cast a thousand dreads and a thousand doubts into her mind. After having defended herself for a long time against agreeing with what they said, she confessed that, until then, she had not seen her husband, but that he had so much charm in his conversation that it was sufficient to hear him to be content, that he was in penitence for two more years, and that after that time, not only would she be able to see him, but she would become as beautiful as the day star.

"Oh, you poor woman!" cried the queen. "How crude the snares that are extended for you are! Is it possible that you believe such tales with such a great simplicity? Your husband is a monster, and it cannot be otherwise, for all the pagodas of which he is the king are true apes."

"I would rather believe," said Laidronnette, "that he is the god Amour himself."

"What an error!" cried Queen Bellotte. "Psyche was told that she had a monster for a husband, and she found that it was Amour; you're obstinate that Amour is yours, and surely he's a monster. At least put your mind at rest; enlighten yourself in such an easy matter." The queen, her mother, said the same, and her son-in-law too.

The poor princess was so confused and troubled that, after having sent all her family away with presents that paid for the purple taffeta and the sleeve-ribbon, she resolved, whatever might happen, to see her husband. Oh, fatal curiosity, which a thousand fatal examples cannot correct, how dear you are going to cost that unfortunate princess!

She would have regretted not imitating her predecessor Psyche, with the result that she hid a lamp in her room and made use of it to see the invisible king so dear to her heart. But what frightful screams she uttered when she saw, instead of tender Amour, blond, pale, young and utterly lovable, she saw the frightful Green Worm, with long bristling hair.

He woke up, transported with rage and despair. "Barbarian!" he cried. "Is this the recompense for so much love?"

The princess did not hear him; fear had made her faint, and Worm was already far away.

At the noise of all that tragedy, several pagodas had come running. They put the princess to bed, they helped her, and when she had come round they found her in a state that imagination cannot attain. How many times did she reproach herself for the woe she was going to procure her husband? She loved him tenderly but she abhorred his form, and she would have given half her life not to have seen him.

However, her sad reveries were interrupted by a few pagodas that entered her bedroom fearfully. They had come to tell her that several ships full of marionettes, with Magotine at their head, had entered the port without obstacle. The marionettes and the pagodas had been enemies at all times; they were in competition in a thousand things, and the marionettes even had the privilege of talking everywhere, which the pagodas had not. Magotine was their queen; the aversion that she had for the poor Green Worm and the unfortunate Laidronnette had obliged her to assemble troops with the resolution of coming to torment them at the moment when their dolors were most intense.

The fay had no difficulty succeeding in her projects, for the queen was so desolate that although she was pressed to gave the necessary orders, she refused to do so, saying that she did not understand war. The greatest captain among the pagodas that were in the besieged cities and in the cabinet were assembled on her orders; she ordered them to take care of everything, and then shut herself away in her cabinet, regarding all the events of life with an almost equal eye.

Magotine had for a general the famous Polchinelle, who knew his métier well and had a large reserve corps composed of wasps, cockchafers and butterflies, which wrought marvels against a few lightly-armed frogs and lizards. They had been in the hire of the pagodas for a long time, and were in truth more redoubtable in name than by their valor.

Magotine amused herself for some time watching the battle; the pagodas and pagodines surpassed themselves therein; but with a thrust of her wand the fay dissipated all those superb edifices. Those charming gardens, those woods, those meadows and springs were buried in their own ruins, and Queen Laidronnette could not avoid the harsh condition of being a slave of the most malign fay there ever was.

Four or five hundred marionettes obliged her to come to where Magotine was.

"Madame," said Polchinelle, "this is the queen of the pagodas, whom I dare to present to you."

"I've known her for a long time," said Magotine. "She is the cause of my receiving an affront on the day of her birth, which I shall never forget."

"Alas, Madame," said the queen, "I believe that you are sufficiently avenged. The gift of ugliness that you bestowed on me to the utmost degree could have satisfied a person less vindictive than you."

"How she talks," said the fay. "Here's a doctor of a new edition. Your first employment will be to teach my ants philosophy; prepare to give them a lesson every day."

"How can I do that, Madame?" replied the afflicted queen. "I don't know philosophy, and if I did, would your ants be capable of learning it?"

"See, see the argumentative chit!" cried Magotine. "Well, Queen, you might not teach them philosophy, but you'll give the whole world, in spite of yourself, a lesson in patience that it will be difficult to imitate."

With that she had iron shoes bought for her so narrow that half her foot would not go in, but it was necessary nevertheless or her to be shod; the poor queen had to weep and suffer all the time.

"By the way," said Magotine, "here's a distaff charged with cobweb; I intend you to spin it as fine as your hair, and I only give you two hours."

"I've never spun. Madame," the queen said to her, "but even though what you want appears impossible to me, I'll try to obey you."

She was immediately taken into the depths of a very obscure grotto. It was sealed with a large stone after she had been given a loaf of brown bread and a jug of water.

When she tried to spin the dirty cobweb, her excessively heavy spindle fell to the ground a hundred times over; she had the patience to pick it up as many times and to recommence the work several times, but it was always futile.

"I know all too well now," she said, "the excess of my misfortune. I am delivered to the implacable Magotine; she is not content to have stolen all my beauty, she wants to find pretexts for making me die."

She began to weep, passing through her mind the fortunate state she had enjoyed in the realm of Pagodia, and dropping her distaff on the ground. "Let Magotine come when she pleases," she said. "I can't do the impossible."

She heard a voice that said: "Oh, Queen, your indiscreet curiosity has cost you the tears that you are shedding. However, there is no means of seeing the person one loves suffering. I have a friend that I have not mentioned to you; she is known as the Protective Fay. I hope that she will be a great help to you."

Immediately, there were three raps, and without her seeing anyone, her distaff was spun and unwound.

After two hours, Magotine, who was seeking a quarrel, had the stone sealing the grotto removed and she came in, followed by a numerous cortege of marionettes.

"Let's see, let's see," she said, "the work of an idler who can neither sew nor spin."

"Madame," said the queen, "I didn't know, in fact, but it has been necessary to learn."

When Magotine saw such a strange thing, she took the ball of spider-silk and said: "Truly, you're so skillful that it would be a great pity not to occupy you. Here, Queen, make nets with this thread that are strong enough to catch salmon.

"Oh, please," she replied, "consider the difficulty with which flies are caught therein."

"You argue a great deal, my beautiful friend," said Magotine, "but that won't do you any good." She left the grotto had the large stone replaced in front of it, and assured her that if the nets were not finished in two hours she would be doomed.

"Oh, Protective Fay," said the queen, then, "if it's true that my woes can touch you, don't refuse me your help."

Immediately, the nets were finished. Laidronnette was surprised to the utmost degree; with all her heart she thanked the helpful fay who did so much good, and thought with pleasure that it was doubtless her husband who had procured that friend for her.

"Alas, Green Worm," she said, "you're very generous still to love me after all the harm I've done you."

There was no reply, for Magotine came in, and was very surprised to find nets so industriously wrought that an ordinary hand would not have been capable of doing such work.

"What!" she said. "Will you really be bold enough to sustain that it's you who wove these nets?"

"I have no friend at your court, Madame," the queen said to her, "and even if I had one, I've been so securely imprisoned that it would be difficult for anyone to speak to me without your permission."

"Since you're so skillful and so adroit," said Magotine, "you'll be very useful to me in my realm."

She immediately ordered that ships be equipped and that all the marionettes should be ready to depart. She had the queen attached with heavy iron chains, for fear that by some movement of despair she might throw herself into the sea.

The unfortunate princes was deploring her sad destiny one night when she perceived Green Worm by the light of the stars, who was approaching the ship quietly.

"I still dread frightening you," he said, "and in spite of the reasons I have for not protecting you, you are infinitely dear to me."

"Can you forgive my indiscreet curiosity?" she replied, and can I say to you without displeasing you:

Is that you, Worm, dear lover, is that you?
Can I see again the object for which my heart sighs?
What! I can see you again, my dear and tender spouse!
O Heaven, what a rigorous martyrdom I have suffered!
How I have suffered, alas,
In not seeing you.

Worm replied with these lines:

How the dolors of absence
Trouble amorous hearts!
In the frightful realm
Where the gods exact their vengeance.
One cannot suffer more rigorous woes
Than the dolors of absence.

Magotine was not one of those fays who sometimes sleep; the desire to do evil always kept her awake. She did not fail to overhear he conversation of King Worm and his wife; she came to interrupt it like a Fury.

"Aha! You're mingling poetry and lamenting in the tone of Phoebus. Truly, I'm very glad. Proserpine, who is my best friend, has begged me to give her some poet for her wages; she has no lack of them, but she wants even more. Let's go, Green Worm, I order you, to complete your penitence, to go to the somber manor and give my compliments to the noble Proserpine."

The unfortunate Worm departed immediately, with long hisses, leaving the queen in the most intense dolor. She thought she had nothing more to lose, in her transport she cried: "By what crime have I displeased you, barbaric Magotine? I was scarcely in the world when your infernal malediction took away my beauty and rendered me frightful. Can you say that I was guilty of anything, since I did not have the usage of reason yet and did not know myself? I am certain that the unfortunate king that you have just sent to the Underworld is as innocent as I was; but finish it—kill me promptly; it's the only favor I ask of you."

"You would be too content," Magotine said to her, "if I granted you that prayer. It's necessary before then that you draw water from the bottomless well."

As soon as the ships had arrived in the realm of the marionettes, the cruel Magotine took a millstone, attached it to the queen's neck and commanded her to climb to the summit of a mountain that was far above the clouds; when she was there she was to pick four-leafed clover and fill her basket with it, and then descend into the bottom of the valley in order to draw in a pitcher pierced with holes the water of discretion, of which she was to bring her enough to fill her large glass.

The queen told her that it was impossible for her to be able to obey, that the millstone weighed ten times as much as she did, that the pierced pitcher could never retain the water that she wanted to drink, and that she could not even attempt such an impossible thing.

"If you fail in it," Magotine said to her, "be assured that your Green Worm will suffer in consequence."

That threat caused the queen so much fear that, without examining her weakness, she tried to walk; but alas, it would have been futile if the Protective Fay, to whom she appealed, had not come to her aid.

"This," she said to her, as she approached her, "is the just payment for your fatal curiosity; you only have yourself to blame for the state to which Magotine has reduced you."

Immediately, she transported her to the mountain and put the four-leafed clover in her basket, in spite of the frightful monsters that guarded it. They made supernatural efforts to defend it, but with a stroke of her wand, the Protective Fay rendered them meeker than lambs

She did not wait until the grateful queen had thanked her to finish giving her all the pleasure that depended on her. She gave her a little chariot drawn by white canaries, which talked and whistled marvelously. She told her to go down the mountain, to throw her iron shoes at two giants armed with clubs that were guarding the spring, and that they would fall unconscious. She advised her then not to stay at the spring, nor to go back up the mountain, but to stop in an agreeable little wood that she would find in her path; that she could spend three years there; that Magotine would always think that she was still occupied in drawing water in her pitcher or that the other perils of the journey had caused her death.

The queen embraced the knees of the Protective Fay and thanked her a thousand times for the particular favors she had received from her. "But Madame," she added, "neither the fortunate success that I ought to have, nor the beauty that you promise me, will be able to touch me with joy until Worm has been devermified."

"That is what will happen after you have been in the wood on the mountain for three years," the fay said to her, "and on your return you have given the water in the pitcher and the clover to Magotine."

The queen promised the Protective Fay not to fail in anything that had been prescribed to her. "However, Madame," she added, "will I be three years without hearing mention of King Worm?"

"You deserve to be deprived of his news as long as you live," replied the fay, "for can there be anything more terrible than to condemn that poor king, as you have done, to recommence his penitence?"

The queen made no reply; the tears that flowed from her eyes and her silence were evidence enough of the dolor she felt. She climbed into the little chariot; the canaries did their duty and conducted her into the depths of the valley, where the giants were guarding the spring of discretion.

Promptly, she took off the iron shoes, which she threw at their heads; as soon as they were touched they fell like lifeless colossi. The canaries took the pierced pitcher and repaired it with such a surprising skill that it did not appear that it had ever been broken.

The name the water bore gave her a desire to drink it. *It will render me*, she thought, *more prudent and discreet than I have been in the past; if I had had those qualities, I would still be in the realm of Pagodia.* After she had drunk a long draught she washed her face, and became so beautiful, so beautiful, that she might sooner have been taken for a goddess rather than a mortal person.

Immediately, the Protective Fay appeared and said to her: "You have just done something that pleases me infinitely. You knew that that water could embellish your soul and your person; I wanted to know which of the two would have preference. In the end it was your soul that had it; I praise you for that, and that action will abridge your penitence by four years."

"Don't diminish my punishments," relied the queen, "I merit them all; but relieve Green Worm, who does not merit any."

"I will do what I can," said the fay, embracing her, "But wait, since you're so beautiful, I want you to quit the name of Laidronnette, which no longer suits you. It's necessary that you call yourself Queen Discreet."

With that she disappeared, leaving her a small pair of shoes, so pretty and so well embroidered that she almost regretted putting them on.

When she had remounted her chariot, holding her pitcher full of water, the canaries took her straight to the wood on the mountain. There has never been a more agreeable place; the myrtles and the orange trees linked their branches to form long covered pathways and arbors that the sun could not penetrate; a thousand steams hat flowed gently contributed to refreshing that beautiful abode; but what was rarest of all was that all the animals there talked, and they gave the best welcome in the world to the little canaries.

"We thought," they said to them, "that you had abandoned us."

"The time of our penitence is not yet finished," replied the canaries, "but here is a queen that the Protective Fay has charged us with bringing; take care of diverting her as much as you can."

At the same time she found herself surrounded by animals of every species, which paid her great compliments.

"You shall be our queen," they said to her. "There are no cares and respects that you ought not to expect from us."

"Where am I?" she exclaimed. "By means of what supernatural power can you talk to me?"

One of the little canaries, which had not quit her, twittered to her: "It is necessary that you know, Madame, that several fays, having set out to travel, were chagrined to find people falling into essential faults; they thought at first that it would be sufficient to warn them in order to correct them, but their cares were futile, and, suddenly becoming irritated, they put them in penitence; they made parrots, magpies and chickens of those who talked too much, pigeons, canaries and little dogs of lovers and mistresses, monkeys of those who mimicked their friends, pigs of certain people who were excessively fond of good cheer and lions of angry people. In the end, the number of those they put in penitence became so large that this wood is populated by them, with the consequence that one finds individuals of all qualities and humors here."

"By what you have just told me, my dear little canary," the queen said to him, "I have reason to believe that you are only here for having loved too much."

"That's true, Madame," relied the canary. "I was the son of a Spanish grandee: Amour has rights so absolute over all hearts in our country that one cannot escape him without falling into the crime of rebellion. An English ambassador arrived at the court; he had a daughter of extreme beauty, but whose arrogant and piquant humor as insupportable; in spite of that I attached myself to her, I loved her to the point of adoration; she sometimes seemed sensible to my cares, but at other times she rejected me so forcefully that she drove my patience to the limit.

"One day, when she had driven me to despair, a venerable old woman accosted me, reproaching me for my weakness, but all that she could say to me only served to make me more obstinate. She perceived that, and became irritated. 'I condemn you, she said, to become a canary for three years, and your mistress a wasp.' Immediately, I sensed the most extraordinary metamorphosis take place in me.

"In spite of my affliction, I couldn't help flying into the ambassador's garden to discover the fate of his daughter, but I was scarcely there when I saw her become a huge wasp, buzzing four times as loudly as any other. I fluttered around her with the urgency of a lover whom nothing can detach; she tried several times to sting me. 'If you want my death, beautiful wasp,' I said to her, 'it isn't necessary for that to employ your sting; it's sufficient for you to order me to die.' The wasp made no reply; she alighted on flowers that were to suffer her ill humor.

"Dejected by her scorn and my condition, I flew away without taking any particular route. I eventually arrived in one of the most beautiful cities in the world, which is called Paris. I was tired; I threw myself into a clump of large trees enclosed by walls, and without knowing who had caught me I found myself at the door of a cage painted green and garnished with gold. The furniture and the apartment had a magnificence that surprised me; immediately, a young woman came to caress me, and spoke to me with so much affection that I was charmed.

"I had not been in her room long before I was informed of the secret of her heart. I saw a kind of braggart come to see her, always furious, who could not be satisfied, not only charging her with unjust reproaches but beating her and leaving her for dead in the hands of her women. I was not a little afflicted to see her suffer such unworthy treatment, and what displeased me even more was that it seemed that the blows with which he hurt her had the virtue of reawakening all that pretty lady's tenderness.

"I wished day and night for the fays that had rendered me a canary to come to put some orders into such ill-matched amours. My desires were accomplished; the fays appeared abruptly in the room as the furious lover was commencing his ordinary Sabbat; they charged him with reproaches and condemned him to become a wolf. As for the patient young woman who allowed herself to be beaten, they made her a ewe and sent her to the wood on the mountain. As for myself, I easily found the means of flying away.

"I wanted to see the different courts of Europe. I went into Italy, and hazard caused me to fall into the hands of a man who, often having affairs in his city, and not wanting his wife, of whom he was very jealous, to see anyone, took care to lock her up from morning until evening, with the result that he destined me with the honor of diverting that beautiful captive, She was, however, occupied with other cares than that of listening to me. A certain neighbor whom she had loved for a long time, came to the top of the chimney in the evening and let himself slide down, blacker than a demon. The keys that the jealous man had taken away only served to put his mind at rest.

"I always feared some unfortunate catastrophe, and the fays came in through the keyhole, causing the tender couple a surprise that was not mediocre. 'Go in penitence,' they said to them, touching them with their wands, so that the chimney-sweep became a squirrel and the lady a she-monkey, because she was adroit; and the husband who took so much care to keep the keys of his house became a mastiff for ten years.

"I would have too many things to recount to you, Madame," added the canary, "if I told you all the different adventures that have happened to me. I am obliged to return, from time to time, to the wood on the mountain, and I hardly ever come without finding new animals, because the fays are till traveling, and people continue to irritate them with infinite faults; but during the sojourn you spend here, you will be able to divert yourself with the stories of all the adventures of the persons who are here."

Several immediately offered to tell her theirs whenever she wished; she thanked them very politely, but as she had more desire to think than to talk, she searched for a solitary spot where she could be alone. As soon as she had marked one, a little palace appeared there, where the finest meal in the world was served to her; it only consisted of fruits, but very rare fruits; the birds brought them, and for as long as she was in the wood, she did not lack anything.

Sometimes there were fêtes more agreeable by their singularity than anything else; lions were to be seen dancing with lambs there, bears sweet-talking doves and snakes showing affection for linnets. A butterfly could be seen intriguing with a panther. In sum, nothing was matched in accordance with its species, for it was not a matter of being a tiger or a sheep, but only people that the fays wanted to punish for their faults.

They loved Queen Discreet to the point of adoration; they all rendered her the arbiter of their disputes. She had an absolute power over that petty republic, and if she had not reproached herself incessantly for the misfortunes of Green Worm she would have been able to support her own with a kind of patience; but when she thought about the state to which he was reduced, she could not forgive herself or her indiscreet curiosity.

When the time came for her to leave the wood on the mountain, she informed her little conductors, the faithful canaries, who assured her of a fortunate return. She slipped away one night in order to avoid adieux and regrets that would have cost her a few tears, for she was touched by the amity and deference that all those reasonable animals had testified to her.

She did not forget the pitcher full of the water of discretion or the basket of clover, nor the iron shoes, and while Magotine believed her to be dead she suddenly presented herself before her, the millstone round her neck, the iron shoes on her feet and the pitcher in her hand. On seeing her, the fay uttered a loud cry, and then asked her where she had been.

"Madame," she said to her, "I've spent three years drawing water with the pierced pitcher, and the end of which I found the means of making it hold some."

Magotine burst out laughing, thinking about the fatigue the poor queen had had, but, looking at her more attentively, she cried: "What's this? Laidronnette has become quite charming! Where, then, have you obtained that beauty?"

The queen told her that she had washed herself with the water of discretion and that the prodigy in question had occurred.

At that news, Magotine threw the pitcher to the ground.

"O power that is defying me," she cried, "I shall be able to avenge myself. Prepare your iron shoes," she said to the queen, "it's necessary that you go on my part to the Underworld, to ask Proserpine for the essence of long life. I always fear falling ill, and even dying; when I have that antidote, I shall no longer have any reason for apprehension. Refrain, therefore, from taking the stopper from the bottle or tasting the liquor she will give you, for you'd diminish my share."

The poor queen had never been more surprised than she was by that order. "By what route does one go to the Underworld?" she asked. "Can those who go there come back? Alas, Madame, will you not weary one day of persecuting me? Under what star was I born? My sister is far more fortunate than me; it's necessary no longer to believe that the constellations are equal for everyone."

She started to weep, and Magotine, triumphant at seeing her shed tears, burst out laughing. "Let's go, let's go," she said. "Don't defer for a moment a journey that will bring me so much satisfaction." She filled a satchel with old nuts and brown bread for her.

With that good provision, she departed, resolved to break her head against the first rock for her pains. She walked for some time without taking any route, going one way and turning the other, thinking that it was a very extraordinary command to send her thus to the Underworld. When she was tired she lay down at the foot of a tree and stated to dream about the poor Worm, no longer thinking about her journey; but she suddenly saw the Protective Fay, who said to her: "Don't you know, beautiful queen, "that in order to extract your husband from the somber abode where Magotine's orders retain him, that it's necessary for you to go to Proserpine's dwelling?"

"I'd go much further if it were possible for me," she replied, "but Madame, I don't know where to descend into that tenebrous domain."

"Here," said the Protective Fay, "this is a green branch; strike the earth with it and pronounce verses distinctly."

The queen embraced the knees of that generous friend, and then she said:

You who are able to disarm the master of thunder,
Amour, give me aid,
Come to stop the course
Of rigorous ennuis that are tearing my soul.
Open for me, as you can, the path to the Underworld;
In that subterranean realm you can make your flame felt,
Pluto for Proserpine has moaned in your irons;
Open for me, tender Amour, the path to the Underworld.
A faithful husband has been snatched from me;
I feel the rigors of the most terrible fate.
My dolor is more than mortal,
And I cannot find death.

She had scarcely finished her prayer when young child, more beautiful than anything we see, emerged from the depths of a cloud mingled with gold and azure; he flew and came to alight at her feet; a crown of flowers circled his head. The queen knew by his bow and his arrows that it was Amour. He said to her as he approached:

Your sighs have been heard,
I have abandoned the heavens,
And come to dry the tears flowing from your eyes.
For you I can attempt anything;
You shall see again the object you love the most;
Recall Worm to the pleasures of life,
And punish thus his cruel enemy.

The queen, astonished by the splendor that surrounded Amour, and delighted by his promises, cried:

Into the Underworld I am ready to follow you;
That horrible abode will seem charming to me,
If I see again the lover
Without whom I can no longer live.

Amour, who rarely speaks in prose, struck three blows, singing these words marvelously well:

Earth, obey my voice,
Recognize Amour, open a passage
All the way to the dismal shore
Where Pluto imposes his laws.

The earth obeyed; it opened its large bosom, and by means of an obscure descent, in which the queen had need of a guide as brilliant as the one who had taken her under his protection, she arrived in the Underworld. She feared encountering her husband there in the form of a serpent, but Amour, who sometimes mingles rendering a few good offices, having foreseen everything that could be anticipated in that regard, had already ordered Green Worm to become what he had been before his penitence. However powerful Magotine was, alas, what could she do against Amour?

The first thing that the queen found, therefore, was her amiable husband. She had never seen him in such a charming form, nor had he seen her as beautiful as she had become; however, a presentiment—and perhaps Amour, who made a third party with them—enabled them to divine who they were. The queen immediately said, with an extreme tenderness:

I have come to his place in order to bend destiny's law,
If you are arrested here by a barbaric order
Let us unite our hearts, let nothing separate us;

The king, transported by the most intense passion, responded to his wife everything that could mark his ardor and his joy; but Amour, who does not like to waste time, invited them to approach Proserpine.

The queen paid her a compliment on behalf of the fay, and begged her to charge her with the essence of life. That was a password agreed between those good persons; she immediately gave her a phial rather poorly sealed, in order to facilitate the desire to open it. Amour, who was not a novice, warned the queen to refrain from a curiosity that might again be fatal, and, emerging promptly from that sad abode, the king and the queen saw the light again.

Amour did not want to abandon them; he conducted them to Magotine, and in order that she would not see him he hid in their hearts. However, his presence inspired sentiments so humane that the fay, although she did not know the reason for it, received the illustrious unfortunates very well; making an effort of supernatural generosity, she returned the kingdom of Pagodia to them; they went back there immediately, and lived with as much good fortune as they had previously experienced disgrace and annoyance.

Don Fernand had attracted that attention of his audience so strongly that daylight was beginning to appear without Lenore and Matilde having had any desire to sleep. He begged them insistently to go into a cabin and seek some repose in the midst of all the anxieties by which they were agitated.

They were on the point of entering the Gulf of Venice when the weather suddenly changed, and put them in a state of fear for their lives. After having tried in vain to rest the winds it was finally necessary to yield to them. They were drawn away to such an extent that they found themselves more than two hundred leagues from the entrance to the gulf. The sea was beginning to calm, down when two brigantines attacked them. They were commanded by Zoromy, the famous corsair, who had acquired such a reputation that he was feared in almost every sea.

Having perceived and approached them, he surprised them with such great diligence that, being still in the disorder in which the tempest they had endured had left them that they did not even have the leisure to think of defending themselves. After having resisted with a volley of cannon shots, the Spanish captain surrendered, and our young lovers saw themselves in the harsh necessity of recognizing a corsair for a master.

I cannot pretend to represent the excess of their dolor; it is easy to understand and difficult to describe well. The ship was immediately filled by Turks, who took away their disposition in all things, and particularly their liberty. However, as they were able to judge by the respect that people had for the ladies and the magnificence of their garments that they were of distinguished quality, they treated them with more honesty than they had reason to expect of those barbarians.

Zoromy took them on to his own ship, with Don Fernand and Don Jaime. He said to Leonore and Matilde, in French, that they should not be so afflicted, and that he would try to reduce the bitterness of their captivity. They could only reply to him with tears that marked the excess of their affliction. The two Spanish cavaliers were penetrated by their own, although they sustained themselves with more courage.

When Leonore was able to speak to Don Fernand she told him that since they could not foresee what their destiny would be, she judged it appropriate to make him pass for her brother, and that if they were separated, he could console himself with the certainty that she would rather cease to live than change.

"Oh, Madame," cried the amorous Don Fernand, "What are you saying to me? Is it possible that I shall have the misfortune of being far from you?"

"It is necessary to anticipate anything," she said, "in the deplorable state that we are in, and prepare ourselves for it without weakness."

"You have so much firmness," he said to her, "that I fear that indifference might enter into it."

"Can you form such suspicions?" she replied, looking at him sadly "Does not what I have done for you, when I quit my father' house, prove my amity sufficiently?"

"I'm not a ingrate," replied Don Fernand, "but Madame, I am an unfortunate overwhelmed by the most disastrous blows with which fortune can persecute a man, so pardon my alarms; if you were less dear to me, perhaps I would be less unjust."

Sentiments so tender gave a good deal of consolation to the lovely Leonore; she gave evidence of her own to Don Fernand in terms appropriate to soothe his irritations. They agreed that he would go to speak to Zoromy in order to know his intentions and what sum he wanted for their ransom. He had scarcely opened the proposition, however, than the corsair imposed silence on him.

"Those ladies only ought to think," he told them, "of pleasing the great vizier Achmet, to whom I am resolved to present them, in order to acquit myself of an infinite number of obligations that I owe him."

What news, alas, for persons who love one another and who had flattered themselves with emerging from slavery soon!

When Don Fernand came to inform Leonore of that, she was penetrated by the sharpest dolor; but in the end, finding too much weakness in abandoning herself entirely to her displeasures, and seeing the pain of her generous lover, she resolved to have recourse to her courage in order to stifle a part of them, and to hide the rest to the best of her ability.

For their part, Don Jaime and Matilde spoke to one another no less tenderly and no less generously; they swore an eternal love a hundred times over; it was their unique consolation.

The wind was so favorable that they arrived in Constantinople in a short time When the ladies were disembarked, Zoromy hid them carefully; they were taken to his house. He gave them time to repose in order that it would not appear that the fatigue of the voyage had stolen anything of the vivacity of their eyes or the freshness of their complexion. He had them dress in the Turkish fashion, in magnificent gold fabric, and having had chains made of all the precious stones that he had taken from them, he bound their hands and their feet.

Don Fernand and Don Jaime also had slave costumes of the same cloth; their good looks ornamented them even more than the gems with which Zoromy had their jackets covered. He took all four of them in that new equipage to a country house near Constantinople that belonged to the grand vizier, who went there to divert himself and only wanted to be accompanied by a small court.

Zoromy asked him for permission to salute him. Achmet received him obligingly; he admired the good looks of his slaves and said that he had never seen anything as beautiful as Leonore. He spoke the Spanish language very well, and gazed at her with an expression full of tenderness and pity.

"Quit those chains," he said to her. "Heaven has given birth to you in order to give you to all those who see you." Leonore made to reply to that gallantry. She lowered her eyes and could not hold back her tears

"What!" continued the grand vizier. "Have you a great dolor in finding yourself among us? I assure you that you will have no less power here than you had in your own country."

"Sire," she said, "Whatever bounty you promise me to generously in yours, it seems to me that I will always distrust my fortune, after the misfortune that has overtaken me, so I beg you not to think me ingrate to those same generosities, although I am not testifying all the sensibility to them that I ought. But Sire," she added, throwing herself at his feet with a utterly charming grace, "if you wish to dry up the source of my tears, deign to set a price on our liberty, in order that we can put ourselves in a state to see our parents and our homeland again soon."

"Since this beautiful girl is your sister and these slaves are your brothers," he said, "I shall immediately grant what you ask for them; in your regard, I ask for time to think about it."

They recognized clearly by that response that Achmet was only rendering them liberty in order to separate them from Leonore. Being engaged not to abandon one another, however, as long as they could, they responded to the vizier with a great deal of respect: "We would not merit, Sire, the favor that you deign to accord us, if, before profiting from it, we had not tried to render ourselves worthy of it; thus we dare to beg you to permit us to remain for a sufficient time in the number of your slaves, in order to make you know a part of our gratitude."

Achmet consented to that, and after having told the corsair that he had made him a present the price of which he would never forget, he had Leonore and Matilde taken to the women's quarters.

It was in that house, destined for his pleasures, that he kept the most beautiful women in the world. There was no man whose life was more delectable than his. He was the grand vizier in an era when the others were hardly in favor. The burden of affairs stole nothing from his pleasures, and his pleasures stole nothing from his duty. He was well made and his person was as generous and gallant as it was possible to be in a place where delicacy is so little known. But it was not in Constantinople that he had become so polite; he had seen other courts, and if he had been able to spend more time there, there would not have been a more honest man than him in the world.

He had the two Spaniards lodged in an apartment, the beauty and magnificence of which surprised them. He came to see Leonore every day, assiduously; he sent her considerable presents and the cares that he took to please her made that beautiful young woman understand that she would have terrible combats to sustain, and that he was not disposed to wait for a long time for favors that he could demand as a master.

She sometimes said to him that the goods that are only possessed in that manner are always mingled with chagrin; that the heart wants to render itself by inclination and never by violence; and when he pressed her harder, she implored him to leave her enough liberty to be able to say to herself that it was to his tenderness, and not to his authority, that she granted her esteem. He found something delicate in that proposition, and promised her that he would never neglect anything to please her.

He treated Matilde with a thousand kindnesses; he gave her presents in order to put her in his interests, and with regard to Don Fernand and Don Jaime, he softened the rigors of their captivity by means of manners so generous and easy that they appeared to be with him under the title of friends rather than that of slaves. But alas, what a sad abode it was for Don Fernand; he no longer saw his mistress, and he knew that she was in the power of an absolute rival; in what continual alarms his soul floated! He feared the weaknesses of the fair sex, he dreaded the authority of the vizier; in sum, he was in a deplorable state.

Don Jaime, who had fewer anxieties for his dear Matilde, consoled him, and tried to soothe the frightful pains by which he was devoured.

For her part, Leonore prolonged adroitly the term that Achmet prescribed for giving her his faith and receiving hers; and although she had good reasons for praising his procedure she was nevertheless afflicted by it. That affliction was caused by the fact that, in spite of all the politeness it was necessary to have, and the particular regards that she owed him, there was often reason to suffer from them; sometimes, too, he adopted such abrupt manners with her, full of impatience, that announced a terrible future.

Finally, he pressed her to make a determination. "I shall not treat you like the others," he told her. "I want to marry you and render you happy. Think, therefore, of what response to give me the next time I come to see you."

Leonore remained sad and pensive. Matilde came to find her when he had quit her; seeing the tears that were flowing in abundance from her eyes, she implored her to tell her whether she had new subjects for displeasure. Leonore told her what had happened; she spoke thereafter about Don Fernand with an extreme tenderness, but she perceived the vizier, who was listening behind the door of a cabinet that could be entered by another door; he had wanted to hear the conversations that she had with her sister, and for several days he had remained hidden in various places in her apartment

Leonore pretended not to have seen him; she continued her discourse and said to Matilde: "I sense that if Don Fernand had been faithful, I would be incapable of neglecting any of the oaths that we have made; I would conserve my heart for him at the expense of my life, and our distance would not change my dispositions, but the ingrate has sacrificed me; you know, my sister, the unworthy procedure he has had for me. I am resolved to forget him, for my repose; I even sense that this is the last time that I shall mention him to you."

The vizier withdrew with an agitation difficult to express; he could not prevent himself talking to Matilde about it;

she responded to his questions like an intelligent person. Leonore learned from her what had happened, and as a thousand reasons obliged her to be careful of the mind of a lover who was her master, she sent word asking him to come to her room. He would have liked not to see her again, but what means is there of fleeing a person one loves? Heroes, like the rest of men, have their moments of weakness in that regard.

He went to Leonore's apartment; she knew by his expression the chagrin by which he was overwhelmed

"Don't complain of my heart," she said to him. "It was engaged before knowing you. I could not have resolved to make you the confession; you have learned it, and you know as well that the infidel who loved me has ceased to love me; you had a rival, Sire, but you no longer have one, and if you grant me some time to soothe my pains, I can promise you all the marks of gratitude that I owe to your generosity."

"I admit to you," he told her, "that my amour and my delicacy are equally offended by knowing that I have a competitor in your heart. I was not surprised by your indifference; I blamed your youth for it, and promised myself everything of my cares; I was even piqued by an agreeable emulation that made me desire to be the first who had touched you with esteem and tenderness. But, cruel woman, I know my misfortune and flatter myself in vain of your tenderness; alas, I dare not hope for it."

As he finished speaking he cast his eyes upon Leonore, in order to seek in hers some relief for his anxiety; she looked at him then in a favorable manner; he was no less satisfied by that than by all the obliging things she said to him. She used that stratagem because she was meditating flight, and in order to succeed in that, she neglected nothing in order to gain time and to take advantage of the first opportunity that she could find.

Fortune presented her with one that she seized with the utmost urgency. The Sultan was returning to Constantinople, the vizier was obliged to accompany him, and as Leonore's health was ailing, he did not want to commit her to the fatigue of a journey. When he was ready to depart he went into her room.

"I am going to quit you, charming Leonore," he said, "although it is only for a few days, it seems to me that I am tearing myself way, and I have even more need to remember all your promises. Alas, what will I do if you do not keep any, and if I lost you, what would I do. O gods..."

He stopped at that point, and remained in a profound reverie.

Leonore shivered, apprehensive that he might have discovered something of her design, but the vizier resumed his discourse: "No, terrors, no, vain alarms," he cried, "I shall no longer listen to you. Leonore has given me her tenderness..."

"Yes, Sire," she said, interrupting him, "you possess it entirely and I would be unworthy to live if I could respond with more indifferent sentiments than those you have for me. Go where your duty summons you, but do not listen to it so much, Sire, that you do not return soon."

Penetrated by what she said, Achmet responded to that prayer with a thousand assurances of an eternal passion. When he said adieu, it was in a manner so touching that one could have believed without difficulty that some presentiment was acting upon him.

Don Fernand and Don Jaime, having been alerted to the designs of heir mistresses, had seconded them with a success so fortunate that they had found the means of ensuring themselves of a ship. They informed them. Leonore had Christian slaves who were entirely devoted to her; the signal was given; they set fire to several parts of the seraglio; the confusion and disorder that those sorts of accidents bring with them facilitated the entry of the Spanish cavaliers into the women's quarter and gave them the opportunity to rescue Leonore and Matilde.

They took with them those of their slaves in whom they had confided. The palace where they were was built on the shore of the sea; launches were waiting for them and they went as far as the ship without encountering any obstacle. The anchor was raised immediately and the sails extended; the tender lovers savored the pleasure of being together and finding themselves free with a thousand transports of joy.

A favorable wind that rose impelled them rapidly into the Gulf of Venice, and no navigation had ever been more agreeable or more fortunate than theirs.

Leonore and her sister had the design of going into a convent on arrival until Don Fernand and Don Jaime had obtained permission to marry them from the Count de Fuentes and the Marquis de Toledo. After long reflections, however, they all agreed that if they delayed, their irritated patents might prevent them from marrying, whereas if the thing were done, after a time of anger, everything would calm down.

The lovers were delighted with the resolution that their mistresses made in their favor. They had bought the most beautiful gems in the world, which the vizier had given to Leonore, with the consequence that they found themselves in a state to obtain an equipage and make a figure proportionate to their birth.

Meanwhile, the old Marquis of Toledo had no sooner learned of Leonore's abduction than he set forth on campaign to follow her. The Comte de Fuentes, who found himself very interested in that, departed with him; the neglected nothing of all they thought necessary to overtake the fugitives, but while they were searching in one direction they had escaped in the other.

Sensible as the Count de Fuentes was, that did not equal in the slightest the vivacity and the dolor of the Marquis de Toledo. He was veritably touched by Leonore, and was threatening his son with disinheritance when he felt overwhelmed by anxieties to such a point that he no longer had the strength to torment himself further. The physicians found his woes so pressing that they warned him about them. All his son's friends tried to appease him; he received respectful and submissive letters from them. Finally, the approach of death relented his passion, and he forgave Don Fernand.

The Count de Fuentes had the same generosity for his daughters. What could he have done? They were married, and their choice could not have been better, when their entire family would be mingled by it.

The Marquis de Toledo did not linger for long; Don Fernand rendered his memory all the honors that he owed to it. He and Don Jaime returned to Cadiz with their wives; everyone found them embellished, so much is mental satisfaction an excellent enhancement. Don Francisco continued to serve them as the most generous relative in the world, and Don Jaime, penetrated with gratitude, asked him one day whether he would not like him to give him some means of acquitting all that he owed him.

"You can do that easily," said Don Francisco. "Accord me your charming sister; I've adored her for a long time; she suffers it without anger, but in the end, without you we cannot be happy."

Don Jaime embraced him with all the testimonies of amity that he had reason to promise him. "I lament," he said to him, obligingly, "the secret that you have made of a passion in which I am in a state to serve you; my sister will never belong to anyone but you, and I shall work so well on her behalf that you will have reason to be content."

Don Francisco felt a joy difficult to comprehend; he said to his friend everything he could imagine of the most engaging, and the same day they went to the home of Don Jaime's sister, who had always been raised in a convent; her mind was no less cultivated than his, and whatever care she took to hide her sentiments, she could not help her brother penetrating them. He took her out of the religious house, and the wedding was held in his home, with a great deal of magnificence.

Thus, our three lovers and their mistresses found themselves content with their lot; there are few who can boast of a similar good fortune.

CLASSIC FRENCH FANTASY

Honoré de Balzac. *The Last Fay*
Gabrielle-Suzanne Barbot de Villeneuve. *The Naiads / Beauty and The Beast*
Chevalier de Béthune. *The World of Mercury*
Jean Carrère. *The End of Atlantis*
Charlotte-Rose Caumont de La Force. *The Land of Delights*
Comte de Caylus. *The Impossible Enchantment*
Félicien Champsaur. *Pharaoh's Wife*
Jacques Collin de Plancy. *Voyage to the Center of the Earth*
Gaston Danville. *The Perfume of Lust*
Comtesse D.L. *The Tyranny of the Fays Abolished*
Marie-Antoinette Fagnan. *The Enchanter's Mirror*
Paul Féval. *Anne of the Isles*
Charles de Fieux. *Lamékis*
Judith Gautier. *Isoline and the Serpent-Flower*
Nathalie Henneberg. *The Green Gods*
Gustave Kahn. *The Tale of Gold and Silence*
Edmond Haraucourt. *Dieudonat*
Françoise Le Marchand. *Florine and Boca*
Marie-Jeanne L'Héritier de Villandon. *The Robe of Sincerity*
André Lichtenberger. *The Centaurs; The Children of the Crab*
J-M. & Randy Lofficier. *The French Fantasy Treasury 1-3*
Charles Lomon & P.-B. Gheuzi. *The Last Days of Atlantis*
Maurice Magre. *The Marvelous Story of Claire d'Amour; The Call of the Beast; Priscilla of Alexandria; The Angel of Lust; The Mystery of the Tiger; The Poison of Goa; Lucifer; The Blood of Toulouse; The Albigensian Treasure; Jean de Fodoas; Melusine; The Brothers of the Virgin Gold*
Marie-Madeleine de Lubert. *Princess Camion.*
Camille Mauclair. *The Virgin Orient*
Hippolyte Mettais. *Paris Before the Deluge*
Victor-Emile Michelet. *Superhuman Tales*

Henriette-Julie de Murat. *The Palace of Vengeance*
Charles Nodier. *Trilby / The Crumb Fairy*
Edgar Quinet. *The Enchanter Merlin*
Henri de Régnier. *A Surfeit of Mirrors*
Restif de la Bretonne. *The Fay Ouroucoucou* (2 vols.)
J.-H. Rosny Aîné. *Pan's Flute*
Marie-Anne de Roumier-Robert. *The Voyage of Lord Seaton to the Seven Planets*
Nicolas Ségur. *Penelope's Secret*
Brian Stableford (ed.). *Funestine; The Queen of the Fays; The Origin of the Fays*
Kurt Steiner. *Ortog*
C.-F. Tiphaigne de La Roche. *Amilec / Giphantia*
Simon Tyssot de Patot. *The Strange Voyages of Jacques Massé and Pierre de Mésange*